Chewing the Scenery

Davina Elliott has worked on over 80 theatre productions in a variety of jobs from dresser to small time producer. None of them include performing. She lives in London with no children, no pets and is inseparable from her laptop called Leo.

Chewing the Scenery is her first novel.

Chewing the Scenery

Davina Elliott

PUCK BOOKS

Published by Puck Books
www.puckbooks.com

First published 2008

British Library Cataloguing in Publication Data
A catalogue record for this book is available
from the British Library.

ISBN 978 0 9560960 0 5

Printed and bound in Great Britain
by CPI Bookmarque Ltd, Croydon, Surrey.

ACKNOWLEDGEMENTS

Thanks to my wonderful editor Kathy Kerr for all her hard work, patience and support, and to my agent Judith Chilcote for her great faith in my book. Thanks also to Caroline Baron for patiently listening to each chapter and providing constant feedback and reassurance, and to Su Gilroy, grammar expert extraordinaire, avid reader, character analyzer and all round good egg. Finally to all my family, friends and work colleagues for their encouragement and participation, especially Christopher Cazenove who told me I should be a writer in the first place!

For M

Wesley Bartlett presents:

BLITHE SPIRIT

By Noel Coward

Cast in Order of Appearance:

Edith, the Condomine's maid	Scarlett Montgomery
Ruth Condomine	Miranda Flynn
Charles Condomine	Rupert Blake
Dr Bradman	Adam Lane
Mrs Bradman	Isabelle Whiteside
Madame Arcati	Judith Gold
Elvira	Echo

Director Alexander Columbus
Designer Jasper Fleming

For Blithe Spirit Productions:

Company Manager	Declan Shaw
Deputy Stage Manager	Rebecca Cross
Assistant Stage Managers	Lucy Foster
	Matthew Scott
Wardrobe Mistress	Libby Bennett
Miss Gold's dresser	Fred Walker
Dresser	Cassie Stewart
Wigs Mistress	Tasha Healy

The play takes place in the living room of
Charles Condomine's house in Kent.

Scene Synopsis

Act One
Scene 1   Before dinner on a summer
              evening.
Scene 2   After dinner.

Act Two
Scene 1   The next morning.
Scene 2   Late the following afternoon.
Scene 3   Early evening. A few days later.

Act Three
Scene 1   After dinner. A few days later.
Scene 2   Several hours later.

There will be two twenty minute intervals.

PROLOGUE

The first day of rehearsal: an awkward affair. Polite introductions. Greetings of old acquaintances. A chorus of "darling"s from people who didn't consider them darlings at all, but couldn't be bothered to recall the name of their understudy three years ago, or the assistant stage manager who always forgot the sugar in their tea on a second-rate tour round the seaside venues of England.

"OK, people, gather round!" The young, trendy director clapped his hands together.

The elderly, famous and respected theatre actress gave a sniff of disapproval; she didn't consider herself 'people'.

"I want to say a big welcome to you all on this our first day of rehearsals on what promises to be a revolutionary production."

"Oh, Christ!" said the actress.

"How revolutionary can a production of a Noel Coward play be?" muttered the actor playing the male lead to the woman playing his wife, who shrugged non-committally.

The young actress, straight from drama school, looked up at the director, eyes huge with excitement. "Isn't he wonderful?" she mouthed at her neighbour. Then, remembering her neighbour was apparently a famous American TV actress making her theatre debut, added, "And I'm sure you are too."

The TV actress smiled, showing the teeth which had cost her mother a small fortune, and wondered whether this other girl was also in the show and if so would they become friends?

The remaining two members of the cast, playing the other married couple, were reacting in different ways. The woman's eyes darted everywhere as if making certain she wouldn't miss a thing; by contrast the man stared into space as if hoping to find the answer to life out there.

The four members of the stage management team clustered around a table, ready to prepare notes on the director's instructions: where the actors were to move on stage, how he wanted the rehearsals to run, the times and days each actor was to be called, and what props were needed.

The wardrobe mistress, having met everyone, was no longer needed and decided to go and search for period-looking tights in John Lewis. If she didn't do it now the designer would no doubt demand them at the last minute. 'Be prepared' wasn't only a good motto for Boy Scouts.

"Right, people!" The elderly actress sighed again. She was going to have to have words with this director. The director paused, and looked round expectantly as if to make an exciting announcement, then spoke with a pause between each word. "I want to talk about emotions and characterisation, before we start to block the play."

"What's 'block'?" asked the TV actress audibly.

"Oh, Christ!" said the elderly actress.

"It's when the director tells you where to stand and when to move," explained the girl from drama school.

"Oh, like on my mark for the cameras for TV. But my director always keeps it real simple so I don't get like totally stressed."

"Oh, Jesus Christ!" said the elderly actress loudly.

The company stage manager approached the director requesting designs of the set for everyone to look at.

"Oh no, our wonderful designer is still working on that, but it'll be gorgeous, I assure you."

"He would say that," said the female assistant stage manager to the male, "the designer's his boyfriend."

"So," demanded the elderly actress, "how are we supposed to know where the furniture is during rehearsals?"

The director decided to make the joke he'd been dying to use: "Well, you're playing a psychic; can't you predict where it'll be?"

The look the actress gave him would have turned the bravest and smartest of men into quivering wrecks. This man merely ploughed on: "First I want to discuss motivation; we'll have a general discussion to start and then I'll speak to you all individually. I promise this rehearsal process is going to be the most exciting and innovative Noel Coward will ever have known."

In the corner of the room the elderly actress was on her mobile to her agent – a call which left her agent in little doubt of the actress's opinion of innovative rehearsal processes.

CHAPTER ONE

Alexander Columbus had become a successful director by fluke. When anyone asked him his ambition he'd announce, "I'm going to be the next Steven Spielberg."

The suggestion of the school careers advisor that then perhaps he should try and get into film school was met with derision. Alexander had no intention of studying any more than was necessary. As far as he was concerned he knew everything. The fact that he actually knew nothing wasn't going to stop him. If truth be told the only thing he did know everything about was fish and chips, that being the family business from which he escaped as soon as he legally could. Watching movies all his life, he had lost his Yorkshire accent within weeks of moving to London, speaking with a drawl which was a cross between Cary Grant, Sean Connery and Kathleen Turner.

Pestering anyone he could in the entertainment industry, he eventually got a job as a runner for a film company, undertaking errands, fetching coffee and being a general dogsbody. Changing the loo roll in the Ladies for the umpteenth time one day, he resolved that before long he was going to be surrounded by people to do this kind of thing for him.

At this point Alexander was using his given name, Mark Ruck; that was his mother's final legacy to him as far as he was concerned. Why on earth couldn't she have married someone with a name like De Niro, or Coppola, or Kubrick or even Chaplin? But no, he was stuck with Ruck. And when there were names like Ferris, or Mikhail, or Clark, or Brad, how come he'd got Mark? Eventually, like the accent, his name had to change and he decided on Alexander, after the director Alexander Korda, and Columbus after Christopher Columbus who discovered America, one of the few facts he had learnt at school – America being where the former Mark Ruck intended to make his mark.

He'd originally chosen Alexander Spielberg, but that was greeted with derision and questions like how the next *Indiana Jones* film was coming or was it true he was going to be filming *Jaws 73*? But apart from switching surnames Alexander didn't let it get to him; he knew geniuses were always misunderstood and that their gifts were often not recognized until after their death. He had no intention of waiting that long though; there seemed little point in being idolised when you couldn't revel in it.

There was only one area in which he showed sensitivity: his looks. In a pub one night a rather drunk colleague had remarked that if he were to make the sequel Alexander could play ET himself as there were so many similarities.

Alexander spent the whole of that night staring at himself in the mirror. The next day he requested a loan from the bank and went to see a plastic surgeon.

"I want my ears pinned back, a nose job and a tummy tuck," he stated. He had all his teeth capped, and his red hair dyed blonde. This looked strangely at odds with the attempt he made at a Steven Spielberg-type beard, which, not surprisingly, grew red. After a week of ribaldry he reluctantly shaved off the beard.

After two years as a runner, one of the production assistants called him outside.

"A friend of mine is performing in a production of *Twelfth Night* and their director walked out yesterday. It's a profit-share production, which means no money, and it's only at a pub theatre when I know you have your eye on Hollywood, but it would be a start and they're desperate."

Alexander quit his running job on the spot and started his first directing job the following day.

Having slept through most of the classes on Shakespeare at school (there seemed no point in being interested, Kenneth Branagh having already cornered the market in filming the Bard's plays), and unable to find a copy of *Twelfth Night* until 9am the next morning when rehearsals started at 10, Alexander was less than well prepared. He read the first line as he reached the tiny rehearsal space in the middle of nowhere: 'If music be the food of love play on.' At that point he determined that food and music should play a large part in his production – whether appropriate or not.

As the cast, seated on the floor at his feet the way he'd requested, looked expectantly up at him, he drew a deep breath and stared round at them in a way that was to become his trademark. "We are going to set this production at a rock concert."

There was silence.

He warmed to his theme. "Like Glastonbury. So there will be food, cooked on camp fires and shared while the music plays." He flipped through a few more pages.

"But how does the shipwreck fit into Glastonbury?" asked one of the actors.

"Good question," said Alexander. It was a very good question. Why hadn't Shakespeare mentioned a shipwreck on the first page? Then he could have set it on a pirate ship, all those hunky men in silk shirts slashed to the waist waving cutlasses. But there was no going back now; he couldn't risk anyone discovering he hadn't a clue what he was talking about. "Ah yes!" God, he was a genius. "The shipwreck will be an allegory for the storm at Glastonbury a few years back, when all the tents were drenched and everyone was covered in mud. In fact ..." here he gave a long pause for effect, "this whole production is going to be set in mud."

Understandably, the pub theatre was less than keen that their venue was to be covered with a foot of dark slime but, after promises of plastic sheeting underneath and of scouring the place at the end of the run, they reluctantly agreed.

After a few initial problems, such as all but the back two rows of the audience being splattered with mud, solved by providing them with disposable rain coats, the production became a huge success.

"Original!" proclaimed Time Out.

"An exciting debut from this first-time director," announced The Stage and then went on to name the entire cast.

"A mud bath orgy!" proclaimed The Sun, unaware until then that they had a theatre critic.

Alexander found himself a sought-after commodity and was invited to The National Theatre where he staged *Romeo and Juliet* with a happy ending and to the West End where he directed *The Sound of Music* where it was strongly suggested Maria was having a passionate affair with the Mother Abbess.

It was when one of the nuns in *The Sound of Music* (it was hard to tell which one, they looked so different when they weren't wearing their habits and like identical penguins when they were) propositioned him at the first-night party, that Alexander concluded something he had first suspected cleaning the Ladies loos in his first job: women did nothing for him.

Prising the nun off, Alexander caught the eye of a particularly cute waiter handing round the canapés. It wasn't something his mother would approve of, but as he got into a cab with the waiter at the end of the evening he thought anyone who could call their son Mark Ruck didn't understand artists, and artists needed to let their juices flow – in whatever way they wanted. And this was definitely the way he wanted.

The waiter didn't turn out to be more than a two-night stand, but others followed: the guy serving drinks at his local wine bar (Alexander didn't do pubs, he considered them too common for a future director of his calibre), a young man walking his dog in the park and a charming Australian tourist he'd picked up in Piccadilly Circus, fittingly under the statue of Eros.

True love finally found Alexander when discussing a future project at The National Theatre where he noticed a very handsome young boy who worked at stage door. After two days of checking for non-existent post and pretending to wait at the stage door for friends he didn't have, Alexander asked this Adonis in tight leather for a drink in the theatre's green room. It turned out that this boy, Jasper Fleming, wanted to be a theatre designer.

"As in designing the theatres themselves or designing sets for plays?" asked Alexander jokingly.

"Oh, I want to do the sets and costumes," said Jasper earnestly. "I've got tons of ideas. I'll bring my portfolio in to show you tomorrow."

Jasper didn't bring in the portfolio the next day, since he never made it back to his own bed-sit. But that night Jasper made the transition from stage door keeper to designer without the need for a portfolio.

Within a week he had also made the transition from bed-sit to Alexander's Hampstead home.

It was at that point in his career that Alexander was contacted by a successful West End producer. Alexander settled himself in a hard-backed chair in the producer's office. "How can I help you?" he asked as if he were doing the favour.

The youngish producer looked a little taken aback. "Yes, right. I trust you've heard of Judith Gold?"

Alexander nodded. Who hadn't heard of Judith Gold? She was a theatrical legend.

"She has expressed an interest in playing Madame Arcati in *Blithe Spirit* and has approached me to produce it. Since your name seems to be on everyone's lips at the moment I wanted to ask you to direct it. Are you interested?"

At that moment Alexander did something which was going to start a chain of events resulting in a rollercoaster ride, climaxing in the theatrical experience people would talk about for years. He said yes.

CHAPTER TWO

Judith Gold slammed the door of the taxi (paid for by the *Blithe Spirit* producer, her agent wasn't that useless) which had brought her back from the first day of rehearsals. As soon as she opened her front door, Max X (that is X as in Roman numerals, not as in X-rated) shot out the kitchen and rubbed himself against her.

"Careful, Max, the way I feel at the moment I'm tempted to throw or kick something very hard so you may be wise to keep clear."

Max X merely mewed and sat on her foot. "Don't say I didn't warn you." Judith kicked him off, though gently. Max X trotted towards the kitchen. "Didn't that bloody stupid housekeeper of mine feed you?" Judith marched into the kitchen and looked at the shelf where the cat food lived; it was untouched. She snatched down a tin and emptied half of it into a bowl. "Right, that woman is fired! What the hell is her name anyway?" Since this was the latest in a long line of housekeepers, none of whom stayed for any length of time, names were rarely remembered. Judith's acerbic tongue and constant criticism were too much for all but the most hardened. Only one had stayed for any length of time, a woman called Mrs Hudson, a name which amused Judith as she'd once played Sherlock Holmes's housekeeper of that name.

On Mrs Hudson's first day Judith had got up at her usual time of 1pm, to find Mrs Hudson vigorously cleaning the cooker. "That's a fine time to get out of bed I must say," she said to Judith.

"How dare you speak to me in that manner? I am a fucking actress and I need to get a lot of fucking rest so I have the energy to give my best fucking performance for my public every night."

"Well, I'm a fucking housekeeper, and I need a lot of energy to give a good fucking to my husband every night, but you won't see me wasting half my day lying around in bed."

Judith stared at her, stunned. Then she started to laugh. "Mr Hudson is obviously a very lucky man!"

Mrs Hudson stayed with Judith for five years until the lure of her first grandchild sent her back up to her native Scotland. Judith missed her more than she'd ever admit.

Judith had one philosophy in life: she wouldn't tolerate weak people, idiots and those who couldn't do their jobs properly and that job could be anything from a housekeeper to a doctor to an actor. Once, on a plane to Los Angeles, she had got up and performed the safety display herself because the stewardess wasn't doing it properly, pointing out the lavatories instead of the exits and wearing her lifejacket inside out. Judith, of course, had done it with such panache that the passengers gave her a round of applause as she sat down again.

Judith poured herself a large glass of whisky and threw herself down on the sofa and got out her *Blithe Spirit* script. Max X came and curled up on her lap.

"The director is an idiot, Max. I don't know why I agreed to let this stupid producer employ him. Just because he's flavour of the month – what the fuck does that matter?"

Max X purred contentedly. Judith stroked him gently. Max X was so named in that he was the 10th Max that Judith had owned. Max I had been dead about 40 years now. Not that she'd had cats as a child. Judith had been born just before the war, and her mother had struggles enough with rationing and a husband in the army to want the extra hassle that pets brought. Then when Judith's father had come back he announced he had met another woman and was divorcing Judith's mother. Judith found herself shuttled back and forth between parents on the train, like some child commuter, and pets were definitely not an option.

Judith had acquired Max I at the Oldham Repertory Theatre. This was Judith's first theatre job after leaving RADA and she had been hired to play a variety of roles, from maids to children to dramatic heroines to old ladies – all at 20 years old.

"The Repertory Theatre System," Judith would say in interviews, "was a wonderful way of learning the theatre business. Every week we had to play one role, while rehearsing another in the day for the following week. I always preferred the period pieces; that way we got the costumes provided for us. If it was a modern play we had to supply our own, and as you can imagine at 20 I had very few old lady clothes. On some shows I would double as an assistant stage manager and have to help with props and setting scenery. Actors nowadays don't know they're born."

Max I had been bought as a theatre cat, for the purpose of mouse removal. Unfortunately for the theatre he proved exceptionally lazy, having no intention of either chasing mice or bothering to find his litter tray. What was the point when there was so many delightful places on which to relax and empty his bladder? Consequently, actors would find wet patches in the middle of the carpet during an Agatha Christie play or inside a pair of costume shoes, while the auditorium seats were covered in cat fur. His fate was sealed when, during a bedroom scene of a new play, the leading lady and man lay back onto the covers to find them saturated in cat pee. Max I was fired on the spot.

"What's going to happen to him?" Judith asked the stage manager.

"He'll have to be put down. I'm sorry but we can't keep him."

"I can," said Judith. A gallant pronouncement, resulting in her having to change digs four times, before she found a woman with three cats of her own who soon ensured Max I learnt to use the litter tray.

As a jobbing actress, having a cat was not easy but somehow Judith managed, even though on occasions she had to sneak him into various digs and hotels in her suitcase. When, after a heart attack, Max I died in Clacton-upon-Sea during a UK tour of a rather bad thriller Judith was appearing in, she was gutted.

At the performance that night she was so emotional in the scene where she discovers her murdered husband that a leading London agent, in Clacton-upon-Sea to visit his aunt, was mesmerized and offered to represent her. Judith kept him waiting for two days so as not to appear too keen and then signed up with him.

Alan East, the agent, was exactly what Judith needed, and, unlike most actors who always claim their agents don't do anything for them and constantly try to change to another, Judith stayed with him. Of course she gave him hell, but he got used to it. People said Alan only put up with Judith because she made him a lot of money, and of course she did. But he also had a huge admiration for her talent and besides he'd known her before she was a star and understood her a lot better than most people. When he had first taken Judith out to lunch in London to discuss his future plans for her, she'd confided the real reason for her emotion the night he'd seen the play.

Alan had laughed a lot. "You mean to say I've taken on a one hit wonder!"

"It's too late now, I've signed the contract. You're stuck with me!"

The following day Alan had arrived at Judith's door carrying two tiny kittens. "I couldn't decide which one to choose, so I got both," he explained.

"How am I going to look after two of them?" Judith demanded, at the same time gently stroking the heads of the kittens destined to become Max II and Max III.

"You are going to be such a star reams of people will be falling over themselves to look after them for you."

A week later Alan persuaded an established director to audition Judith for the role of the self-assured Raina in a West End production of George Bernard Shaw's *Arms and the Man*. The director was charmed by Judith's remarkable looks, talent and forthright manner. She got the role. Her performance garnered rave reviews and Judith was on her way.

Though many critics commented on her striking looks, Judith never considered herself a beauty. Though her jet black hair, emerald green eyes, and perfect size ten figure had many men drooling, she also had a distinctly angular nose. In her second West End play, Somerset Maugham's *The Circle,* one critic had written: 'Miss Gold may find it hard to continue getting roles as pretty young things unless she considers having some cosmetic work to her nose. She would, however, be perfect casting as the Wicked Witch of the West in *The Wizard of Oz.*'

To most young actresses this would have led to an immediate appointment with a plastic surgeon, an emerging fashion in London. Judith took a different approach. Dressed in full Wicked Witch of the West costume, complete with green face and hands, she arrived at the offices of the critic's newspaper, and presented him with a writ for libel. This was virtually unheard of at that time. The newspaper tried to settle out of court, but Judith would have none of it: she wanted to be publicly vindicated. A sympathetic judge, a substantial amount of damages and Judith emerged beaming. She wasn't going to give in to anybody.

Eight years after her first job in Oldham, Judith was the darling of the West End, playing leading roles in plays by William Shakespeare, Noel Coward, Henrik Ibsen, Christopher Marlowe, Anton Chekhov, Arthur Wing Pinero, Terence Rattigan and JB Priestly.

"These classics are all very well, Alan,"

Judith complained one day while she was having coffee in her agent's office.

Alan East raised him eyebrows. Most of the other actors on his books would give anything to play the roles Judith was getting.

"Oh, put your eyebrows down, Alan, for fuck's sake; you look like some Victorian melodrama villain."

"So what do you want to do, Judith?"

"A musical. I've never done one."

Alan, who wasn't sure he could picture Judith kicking up her heels in a show like *Oklahoma!*, thought for a minute. "There's *Peter Pan* at the London Coliseum this Christmas. A couple of my other clients are auditioning for pirates and Indians. How would you fancy playing Peter? I don't think it's cast yet and I'm sure they'd be thrilled to employ someone of your calibre."

Judith grabbed the half finished mug of coffee from his hand. "Well, get on with it Alan. NOW!"

The rehearsals started well enough, but after a few days Judith found her numbers were being cut or given to Wendy or the Lost Boys to sing.

"Why?" she demanded. "Is there something wrong with my singing?"

The director, terrified of his temperamental star, muttered something about the show being too long and the songs detracting from the story.

"Bollocks!" Judith said and phoned Alan,

who turned up, listened to Judith performing one of her numbers and then took her out to lunch.

"You can't sing."

"I can, I was singing perfectly."

"No, Judith, you were completely off key. You and the tune were not compatible. Couldn't you hear that?"

Judith shook her head.

"I think you're what they call tone deaf, Judith. I'm sorry."

"I could take lessons."

"You don't have time. Besides, if you're totally tone deaf there's little anyone could do. Look, you're going to be a terrific Peter Pan and everyone will rave about you. Don't spoil that by trying to do the only thing you can't. OK?"

"Why didn't the bloody director tell me that?"

"Probably because he's scared of you."

"Stupid fucker!" Judith stalked off. Alan sent his secretary to the local pet shop, and Max IV joined Judith's growing feline household.

She might not be able to sing, but Judith loved the chance to fly way up above the stage. Where her co-stars looked nervously down and clung to their wires, Judith demanded to be taken higher and higher. When Wendy screamed one night after she unexpectedly dropped a few inches, Judith tore her off a strip as they came into the wings.

"The audience is hardly going to believe we're having a magical time flying over Neverland, when Wendy is screaming her fucking head off."

"I wonder if she'd have been sympathetic if I'd actually crashed to the ground," Wendy muttered to one of the Neverland Indians who was standing in the wings waiting to go on stage for the pow-wow scene.

"I doubt it!" said the Indian, checking his make-up. "I don't think she cares for anyone except herself." Judith sat in her dressing room cuddling Max IV and wondering why she was surrounded by amateurs.

Max V was a first-night present to Judith from Victor Lewis on the opening night of Hedda Gabler ('A tour de force from this magnificent actress': the Times). Victor was a young actor understudying the role of Eilert Loveberg. Unlike Judith's usual co-stars, he wasn't intimidated by her in the least. On the first day of rehearsals, Victor had done an excellent impersonation of the director and had made Judith cry with laughter. An instant friendship became a passionate affair.

When, however, at the end of the run Victor had got down on one knee and proposed, Judith had stared at him in astonishment.

"I can't possibly marry anyone at the moment. I've got to concentrate on my career. Besides, you're merely an understudy; I am a leading lady. I have to think of my reputation."

Victor had never acted again. Nor did he ever see Judith again. Judith had plenty more affairs, and with some of the biggest names in the business as well as a member of parliament, but no one made her feel the way Victor had. On occasions she would claim he was the great love of her life, and would hint that some dreadful event had befallen him, rather than it being her own ambition which had destroyed their relationship.

'**Judith Gold loves nobody but Judith Gold**' screamed the headline of an article by one of her leading men in Hollywood.

Hollywood had been the natural step after playing so many leads in the theatre. Three top studio heads fought to get her under contract. Each one, on hearing that she liked cats, and aware the British quarantine system prohibited them from joining her if she decided to return there, secretly sent out their assistants to get her a kitten. She made a few movies, but not being a conventional beauty and refusing to fit in with the Hollywood Studio system, she grew bored and headed back to England. Her only regret was being forced to leave the Maxes (VI, VII and VIII) behind, even though she found them all good homes.

"Thank God!" exclaimed one of her directors on hearing the news of Judith's departure. "That woman gave me more sleepless nights than all three of my children."

On hearing that remark, the director's wife snorted derisively. His three children had hardly given him sleepless nights since she'd been the one who always got up.

Judith continued her film and TV career in England and won a British Academy film award for her performance as a prostitute in the movie *Don't Knock It Until You've Tried It*. She already had two Society of West End Theatre awards. One for *Hedda Gabler* and the second for *Who's Afraid of Virginia Woolf?* She kept these three proudly on the table in her sitting room. But if anyone came round she would quickly stick them in front of her doors and say, "Oh, those silly things, they mean nothing, do they? But they're perfect doorstops."

After a few years of non-stop work, Judith decided she'd take a break. It didn't last long.

"Alan, it's Judith."

"Judith. I was beginning to think you'd gone into retirement. You haven't returned any of my calls."

"I've decided it's time to return to the West End stage. I've been away from my theatre-going public for too long."

"Really? How thoughtful of you."

"Don't be such a supercilious bastard, Alan. OK, in truth, I'm 55," Alan smiled, Judith had been 55 for well over five years by his reckoning, "and no one wants older actresses on film and TV, do they?"

"Well …"

"Oh come on, Alan, you don't have to do

your client support act. You know I'm right. It would be fine if I were a man of course. No doubt fucking Sean Connery and bloody Harrison Ford will go on making movies on day release from their old people's homes on Zimmer frames!"

Alan chuckled. "OK, so have you anything in mind?"

"Yes, Saint Joan."

"Judith, she was a 17 year old virgin."

"So? Sarah Bernhardt played her when she was about my age, and she had a wooden leg."

"Yes but ..."

"Do you think I couldn't play the part?"

"Yes of course you could only ..."

"I could look young at a distance."

"How far a distance? She's 17, as in a teenager."

"Oh for fuck's sake, how did I end up with an agent without a sense of humour?"

"You were kidding? You mean you don't really want to do Saint Joan?"

"What do you take me for, Alan, a complete idiot?"

"Thank God. Don't do that to me again, Judith, you've aged me ten years in the last two minutes. Now, have you any better suggestions, or shall I hang up?"

"Yes, Madame Arcati in *Blithe Spirit*. You know how I adore dear Noel's plays, and I've never had the opportunity to do *Blithe Spirit*."

"But Madame Arcati isn't the largest role in the play."

"No, which means far fewer lines to learn, thank God. But every time she appears she steals the scene: perfect. Think of the film; who's the person you remember?"

"Rex Harrison."

"Alan, don't be so fucking insufferable."

"Well, he used to be one of my clients so of course I'd remember him."

"Say he hadn't been your client."

"Margaret Rutherford."

"Precisely. Everyone considers her the archetypal Madame Arcati, but that's because they haven't seen mine yet."

"I'll get on to it in the morning, Judith."

"What's wrong with now?"

"It's 6pm; I'm on my way home."

"Not any more."

Alan sighed, bid Judith goodbye and started ringing round producers. Not that it was hard; a play with Judith Gold was a sure fire hit and would pay great dividends. Alan decided to deal with a producer who had worked with Judith before and therefore aware of the stress involved.

The producer suggested a new young director who had wowed critics at the National Theatre and in the West End. Judith hadn't seen any of his productions.

"But at least if he's young I'll be able to tell him what I require," she said to Max X when Alan had phoned to tell her of the deal (Max IX had been a brief visitor, a stray who decided one night he preferred being a stray and never came back). But after one day of Alexander Columbus's direction Judith was no longer sure she was going to be able to get the sort of production she wanted, and she liked to get what she wanted. She certainly had no intention of failing this time.

CHAPTER THREE

Rupert Blake and Miranda Flynn were going at it hell for leather. This was nothing new; they'd been married for 10 years and spent at least half of that fighting. It was the way their relationship worked. Yet outwardly they were the perfect theatrical couple.

"We're the English equivalent of Jennifer Aniston and Brad Pitt," Miranda used to joke in interviews, but she'd had to change that. Rupert, who had a huge respect for older movie actors, preferred comparisons with the likes of Paul Newman and Joanne Woodward or Mel Brooks and the late Anne Bancroft.

"I don't want to be compared to some grey haired old lady," Miranda would snap. "I'm young and glamorous."

Rupert would think of Anne Bancroft seducing Dustin Hoffman in *The Graduate* and comment that he'd have slept with her anytime.

"Oh, that's gross, though of course I'm aware you'd sleep with anything female, but she's not even alive any more. Besides, do you want to be compared to some old man who makes salad dressing or writes silly comedies?"

"If I could give a performance like Paul

Newman in *The Hustler* or *Cool Hand Luke* or write and direct a movie like *The Producers*, I would be a happy man."

As an acting couple, they were sometimes employed jointly for plays and TV. *Blithe Spirit* was the third West End show they had done together, this time playing husband and wife, Charles and Ruth Condomine.

Both Rupert and Miranda considered they were the actor the producers wanted to employ and that the other came along as part of the package. Since each of them was confident in this view neither of them mentioned it to the other and both were happy.

"You were practically drooling over that young girl playing the maid," Miranda announced, dramatically throwing herself onto the sofa with her hand clasped to her heart, or at least roughly where she thought her heart was. In their worst quarrels Rupert frequently told her she had no heart, and since she was the only person in her form at school that had been requested to no longer partake in biology classes, her knowledge of anatomy was sketchy.

"I have no interest in cutting up frogs or learning how plants reproduce," she stated to her teacher. "I'm not a plant, nor do I ever intend to be one, so why should I care?"

Her parents, having spent a fortune sending her to a private school, were less than happy. Miranda considered education a waste of time except for drama classes; that was all she needed to become an actress. She virtually lived in detention since she rarely bothered to do any work. Her parents threatened to withdraw their funds for her drama school if she didn't stay on at school until she was 18. Miranda stayed until her 18th birthday and then walked out the school gates never to return, regardless of the fact her A levels weren't for another three months. As far as she was concerned she had kept her side of the bargain.

Much to her chagrin, Miranda failed to get a place at RADA. "But that's where everyone good goes," she'd said in horror on opening the envelope denying her application. She applied for The Central School of Speech and Drama, Webber Douglas Academy and The London Academy of Music and Dramatic Art and got nowhere.

Eventually, after astounding the auditioning panel with her spirited, if naïve, version of one of Cleopatra's speeches from *Anthony and Cleopatra*, she got into Mountview Theatre School.

Three years later, at the graduation showcase, Miranda played the leading role of Sally Bowles in *Cabaret*. In spite of a less than stunning singing voice and not possessing some of the talent of her fellow students, Miranda, with her vibrant auburn hair, long legs encased in stockings, and smouldering glances, was enough to electrify many of the men in the audience.

Among these men was Mike Hopkins, a young up-and-coming agent, who made the mistake of falling madly in love with her and immediately offering to represent her. Much to his disappointment, being her agent was as far as he got; Miranda's interest in Mike was professional only, but as long as he was in love with her she could twist him around her little finger, and she did.

"I want to be famous, Mike, whatever that takes, and I want it soon."

Miranda's first professional role was as an obnoxious teenage daughter in an Alan Ayckbourn play. A few years later and she'd progressed to the adult lead in another Alan Ayckbourn. She worked steadily, got a nice role in a TV drama series, a cameo in a BBC adaptation of a Charles Dickens, more theatre, a guest slot in Midsomer Murders (but then which actor hasn't?) and an advert for low calorie margarine which paid for a deposit on a flat in Chelsea. For an actor it was a good career, but Miranda never felt she was as famous as she deserved.

Rupert, on the other hand, was noticeably more successful, partially, at least to start, helped by his good looks and enormous charm. People who had previously worked with him would recollect how he'd be familiar with the names of their spouses and children and seem to be genuinely interested in their problems. He never caused any trouble in rehearsals, was never late for filming and was always fully prepared with his lines or moves. This, combined with a definite talent, made Rupert a director's dream and the perfect co-star. He was never out of work for more than a few weeks.

Unlike Miranda, Rupert hadn't always dreamt of being an actor. He'd actually fallen into it after his career dream, being the first English man to win Wimbledon, disappeared after he was continuously knocked out in the first round of every tournament on the tennis circuit.

"I was the man who encouraged Tim Henman," he used to joke. This was possibly news to Tim Henman who had started to play tennis well after Rupert had given up. But undeniably it sounded impressive.

Rupert's tennis career finished one June day after losing on one of the outside courts at Wimbledon 4-6, 2-6, 0-6 to some Hungarian player with an unpronounceable name. As he walked back to the locker rooms he was approached by a young woman in a smart designer suit and dark glasses.

"Mr Blake – Jane English. I work for a leading London modelling agency. I wondered whether you had ever thought of trying some modelling."

"No!" Rupert was a little shocked. He was very proud of his masculinity; posing for a camera in make-up and Calvin Klein underwear was not for him. "But thank you for the offer." After all, it was flattering.

"Shame," said Jane, "with your looks you could go far. Perhaps you should try the movies."

Rupert considered this as he left Wimbledon that night. Now he was out of the tournament he had nothing else to do for the next two weeks while his opponents went on to fight for the winner's crown. Perhaps he should give up trying for a sporting trophy and go for an acting one instead: an Oscar or a BAFTA maybe. He did some research, bought a copy of Contacts, a sort of theatrical who's who, and called round to all the agents.

"Are you appearing in anything at the moment that we could see you in?" was the identical response from every agent. "You're not. I'm sorry, then we couldn't consider you at present. Get back to us when you are."

This was turning out to be harder than he'd thought. He called Jane English. "Would you take me on as an actor?"

"But I don't know much about acting work."

"How much do you normally charge your modelling clients?"

"10%."

"I'll pay you 15%. How much do you know about acting now?"

"I'm a quick learner."

Jane turned out to be a very quick learner and within a week had got Rupert a small role in a TV comedy. As she'd predicted, Rupert came across well on screen and was quickly snapped up for the lead in a new Lynda La

Plante TV drama. He followed that with the lead in that rare phenomenon, a successful British movie, in turn leading to a small but critically acclaimed role in a Hollywood blockbuster. Jane was certainly earning every penny of her 15%, and in more ways than one when she and Rupert had an affair lasting six months. It wasn't serious on either side, so caused no bad feelings or problems in their working relationship when it ended. Jane was virtually certain Rupert had slept with other girls while she was seeing him, but that was Rupert; you either accepted it or you got out. Being constantly surrounded by pretty young actresses was far too much of a temptation for someone with Rupert's libido. Besides, Jane had taken on to her books an 18 year old male model and was very happy enjoying the experience of a toy boy.

In spite of his success on screen Rupert missed the excitement of performing live in the way he had when playing tennis. In film and TV you had no one to cheer you or laugh or clap. Additionally, if you made mistakes you could do them again. There could never be the same adrenalin rush as being in front of an audience.

"I want to hear the proverbial 'roar of the crowd', Jane. Can you get me some theatre work?"

"Are you crazy, Rupert? Your career is going great in the movie industry. Once you start taking time off people forget you instantly."

"And my darling Janie, movies pay far more than theatre, and agents like to get as much commission as possible, don't they?"

"How can you say that, Rupert? You know I'm only thinking of your career. Besides, how do you know whether anyone wants you on the stage? You're thought of as movie actor."

"Funny you should say that. The National Theatre has asked me if I'd like to join them for a couple of plays. Or to be precise I slept with one of the casting people and persuaded her in a moment of passion."

"WHAT? Have you any idea how badly they pay? In the West End I could have got you a good deal, but the National pay peanuts! People only go there for the kudos."

"Exactly," said Rupert. "I want to prove I can act, not that I'm merely a pretty face. And that is what I'm going to do, however hard I have to work at it. I was a second-rate tennis player, but I'm going to be a first-rate actor."

Actually it was harder than Rupert had imagined, but he never gave up. Realizing that most actors at the National had years of training and theatrical experience, he was careful to watch and learn and would humbly ask for help from anyone.

On the first performance of Shaw's *Man and Superman,* his stage debut in which he only had a small role, Rupert experienced a euphoria as the curtain came down which he'd never felt before, not even when he'd taken a game off Jimmy Connors in the US Open 6 years before.

Rupert's second role was as the lead: American newspaper reporter Hildy Johnson in Charles MacArthur and Ben Hecht's 1928 play *The Front Page*. His reviews were excellent, but far more importantly to Rupert, Anthony Hopkins stopped him in the backstage canteen after a matinee and told him how much he'd enjoyed his performance. How much more could any actor want? He loved the stage and when he was offered further roles at the National he stayed on. After a year they offered him the chance to play Hamlet, every actor's dream role, and he jumped at it.

The critics weren't over enthusiastic with his portrayal, but neither were they damning. Rupert himself admitted he might not have been entirely ready for the role. There was so much depth in the Danish Prince and Shakespeare was a playwright you couldn't just wing, but he might never have got another chance and he didn't regret taking it.

There was another reason *Hamlet* was a significant experience for Rupert. Cast as Ophelia was a young actress called Miranda Flynn. Lovers on stage, they also became so off stage and a year later they married. It was mostly a successful relationship, in spite of the rows and Rupert's magnetism to women. Not that the magnetism was one sided; his reputation as a womanizer was notorious and the cause of their argument tonight after their first day of rehearsals for *Blithe Spirit*.

"Come on, Miranda, I hardly noticed that girl."

"Rupert, you were looking down her top when you shook her hand."

"Rubbish! She's a child. I'm hardly going to be interested in some 18 year old; what the hell would we have to talk about?"

"Talking would be the last thing on either of your minds, I suspect. Besides, she's been to drama school. That's a three year course; she must be at least 21."

"Well, if I'm to make passionate love to a 21 year old, perhaps you should do the same with our young director."

"Oh please! That man is an idiot. He's done nothing all day but talk about concepts and motivation. I don't think I've ever spent a day of rehearsals without a single bit of acting before. Why on earth has he been employed?"

"It beats me, darling." Rupert wandered into the kitchen and brought out a bottle of wine and a couple of glasses. "Do you want a drink?"

"Do you need to ask? But forget those tiny glasses; get me a tumbler."

Rupert returned with two huge tumblers and settled down on the sofa beside Miranda, her auburn tresses contrasting with his dark locks.

"So how do you think it's going to go?" Rupert asked.

"Like hell." Miranda yawned and stretched her legs onto Rupert's lap. "I can't see Judith and Alexander hitting it off. Can you?"

"No. But I hope it doesn't ruin the play; I've always wanted a crack at a Coward play. I love the wit and speed of the dialogue."

"Well, we have several scenes with only us, darling. I'm sure we can make the most of those: how about a bit of private rehearsal?" She wiggled her toes in what she hoped was a seductive manner. Arguments always made her feel horny.

"You're right." Rupert pulled his script from his bag. "Shall we go from the top of the play?"

"That wasn't quite the rehearsing I'd meant." Miranda smiled up at him.

"Come on, Miranda, I want to get a grip on this role before Alexander and Judith re-do the whole play."

"Great!" Miranda snapped. "You want to sleep with everyone but me. Fine. I'll get my script." She walked across the room picked up her bag, managing to crack Rupert across the head as she did so.

"Christ, Miranda!"

"Oh, sorry darling, I was giving you some motivation for being a henpecked husband."

"Charles is not henpecked."

"Oh yes?"

"No, it's just that Ruth is a bitch."

"She is not. She's being totally supportive of Charles and what's the thanks she gets? He becomes all gooey over the ghost of his first wife."

"Gooey? Honestly, Miranda, that's not very Noel Coward, is it?"

"Oh, who cares?"

Rupert got off up the sofa and headed into the kitchen with his script. "I do."

That, he thought, was the main difference between him and Miranda. He cared passionately about his craft; Miranda cared about being famous and looking good. He hoped working together on this particular show wasn't going to be a problem.

Miranda, on the other hand, was hoping her costumes were going to be glamorous. She flipped through her script wondering how many different outfits she could be permitted. Oh, and she must make sure she had a say in her wig; she'd seen some horrors in her career and she couldn't risk something which made her resemble a scarecrow.

"Rupert," she called out, "who made my wigs for that TV Agatha Christie I did? They were beautiful."

Rupert, engrossed in Noel Coward's language, sighed. "It was a Mr Stein, I think, darling. Yes, Frank N."

"Frank N Stein," said Miranda frowning. Then stopped, scowling.

"You bastard, Rupert!"

Rupert smiled and returned to his script. Miranda found her contacts book and started rifling through for wig people. Frankenstein indeed, sometimes she could kill Rupert.

CHAPTER FOUR

Echo would have been terrified by the first day of *Blithe Spirit* rehearsals, if she hadn't been two sandwiches short of a picnic. She'd never acted on stage before, in fact the majority of people who'd seen her on TV in America considered she'd never acted full stop. Nor had she ever been to England.

"I had to get a passport to come here," she'd told Miranda with wide eyes over coffee that morning.

"You've never had a passport before?" Miranda considered trips abroad an essential deduction on her tax return.

"Oh sure, I had one to go to Disneyland in LA; it was a special one too, because I was a VEP."

"A Vep?"

"A Very Emportant Person."

Miranda spluttered into her coffee. "Emportant?"

"Yeah, 'cos I was a celebrity. I got to skip to the front of the line and everything."

"You and Mickey Mouse probably got on famously."

"Oh, he didn't speak to me."

"No, he probably has too much of an IQ, or in your case an EQ!"

"Oh no, it's IQ. I was tested once."

"Did they find anything?"

"Huh?"

"Never mind, Echo." Miranda couldn't stand it any longer; her patience was exceedingly limited. Leaving the American standing alone she went in search of Rupert to relate Echo's pearls of wisdom. Echo, honestly, what kind of a name was that?

Echo was very proud of her name. It sounded so romantic. Her mother, Storm, a failed beauty queen entrant whose obsession was now her precious daughter, told Echo she'd been through every name in three books of baby names, and this was the only one which fitted her blonde, blue eyed daughter to perfection.

As Echo grew older her blonde hair started to change to a darker shade. Immediately, Storm whisked her off to the best hairdressers in town to bleach it back; she was five years old at the time.

Storm, determined her daughter would succeed where she had failed, dragged her round the children's beauty pageant circuit. Echo had an entire wardrobe of fancy clothes, pretty shoes and enough hair ribbons to create her very own maypole, if she'd known what a maypole was. Since they were constantly travelling from town to town Storm elected to home tutor her daughter. Sadly, Storm's own education had been along a similar line so Echo never stood a chance. A typical lesson would go something like this:

"OK, Echo, can you tell me which state we're going to tomorrow?"

"Texas."

"That's very good honey. Now can you tell me what the capital of Texas is?"

"Austin."

"Really? I thought it was Houston."

"No, Mommy, one of the other girls in the pageant, you know Bethany, she comes from Austin and she said it's the capital."

"Well, aren't you the cleverest little thing to remember that?"

"Yes, Mommy."

"And what is Texas most famous for?"

"Oil? That's what Bethany's dad works in."

"No, Echo, far more famous than that. Let me give you a hint: Miss Ellie, JR, Bobby?"

"*Dallas*!"

Echo had grown up watching her mother's collection of *Dallas* videos until she felt as if Lucy Ewing was her sister and Bobby a kind of uncle. Together she and Storm would examine every costume and hairstyle; in fact, several of Echo's outfits were mini versions of *Dallas* designs.

"OK, baby, one more question. And this is the most important one of all. Are you ready?"

"Yes, Mommy."

"What dress are you going to wear for the pageant Saturday?"

"The pale blue with the lace, my two tone

satin Mary Jane's, that blue bow with the flower on it, and the new pink sugar lipstick we got last week."

"Who's a clever little girl then? Now, you've worked real hard so shall we go get a treat to eat?"

"Candy?"

"Echo, you know you can't eat that. It'll do terrible things to your complexion and your teeth, not to mention your figure. How about some carrot sticks?"

"Oh, Mommy, please, no more carrot sticks."

"Oh all right, how about some raisins as a special treat?"

"Thanks, Mommy, you're the best."

Where most American kids tell the passing of years in school grades, Echo notched them up in competitions: Toddler, Pee Wee, Little Miss, Pre-Teen. By the time she'd reached Teen proper Echo had a collection of awards, varying from trophies to bikes, from radios to cash, and had more photographs printed in local newspapers than the President of the United States had in the nationals in his entire tenure of office. Her wardrobe alone would've clothed a juvenile *Sex and the City* show for several seasons. The last time Storm and Echo had gone home to Alabama, Storm had demanded Echo's father, Pete, build them an extension to house all their stock.

"Why?" her long-suffering husband demanded. "Can't you give them to a thrift store? Help someone less fortunate than yourselves."

"Absolutely not, those are Echo's legs-lacey, to keep for her kids. Don't you know nothing?"

"I may not know much, Storm, but I believe the word is legacy, which surprisingly has nothing to do with legs or lace. And there's another thing I know: Echo is 13 and, as they say round here, a few fries short of a Happy Meal."

"But we never go near McDonald's, and Echo could never have fries."

"It's an expression; it means she's thick. Not that it's her fault; she doesn't have a chance, rushing all over the country for these beauty contests with only you as tutor. Kids are supposed to come home and go to school between, but no, you want to jump from one venue to another."

"We need time to prepare. It's not only the clothes, she has to walk proper and dance and have poise; that all takes practice. Have you any idea how heavy some of them tiaras are to wear?"

"Nope, funny thing, I don't. But I ain't finished talking yet. When Echo was little it was OK, though I always found it pretty grotesque plastering kids in make-up, pulling their hair into ringlets and dressing them like mini Joan Collinses. Still, it made you happy and Echo seemed unbothered. But it's got to stop. It's time Echo was allowed to try a Big

Mac and go to movies with her friends and spend Sundays playing softball in the park with other teenagers."

"Softball! Are you insane? Have you any idea of how dangerous these sports are? What if she got hit on her eye? She couldn't enter a contest with a black eye, although one of the other mothers told me there was some sort of amazing make-up that could cover all sorts of ..."

"Storm, you're not listening to me. I don't want Echo to enter any more competitions. I want you both to stay home with me. I never see either of you for more than a week at a time and often not for months on end and I've had enough. I wanna have my wife around and to see Echo grow up; I've missed too much of that anyways."

"Now, Pete, I can't take poor Echo off the circuit now, she'd be broken-hearted. Perhaps we could do a few less competitions and come home more often between 'em."

"You stay here permanently or you find some place else to live."

Storm stared at Pete in shock. He'd never spoken so masterfully before. It kind of excited her. She contemplated it for a minute. But what the hell would she do around here all day – in Alabama? Besides, she'd worked too hard to give up now. "I think it's cruel of you not to co-promise, honest I do."

"Compromise, Storm, I won't compromise."

"That neither. Well that's your loss 'cos me and Echo is going."

"Where 'is' you going?"

Storm had to think for a second. Snap decisions weren't her strong point. "We'll go to California. To Hollywood. Echo would make it big in the movies."

"If you do you're paying. I'll help out if Echo goes to a proper school, but not otherwise."

"Fine! We won't need help; when they see Echo do a screen test they'll be paying her millions a week."

"But Echo has never acted in her life. Beauty pageants ain't acting."

"Oh, how hard can it be? Look at all these young actresses: Kirsten Dunst and Reece Witherspoon, how much experience do you think they had?"

Pete sighed. He loved Storm, he really did, and he knew he was hardly the smartest guy around, but honestly she was so dumb. It distressed him that Echo was probably going to turn out the same. He should have done something about it a long time ago, but he'd always been weak. Too late now. "If Echo ends up acting like Kirsten Dunst or Reece Witherspoon, I shall personally come and beg for her autograph outside Grauman's Chinese Theatre where she will no doubt be laying her hand-print in cement on the sidewalk."

"We'll see you there." She called upstairs, "Echo, start packing: hot weather clothes."

She turned back to Pete. "It is always hot in Hollywood, right?"

"No, I don't think always. You might need some sweaters and jeans too."

"Oh." Storm relayed the message to Echo. "So you'll find somewhere to store the rest of Echo's wardrobe."

"No. I told you, I'm washing my hands of this whole thing."

"Fine, then I'll have a removal firm bring them out to California."

"I hope you find a big apartment."

"Apartment? We'll have a huge mansion, maybe overlooking the sea. Yes, Echo would like that."

"Echo would, or you would?"

Storm gave him a filthy look and called up the stairs for Echo to hurry up. Echo came downstairs carrying a designer suitcase she'd won a few months back. "Where are we going, Mommy?"

"To Hollywood. We're going to live there, and you're going to be a movie star."

"OK, Mommy. Is Daddy going to live there too?"

"No, so say goodbye for a while, OK?"

"Yes, Mommy. Goodbye, Daddy."

Pete hugged her. He was sure gonna miss her, but it was hardly as if he wasn't used to her not being around. Besides, he felt this idea was going to go belly up and they'd both be back before long and maybe this time Storm would agree to his requests. Successful as

Echo might be, it wasn't a hugely profitable hobby, and he had always supported them financially.

"Mommy," Pete heard Echo say as she and Storm walked down to the car, "I won't have to remember words if I'm a movie star, will I?"

"No, I'm sure they can write it all out for you, sweetheart."

Oh yes, Pete thought, they might be back real soon.

Pete might have been right with most women but he'd underestimated Storm.

Storm however, had underestimated Hollywood. Much to her annoyance there seemed to be literally hundreds of blonde, blue eyed teenagers all trying to break into the movies.

Determined not to have to ask Pete for money, Storm moved her and Echo into a tiny, run down apartment in West Hollywood, conveniently forgetting to send for Echo's clothes, and got herself a job as a make-up consultant at a department store; make-up she knew about. In the evenings she waited tables to pay for the acting classes she'd enrolled Echo in.

Echo liked LA. The sunny warm weather, the orange trees in people's gardens, the beach, the stores, the movie houses and constant movie premieres: she used to go and stand outside them and watch the famous actors walk up the red carpet. But most of all she loved being in only one place. It was a pretty grotty place: the air conditioner rattled constantly, if you ran the hot water in the tiny kitchenette the shower would go cold, their nearest neighbours rowed ceaselessly, and as for the cockroaches ... But it was home.

The acting classes, on the other hand, were torture. Everyone seemed to have done so much and she'd done nothing. At her first class the tutor had asked everyone to prepare a speech from Shakespeare.

"Is it a long play this Shakespeare?" she asked one of her fellow students.

"Huh?"

"We have to learn a piece from Shakespeare; I wanted to know if it was a long play."

"Are you messing with me?" The other girl looked at her suspiciously.

"No. At least, I don't think so."

"You really think Shakespeare is a play?"

"Isn't it?"

"Hey, guess what, guys? New girl here thinks Shakespeare is a play!"

There were screams of laughter.

Echo stood there, stunned. What had she said?

Having eventually tracked down a piece of a play by Shakespeare Echo then found it impossible to understand it, let alone learn it.

"Please can't I give up the classes, Mommy?" she'd begged.

"No, you're gonna be an actress and you're gonna take the classes."

"But Mommy, everyone else is so good and they get to go to auditions."

"They do?" Storm marched to see Echo's teacher who told her in no uncertain terms that Echo had very little talent.

"What the hell do you know?" Storm demanded and removed Echo from classes.

Echo happily went back to daydreaming, watching TV and visiting the wonderful clothes stores on Rodeo Drive. She often thought she wouldn't mind working there; she'd be surrounded by lovely clothes, and movie stars would come and ask for her advice.

But Storm had other ideas and eventually managed to get a make-up job on a movie at one of the studios. Talking to one of the actresses as she did her mascara one Tuesday, she learnt the young actress about to play a leading role in a daytime TV soap was on a sudden visit to the Betty Ford Clinic. A replacement was being sought at exceedingly short notice. "Isn't your daughter an actress?" the actress said. "Would she be interested?"

"Do Popes shit in the wood?" Storm demanded.

The actress looked startled. "Isn't that bears?"

"Huh?"

"Do bears shit in the wood? I think that's the expression."

"Oh. So what do Popes do?"

"I think they're Catholic."

"Of course Popes are Catholic; everyone knows that."

"Right, so why don't you check it out?"

The pilot began filming in two days' time, so when Storm turned up with Echo the soap's producers were thrilled. She was perfect: the right age, beautiful, blonde, and believable as the daughter of Tasha Lawson, the star. Echo was signed to a minimum five year contract on an accelerating scale of pay, sent to get her costumes fitted and given her first call. No one bothered to see if she could act.

Thankfully for Echo, the viewers of *Acacia Drive* ('Discover the lust, loves and heartbreaks of the families of Acacia Drive in our new afternoon soap': the Daily Soap Guide) were not greatly worried by acting ability and took Echo's character of sweet young Kimberly O'Connor to their hearts as she struggled with school, boys and her heavily drinking father.

Echo had struggles of her own.

"How can I learn all them words?" she'd asked Storm, horrified, as the first script had arrived.

"Don't worry, Honey, I'll help you."

Echo turned up on her first day excited and prepared, only to be given pages of rewrites to learn on the spot. It was a disaster. The director tried a teleprompter. That proved useless since Echo read so badly and with no expression whatsoever. Eventually, she was given an ear-piece through which she was fed her lines.

This was such a success that for the next 10 years that the series ran, Echo never again bothered to learn her lines. What was the point when there were lovely ear-pieces? Sure, she'd look at the lines first so when she heard them again they sounded familiar, and she could show the appropriate emotions, which in Echo's case were:

1. Horror/Fear: eyes wide open.
2. Cute: eyes fluttering.
3. Sad: eyes closed, sniffing.
4. Everything else: eyes vacant.

But the audience didn't care. 'I just want to be loved' became Kimberly's catchphrase and hundreds of viewers wrote in offering to adopt her, date her or merely be her friend. Her fan mail outstripped anyone else's on Acacia Lane. After one episode in which Tasha Lawson locked Kimberly in her room for calling the cops on her father, Tasha received so much hate mail she had to have a twenty four hour body guard until the writers came up with a reconciliation scenario.

There were quantities of photographs of Echo in magazines, and the National Enquirer linked her with a variety of well-known young actors. Echo did date a few, but most of them felt that having Storm come along was somewhat of a turn off.

But for Storm the important thing was her baby was a success. She called Pete.

"OK, so when are you gonna come beg for Echo's autograph?"

"When Echo can act."

"Whaddya mean? She is acting."

"Sure, if they ever need robots for a movie."

"Pete, how can you say that?"

"I watch the programme, Storm, or at least I did until I couldn't bear the scripts and the acting no more."

"But she's a star."

"Of a day time soap opera – that ain't saying much. She's a pretty blonde girl who's on TV. She ain't no actress."

Storm was furious. What did you have to do to be recognized as a proper actress? She bought a copy of Variety and for once read all of it. Hey, there was a theatre section, whaddya know? One of the articles caught her eye: 'Major Hollywood stars head to London to appear on West End stage'. Storm was fascinated. So that was what proper actors did. Geez, look at those names: Christian Slater, Matthew Perry, David Schwimmer, Minnie Driver, Kim Cattral, Holly Hunter, Madonna, Kathleen Turner, Luke Perry, Molly Ringwald, Jessica Lange, and Brendan Fraser. Mentally, she added Echo to the list.

Initially, Storm had been a little nonplussed to find it wasn't as easy as she'd thought. She obtained a list of noted English directors and stared to work through the list of unfamiliar names: Trevor Nunn, Richard Eyre, Nicholas Hytner, Sam Mendes, Peter Hall, Edward Hall, but none returned her calls. She continued down the list. Finally, a young man called Alexander Columbus answered his phone, informing her proudly that he was about to do a new production of Noel Coward's *Blithe Spirit.*

"I am currently looking for a well-known actress to play the role of Elvira," he told Storm importantly.

"Elvira. Isn't she some sort of vampire?" Storm asked suspiciously.

"No." There was a long pause from Alexander's end. "At least, I don't think so. She's a ghost. She swans around a lot in a white frock ... I believe."

"So she wouldn't have to take her clothes off or do sex scenes?"

"Certainly not!" Another pause. "Unless she wants to."

"No."

"Oh. Oh well, never mind. OK. So is she a big TV star then? Has she been on *ER* or *Friends*?"

"She's a huge star. She has her own TV show. But I don't think you get it in England. Of course they begged her to guest on *ER* and *Friends*, but she couldn't fit it in her busy shooting schedule."

"Can you send me her photo and her CV?"

"CV?"

"You know, everything she's been in and what theatre work she's done."

"Oh, you mean a résumé. Sure. I'll send them both out right away."

Storm sent a glamorous studio photo of Echo and a résumé stolen from a bit part actress in Acacia Lane who had done a lot of stage work in summer stock.

Alexander presented his negotiations with Storm as a fait accompli to the *Blithe Spirit* producer; he hadn't had much say on previous casting and was proud of his scoop. "Besides, if we have an American star in the show it might be easier to take it to Broadway," he told the producer. Mention Broadway to a producer and they start to see dollar signs. The role of Elvira was cast.

Meanwhile, Storm announced Echo would not be taking up her contract for another year on *Acacia Lane*. And Echo found herself on her way to her first stage appearance in London, England, with a passport – and with Storm.

CHAPTER FIVE

Scarlett Montgomery was, in all probability, the only person to go home from the first day of *Blithe Spirit* rehearsals in a state of excitement. Not only was this her first professional engagement, but she was working with some of the biggest names around and the trendiest director. Unlike her fellow cast members, Scarlett had seen all Alexander Columbus's productions, even *Twelfth Night* in the pub theatre where she'd insisted on sitting in the front row wearing a bright yellow raincoat in the hope she would get noticed.

She didn't.

When she saw Alexander's directorial version of *Romeo and Juliet* she wore a T-shirt that said: 'Sod Juliet try me' and stood outside the stage door when the young actor playing Romeo came out to sign autographs.

The actor didn't take up her offer.

For *The Sound of Music* she wore a nun's wimple, a Von Trapp child's sailor dress and Nazi boots, and once again sat in the front row.

That got her noticed.

It didn't, however, get her work, but that was OK. She still had a few more months left at her drama school and then she'd worry about her career. No, Scarlett loved acting, but her obsession was with the famous. She wanted to meet them, to talk to them, to work for or with them and preferably to date them – if they were male. The females would, in Scarlett's fantasies, become inseparable bosom buddies.

A dictionary could well define star-struck as:

1. Fascinated by or exhibiting a fascination with fame or famous people.

2. See Scarlett Montgomery.

As a child she would beg her parents to introduce her to famous actors, even though they were both trial lawyers and didn't move in theatrical circles.

"Honestly, why can't you ever defend anyone famous?" Scarlett would demand. "They commit crimes too, you know. Look at OJ Simpson and Michael Jackson."

"I'd much rather not," replied her father in the midst of trying to figure out a defence for a shoplifter who had been caught red-handed not only by two shop assistants, but the manager and store detective. In spite of that she was pleading not guilty. There were occasions you needed such a good imagination in his job: something Scarlett seemed to have inherited.

At 12 years old Scarlett finally got through that hallowed portal called the stage door to visit her best friend's aunt who was appearing in a play in the West End. She looked round the dressing room as if she'd arrived in heaven and was only removed with difficulty.

"I'm going to be in this dressing room one day," she had announced. "And everyone will come and visit me, like other actors and movie stars and ... and my family and old friends too, I suppose."

She created her own dressing room in her bedroom at home, copying pictures from books. There were lights round the mirror, a dressing table full of make-up (mostly for display purposes), a star on the door, a stereo system playing non-stop show tunes, piles of scripts and walls covered in theatre posters and signed photographs she'd collected. She'd had Judith Gold's signed photograph up there which she'd written to ask for after seeing her in Hedda Gabler. Now she was working with her; it was a miracle.

At the age of 14 she got herself a paper round to pay for several backstage theatre tours. She was very disappointed that at neither the Haymarket nor Drury Lane theatres did she see anyone famous at all. But at the National she was certain she'd seen Judi Dench walking round the ground floor level carrying a sandwich and looking a little disoriented.

"Everyone gets lost here," the guide told them. "It's like a rabbit warren backstage. When I first started I used to tie pieces of string on the stairwells and doorknobs so I could find my way around. One night I got so muddled I was wandering around for about 30 minutes before I could find someone to show me the way out!"

As they continued the tour Scarlett allowed herself a short fantasy where she rescued a lost Judi Dench from the bowels of the National, just in time for her to make her entrance on stage, and Judi said: "Thank you so much Scarlett, I could have been here for days. How can I ever thank you? Perhaps you'd like to co-star in a play with me. Whichever play you'd like. And of course you must come and stay with me while we do it, and we'll become great friends."

Luckily, Scarlett could act as well as she could worship, so getting into drama school wasn't a problem. A month after she'd left she had her first job, and what a job. Scarlett hardly slept for a week before the first *Blithe Spirit* rehearsal and would leap out of bed at 4am to scrawl an idea in her well-thumbed script. Edith wasn't a huge role; in fact in Act One her lines were virtually monosyllabic. But the last scene, where it emerged she'd been responsible for the whole ghost scenario, was a joy. And the scene was with Judith Gold (and Rupert Blake); what more could she want? She, Scarlett Montgomery, and Judith Gold acting on stage together.

"So how did it go today?" Scarlett's flatmate, Holly, had arrived back from work.

"Great, terrific. Oh I can't believe it's really happening to me!"

"OK, don't rub it in."

"Oh, I'm sorry, Holl. You'll get something soon, I know you will."

Holly grimaced. "Yeah right. Remember our end of year showcase? The pile of photos we each had for prospective agents to take? Every one of yours went. Me? How many did I get rid of? Let's count. Oh yes, I remember – one! And I'm not sure that wasn't my mother taking it out of pity when I wasn't looking. And the party afterwards – you were surrounded by important theatre people. I stood in the corner and talked to the pot plant and even it wasn't really interested. I think I put on half a stone that day because I ate everything in sight so I would appear like I was busy. But you, you're talented and you're gorgeous; that's a great combination."

"Come on, Holl, you're hardly a dog."

"I might do better if I was. I could play Sandy in the revival of *Annie,* or one of those dogs in *Chitty Chitty Bang Bang.* Instead I get to temp at the most boring offices in London. Do you know how long eight hours is when you spend it doing nothing but stuffing envelopes? You have no idea how much I long for the tea break, and I don't even drink tea! The main excitement of the day is when the manager brings in biscuits and I have the huge task of choosing whether to have one or not."

"To be scuit or not to be scuit, that is the question, Hobnoblet Act IV," said Scarlett flipping through her *Blithe Spirit* script yet again. Holly laughed "Alas poor Rich Tea, I knew him well." She studied Scarlett thoughtfully. She was stunning. With a Greek Mother and English father, Scarlett had a dark, exotic complexion with huge brown eyes and long thick black hair with a natural wave. Her whole body seemed to exude life and energy. Holly, on the other hand, felt she exuded nothing but exhaustion at present, and her curly hair was a frizzy mess thanks to the rain. It is a known fact that something like 80% of the acting profession are out of work at any one time. Holly had a horrible feeling she would probably spend most of her career in that percentage whereas Scarlett would no doubt be in the 20% success rate. If she was still temping in ten years time she would throw herself off Westminster Bridge. No, better make that off Waterloo Bridge; at least that way she'd be in front of the National Theatre, possibly the closest she'd ever get to performing there.

"I really should call Mike," Scarlett said suddenly.

"Why?"

"To tell him how it went today." Scarlett was so proud she'd landed a big agent she mentioned his name as often as she could.

"It's 7.30 pm; I doubt he'll still be in the office."

"Oh. Did you know he was also Miranda Flynn's agent?"

"I believe you mentioned it once or twice."

"Do you think that had anything to do with my getting the job?"

Holly was certain it had a lot to do with it. That was how agents worked. The producers would probably have phoned up Mike Hopkins about having Miranda in the show and Mike would have said something like: "I've got a young actress I've just taken on my books. Isn't there a maid in *Blithe Spirit?* Edith, yes. Well she'd be perfect for that role. Why don't we set up an audition for her?"

The rest of course would have been up to Scarlett. Secretly Holly thought Scarlett was too beautiful and unusual looking to be the awkward maid, but perhaps that was just jealousy.

"So was Miranda Flynn nice?" Holly knew Scarlett was desperate to talk.

"Oh yes, at least I think so. I didn't get a lot of opportunity to chat to her. She was talking to Rupert Blake quite a lot; they're married, you know."

"I'd heard!" Holly raised her eyebrows. "I have read the gossip columns for the last 10 years too, you know!"

"Sorry. She was talking to Echo too; she's really beautiful. But can you believe her mother was there too? I would just die to have my mother with me in rehearsals. And Judith Gold, wow – I grew up wanting to be as good as her."

"You didn't tell her that?"

"Of course I did. No one else was talking to her, apart from Alexander of course and she kept ignoring him. It was kind of funny. Are people allowed to ignore directors? I thought they were like God; actors are supposed to hang on their every word. So anyway, in the lunch break I went over to Judith and told her all the things I'd seen her in and how wonderful I think she is and that I did one of the speeches I'd seen her do on stage for my audition speech for drama school, and I was sure I'd got accepted because of that, and that I had a signed photograph of her when I was a kid, and how excited I was to be working with her."

"And did you manage to breathe at all during that monologue?"

"Holly!"

"Sorry. So what did she say?"

"'How nice, dear'. Wasn't that lovely of her?"

Judith had indeed used those words; however, they were spoken with complete irony. But that was lost on Scarlett. Judith was her heroine and could do no wrong. Neither could Alexander or Miranda or Rupert. She had worshipped them from afar and in her book they were perfect. Nothing or nobody was going to stop this job from being heaven.

CHAPTER SIX

Adam Lane arrived home from rehearsals to find three messages on his answerphone.

"Hi, Dad, it's Justine, just wondered how the first day went. Call me."

"Hello, Dad, this is Hattie. I was checking everything was OK. I've got to go to parents' evening at 6, but I'll be in after that. Give me a ring."

"Oh hi, Dad, it's Justine again, I guess you're still at rehearsals, um ... that's all really. Speak to you later."

Adam clicked off his machine. Justine and Hattie did worry so; sometimes it made him feel like he was the child and they his parents. But they could relax now; he was much better. Dr Bennett had said that several months ago at his counselling sessions. Ironic, wasn't it? Here he was playing a doctor on stage when he still needed one himself.

"But Dad, that puts you in the perfect position to study them, doesn't it?" Hattie had said. Hattie was a school teacher and into analysis.

She was probably right, except the doctor in *Blithe Spirit* was a GP not a shrink.

He picked up the phone. If he didn't call Justine soon she'd doubtlessly be round here checking up on him. Hattie would still be at parents' evening so he'd wait until later to contact her.

"Hello, Justine darling."

"Dad, how did it go?"

"Fine."

"Oh, great. How are the rest of the cast?"

"Hard to say. Nobody did much except listen to our renowned director talking on and on. Never did any acting."

"Oh. Well perhaps that's a good thing. Ease you in gently."

"Justine, I eased in gently with that small role in *The Bill*. Remember?"

"Dad, you were murdered in the first scene. Your only line was: 'Who the hell are you?'."

"Thank you for your confidence, Justine. At least they were willing to employ me."

Justine hadn't the heart to say that *The Bill* went through so many actors most of Equity had made an appearance at some point. And not many actors could mess up one line.

"Yes of course they did, Dad. It's only that this is theatre and it's quite a big role and ..."

"And I could go all loopy, yes I know, thank you, Justine. However, it isn't really a big role, only one major scene and a tiny one later on. Rupert Blake and Miranda Flynn do most of the work, though of course Judith Gold will steal every scene she's in. There'll be no pressure on me. Oh, and the girl playing Elvira, some American called Echo, looks so completely lost by everything, I don't think she's ever acted on stage before. Her mother insists she has, but I very much doubt it. Compared to her I'm going to be all right."

"That's great, Dad. You do sound more confident. Now, is there anything you need help with? I could come over and we could go through some lines."

"No I'm fine. It's been quite a long day, even listening to Alexander go on and on. I think I'll just have something to eat, look over the script and have an early night."

"Have you got any food in?"

"Justine, I had mental problems, that did not affect my abilities to cook or shop."

There was a chuckle on the other end of the line, Justine said goodnight and hung up.

Mental problems: how he loathed that expression. It sounded like something out of *One Flew over the Cuckoo's Nest*. Not that he would mind playing the lead role in that play, but in his early 50's he had to admit he was a little too old.

"Come on, Adam," he admonished himself. "Do some work on the role you do have." He ran over the plot in his head.

Dr Bradman, GP and acquaintance of Charles and Ruth Condomine, is invited to the séance with his wife. Later he comes back to see to Charles's sprained wrist, end of part.

"Nice and simple," his agent had said. To be precise, his agent's assistant, junior assistant. His agent didn't bother dealing directly with him any more; she had more important clients, ones that were employable, ones that didn't blank out in the middle of a play.

Oh God, he mustn't start thinking about that now; he needed all the confidence he could get.

But it wasn't easy. Dr Bennett had told him it was hard not to think about an obsession. "If, for example, you were told not to think about a pink elephant, the first thing you would think about would be a pink elephant."

Adam found this of no great help as he very rarely thought about pink elephants, apart from that wonderful song from *Dumbo*: 'Pink Elephants on Parade'. His obsession continued. Even last night he'd woken up in a sweat, dreaming he was in front of an audience not knowing what play he was in or any of his lines and completely naked.

A typical actor's nightmare, but in Adam's case it had been a reality – apart from the bit about being naked. Of course on the night it happened he might as well have been naked or wearing the back-end of a pantomime horse for all he was aware.

He'd been a young actor of 28, fairly successful, a TV comedy show under his belt, a couple of plays out of London, one in the West End and then the chance to join the Royal Shakespeare Company to play Lysander in *A Midsummer Night's Dream*, Cassio in

Othello and Jerry in Moss Hart and George Kauffman's comedy *Once in a Lifetime*, the token non-Shakespeare play for that season.

Initially, this challenge suited Adam, and the two Shakespeare plays opened with good reviews for both him and the productions. ('TV sitcom actor knows his stuff': the Evening Standard).

It was *Once in a Lifetime* which proved his undoing. The rehearsals had gone reasonably well, as had the previews. Adam enjoyed the role of the ambitious, if slightly arrogant, Jerry, and it was a wonderfully funny play. The audiences appeared to agree and their response was excellent. There was a real buzz on the opening night with the press and friends watching. Adam got dressed with a feeling of nervous excitement and waited in the wings for his entrance.

It was going well; the actress and actor playing May and George were getting all their laughs. His character had been set up ('Where is Jerry?' 'Jerry lets me do such and such,' etc).

"Have a great show," Katie, the pretty ASM, whispered to him. He smiled at her, opened the door to the set, representing the one to their drab lodgings, and walked on stage. Both May and George looked at him expectantly. He looked back at them; he was supposed to say something, but what the hell was it? May, seeing something in his face, improvised a line which should remind Adam of his. It worked. He said the line, relief flooding over him, and then the next. After that he froze again. May came up with another helpful line, but he failed to pick up on that one. He stared at her gormlessly and then out at the audience. Was this how rabbits felt when caught in headlights? Behind him he could hear May and George ad-libbing an entire new scene. But they couldn't do that forever; Jerry was the one who had to announce they were going to Hollywood to teach the silent movie stars how to speak properly for the talkies. He had to do something. The song 'Hooray for Hollywood' came into his head and he started to sing it loudly, whilst doing a sort of soft shoe shuffle. May and George stopped ad-libbing and stared at him in astonishment. Up until now *Once in a Lifetime* had not been a musical.

Once he'd sung it twice through Adam stopped and in one breath said, "Right guys," – he'd even forgotten May and George's names – "we're going to Hollywood now because there are people over there who can't talk."

"Can't talk?" May questioned, before the audience pictured a city of mutes. "Do you mean the actors from the silent movies can't talk well enough for the advent of talking pictures?"

"Yes that's it. And we're going to help them. I've got the plane tickets so start packing."

"Plane tickets?" Poor May was thinking of the next scene which was set aboard a train.

"Um, I'm afraid to fly so how about we go by train?"

Adam, vaguely recalling something about a train, nodded gratefully. "Come on." He rushed off stage and grabbed the script that Katie was holding out to him.

On stage May and George were trying to finish off the scene and summarize what the audience had missed, in lines which had never seen Moss Hart or George Kauffman's pen.

In the wings Adam was running his eyes down the script.

"Adam, you're on," Katie was calling him urgently. May and George were on stage sitting in a railway carriage supposedly on the way to Hollywood. He dumped the script in Katie's hands and sat down praying for the lines to come. It wasn't just May and George in this scene, there were several other characters, though at present he couldn't recall how many or who the hell they were.

He heard his first cue coming. He knew his line was about a crossword clue and May had to give him the answer. But what was the clue? All he could think of was a general knowledge crossword he'd done last Sunday which had involved a film question; surely that was appropriate for this play about movies.

"Christian name of man who doesn't give a damn, five letters."

He'd said something. Did it make sense? He looked at May's horrified face. Oh God, the answer was Rhett, Rhett Butler from *Gone with the Wind,* a book that hadn't even been written in the 1920s when this play was set, let alone been made into a movie.

May obviously decided not to reply to his question and to skip on to the next line. She, George and the porter had a page of dialogue before Adam had to come in again. Sweat poured down his face. What was it? His old drama teacher always said: "Don't worry about drying on stage; it'll always come back to you" – yeah right! May had turned back to him looking worried. May was supposed to look worried at this point, but there was real fear in her eyes, no doubt wondering what the hell was Adam going to come up with next. The answer was sod all.

May made one last try. "Aren't you gonna tell me that we need to put up a front to make our scheme work?"

"Yes. Absolutely. Definitely. No doubt. Indubitably."

May cut him off before he could think of any more affirmatives, delivered her next speech and made her exit. This left him and George on stage. The actor playing George was not as sharp as the one playing May and therefore not as well equipped to adlib and help Adam out, besides he was supposed to be the thick character; he couldn't be giving the smart Jerry ideas.

Adam knew he was supposed to start. Yet he couldn't. He did something virtually unheard of for actors – he asked for a prompt. The DSM's voice came calmly out from the wings. He repeated his words, hoping it would get him back on track. It didn't. On his next line he had to ask for another prompt, and another.

After a page of this he could feel the audience getting restless. He couldn't continue like this. He stood up from his train seat.

"Ladies and gentleman, I am terribly sorry about this, but I seem to have totally blanked out. The only way I think I can continue is to use the script." He walked into the wings where an open mouthed Katie handed him one.

Walking back on that stage holding the script in front of a first-night audience was the hardest thing he'd ever had to do in his life, but at least he got through the show.

The first-night critics amazingly didn't dwell on the matter, some didn't even mention it, but the gossip columnists were in their element. Adam, holed up in his flat, didn't read any of them. He'd called all his fellow actors to apologize, spoken to the director, the stage management and had a long talk to his agent. Everyone was hugely supportive; they told him not to worry, that he should go on that night, that he'd be fine.

"If you run away now," his agent had said, "you'll never get back on stage again."

And Adam hadn't gone on the stage again, not until today. He'd got as far as the theatre, that second night, but he couldn't get past the wings. His understudy took his place in all three plays and Adam had given up acting for 20 years.

Instead he took a teacher training course and taught English in a failing secondary school; it seemed appropriate to teach in a failing school since he too was a failure. But God it was so dispiriting.

"Can anyone name me three of Shakespeare's comedies?"

Silence.

"Can anyone name me any of Shakespeare's plays?"

Silence.

"If no one can name me a single play you will all be staying through break-time to research it. Yes, Jenny?"

"*Romeo and Juliet.*"

"Very good, Jenny. Now someone else. Was *Romeo and Juliet* a tragedy, a comedy or one of his history plays?"

"A comedy, Sir!"

"So Ryan, the fact that both Romeo and Juliet die at the end is funny, is it?"

"Yeah."

"I want you all to read the play for homework and write about the tragic aspect of it."

"But we don't have a copy of it, Sir. It's not on our syllabus."

"Go the library, or ask your parents or relations; surely somebody will have a complete copy of Shakespeare."

"My dad has a complete copy of *Playboy*, Sir."

"I'm sure he does, Ryan."

What was the point teaching these kids something they weren't interested in and would doubtfully ever have a use for? It was depressing, but less frightening than the alternative. The only decent thing to emerge from the experience was meeting his future wife Elizabeth, the geography teacher. The marriage didn't last; Adam was too unhappy with his life and failure to be a loving husband, but it did produce his two beloved daughters.

It was Justine and Hattie's pushing that had got him back into acting. Both loved to hear his theatre stories and avidly watched his old TV sitcom on UK Gold.

"Daddy, why don't you act any more?"

"Go on, Daddy, act again, we want to see you."

"But I'd never see you if I was always at a theatre or on a movie set," was Adam's constant excuse.

When Justine was 20 and Hattie 18, Adam could no longer use that defence. Besides, his sessions with Dr Bennett were finally beginning to pay off. After one such session Adam dashed home and, before he could lose his nerve, phoned his agent.

"Hello, it's Adam."

"Adam?"

"Adam Lane."

"Good God, I thought you were dead. Or at least retired."

"I was, only I'm thinking of going back into the business. Is there anything out there for me?"

"To be honest, Adam, after 20 years I don't think anyone's going to remember you, or if they do it'll be as the actor who had to take his script on stage. What have you been doing all this time?"

"Teaching."

"Take my advice, keep on with that. I don't think I can help you."

Adam hung up more depressed than in 20 years. He went for open auditions and castings, doing supply teaching to earn money, but it seemed his agent was right.

After three years he eventually got a small role in *The Bill*. It was wonderful to be back among actors again, doing what he loved. Then it was back to the teaching. It was a further two long years before he heard about *Blithe Spirit*. When Adam had first started out he had appeared in a play for a theatre company in Northern England which had been run by the parents of the *Blithe Spirit* producer. The producer, then a child, had also appeared in a small role and he and Adam had got on well and vaguely kept in touch. The producer had long ago given up acting and gone into the production side of the business. Adam called him up and suggested they meet for lunch.

"Is there anything for me in *Blithe Spirit*?"

Adam had asked before they'd even had a chance to look at their menus. "Something small."

The producer raised his eyebrows. "Do you know the play?"

"Yes."

"So you have something in mind?"

"Dr Bradman."

"Hmm. Do you think you're up to it?"

"I wouldn't ask if I didn't think I was."

The producer thought for a while. "What if you're not? How long have you been away from the stage?"

"25 years."

"That's a long time."

"I can do it. I just need the chance."

"You'll have to audition. For me and for Alexander Columbus."

"No problem."

Adam did a great audition, and, having done a lot of research, charmed a rather disgruntled Alexander, who wasn't happy with the producer once again going over his head.

"I wanted my return to the stage to be with an exciting director such as you," he told him. Alexander beamed. Maybe this guy would do, he looked a bit like a doctor after all. And he had cast Echo himself, so maybe it was OK if the producer cast Adam.

The producer was still uncertain, but he liked Adam and wanted to give him a break. He must make sure they employed a good understudy though, just in case he couldn't hack it.

Strangely, Adam's agent suddenly became interested at the sniff of potential earnings and instructed her junior assistant to talk money with the producer. It's a fascinating thing about agents: even if they don't get you a job, or in Adam's case don't even want to know, they still demand their percentage.

Adam's phone rang, jolting him back to the present.

"Dad, it's Hattie."

"Hello, darling, how was parents' evening?"

"Chaotic. Lots of neurotic parents complaining that their precious offspring aren't all being treated like child protégées." In the background Adam could hear Hattie's own daughter Millie demanding attention. "Ssh, I'm talking to Grandpa." He listened as Hattie tried to quieten her. "Sorry about that, Dad. She'd been sulking because I went out again and she was left with her daddy. So how were rehearsals?"

"Good thank you, though I'm sure Justine has already filled you in, hasn't she?"

"Well maybe! But I'm dying to know what the actress playing your wife is like. Are you going to get on?"

"I don't know, Hattie. I've hardly spoken to her."

"Does she have a name?"

"Yes, she does."

"Dad!"

Adam chuckled. "Alright, I give in. It's Isabelle. Isabelle Whiteside."

"Is she single?"

"Hattie!"

"OK, OK. But I wonder what she thinks of you."

"I doubt she's thinking of me at all, darling. Now I must go and do some work on my lines. I'll keep you posted when there's anything to report, OK?"

"OK, Dad. Love you. Take care."

Adam was wrong. Isabelle was thinking about him. In fact, she was thinking about the entire cast. With her new laptop she was trawling through various internet websites looking for information and unusual titbits on any one of them.

Isabelle loved gossip. If there wasn't any on a production she normally created some. It was fun watching how people reacted.

At school she'd started an in-house newspaper, which basically comprised of who was dating who, who wore the dreaded school uniform in the most fashionable way, and her favourite of all: who was the most popular girl in the school. A secret ballot of course, but Isabelle had a surreptitious way of colour marking each vote so she could discover who liked who.

On her first acting job, a small role in a TV movie, she was nicknamed Louella, after Louella Parsons, the Hollywood gossip columnist, a name which stuck with her throughout her career. Isabelle didn't mind; she found it quite flattering. She only wished she had Louella's power.

But for all this Isabelle wasn't as unpopular as she could've been. She was immensely friendly, and generous, and since the theatre world thrives on gossip, Isabelle was frequently inundated by her co-actors wanting to know who was gay, who was available, who had a coke habit and so on.

"You can't dislike her," said one cat to another when Isabelle was playing Grizabella in Andrew Lloyd Webber's show, "but you sure as hell can't trust her."

Isabelle ran her eyes down the list of the *Blithe Spirit* cast. This was going to be so much fun; she couldn't wait for the sparks to start flying. She opened Word on her laptop and created a new document: *Blithe Spirit: A Day to Day Diary of a Production.* She typed in the company's names and what she had discovered about each one, password protected it and picked up the phone.

"Adam, it's Isabelle Whiteside here; I got your number off the contact sheet. I'm sorry to disturb you at home, but I wondered whether you'd like to meet for coffee tomorrow before the rehearsal? Since we're playing husband and wife it might be an idea to get to know each other better."

On the other end of the phone Adam made a face. That would mean not being able to take little Millie to nursery in the morning which he loved to do. But it seemed churlish to refuse when Isabelle was making an effort to be friendly. "Sure, that'll be great."

"Lovely, see you then." Isabelle hung up smiling. He sounded a bit nervous, which wasn't surprising after a 25 year absence from the theatre. And of course the way he left ... too, too awful! She was longing to hear the entire story of that first hand. Then if necessary she could add a few little dramatic touches of her own and relay it to all her acquaintances. Perhaps there were people in the *Blithe Spirit* company who didn't know about his history, and she could enlighten them! She could hardly wait until tomorrow.

CHAPTER SEVEN

Declan Shaw, the company manager for *Blithe Spirit,* had also decided a morning meeting with his colleagues was a good idea, though not for the same reasons as Isabelle's. The first day of rehearsals had been a nightmare. His only achievement had been the collection of P45s, schedule D numbers and bank details from members of the company. In spite of constant questions and requests Alexander had given him no idea how rehearsals were going to proceed, what the set looked like or what props would be needed. Declan had been a company manager for 14 years and never known anything like it. Before going into stage management he'd been a dancer, but given that up 21 years ago at the age of 30, before it gave him up. He'd never regretted his change of career as he watched young dancers put themselves through a mass of classes and injuries only to spend months on the dole. Still, yesterday he rather wished he were back there again without the problems he could foresee on *Blithe Spirit*.

For rehearsals the stage management team arrived an hour or so before the actors and director to set up what furniture and props they had to practice with, but since they had none Declan suggested they open up the rehearsal room, in case any actors arrived early, and then go on to the local Starbucks. A tea urn had been set up in the rehearsal room with tea, coffee and biscuits, but Starbucks had better coffee and was a lot more private.

Declan surveyed his team comprising of a deputy stage manager and two assistant stage managers, all of whom looked about as shell-shocked as he felt.

"Right, I know yesterday wasn't exactly how we'd expected so I thought it was a good time to put our heads together and air our views."

Lucy Foster, the 28 year old ASM, put her hand up. "Please, Boss, I'd like to say this production is going to be a stinker."

There was general laughter.

"Thank you, Lucy." Declan was trying to keep the mood serious, but with Lucy it was hard; she had quite a reputation in the business for being more than a little zany. The story of how she ended up trying to ride one of the bronze horse statues in the fountain in Piccadilly Circus at three in the morning, after an opening night party, was notorious round the West End. But she was also efficient, easy going, and a good ASM. Declan had worked with her before and liked her.

"OK, seriously, Declan," Lucy continued, "I think we're going to have a lot of problems with this one. Alexander is waffling on and on and we have nothing to work with. All I did yesterday was make endless cups of tea for everyone when I should be out searching for props or making notes. Judith Gold looks like she's about to explode, I'm sure Rupert was checking out Scarlett's tits yesterday, which Miranda didn't look happy about, and who the hell is this Echo – and why do we have her mother in rehearsals?"

Declan smiled. Lucy didn't miss a trick or hold back on an opinion.

"Rebecca?" he asked his DSM.

Rebecca Cross frowned. "I'm inclined to agree with Lucy, well mostly anyway. Perhaps not the bit about Rupert, I didn't notice that."

"You wouldn't, Bec, you always think the best of everyone," said Lucy, having worked with Rebecca last year. Rebecca was an excellent DSM, nothing worried her, or if it did she never let it show. Lights could go off, sets break down and actors miss their cues and Rebecca would calmly deal with each problem until it was resolved.

"Honestly. Rebecca, if the end of the world was coming, you'd probably sit at the prompt desk and organize it the best way you could," another ASM had said to her after a particularly stressful show. She was the perfect person for a high profile show like this one, as even Judith Gold was unlikely to ruffle her. In contrast to Lucy, Rebecca rarely socialized or got drunk. She was very happily married to a university professor and preferred to go home to him after the show rather than going to the pub.

"Do we know if the set builders and painters have seen a plan of the set?" she asked Declan.

"I don't believe so."

"Will they have time to build it?"

"I have no idea. Thankfully at the moment that isn't my problem; that's up to the production manager and the producer."

"It will be your problem when we get to the theatre in four weeks and have no set," Lucy pointed out as she tilted her cup upside down to get the last bit of cappuccino out.

"Thank you, Lucy."

"Any time, Declan."

"And you have a milk moustache."

"Don't all the best people?" She looked at him pointedly.

Declan surreptitiously wiped his mouth before remembering he'd had black coffee. "However, my more immediate problem is rehearsal furniture; the plastic chairs provided in the rehearsal room can't double for everything."

Matthew Scott, the rather serious and young ASM, put his hand up.

"It's OK, Matthew, you don't need to put you hand up to speak," Declan said.

"Oh, right," said Matthew, looking at Lucy.

"Lucy was being facetious when she did," Declan explained. "Though of course some respect would be nice."

"Yes Sir, boss Sir," said Lucy.

"So what was your comment, Matthew?" Declan continued.

Matthew produced a huge typed list from his backpack. "I went through the script and made a list of everything we might need."

"Oh yeah, me too," said Lucy pulling a dog-eared notebook from her psychedelic shoulder bag.

"Great," said Declan. "Those will be vital – even yours, Lucy!" Lucy made a face at him. "Go on, Matthew."

"Don't we require a séance table that has to rise up and bump around?"

"Yes."

"So what do we do about that?"

"Excellent point," Declan said. "The table is but one effect on this show. We also have to have record players work by themselves and the set more or less collapse at the end. We'll need a specialist to sort those out, but that's Alexander's decision, unfortunately."

"Perhaps we should give him some names," Rebecca said.

"Like who?" Matthew asked.

"An expert in magic. A member of the Magic Circle."

"We had one of those on a production of *The Invisible Man* I did," Lucy said, "and we all had to sign a disclaimer vowing we wouldn't give away any of the illusions. It was quite scary, like Paul Daniels would arrive in a clap of thunder and wreak havoc on you if you broke the vow."

"And you managed not to?" Rebecca pressed her.

"Absolutely! Never breathed a word! Imagine having Paul Daniels turn up in your flat ..." She gave a pretend shiver of horror.

"So special effects, props, furniture, disgruntled actors, what other problems can you foresee?" Declan asked.

"How long have you got?" Lucy quipped.

"I'm sure it'll all work out," Rebecca said positively.

"I think it's going to be rather exciting," said Matthew.

"This is your first show, right?" Lucy enquired. Matthew nodded. "I thought so; you still have that charming optimism. What made you want to join this crazy world?"

"I more or less grew up in the business; my father was a children's TV presenter so I was always around studios. In fact, I was on his show when I was 8 in a Christmas play. But I was a bit awkward to be an actor so, since I had a lot of technical knowledge, I decided to go into stage management. Ultimately, I'd like to work on TV as a floor manager maybe, but I should get some experience first."

"Oh great, so we get stuck with you!"

"Lucy!" Rebecca admonished her. "Just ignore her, Matthew, she doesn't mean any of it."

"Oh right. And don't worry, I do know what

I'm doing, and I can fix almost anything."

"Oh, thank God," said Lucy. "I can't fix a thing. The fuse blew in my flat last week and it took me two hours to figure out how to fix it. I totally missed *Desperate Housewives*, and by the time I had power again I was far more desperate than they were. So any props that break, you're the man. I'll be the ASM who runs around reminding actors they've missed their cues and making the sandwiches. I take it there will be sandwiches in this production, Declan, since they are mentioned in the script, or do you think Alexander is the kind of person to believe in abstract theatre?"

"God knows."

"I thought company managers *were* God."

"No, some of them simply think they are. I hope I'm not one of them."

"No, Declan, you're not. But I think Alexander thinks he is."

Declan smiled but he could hardly admit out loud that he thought Lucy was right. He was supposed to be impartial, to keep some sort of discipline and not gossip too much.

Lucy, understanding she had gone far enough, had moved back on to her hapless colleague. "Hey Matthew, perhaps you could make some of our props out of sticky back plastic; isn't that the kind of thing your dad would do?"

"I guess so, sometimes." Matthew began to wish he'd never mentioned his father.

"Cool. Hey, we could save some washing up

bottles and make rockets; I've always wanted to do that and I'm sure we could sneak them on the set somewhere."

"I don't think they had rockets in Noel Coward's day." Matthew looked doubtful.

"Well, duh!"

"OK, Lucy." Declan hoped Matthew would get used to Lucy's ribbing. "Has anyone got anything else of use to say?"

"What about Judith Gold?" Rebecca asked. "Has anyone worked with her before?" Everyone shook their heads. "I think we're looking at a lot of TLC."

"I wouldn't mind doing some TLC to Rupert," Lucy said. "He's cute. What about you, Matthew? You could do some with Echo; she looks about your age and she's pretty."

Matthew went red. "No, I couldn't, I mean ..."

"Oh sorry, are you gay?"

"No! It's just she's not my type."

Matthew was saved from any further embarrassment by Declan's mobile going.

"Hello, Declan Shaw. Libby, hi. Where are you? No, we're in Starbucks on the main street. Come and join us. I'll get you a latte, is that right?" He hung up and went over to the counter. He was carrying the mug back to the table as the wardrobe mistress walked in.

"Thanks, Declan," Libby took a sip. "Oh, that's better; honestly, I only work in theatre so I don't have to get up in the mornings. This 10am start thing is too much."

"And there was I thinking you only did it

because you loved working with me," said Declan. This was the third show he and Libby had done together. Libby had been around almost as long as Declan, though she rarely admitted to being over 21.

"Well, there's that too of course, Declan. I wouldn't mind as much if it wasn't such a trek. I seemed to be on the tube so long I was convinced I must have boarded the Eurostar in error and would soon arrive in Paris. Why are rehearsal rooms always in the middle of nowhere?"

"Because they come cheaper that way," Declan pointed out.

"I liked that one run by the nuns; it made me feel at peace and at one with God," said Lucy.

"Since when did you believe in God?" Declan asked, amused.

"One should always keep ones options open."

"Why are you in again today?" Rebecca asked Libby. "You're not called, are you?"

"No, just for the meet and greet yesterday, but I wanted to get some of the actors' measurements, in case the designer suddenly wants me to buy something. I can't get hold of him to see if he or his supervisor already have them."

Declan glanced at his watch. "You'd probably better get that coffee to go, Libby, it's getting on for 10 and we don't want be late."

CHAPTER EIGHT

Declan needn't have worried about their being late. Alexander finally rolled in about 10.45 and immediately sent Matthew out to get him breakfast.

"Nothing too much," he said. "Bacon, eggs, sausage, toast and coffee."

Alexander gave Matthew no money for this errand so Declan dug into his pocket and gave him £10. "Get a receipt and I can claim it on petty cash," he said. Matthew set off wondering where he was going to get a full English breakfast to take away around here at 11am.

As he left the room there was a blast of cold air from the outside door, yet that was nothing to the icy atmosphere which already existed in the rehearsal room. Nobody was impressed by Alexander's late entrance, having struggled up themselves to be there promptly. Theatre actors are used to working late and sleeping late, unlike film and TV work where a 5am call is not unusual.

"Problems getting up?" Judith asked.

"Yes, isn't it hard?" Alexander had either missed the irony in Judith's voice or decided to ignore it.

Judith stared at him for a second. "That

all depends on how professional you are. Apparently some of us are more so in that department than others."

Isabelle's eyes were wide with excitement. In her head she was already writing up today's entry and it wasn't even lunchtime yet. It was certainly going to make up for the disappointing breakfast she'd had with Adam; he had steadfastly ignored all her attempts to discuss his breakdown, and instead bored her rigid with the exploits of his daughters and granddaughter. Although she had made all the right noises and laughed in her charming way over the story of how little Millie called Adam a hacksaw because she couldn't say actor, this was not what she wanted to hear. Getting Adam to confide in her was obviously going to be harder work than she'd anticipated.

Alexander was looking at Judith, unsure of what to do next. He was used to having people hanging on his every word. He decided to retreat to more familiar ground. Once he started directing them, they'd soon recognize his genius. And if geniuses needed an extra hour in bed in the morning because they'd had hours of rampant sex with their designer boyfriend the night before then they should be allowed. He took his customary deep breath and looked at every person in silence. That always worked, but he hadn't reckoned with Judith.

"Cat got your tongue?" she asked acidly. "Or are you having an asthma attack?"

Alexander decided to abandon his usual meaningful pauses before Judith shoved an inhaler down his throat. "OK, come along everyone, we mustn't waste time. We've got a tight schedule here."

"Really?" said Miranda who was also not a morning person. Rupert, with years of practice, had only got her out of bed with the aid of a wet sponge, removal of the duvet, a blast of Capital Radio, and a large coffee. He then, wisely, proceeded to disappear to the kitchen until Miranda was worth speaking to. "Perhaps as director you could show us by example."

A slight smile crossed Judith's face; she felt Miranda had the makings of an ally. Miranda caught the smile and mentally congratulated herself. She had heard the horror stories of Judith making life miserable for her co-stars if she didn't like them, and Miranda was determined not to be in that position, however hard she had to work.

Alexander, finding both his leading ladies attacking him at once, decided to fall back on his allies. "Scarlett."

"Yes, Alexander."

"I've been reading the play."

"Now there's a novelty for a director." Judith's caustic tones would have silenced a better man than Alexander, but he struggled gamely on.

"I was thinking about your role last night. I mean, you open the play, don't you?"

"Um, well, sort of. I carry a tray of drinks on stage. But Ruth, or should I say Miranda, has the first line."

Damn, Alexander thought to himself, he really must study the script properly and not flip through it. He'd seen Edith's name at the top of the page last night in bed, and not bothered to look very carefully after that. Imagine the first character to appear not speaking; it was ridiculous. He improvised quickly.

"Yes of course. But that tray of drinks is very important. It's totally symbolic of the play."

"Why?" Rupert asked. "Are we all alcoholics?"

Alexander looked thoughtful for a moment. "That is a theory; you do all drink a lot, especially Charles. That's the character you're playing, Rupert."

"Yes, I believe my agent did mention the role before I signed the contract," said Rupert dryly, raising his eyebrows upwards. Lucy turned her laugh into a cough. "But I don't remember a mention of Alcoholics Anonymous."

"Echo doesn't drink." Storm was determined to have her say. "She can't be seen to endorse alcohol, not with her career."

"Don't worry, it won't be real alcohol," said Isabelle, determined to impart information, gossip or otherwise.

"Oh," said Storm. "What will it be?"

"Probably coloured water or ginger ale or watered down coke, it depends what it's supposed to represent."

"I'm all for using the real stuff," said Rupert. "It would help my performance enormously if I'm playing the role as an alcoholic."

"You hardly need practice at that, darling," said Miranda.

Isabelle looked from Rupert to Miranda; was there animosity there? Was their perfect showbiz marriage not so perfect? But much to her disappointment Rupert merely laughed.

Declan didn't consider it his job to put pressure on directors, but otherwise he could foresee another totally wasted day. "Alexander, do you have any kind of schedule for today, or actually any day?"

Alexander shook his head. "I don't believe in schedules. I believe in spontaneity. I have to go where the mood takes me."

"I wonder where that would be, fairyland?" Libby muttered to Declan. "I hope that laissez-faire attitude doesn't apply to the costume designs. I haven't seen a single one yet."

"I'll ask," Declan said. "Alexander, Libby, our wardrobe mistress here, was wondering if there were any costume designs yet."

"Jasper's working on it, don't panic."

"As long as we get them in time," Libby said doubtfully as she left, Alexander's late entrance having given her the chance to already measure up the actors, "or your cast will be going on naked."

"Oh, my God," said Miranda to Rupert. "Look at Alexander's face; please, please, don't tell me he's going to consider that! I want gorgeous frocks! And stop smirking, just because you want to see Scarlett naked, and probably Echo too."

"Oh, Miranda, don't talk such nonsense," said Rupert, even though the thought had crossed his mind. Then to change the subject added, "Wait for it," and pointed at Storm. Bang on cue she started to protest that Echo would no way be going on stage naked. It took Declan a good ten minutes to calm her again down and persuade her that Libby was only joking.

"Are we going to rehearse anything today?" Judith enquired from where she was having a cigarette in the corner. Declan knew he should tell her she shouldn't smoke in here, but somehow he couldn't face it. Alexander on the other hand had no such inhibitions.

"No smoking, no smoking, it upsets the aura. I need to be able to breathe to create."

Judith sauntered over to him, even the thick-skinned Alexander took a slight step backwards, and slowly breathed a large mouthful of cigarette smoke in his face. Then she collected her bag and coat and walked to the exit. "Do let me know how this fucking show goes. I shall be at the Priory having a nervous breakdown."

There was a stunned silence after she left. Declan put his head in his hands; he couldn't wait to tell the producer he had lost his leading lady on the second day of rehearsals. Or at least temporarily mislaid. She would come back; she had to – she had a contract. The whole show was being financed on her name.

The tension in the rehearsal room was unbearable. It was at this point that Matthew made his entrance carrying a tray on which was a plate with bacon, egg, and sausage, another plate with a pile of buttered toast, while a mug of coffee sat gently steaming beside a napkin and a bottle of brown sauce.

"How can I eat at such a time as this?" Alexander snapped. Poor Matthew's mouth fell open.

"How dare she?" Alexander was fuming. "She can't treat me like that."

"I'm sure she'll come back," Declan said.

"I don't care whether she comes back or not. All that smoke in my face, I need to go home at once and recover. Rehearsals are finished for the day. I may never return."

With that he too picked up his coat and bag and left, clasping his hand to his forehead in a gesture that would've looked great in silent movies. Nobody spoke. Within an hour they had lost their leading actress and their director. Isabelle was unobtrusively taking notes of the exact wording each party had used; she must have this record of events, especially if the show got cancelled.

Lucy eventually broke the silence.

"Matthew, wherever did you get food served like that? You've even got brown sauce. I've never seen a café do anything like that."

"It wasn't a café; I couldn't find one anywhere round here. I got it from a woman who lives in that cul de sac round the corner, no 28."

"You what?" Lucy asked.

"You see, I met her in the road and asked her if she knew of anywhere I could find a full English breakfast, and she said no, but she lived round the corner and did a lovely fry up and she'd only charge me a couple of quid. Sorry I couldn't get a receipt though, Declan."

"No problem. What about the crockery?"

"Oh, I promised I'd return those later."

"Matthew, I take back anything I might have thought about you," Lucy chortled. "If you can get a cooked breakfast out of some woman in the street, you'll be a wonderful ASM!"

Matthew blushed; damn, he wished he wouldn't do that, it was so embarrassing. "Rather a wasted effort though now Mr Columbus has gone," he said.

"Not in the least," said Lucy picking up a sausage with her fingers. "Ooh look, a big one! Does anyone want to help me?"

"I'll take the coffee," said Miranda gratefully. Rupert nabbed a piece of toast and dipped it in the egg.

"What number did you say the woman

107

lived at, Matthew?" asked Isabelle, scribbling madly.

"28."

Miranda looked at Isabelle thoughtfully. She knew of her reputation and didn't want to feature badly in anything she might be creating. She'd have to watch what she said around the famous 'Louella'. This show was going to be exhausting backstage – if it happened: keeping in with Judith; watching her back with Isabelle; making sure Rupert didn't jump into bed with Scarlett, and Lucy didn't look like she'd turn him down either. At least she didn't have to worry about Echo. She looked like the proverbial fish out of water. As far as Miranda could remember, she hadn't said a word all day; in point of fact not since they'd had that conversation about Disneyland and passports yesterday. But with a mother like Storm, currently creating havoc with Declan over what was happening, she probably didn't get a chance. She turned to discuss the morning's events with Rupert. Neither of them believed Judith and Alexander wouldn't come back; they both had their reputations to think of. Still, it wasn't an auspicious start.

Scarlett on the other hand had no such confidence and was gutted at the prospect of losing her precious job. She glanced round the room. Declan was busy trying to appease Storm; Miranda and Rupert were talking to each other; Isabelle seemed to be busy writing something, while Lucy was filling Matthew in on what happened during his absence. Rebecca was attempting to make her daily rehearsal notes, which consisted of 'Rehearsals abandoned' with a few details. That only left Echo, who was staring vacantly at the coffee and tea area, and Adam, who was sitting on his own looking utterly lost. Scarlett went over to him.

"Adam, hi. Look, I was wondering, you've been in this business for a while, haven't you?"

Adam looked at her in surprise. Was it possible she hadn't heard about him? Perhaps not; she was virtually a child, probably younger than Hattie and Justine. "I've done a fair amount of stuff," he said, "though I've taken a break recently." It was after all only a small exaggeration of the truth.

"Do you think the play is going to continue? I mean, if you lose both your leading lady and your director isn't that like the end?"

Adam wished he knew the answer. All he could do was talk about star temperaments and the old adage of 'the show must go on.' It wasn't especially helpful, but it was the best he could do.

"It's just that this is my first ever acting job, and I don't want to lose it. It's what I've dreamt of for 20 years, ever since I saw my first pantomime."

How ironic, Adam thought, this was all he'd dreamed of for the last 20 years too; why the hell had he bothered if this was all it was going to come to?

Storm, still haranguing Declan, spotted Echo who had moved to the tea urn wistfully eyeing a chocolate digestive. Marching over, she dragged her daughter away from temptation.

"Poor kid," said Declan, moving across to Rebecca where he remained in serious conversation with her for several minutes before he made an announcement.

"Ladies and gentlemen, there seems very little point in keeping you hanging around here. We could have continued temporarily without Judith, but without a director as well we can do nothing."

"To lose one member of the company may be regarded as a misfortune, to lose two looks like carelessness," Rupert observed, neatly misquoting Wilde.

"Indeed," said Declan. "I'll phone you when I've got any news. Please ensure I have phone numbers where I can reach you later this afternoon or tonight. Thank you all very much."

There was a gentle muttering as everyone got their stuff together and left the rehearsal room. Miranda and Rupert were arguing about what to do that afternoon: Miranda wanted to go to the latest Brad Pitt blockbuster, Rupert to see an old movie at the National Film Theatre. Storm was trying to find a hairdresser because she was sure she could see Echo's roots coming through. Isabelle couldn't wait to start phoning round that morning's events, while Adam wondered if he could go and pick Millie up from nursery. The stage management were the last to leave, making sure the tea urn was off and the chairs stacked neatly.

"Now that," Lucy announced as they left, "was the shortest day of rehearsals I've ever done. I only hope it wasn't the last."

CHAPTER NINE

Wesley Bartlett was having a terrible afternoon. When he had agreed to produce *Blithe Spirit* as a vehicle for Judith Gold, he knew it wouldn't be easy, but he wasn't ready for the trouble to be so immediate. Or that she would actually walk out; that wasn't like her at all. Perhaps getting a young director like Alexander Columbus hadn't been such a smart move, but he'd hoped he and Judith might hit it off – opposites attract and all that. Plus, it was fairly hard to find theatre directors who would work with Judith, most of them remarking that since she directed herself there was little point in them bothering to turn up.

When Declan had first phoned Wesley to tell him that morning's events, Wesley was in the middle of talking to the publicity company promoting *Blithe Spirit.* A huge marketing operation had already started, using both Judith and Alexander as the draw. The daily newspapers had it in their listings, there were posters all over London and the Southeast and booking had already opened at the theatre where there was a steady stream of customers. It promised to be one of the hottest tickets in town; he could hardly start changing all that now, besides, he needed them. Who would come and see some unknown actress play Madame Arcati, with a director who might once have, say, run Bognor Regis rep? No, names were essential.

Before he could even get on the phone to Judith, Alan East had been on the phone to him regarding Alexander's behaviour towards his client, having received an earful himself. Judith had rung him as soon as she'd left the rehearsal room. "Alan, the man is a complete arsehole. I can't work for him."

"I'm sorry, Judith, but I don't know what I can do about that."

"You can get me out of my contract; isn't that what agents are supposed to do? Or even better get rid of the director."

"No can do, sorry. He has a contract the same as you do; I can't demand that he's fired."

"Why not? Isn't there a clause about complete morons not being allowed to direct Noel Coward plays?"

"I don't believe so, though I certainly agree there should be. Let me phone Wesley and explain the situation; I'm sure we can sort something out."

"Fine, you do that and get back to me. I'm going home. Christ, I suppose because I've left early my taxi isn't here and I'll have to get the fucking tube."

"Couldn't you hail a taxi in the street?"

"Are you mad, where would I find one round

here? It's in the middle of fucking nowhere."

"I'll order you one then."

"Forget it, if I hang around here much longer I'll probably be mugged, raped and sold into white slavery."

"You should be so lucky."

"Oh, fuck off, you stupid bugger," Judith said, but after years of experience Alan could detect a slight note of laughter in her voice. He wished other people would give back to Judith as good as she gave; she respected that. Of course one day he might go too far, but so far he'd got away with it.

Alan and Wesley had a long chat; since Judith had worked for Wesley before, this was hardly virgin territory and between them they had sorted out a fair amount of problems. This, they both agreed, was a real humdinger.

"What possessed you to hire such an experimental director to work with Judith?" Alan asked.

"What possessed you to agree?"

"Touché! Have you actually seen any of his productions?"

Wesley scuffed the carpet with his shoe, embarrassed. "I heard great things."

"Yeah, me too!" Both laughed.

"Next time we'll go together," Wesley said.

"At this rate there may not be a next time."

"OK, let's get negotiating."

Half an hour later and the only decision

they'd reached was that Wesley would talk to Alexander and see what he could achieve. In fact, Alexander was already on hold when Wesley finished with Alan, full of complaints which had something to do with smoke rings and a loss of aura. Wesley sighed inwardly as he listened to Alexander prattling ceaselessly. Trying to placate both sides made him feel like he was trying to sort out an inter-galactic space treaty. Alien vs. Alien. Or a boxing match. On the one side Judith Gold representing the old school of theatre, on the other, the way of the future, though if this was what the future held Wesley wasn't sure he liked it. Perhaps he truly had screwed up. Too late now; they would have to learn to get on.

"Alexander, could you come over to my office and we could talk properly?"

"I'm far too stressed to leave my home. It is my haven at a time of crisis like this."

Wesley took a deep breath and mentally counted to ten. "I'll be over in about an hour," he said. Perhaps this way he could also corner Jasper about some designs. The set builders had been told to build a basic box set and that was it. Not helpful when you had less than a month in which to build, paint and furnish it. He also hadn't specified any doors, which would mean the actors could neither enter nor exit.

Alexander's house in Blackheath was stunning. Wesley wondered whether he should go into directing rather than producing. Producers constantly gamble with their own money, whereas directors get paid for directing and then get a continuous fee while the production runs, even if they never hold another rehearsal or go near the theatre again.

Wesley had always been involved in the theatre world. His parents had passionately run a fairly unsuccessful regional theatre in Northern England called the Montage Theatre. Here Wesley made his first theatrical performance as the changeling baby in *A Midsummer Night's Dream*, followed by numerous other roles whenever a small child was required, including, much to his chagrin, playing girls wearing a variety of long and usually curly wigs.

"Mum, everyone will laugh at me," was his usual moan.

"Only because they're envious," would be his mother's reply. "You don't know how lucky you are." This left the young Wesley wondering if every young boy had a secret hankering for long curly wigs.

Surrounded by other young actors in their production of *Goodbye Mr Chips* when a teenager, Wesley realized that, in spite of his experience, he was by far the least talented and that perhaps acting wasn't for him. He went to university, studied economics and took over running the Montage Theatre when his parents decided to retire. Under his leadership the theatre finally began to make a decent profit; Wesley had a definite flair for producing popular, well-staged shows and still making money.

Wesley's move to West End producing came after staging the first play of a new writer he had discovered at the Montage Theatre and, realizing its potential, he transferred it to London. The play was a huge hit and Wesley found himself a producer to be reckoned with.

In an interview with an entertainment magazine, he was quoted as saying: "I like to put on quality productions without cutting corners. Also, my actors know I am always there for them; if they want to phone me at 3am with a problem then they can."

"Don't you find that's a problem with your private life?" the interviewer had asked and Wesley had told the only lie of the interview when he stated: "No, not at all."

In fact, his first wife left him, quoting the old cliché that he was married to his work. He was now married to Henrietta, an actress 10 years his junior and 8 months pregnant. She was more tolerant of his long hours, but Wesley knew once the baby arrived his home life must have priority. He needed to get these *Blithe Spirit* problems sorted out now.

Judith had first worked for him many years ago, when he produced her in *Who's Afraid of Virginia Woolf?*, when no other producer was interested, citing the depressing subject matter. Judith had won an Olivier Award for her performance and Wesley had made a tidy sum for himself. Like any producer, even Cameron Mackintosh, he'd had his fair share of flops, but to date none of the plays Judith had done for him had ever lost a penny. He hoped that *Blithe Spirit* wasn't going to be the first. Wesley sighed and rang Alexander's doorbell.

Jasper opened the door. He was dressed in a vibrant orange T-shirt and the tiniest pair of denim shorts Wesley had ever seen. "Alexander is out by the pool," he said. "He's very emotional." He led the way out the back door and down across the lawn to where Alexander was lying under a large outdoor heater beside an immaculate swimming pool. This kind of pool was for display purposes only, Wesley decided; no child had ever jumped into that pristine designer lido.

"Wesley, how good of you to come," Alexander said, putting his hand up to his brow in a way that reminded Wesley of a Victorian melodrama heroine. "I just couldn't come to you; I'm far, far, too distressed." Yes, definitely Victorian melodrama. "I have never been so insulted in my life."

"You should get out more." Wesley couldn't resist it.

"What are you insinuating? That I don't have enough experience?"

"No! It's a joke, one of the oldest pantomime gags around."

"I don't do pantomime."

Wesley sighed. Why didn't that surprise him? "So, Alexander, what seems to be the problem?"

His question was a big mistake, as Wesley received a non-stop tirade about smoke rings and how Judith was destroying him. These were not new sentiments to Wesley; somewhere there was probably a support group for survivors of the Judith Gold experience. Usually she didn't chew up her victims quite so fast, but after ten minutes of Alexander not drawing breath Wesley could see why it had been so instant.

After another five minutes Wesley cut in. "Look, Alexander, I know Judith isn't easy, but she's a wonderful actress, and her Madam Arcati will be an asset to your production. You're a great director; you mustn't blow your chance to be involved with this production because of a few differences. Don't you want to be known as the man who directed Judith in her best performance to date?"

Wesley could see Alexander's eyes light up. He paused, wondering if Winston Churchill felt this way when he made his rousing wartime speeches. "You could be the director who brought something out in her that no other director has managed." Silently, Wesley considered the only thing Alexander was likely to bring out in Judith at present was venom. Out loud he said, "So, what do you think? We could lay down some guidelines for both of you. Who knows, you might even win an

Olivier award for best director." Wesley was fully aware this accolade had so far eluded the director.

"I'll do it!" cried Alexander.

Winston Churchill nothing, Wesley thought, he felt like he'd won World War Three single-handedly. It took another two hours of negotiations for them to reach a compromise for rehearsals. The gist was Alexander agreed to try and run his rehearsals in a more conventional manner if Wesley convinced Judith not to smoke or blunt his inspirations. "You have to understand that Judith knew Noel Coward personally," Wesley told Alexander as he left. "So she has fixed ideas of how his plays should be performed."

That shook Alexander; he wasn't used to personal knowledge of authors. It was hardly as if a member of his *Twelfth Night* company would have informed him they had insider knowledge that Shakespeare would never have set it at Glastonbury. He'd better read the script again.

"Why don't you watch the movie?" Jasper asked later, producing another sample of fabric from a huge bag he'd got from Berwick Street that morning. Wesley had tried to quiz Jasper about his concepts for the sets and costumes before he'd left, but found the designer had mysteriously vanished, at least temporarily.

"There's a movie?" asked Alexander in amazement.

120

"I'll see if I can get a copy cheap on Amazon."

"Darling, you are my muse," said Alexander. "But I'd better read the play for tomorrow anyway. Judith Gold wasn't in the movie, was she?"

"I think that would make her about 100," Jasper pointed out.

"That wouldn't surprise me; I'm not entirely convinced that she's not a vampire," said Alexander mixing himself a large drink. If he had to read this darn thing again, he needed something to numb him.

Wesley meanwhile got into his car and drove towards Judith's house. Now all he had to do was convince her to give Alexander a chance. He'd better call Henrietta and tell her not to bother to wait for him for supper tonight – again.

CHAPTER TEN

At 9.59 am the following morning a deathly silence hung over the rehearsal room. Judith had walked in two minutes before and was sitting in the corner staring pointedly at her watch.

"Please let him be on time," Scarlett whispered over and over to herself. Even the usually laid-back Rupert was feeling the tension. Miranda had shouted at him when they'd run out of milk at breakfast and he'd shouted right back. Normally, he would either have ignored her or gone out and bought a pint. He was quite surprised to realize how much this show meant to him.

At 10.01 the door opened and both producer and director walked in. Wesley was exhausted; since 9.00 he had been sitting outside Alexander's house, in the taxi he'd ordered for him, trying to ensure he arrived on time. Only one minute late was a miracle. He looked pointedly at Judith, daring her to say anything and, although she lifted her eyes to the ceiling, she kept silent. He'd also brought a large box of assorted fresh cakes in an attempt to start the rehearsal off on a good note. Echo, under Storm's watchful eye, looked sadly on as everyone else made a grab for one.

"Chocolate éclairs, my favourite," said Judith as Miranda's hand hovered over the largest one. Miranda grabbed it, put it on a napkin and handed it to Judith. Rupert smiled; he had to admire his wife. She knew which side her éclair was chocolated, but fawning simply wasn't his style. Scarlett and Isabelle on the other hand were mentally cursing themselves for not acting faster themselves. Wesley, watching what was going on, wished he'd brought nothing but sodding chocolate éclairs! He noticed Adam sitting silently in the corner, the only one not crowding round the cakes. He looked terrible. Please don't let him be cracking up on me, Wesley thought. That was all he needed. He crossed over to him.

"Are you OK?"

"Yep, I'm absolutely fine. In fact, never been better." Adam was protesting a little too hard.

"Truthfully?"

"Yes. Well, you know, a bit uptight, not certain what's going on."

"You feel uptight, how do you think I feel? I'm applying for my first ulcer at any moment." Wesley was rewarded by a laugh from Adam.

"Don't worry about me; I'm terrific, honest – confident, happy, excited. I'm not going to let you down, I promise."

"No, of course you're not. Now go and get a cake before they all go, but I'd stay clear of the éclairs if you value your life."

Adam nodded as if he knew what the hell Wesley meant and wandered over to the cakes, even though he wasn't hungry. Wesley sighed. That was one of the worst cases of bluffing he'd seen and he was a master bluffer. He'd have to keep a serious eye on Adam.

"So are you here to supervise?" Judith called over to Wesley.

"No, I'm not staying; I merely came in to say hello." Wesley never hung around rehearsals; directors needed their own space. He'd done his bit by getting Alexander here on time; he had to rely on him sticking to the agreement they'd made last night. "If anyone has any problems Declan has my mobile number, or you can call me at the office." With that he gave them all a wave and left hastily. Declan would keep him informed of any problems. Please God, don't let there be too many of them.

"Right, people, let's get started." Alexander was determined to re-establish himself as the boss. "I feel we need to communicate with each other in a physical way so we can learn to trust one another. So, as this play is all about a séance, I think we should all place our chairs in a circle and hold hands."

"And are we also going to try and communicate with the dead?" Judith asked acidly.

"Not at the moment." Alexander thought he'd try another joke: "Unless you've got anyone specific in mind."

124

"There might be someone dead by the end of today," Judith said, looking at Alexander. "But then I doubt I'd be trying to communicate with them; more likely to be opening a bottle of champagne to celebrate."

"So shall we all move our chairs?" said Declan quickly.

There was a shuffling of plastic chairs as everyone moved into a circle. Miranda niftily managed to manoeuvre herself on one side of Judith while Scarlett got on the other. Alexander opted to sit next to Scarlett, recognizing her as his ally, and was a little surprised to find Storm on his other side. "This is for cast only," he said, to her annoyance.

"I guess that counts us out then," muttered Lucy.

"Thank goodness," said Rebecca.

"I quite fancied gripping Rupert's hand," Lucy said, wistfully.

Instead Rupert found himself sitting between Isabelle and Adam; Isabelle had also got herself next to Alexander, which left Echo sandwiched between Adam and Miranda. Storm was perched on a chair right behind Echo's.

"Now, I want you all to hold hands, close your eyes and concentrate very hard on making your mind a blank," said Alexander.

"Isn't that a contradiction in terms?" Miranda whispered to Judith.

"Not in his case, I think his mind is permanently blank," replied Judith, not as quietly.

125

If Alexander heard her he ignored it. "I want you to focus on your neighbours, feel the supportive vibes you are getting from them." This didn't go quite as well as Alexander expected. He certainly got good vibes from Scarlett who squeezed his hand to the extent of real pain. However, on his other side Isabelle had her eyes half open trying to observe other people's reactions; she was well rewarded. Judith and Miranda were openly sniggering; Echo was glancing round at Storm as if to check she was concentrating correctly; Rupert and Adam, embarrassed at holding hands, had quietly dropped them, while Rupert's hand holding Isabelle's was left there politely, but with disinterest.

"I would like to ask the muses of theatre and art to look down on our little project and give us divine inspiration," Alexander continued.

"I thought that was what you were supposed to do," Judith said.

"And help us to all work in harmony and trust," Alexander finished off.

"Christ!" said Judith.

"Now, I think we should all take a break for coffee and then ..." Alexander made his usual pause for effect, "we'll do a read-through of the whole play."

"So you finished it then?" said Judith getting up, going over to her bag and getting out her cigarettes. She cut Alexander off before he could say anything. "Oh, don't

126

worry, I'm going into the corridor; I daren't risk you loosing any more of your aura and inspiration."

Alexander turned to Matthew. "Could you get me another one of those cooked breakfasts? It didn't look bad yesterday and hadn't time to eat anything this morning."

"It didn't look bad?" Lucy spluttered to Rebecca. "It looked bloody amazing! What does he expect, a waiter from the Ritz with a silver trolley?"

Matthew looked horrified. How often could he go back to the lady in No 28? Besides, when he'd taken the tray back yesterday the woman had insisted he stop in for a cup of tea and spent the next two hours regaling him with tales of her family.

"Go to Starbucks," Declan told him. "They do some sort of egg and bacon panini and you can get him coffee too. I'll explain to him that I can't have my ASM running round looking for fry ups all day."

Gratefully, Matthew disappeared in the direction of Starbucks, while Declan had a quiet diplomatic word with Alexander. Alexander said nothing; he was a little in awe of this calm, organized company manager. But he was not happy, and wondered whether he could negotiate with Wesley to provide a cooked breakfast every morning. Yesterday he'd already got him to agree to taxis to and from rehearsals and a hot lunch to be delivered each day. Perhaps if he could show him how well rehearsals went today they could discuss his morning food requirements.

"Right, people, let's start, shall we? All back in your places in our séance circle."

"Shall we hold hands again?" Scarlett asked eagerly.

Alexander looked thoughtful. "That's certainly an idea."

"Won't that make it rather difficult to hold our scripts?" Miranda said.

Scarlett, who had learnt her lines within two days of hearing she had the role, had forgotten that most actors didn't work that way, preferring to learn their lines and their moves as rehearsals progressed.

"Exactly," said Alexander. "I was about to point that out myself; thank you, Miranda. You have the first line, don't you?"

"Give that man a cigar!" Judith drawled, having returned from her cigarette break.

"I don't smoke," Alexander said slowly, as if explaining to a total imbecile – a big mistake with Judith.

"Apparently you also don't have a fucking sense of humour," she snapped. "Now can we get on with this read-through?"

At 1pm, after two hours, they had only read through the first act of a three act play.

"How long is this play supposed to be?" Lucy whispered to Rebecca. "At this rate it's going to run longer that Hamlet, and be about as funny."

Everybody staggered out to get lunch.

Judith and Alexander both had hot meals delivered as agreed. They ate at opposite sides of the room in stony silence. Declan stayed in as well, ensuring there was going to be no bloodshed between them, and asked Rebecca to bring him back a sandwich.

At 2pm they reconvened for Act Two, had a short break for tea at 4pm and finally finished Act Three at 6pm, when the company were broken until 10am the next morning.

Everyone left utterly drained and depressed, even the optimistic Scarlett. The read-through, which should have taken no longer than a couple of hours, had taken almost six. Primarily this was because Alexander kept stopping them to point out things that he considered were important, or alternatively suddenly demanding several minutes of silence as he could feel inspiration striking.

"The cuckoo!" he announced at one point. "I think the fact that Madame Arcati thinks the cuckoo sounds angry is very important."

"Oh, Christ!" said Judith.

Additionally, because of the tension of the last couple of days, the cast were all more nervous and stressed that they would usually be on a first read-through. Several actors tripped over their words or interrupted other people's lines. Judith and Rupert were the only ones who managed to never go wrong and Rupert was rewarded by a fleeting smile from Judith as they left for the evening.

Yet there was a bigger problem than any of the above and it was obvious to everyone who the culprit was: someone who never stumbled over their lines, on the contrary each one came out very clearly ... and very, very, slowly. Even worse, they came out with exactly the same tone of voice regardless of what the scene required: anger, playfulness, charm, even seduction. Every one was identical, and all had a strong southern American drawl.

"Oh, Jesus H Christ," Judith said as Echo finished her final line. And everyone in the room, with the exception of Echo herself and her doting mother, had to agree.

CHAPTER ELEVEN

It was Friday at 6pm and the last day of rehearsals for the week. Alexander had decided there were to be no weekend rehearsals. His reasoning to the dubious Wesley, who considered the production was already behind, was the actors could use the time to work on their lines. In truth, Alexander had plans for his two free days. To be fair, he was going to spend some of them watching a copy of the video of *Blithe Spirit* which Jasper had managed to get him. But that shouldn't take any more than a couple of hours. The rest of the time he was longing to spend in bed, either sleeping (this last week had exhausted him) or preferably with Jasper.

Since Alexander's return on Wednesday with promises of conventionality, rehearsals had, thankfully, been more of a success.

For a start, discussions between Alexander, Declan and Wesley resulted in Storm being requested to no longer attend rehearsals. Unsurprisingly, this did not go down well with Storm, but exceedingly well with everyone else. Even Echo, after an initial look of panic, started to relax and finally got to discover the joys of chocolate digestive biscuits.

Secondly, Alexander began blocking the

play. This was a success on several levels: the actors felt they were at last making progress, stage management could finally make some notes, and Echo was actually quite good at standing and moving where she was told, at least initially. However, by the time the cast had reached the final act the following day she said, "But I don't need to remember all the stuff from yesterday too, right?"

"Yes," Alexander explained. "That was Act One, this is Act Three."

"So I have to remember Act One and Act Three?" Echo asked, panic in her voice.

"And preferably Act Two," Judith snapped. "It would certainly be helpful for the rest of us if you didn't stand in the middle of the floor so we all crashed into you, especially since you are supposed to be ethereal."

"Oh, right," said Echo. "What's ethereal?"

Alexander looked round vaguely; damn, she was looking at him and he was darned if he knew. He was a director not a bloody panel member on *Call My Bluff*. Surely he wasn't going to have to bring a dictionary to rehearsals as well as everything else.

"Oh yes, Alexander, do tell us," said Miranda, wickedly stirring up the situation.

"I think I should let someone else answer that question," Alexander hedged.

"It's what ghosts are, or at least some are; I'm not sure about poltergeists," Scarlett jumped in eagerly. "Sort of light and airy and unearthly."

"A perfect description, Scarlett," said Alexander. "I couldn't have put it better myself."

"Apparently not," Judith drawled.

"So I have to remember all of it?" Echo asked, worried. "That's an awful lot."

"Didn't you have to remember moves for TV?" Miranda asked.

"Oh sure. I was real good at remembering tons of moves all at once; all my directors said so, only once we'd done them I didn't have to remember them no more."

"Oh terrific," Miranda muttered to Rupert. "What a bloody idiot."

Rupert couldn't help but agree, yet he also felt a little sorry for her. From what he'd seen so far she seemed a truly dreadful actress, and stood a good chance of spoiling the whole play, but it was hardly her fault she'd been cast, and as for that ghastly pushy mother.... "Look, if you write down everything in your script," he said, showing her his pencil-marked script, "then you can go through it later at home until it's sunk in."

"Oh yes," Echo said cheering up. "Mommy can help me then, can't she?"

"Of course she can," Alexander said. Judith shot him a filthy look. She had been on the phone to Wesley last night demanding to know what in the world had possessed him to cast Echo. Having eventually discovered it had been Alexander's casting coup she was even less happy with the director than she had been before – if that was possible.

"You have to get her a dialect coach," she had demanded of Wesley. "As far as I know Elvira did not come from America's deep south. Charles took her to Budleigh Salterton for their honeymoon, not New Orleans. No, wait, I've got a better idea. I mean, if you can't beat them, join them. How about we set the whole play in the heart of Atlanta? We could call it *Gone with the Windy Spirit.* We could have Elvira O'Hara, Rhett Condomine, Ruth Wilkes, and I of course shall play the big black servant Mammy Arcati!"

Wesley had roared with laughter. God, Judith could be funny. He adored her when she was like this; it made all the problems worthwhile, almost. "I mean it, Wesley." Judith was back on the attack. "Get a fucking dialect coach. That moron has to be taught to do an English accent if, and I say IF, she is going to continue in this role."

Wesley promised he'd sort it. He had presumed Alexander had checked that Echo could do the appropriate accent before employing her; in retrospect that was obviously stupid of him. He'd ring Julia Morton, a dialect coach he'd used on a production of *The Glass Menagerie,* when the very English leading lady had to sound more like a southern American belle, and less like Lady Bracknell.

Julia told him she was working on a revival of an American musical at the National Theatre (yet another one, Wesley thought; honestly, the National was getting so commercial), but she could do some work with Echo this weekend if that would help. Wesley booked her on the spot and hung up, relieved another problem had been temporarily solved. Julia was the best around; if she couldn't sort out Echo's accent then no one could. He didn't even want to think about that possibility!

Apart from Echo's memory problems, the blocking went fairly smoothly. Much to everyone's amazement Alexander was following fairly traditional moves; no one was asked to make their entrance from a trap door or flying over the audience.

Then Rupert pointed out, during lunch, that Alexander was pretty much following the original moves as marked in Samuel French's Acting Edition, a tradition copied by amateur and rep productions all over the country. It was hardly creative, but everyone felt they'd had enough of creativity at present. Besides, Judith usually ignored what Alexander told her and moved where she wanted, while Miranda and Rupert half listened to Alexander and half worked round Judith. This worked remarkably well on the whole, except occasionally with Scarlett, Adam and Echo all following Alexander to a T and Isabelle trying to keep in with everyone, there were a few head-on clashes.

The first took place during the séance scene where Alexander had carefully seated everyone round the table in the manner suggested by French's edition.

"I think Madame Arcati should sit where you've placed Dr Bradman," Judith stated. "If my seat is where you have stipulated, it will be difficult for me to reach it from my current position at the gramophone without pushing past everyone."

Adam was about to move when Alexander stopped him. "No, that's fine, Adam, you stay where you are." Adam sat down again, nervously looking at Judith. "OK, let's run that bit and see how it goes."

Judith stood where the gramophone was supposed to be, at present marked by an old biscuit tin. She pretended to turn it on, did an eccentric little conducting movement in time with the music and moved towards the table. The seat meant for her was, as she had pointed out, hard to reach, whereas the one Adam was seated in was perfect. Judith approached the seat she wanted, turned round and sat firmly on Adam's lap. Adam looked terrified. Rupert and Miranda laughed openly while Isabelle was mentally composing the line 'Leading lady crushes actor'. Judith got the seat she wanted.

Alexander, refusing to wholly concede his authority, said, "Judith, you should do some dance steps once you turn the record player on."

"Why? Would that be because French's edition says so?"

"No," Alexander lied. "I feel Madame Arcati would dance at that point."

"Bollocks. This Madame Arcati doesn't dance. End of discussion."

Further on in the scene, the ghost of Elvira has to stroke Charles's hair. However, for some reason, in Alexander's staging, Echo and Rupert ended up on opposite sides of the stage.

"How can I stroke his hair from here?" Echo asked plaintively.

"Just move towards him, casually," Alexander ordered. Echo marched over as if on a six mile hike. "Sexily!" Alexander shouted. Echo looked bemused and merely walked a bit slower. She had learnt to walk a lot of different ways in her beauty pageant career, but 'sexily' wasn't in her lexicon. Finally reaching Rupert, she pulled his hair so hard Rupert's eyes watered.

"For God's sake, this is supposed to be a moment of passion," Alexander said. "You're not trying to torture the man."

Echo looked close to tears.

"Here." Rupert took Echo's hand and ran it through his hair. "Like this." She tried again; it wasn't exactly sexy, Rupert thought, but it was perfectly pleasant.

During Act Two, Miranda lost her temper with Alexander. "Alexander, as Ruth I am supposed to be talking to Elvira, but since she's invisible to me I keep addressing the wrong place and talking to thin air. Yet at the moment Echo is in my full view, which somewhat spoils the point of the joke."

Alexander glanced at his script. She was right; he'd been carefully placing Echo in Miranda's sightline instead of the contrary. "Echo, you're in the wrong place, you're not supposed to be in front of Miranda," he told her.

Echo looked at her script where she'd written her moves as Rupert had showed her. "But it says here …"

"You must have written it down wrong," said Alexander. "Now carry on," he added hastily before Miranda, who knew very well it was his fault and not Echo's, could protest.

The definitive mishap occurred at the end of the séance scene, when Judith had to collapse into a trance. Instead of collapsing upstage right as directed, she moved to centre stage. As Rupert jumped up he tripped over her and sprawled on the floor.

"I'm so sorry, Rupert," Judith said as Rupert got up, rubbing his knees. "I should have warned you I was going to change the blocking, but I only decided as I was doing it. What is the point of having the focus of attention being off-centre? It's not only me, everyone has to gather round and we'll look silly grouped over in the corner there. The audience will be wondering whether someone else is going to make a guest appearance in the empty centre stage, conceivably a line of high kicking chorus girls."

Alexander thought he'd try yet another joke; obviously he was never going to learn. "Perhaps I'm leaving it for the ghost of Noel Coward." There was a deathly silence; even Scarlett couldn't produce a laugh.

"Noel would not be seen near this production," Judith snapped. "And do you consider the fact that he is dead a laughing matter? It certainly isn't for me, but perhaps you find your friends dying amusing."

Even Alexander had the grace to look embarrassed. "I'm sorry," he said.

Judith ignored him and turned back to Rupert. "I hope you don't end up covered in bruises."

"I hope I do," said Rupert, who found the whole situation highly comical. "I never want to forget the moment I was floored by Judith Gold."

"I'm just sorry you didn't land on top of me," Judith said with the slightest gleam of a smile. "That could have made for an interesting sub-text: Charles and Madame Arcati having a fling under the séance table!"

Christ, Miranda thought, don't tell me even Judith's after my husband.

Actually Judith was no such thing, but she was very impressed by Rupert's behaviour; there was something about him she liked. She liked Miranda too, but Miranda was more like her, cynical and shrewd. Rupert was something different, a real gentleman, but great fun too. Sex didn't enter into it.

By the time rehearsals had finished on Friday night, most of the blocking problems had been solved, and the cast went home with their scripts to start learning lines and moves. Stage management, however, were not much happier. In spite of constant requests for props and furniture for rehearsals, Alexander insisted that the cast should make–believe with objects nothing like the end product. "It helps with their acting to improvise initially," he stated.

"I wonder whether it would improve his directing to make-believe with his necessities," Lucy said crossly to Rebecca. "We could produce a mug of coloured water for his coffee, give him an empty plate and cutlery for his lunch and leave him a push bike to pick him up in the mornings. It's so infuriating. What is the point in sitting round all day when we should be getting props?"

Alexander, unaware of all the bad feeling, considered he was winning with his cast, hardly noticing that they were changing things, or if he was aware, not actually caring. As long as they made the show look good it made him look good. One thing he was steadfast about though: each morning's rehearsals had to start with his séance motivation exercise. Come 10am (ish, even with a taxi provided Alexander still had a punctuality problem) he and the cast had to be seated in a circle, clasping hands. On the Friday morning Judith made a bee-line to sit next to Alexander. Thrilled to think he'd finally won her over, Alexander grasped her hand eagerly until he discovered she had chopped up a cigarette and stuck little pieces of it all over her hand. After that Alexander, though he stubbornly continued with the seated circle, never again requested them to hold hands.

"Such a shame," Judith announced to Rupert and Miranda. "I was going to try Vaseline tomorrow, and I had an idea about Pedigree Chum ..."

Good grief, Declan thought as he overheard this comment, I suppose I'd better warn Wesley a total truce is a long way off yet. God, he was looking forward to this weekend, perhaps if everyone got away from it all for a couple of days they could start anew on Monday.

As he checked over the empty rehearsal room and turned off the lights, he thought: Who am I kidding?

CHAPTER TWELVE

The phone was ringing as Rupert came downstairs wearing his tennis kit. He was on the way to having a friendly game with another ex-tennis pro on Saturday afternoon.

"Hello?"

"Rupert, it's Judith Gold."

"Judith, hi."

Miranda, who was lying on the sofa with a face mask on, opened her eyes so wide the mask cracked.

"I'm sorry to disturb you at home and on your day off," Judith continued, "but I wondered whether we could all meet up today. This production is going arse over tit and I'd really appreciate your input as to what we can do."

Miranda was scribbling what does she want? on a piece of paper.

Rupert scribbled back to meet up today.

Miranda was nodding madly, trying to grab the phone off Rupert. Rupert moved away holding the phone firmly.

"Yes, that would be fine, Judith, but can we make it later? I'm due to play tennis this afternoon."

"What?" Miranda almost shouted, rushing into the kitchen and picking up the phone in there. "Judith, Miranda here, listen, don't worry, Rupert can cancel his tennis game."

"No I can't," said Rupert. "Not only am I looking forward to it, but it would be rude to Ronnie."

"But that's pleasure." Miranda was almost crying with frustration. Judith Gold was inviting her out and Rupert was going to spoil it all. "This is business, and it's important."

"This is important too," Rupert said. "I'm sure Judith won't mind postponing it until later, or Miranda, you could go now and I could join you when I'm finished."

"No, I'd rather see both of you," Judith said. "But Rupert is right, he shouldn't cancel his tennis, that is as long as it doesn't take all day. It doesn't, does it? It seems to last forever when Wimbledon is on TV. They start at lunch time and finish when it gets dark."

"There are normally several matches in that time," Rupert pointed out.

"Always looks the same to me," Judith said. "Lots of men in unattractive baggy white shorts, grunting and occasionally leaping up and down. Rather like sex really. So how about you, Rupert?"

"I try not to grunt – in tennis or sex."

Judith laughed. "I meant, how long will you play for? Though thank you for the additional information."

"A couple of hours probably," said Rupert, "and then we go for a drink."

143

"Surely you can skip the drink?" Miranda snapped.

"That's not necessary either," Judith said. "How about we meet for supper somewhere, say at eight o'clock?"

"Great," said Rupert.

"There's a nice little Italian round the corner from me, if that's OK with you."

"Wonderful!" said Miranda. She was so relieved that the evening was going ahead that she almost, but not quite, forgot to give Rupert a hard time after Judith had given them the address and hung up. "It's a shame she didn't suggest eating at the Ivy though," she said.

"Probably wanted somewhere a little less high profile if we're going to be scheming," Rupert said, getting his racquet and a box of tennis balls out of the cupboard in the hall. "If you did that at the Ivy the whole conversation would probably be printed in next month's *Hello* magazine. But don't worry, I'm sure you'll get your chance to be seen with Judith at the Ivy at some point."

"It's only because I like the food and service, not because I want to be seen there," Miranda lied.

"Yeah right, and I'm off to play doubles with Pete Sampras, Jimmy Connors and John McEnroe!" Rupert leant over to give her a kiss. "See you later, darling." The front door shut behind him and Miranda could hear him starting up his car. Cheeky bastard, how dare he insinuate she was a snob about the Ivy? It was extraordinary that he didn't care about networking; sometimes she didn't understand him at all. It would have been so wonderful if Isabelle had seen a photo of her and Judith at the Ivy in *Hello,* she would have been green with envy. She wondered how smart Judith's little Italian restaurant was and bounded upstairs to start trying on outfits.

Judith hung up thinking about Rupert and tennis. When she'd first heard he used to play professionally she'd been less than impressed. "Everyone thinks they can be an actor," she'd complained. "Whatever next, David Beckham playing Hamlet?" But she was forced to withdraw her prejudices on this one; Rupert was not a failed tennis player who wanted to dabble in acting, he was a good actor. But that didn't mean David Beckham was to go near the Danish Prince.

Rupert had a great match; he really thrashed poor Ronnie York. Each ball he whacked across the net he imagined to be Alexander's head, or other round parts of his anatomy. Also, after a week being cooped up in the rehearsal room with not enough to do, Rupert had surplus energy. Even shots which normally he wouldn't attempt he went for as if his life depended on it. His serves flew over the net at speeds which almost touched Greg Rusedski's and when he reached a 6-0, 6-2 final score he leapt over the net to shake Ronnie's hand.

"Christl" said Ronnie. "You know, just shaking hands over the net is normal."

If only he'd played like this when he was on the circuit he really might be up there making adverts for washing powder with Tim Henman.

Showering in the tennis club, Rupert emerged to find two messages for him at the desk, both from Miranda telling him he'd left his mobile at home and would he please ring her. Rupert, having left his mobile on purpose so Miranda couldn't call him, decided she could wait a little, and went for a drink with Ronnie. An hour later and he and Ronnie were still in mid-discussion regarding possible Wimbledon championship winners.

Miranda meanwhile, having tried on every outfit she owned, was cursing Rupert. She needed to discuss the evening, to ensure he would behave himself, and that he'd agree with everything Judith said; sometimes he could be so contrary merely for the hell of it. She'd kill him if he was going to mess up this chance, whatever it was. She had at least finally decided on an outfit: a dark blue Oriental style dress which accentuated her size eight figure and showed up her auburn hair, which she had curled into loose ringlets to perfection. While she was at it she also laid out a cream suit for Rupert, which would make him look presentable and tone in with her dress.

Promptly at 8pm Rupert and Miranda

arrived at Il Trovatore. Ironic, Rupert thought, to call a restaurant after an opera where people got killed and the heroine fatally poisoned. Judith was already there and only Rupert's standing firmly on Miranda's foot stopped her from incorrectly apologizing for being late. The waiter handed them two huge menus; there was already a bottle of wine on the table and he poured both Miranda and Rupert a glass.

"I hope you both drink wine," Judith said, "but I thought we all needed a drink. We can always go on to something stronger later."

"A woman after my own heart," Rupert said, perusing the bottle and admiring Judith's choice.

"What's good here?" Miranda asked.

"The food," Judith riposted. She could never resist the chance to make fun of someone, even when she liked them. It was too tempting. Besides, it usually got a laugh, this time from Rupert while Miranda glared at him, and no actor can resist getting a laugh.

Judith opted for seafood pasta for her main course. Miranda, after Judith's last retort, decided not to follow suit as she'd intended and chose chicken instead. Rupert asked for a steak Dianne. This was flambéed at their table by the waiter, so it wasn't until that was done the three actors could really start to talk.

"Let's get down to business. As I see it," Judith began mixing the mussels into her pasta, "we have several problems. Obviously one is our renowned director. But I think we can overcome that fairly simply by merely ignoring everything he says. It seemed to work as we were blocking; I don't see why we can't continue in a similar vein. That is if you two don't have a problem with that?"

Rupert and Miranda both shook their heads. They had no problem with that whatsoever.

"Of course some of the other actors seem more determined to follow him, but maybe we can change that. What do you think?"

"Isabelle will do anything for a story," said Miranda. "But she also wants to look good, so if our staging makes her look better then she'll be fine. What about Adam, Rupert? You're a man; don't men share some kind of male bonding?"

"Oh yes, darling, we all go down the male bonding club, drink cheap beer, play strip poker and pull girls!"

"Rupert!" Miranda snapped. "Please be sensible."

"As far as I can see, Adam is terrified," said Rupert. "I think anyone who helps him will win his undying affection."

"Christ knows why Wesley employed him," said Judith. "I presume you know his background?" Miranda and Rupert both nodded. "It's all very well to be supportive, but why should we have to suffer?"

"What about Scarlett?" Miranda asked.

"She practically worships Alexander. I wouldn't be surprised if she has a shrine to him at home."

"Oh, don't worry about Scarlett," Judith said. "I can deal with her. Her hero worship doesn't only extend to our director; apparently I was her idol from birth. Don't you love it when people say that, as if we need reminding we're old? So, that seems to have solved the minor problem of our director; now we come to our major problem: our American Beauty Queen."

There was a silence as the three actors sat and thought about it for a moment. Around them the waiters cleared away their main course plates, offered them desserts, which were universally declined, and brought over cups of coffee. Judith stirred hers thoughtfully. She had been contemplating this plan all day, but now she was unsure how to put it. That wasn't like her at all, but then this wasn't like anything she'd had to do before. She was aware Miranda would do virtually anything to keep in with her but this was asking a lot of her, and of Rupert.

"Could I have a large cognac?" she called across to their waiter. "Rupert, Miranda?" Rupert accepted; Miranda opted for more wine. "I've told Wesley to get Echo a vocal coach, we have to get rid of that ghastly accent, but that isn't going to help with her acting. Now, between us we might be able to do something, show her how to do things, maybe if we say the line a certain way she will copy us. However, one cannot teach emotion. Elvira is a worldly creature while Echo is not, apart from maybe on the beauty pageant circuit. Do you think she's ever had sex?"

Rupert laughed. "You certainly get straight to the point."

"Well, do you?"

"I doubt it," said Miranda after a few seconds. "For a start that awful mother would probably never let a man anywhere near her precious daughter."

"What about a kiss or a snog at the back of a beauty pageant stage?"

Rupert shook his head. "No, I think Miranda's right. I don't think she's ever done anything. Sexually, I think she's got the experience of an 8 year old."

Judith nodded. "I agree. But Elvira is totally the opposite. Not only was she married to Charles for some time, but also, apparently, had an affair with a Captain Bracegirdle. And who knows who else. So the point is, how can anyone play sexy when they have no experience of how it feels? Remember when Alexander said to walk sexily across the stage and she marched across as if in the army?"

"It's a good point," said Miranda. "But what can we do about it? Find her a boyfriend in the next three weeks, or club together and buy her a male prostitute?"

Judith slugged down her cognac and signalled to the waiter to bring her and Rupert

150

another. "No. I was thinking that Rupert could do it."

"What!" Rupert and Miranda were, for once, in total unison.

"I don't mean you have to totally seduce her, Rupert. Or rather maybe I do mean seduce her, but not go through with full sex. Flirt, charm her, make her feel excited and sensual. Elvira is in love with Charles, so if Echo was a little in love with the man playing Charles, who knows how her performance would improve. I know it's a lot to ask; that's why I had to discuss it with both of you, after all it affects Miranda as much as you, Rupert." She took another mouthful of cognac in the silence that followed. At this rate she'd be too drunk to remember their response. "Please say something you two, even if it's only 'fuck off Judith'."

"Fuck off Judith," said Rupert but without venom. "Seriously though, how could this work? I mean, I'm not some sort of Don Juan. What makes you think she'd be interested in me?"

"Oh please!" Judith said. "She's a 20 something year old virgin who's never been touched as far as we know, and you have half the company trying to get into your trousers. Sorry, Miranda."

"No, that's fine," Miranda sighed. "It's nothing new."

"That's exactly my point."

"OK," said Rupert, "so even if I did try and do this, what about her mother? I'd never get

151

near her with that woman as chaperone, and believe me I don't want some sort of perverted threesome."

"I think Miranda and I can sort something out, keep her occupied, don't you, Miranda?"

Miranda nodded, torn between wanting to be included by Judith and being less than thrilled at the prospect of her husband seducing Echo, sex or no actual sex.

"Look, I've thrown this at you, and I'm sorry. If you want to say no I promise I won't hold it against you. Think about it."

"Do you really think it would help?" Miranda enquired.

"Do you remember your first sexual passion?"

"Yes."

"Did that make you feel different?"

Miranda smiled. "Oh yes." Rupert raised a quizzical eyebrow at her. "Mind your own business, Rupert! It wasn't you anyway."

Rupert grinned, recalling both his first sexual passion at the age of seven in the girls' corner of the school playground, and his first fully-fledged sexual experience seven years after that. Compared to him, Miranda had been a late starter, falling for a fellow student at drama school playing Cliff opposite her Sally Bowles in *Cabaret*.

"So did you play love scenes differently after your experience than before?" Judith continued.

"Point taken," Miranda replied.

At a gesture from Judith the waiter brought the bill over to the table. Judith grabbed it before Rupert or Miranda could protest, and put her credit card on the tray. "My treat, I insist. It's the least I could do."

Judith waved aside their thanks and offers to walk her home. "I may be old," she said, "but I'm not a fucking invalid yet, though I may be by the end of this production." She left them outside the restaurant and strolled home slowly, hoping she hadn't caused too many problems with her scheme. Perhaps it was a stupid idea. No, it was a fucking great idea; it was putting it into action that was hard. She'd sacrificed so much for her art over her career, surely Rupert and Miranda could sacrifice a little something. She let herself in the front door and was greeted by Max X. "Perhaps I could get Echo to love you," Judith said to her cat. "She certainly needs to learn to love, with a passion, something which isn't either herself or her fucking mother."

Rupert and Miranda were silent in the cab on the way home. As Rupert closed their front door behind them, he said, "Let's not talk about it tonight, let's leave it until we're less tired."

"But I'm not tired," Miranda sulked.

"Good," said Rupert and in his best Rhett Butler manner he picked Miranda up, carried her to their bedroom and threw her on the bed. "I don't know what's going to happen with Judith's plan, but I know I'm never going to do to Echo what I'm going to do to you now!"

Sometime later, as she nuzzled happily on Rupert's chest, Miranda came to the conclusion that if Rupert was going to get that turned on by the thought of seducing Echo then perhaps she wasn't going to lose out after all.

"Rupert."

"Mmm?"

"Just make sure you don't do that to Echo on her first time or she won't be able to walk, let alone glide in a ghostly manner."

"You mean you want me to do it?"

"I'm not sure if 'want' is the right word, but if it's really going to help maybe you should, if you don't mind. What the hell am I talking about, why would you mind?"

"Miranda, I know this may amaze you, but I have no desire to seduce a whining American child."

"So you won't do it?"

Rupert thought about it for a while. It would be quite a challenge and how many guys could say they had their wife's permission? "I guess I could."

"No full sex though."

"No."

"And especially what you just did to me."

"Never! That was a Miranda special."

"There's one more condition."

Rupert turned her head upwards so he could look at her. "Yes?"

"I want to be the one to tell Judith."

CHAPTER THIRTEEN

Not everyone was having such a productive weekend as Judith, Rupert and Miranda.

Echo was having an awful time. Or to be precise Julia Morton, the dialect coach, was having an awful time. She felt she'd strayed onto the set of *Singin' in the Rain*, where the dialect coach says in perfect English, "And I can't stand him," and Lena Lamont repeats "Aand I caaan't staand 'im." Julia had commenced their two day session by trying to explain to Echo how the English language worked and the different vowel sounds. Echo stared at her blankly. So Julia went through the entire script, a line at a time, in a Standard English accent, getting Echo to imitate her. This worked well as an instant solution, but on revising later without Julia speaking first, Echo reverted to her American drawl.

By Sunday lunchtime Julia was feeling suicidal. Or possibly murderous, not so much towards Echo, but towards Storm, who, stating that this was not a proper rehearsal, had insisted on being present. Any criticism Julia made of Echo Storm took as a personal slight.

"No one never complained about the way she talks before."

"No one ever," Julia automatically corrected.

"Huh?"

"No one never, that's a double negative. It's no one ever."

"Huh?"

"Please forget I said anything."

While Storm and Echo were out buying carrot sticks for lunch, Julia carefully recorded herself reading all Elvira's lines on tape. When Storm and Echo returned, she gave the tape to them with the suggestion Echo listen to it as often as possible.

"So are we done?" Storm asked.

"Definitely."

When Julia arrived home she called Wesley on his mobile. "I've done my best, but it's an uphill struggle. No, that's an understatement; it's more like trying to climb Mount Everest in a blizzard wearing nothing but a bikini."

"Is that a subject you're speaking about from experience?"

"Not yet, but after this weekend I may consider it."

"You're not giving up on me?"

"I'm sorry but I cannot do another session. I've aged twenty years over two days. Perhaps if Echo listens to my tape enough she'll get the hang of it, but I can't guarantee anything. And please don't give me a credit in the programme; if Echo doesn't improve I don't want people thinking I can't do my job properly."

Wesley hung up feeling utterly depressed. He felt like joining Julia on Mount Everest; he'd even wear a bikini. Judith was going to kill him. Bloody Alexander, what had he been thinking of employing Echo? He was damned well going to phone him right now and tell him he needed to sort out this problem himself.

Jasper answered the phone, informing Wesley that Alexander was out and not contactable. Actually, Alexander was sitting in front of the *Blithe Spirit* video making cuts in his script. He was terribly excited; the film was so much shorter than the play. If he could put these cuts in there'd be far less to rehearse which would certainly suit him. And it finished in an entirely differently manner: Charles was killed by both his dead wives. Now that's what he called an ending. He couldn't wait to change it. That would impress his cast: a new ending to an old classic, once he'd figured how to put a car crash on the stage. He'd like to have Madame Arcati seen riding her bike too, as she did on the film. That would be a creative coup.

"Darling," he said after Jasper finished talking to Wesley, hedging on why the set and costume designs still weren't available, "is there any chance we could have a car and a bike operational on the stage?"

Jasper looked thoughtful for a moment. "I suppose so. You wouldn't like a train would you? I love the idea of a train coming towards the audience. I saw something like that once and everyone screamed; it would be dazzling."

"I love it," said Alexander, not wanting to upset his boyfriend, and besides part of it did appeal to him, "but how would the wives have fixed it for Charles to go under a train?"

"Couldn't they push him?"

"No, the text definitely says that ghosts can't touch people."

"Oh. And I suppose we have to stick to the text?"

"It's probably as well if we do. Cutting is one thing, but I'm not certain about rewriting."

"What a shame. How about if we have the car hurtle at the audience instead?"

"Wonderful!"

"And we could have Madame Arcati biking round the auditorium to make her entrance."

"Jasper, you are a genius and that really turns me on. Come here!"

When Wesley phoned back later, still endeavouring to speak to Alexander, neither the director nor Jasper were in a position to answer the phone.

Isabelle and Scarlett on the other hand answered their respective phones early that Sunday evening and were astonished to discover it was Judith. Though neither was aware of it, both received exactly the same dialogue: Judith was worried about Alexander's not really understanding Noel Coward's text and since Noel had been a friend of Judith's this was hugely upsetting to her. She knew it was a lot to ask, but she felt Isabelle / Scarlett was the only person she could trust to help her out. Would Isabelle / Scarlett work with her? Isabelle agreed with alacrity; Scarlett took a little longer. She'd been taught to always obey the director; it felt wrong to work against him, plus Alexander had been an idol to her. On the other hand, this was Judith Gold, Judith Gold who had been her heroine for years, asking her, Scarlett Montgomery, for help. Of course she must say yes.

"That's wonderful," Judith said to each one. "But you must keep this conversation to yourself; I don't want anyone else to know I've singled you out."

Adam also got a call, but his came from Rupert asking him out for a drink. Adam was torn. He'd planned to go over to Hattie's tonight and put little Millie to bed; he loved reading her bedtime stories and seeing her sleeping face on the pillow. It made him feel centred and serene. Then Hattie was going to cook him supper and they'd watch something on TV together. But Rupert had sounded fairly insistent and Adam liked his fellow actor better than any other member of the cast; a drink with him had to be better than that dreadful coffee meeting he'd had with Isabelle before the second day of rehearsals. That woman could get a job with the Spanish Inquisition. So he dashed over to Hattie's for an hour where he sat watching a worn Teletubbies video with Millie, promised he'd put her to bed the following weekend, and then left to meet Rupert about 7.30.

They chose a pub beside the river, somewhere between their two homes, and over a pint and several bags of crisps Rupert gave him a similar story to that which Judith had given Scarlett and Isabelle. "You see, this will only work if we all stick together. What do you think?"

"What about Wesley?" Adam asked. "I feel responsible to him; he gave me this job. How's he going to feel if we don't listen to the director he's employed?"

"If he's got any sense, exceedingly grateful. Did you see his face the day he came in with Alexander? He didn't look too happy. Anyway, we're not asking you to entirely ignore Alexander; only, if anything starts to feel wrong we may need to sort it out ourselves. Perhaps Noel Coward isn't exactly Alexander's cup of tea, and he needs a gentle helping hand." Or a very ungentle push up the backside, Rupert added to himself. "People think Coward is easy to do but it isn't; it's a very specific style as I'm sure you know, but I don't think Alexander does. This play means a lot to me, and I don't want it to be a disaster. I hoped you'd feel the same."

Adam stared out the window at the ducks carelessly swimming up and down. Did ducks ever worry like humans? Perhaps if there was such a thing as reincarnation he'd ask to come back as a duck. Millie loved feeding the ducks; if he did come back as one, perhaps she'd be feeding him with her daughter or granddaughter one day.

"Adam?"

"Sorry." Adam turned back to Rupert. "I was miles away there."

"Let me get you another pint. Give you a bit more time to think about it."

Rupert stood at the bar watching Adam. Poor guy, he looked twice as worried as he had before – either that or he was communing with the ducks; it was hard to tell with Adam. Perhaps they should have left him alone, after all Dr Bradman wasn't a huge role; they could have worked round him rather than bemuse him further by forcing him into confrontation. But then if Adam needed help or support he was more likely to get it from people like himself, Miranda and Judith, than from Alexander. And somehow he couldn't visualize Judith and Miranda helping anyone they felt wasn't with them.

Adam was starting to realize the same thing. He couldn't afford to alienate his fellow actors, and Rupert was so amiable. He'd inquired about Adam's family, looked at the photos of Justine, Hattie and Millie which he kept in his wallet and appeared genuinely interested. Much to his amazement he'd even found himself confiding his fears in Rupert and recounting the complete details of his breakdown. Rupert hadn't thrown up his hands in horror, laughed or even probed further. He'd simply smiled kindly and said, "I don't think there's an actor alive who doesn't occasionally have nightmares about forgetting their lines."

"What, even Judith?"

"I would imagine even Judith. The difference is she'd never let anyone know. I heard a story that she lost her place in a play once when she had this very long speech; she kept going round in circles with her lines until she got back on track. The rest of the cast were going crazy trying to figure out where the hell they were; one moment they heard their cue to enter, the next she'd gone back a page! But she got herself back on track again. You were merely unfortunate in the way it affected you. There's no reason for it to happen again; you'll be fine."

"Thanks. You're a great listener."

Rupert was a good listener; it was one of his best qualities. He found people fascinating and was forever trying to work out what made them tick. He hated actors who only ever talked about themselves; it was so dull. He couldn't bear interviewers like Frank Skinner, Graham Norton and Jonathon Ross who seemed to invite people on entirely to show off how clever and funny they thought they were. Rupert had refused to go on any of their shows. Parkinson he had done when promoting his Hollywood movie, but then

Parkie was a proper interviewer: he asked sensible questions, listened to the answers and wasn't continually trying to upstage his guests.

Considering he was married to Miranda it was as well Rupert *was* such a skilled listener. Or perhaps that was the reason he was so skilled. Certainly if he hadn't been, their marriage wouldn't have lasted as long as it had.

After two hours of talking and several pints Adam agreed to work with Rupert, on the condition it didn't involve any confrontation with Wesley.

"No problem," Rupert said, wondering how Adam would deal with any confrontation at all. Outside the pub Rupert hailed a cab and offered it to Adam.

"No thanks, I think I'll get the bus," Adam said, thinking of his bank account; supply teaching had not been a very lucrative job. Also he needed the walk at the other end of his journey to clear his head and work out exactly what he'd got himself into.

"Sure," said Rupert easily. "I've got into bad habits. Miranda would probably have a stroke on the spot if I suggested she use a bus or tube." He jumped into the cab, gave the driver his address and sped off.

Tonight had been easy, and actually quite enjoyable. His next task was going to be much more of a challenge: Echo. He was going home now to discuss with his wife the best way of seducing a 20 something year old virgin. And people said tennis players lead interesting lives.

CHAPTER FOURTEEN

Monday morning, after the séance circle, Alexander announced he had some cuts to make in the script. Prepared for all sorts of other contingencies, this one flummoxed everyone.

"Cuts!" said Judith.

"I think Alexander might be about to die," Lucy whispered to Rebecca, who was sitting with her script, ready to make notes.

"Do you realize," Judith continued, "that once Noel wrote this play, which he did incidentally in a week, only two lines were ever cut in production?"

"In which case maybe it's about time they were," said Alexander. "And do I have to remind you that I am the director of this particular version and as such I can cut what I like?"

Everyone stared at Judith, who quietly looked Alexander up and down. "Yes of course, Mein Führer." She gave him a Nazi salute. "Shall we get on with it?"

"That's it?" Lucy whispered in disappointment. "I was expecting her to blow."

"Hmm." Rebecca looked at Judith. "Don't think she won't."

Alexander, most of whose knowledge about

Nazis came from *The Sound of Music*, wasn't sure that Judith's salute was very complimentary, but decided to drop the subject. At least she wasn't refusing to listen, though even Alexander had the sense to begin hesitantly. So far it seemed to be going OK; the cast and stage management were making notes in their scripts with pencils and no one had complained, even though some people were losing large amounts of their lines. Alexander decided he must, finally, be getting through to them. But he was going to save his pièce de résistance for later: the car crash and Charles's death.

"Let's have an early lunch, shall we?" he declared at 12.45. "Then this afternoon I want to run over the cuts I've made with moves."

"Right, lunch everyone, back at 1.45." Declan announced officially. "Judith and Alexander, I'm sorry but your lunches won't be here until 1."

"That's fine," Judith said. "I think I'll go and get a sandwich with the others."

"Oh, right," said Declan.

"Give my portion to Mein Führer; I'm sure all that hard work cutting scripts has given him a huge appetite. Right, where are we going, gang?"

"There's a pub across the road," Rupert said. "They do food."

"Let's go." Judith swept out; Miranda, Isabelle and Scarlett excitedly following in her wake. Scarlett couldn't wait to tell Holly she'd been out to lunch with Judith Gold; what a wise choice it had been to side with her. Rupert, last out the room, realized Adam wasn't with them. He turned back to see him still sitting in the corner. "Adam, aren't you coming?"

Adam crossed over to him. "Well, I'm not sure ... I mean, am I really included?"

"Of course you are; come on, I'm starving."

"What about Echo?"

Rupert looked over to where Echo was standing on her own, looking hopefully in their direction. Rupert hesitated. It was cruel to leave her alone, but she would only be confused if they included her in this lunchtime meeting. He had an idea and went over to where Lucy was getting her bag in preparation for leaving.

"Lucy, I wondered if you could do me a favour."

Lucy smiled. "Anything for you, Rupert."

"Ask Echo to go out to lunch with you."

"That wasn't quite the favour I had in mind."

"I know it's a lot to ask, but she's all by herself and I can't take her with us."

"Why? What's going on? Judith is eating out with the plebs and accepting Alexander's cuts. It's all highly suspicious."

"Look Lucy, I'll buy you a drink sometime to make it up to you, I promise."

"It'd better be a bloody large one," said

Lucy. "And at least two packets of kettle chips to go with it."

"Deal!" Rupert laughed and gave Lucy a quick kiss, after all Miranda was out of sight, and then followed the others to the pub.

Lucy looked after him reflectively, wishing she was going with him or at least being a fly on the wall; she hated to miss out on intrigue. Instead, she dutifully went over to Echo and asked her if she wanted to come out to lunch with her, Rebecca and Matthew.

"Honest?" Echo was not used to being asked anywhere without Storm. "Sure. But I have to have salad with no dressing."

"You'll be lucky round here; the closest thing to salad would be a dollop of coleslaw on the side of your plate."

Echo got a plastic container full of carrots, tomatoes and celery from out of her bag. "Mommy sent this in with me; I guess I could have these while you eat."

"No, you can't," said Lucy firmly. "They don't like people bringing in their own food. Come on, live a little. And I know just the place to introduce you to English food."

Thirty minutes later Echo found herself in the local chippie discovering the joys of cod, chips and mushy peas covered in malt vinegar and tomato ketchup.

"Wow, this is so good," she kept on saying over and over again.

"Echo, you look like a girl who's just experienced her first orgasm!" Lucy said.

"Orgasm?" Echo asked "I thought this was called fish'n'chips."

"You have to be kidding ... aren't you?" Lucy said.

Echo looked at her confused.

Rebecca frowned at Lucy across the table.

"And I thought Matthew was the green one around here," said Lucy, causing poor Matthew to go a similar colour to his ketchup. He certainly knew what an orgasm was.

"So should I say I had fish'n'chips to Mommy tonight, or an orgasm?" Echo asked.

"Fish and chips," said Rebecca, Lucy and Matthew in unison. Although, as Lucy pointed out later, it would have been a joy to see Storm's face if her daughter told her she'd been out to a chippie at lunchtime and been given an orgasm.

In the pub orgasms were, unusually, the last thing on the actors' minds. "Where the hell were all those cuts from?" Miranda asked. "Were they picked at random or did he take against certain people?"

"Actually, I think they were from the film," said Scarlett. Everyone looked at her. "When I knew I was auditioning for this role I got a copy of the video to give me some ideas." Then she blushed, remembering it wasn't done for actors to use other actors' ideas, or at least that's what they always claimed.

"Hopefully not ideas you're going to use,"

Judith said. "It was a terrible film. Noel hated it."

"Didn't he have anything to do with it?" Isabelle asked.

"Not a huge amount, they made it while he was away in South Africa. I think his exact comment was: 'It wasn't frightfully good'."

"Yes, it was terrible," Scarlett rushed on, rather embarrassed at what she'd admitted to. "But I'm pretty certain all the cuts he used were those in the movie."

"So our mini Hitler can't even make his own cuts," Judith drawled. "How very interesting."

"Six ploughman's," said the pub waitress, plonking down the plates off her laden tray. "Cutlery and condlements are over there." She turned and stamped off.

"Condlements, how charming," said Judith. "Do you think condlements would produce such things as mayonnaise for all this sad looking lettuce?"

"Mayonnaise, what kind of a pub do you think this is?" Rupert asked, getting up to head over to the condiment area. "One of those gastro places? Heinz salad cream is what you'll get, like it or not."

"Now that takes me back a few years," said Judith.

"Do they still make it?" Isabelle asked in surprise.

"I'm not that old, Isabelle, dear."

"No, sorry Judith, I ... I didn't mean that,

only I've never seen anyone buy it, so I wondered why they still made it."

"Probably especially for places like this," said Rupert, coming back with handfuls of salad cream, knives, forks and paper napkins.

"And of course for ancient people like me to reminisce," Judith said cruelly in Isabelle's direction. Isabelle tried to smile as if she thought that was very funny and viciously stabbed a tomato.

Judith broke off a piece of bread and covered it with cheese. "Not bad," she said. "Nice and strong, we can all breath over our Führer later. Oh, even better, pickled onions, that should kill his aura stone dead. Talking of which, now little Miss Scarlett Holmes here has deduced the source of his cuts, how shall we deal with it? Any ideas?"

"We could tell him we know they come from the film," Scarlett said. "That might embarrass him into withdrawing them."

"I doubt that," Miranda said, toying with her coleslaw which appeared to have bright red carrots in it. "He doesn't seem the embarrassed type, or the type that would back down easily."

"Or even under great pressure," said Rupert.

"What if we go to Wesley and tell him what Alexander's been doing?" Isabelle suggested, desperately trying to impress Judith after her earlier salad dressing disaster. "Surely, as the producer, he would have some say?"

"That's a bit like telling tales out of school, isn't it?" said Rupert, who hated doing that sort of thing. Judith, having no such qualms, was silenced by this unfamiliar stance. "Surely we should try and sort it out ourselves?"

"Yes, but how?" said Miranda. "He won't listen to us and we can't do what he wants; isn't that what's known in chess as checkmate?"

"Stalemate," said Rupert. Miranda glared at him. Did he have to make her look bad in front of Judith? But it turned out Judith would have known anyway since she said, "Ah, a fellow chess player, I must give you a game sometime. In fact, I have Noel's original chess set; he gave it to me a few months before he died."

"I'd love that," Rupert said. "That's inspiration for doing this play if nothing else."

"Talking of doing this play," said Miranda pointedly, "we have to be back in 20 minutes and we've come up with no plan at all."

"Actually, I do have a plan," said Judith. "I was merely wondering if anyone had anything different." She stopped and looked round them all expectantly in an exact copy of Alexander. Everyone laughed, except Adam who was still trying to swallow his ploughman's even though he had no appetite. He kept dreading that someone would ask his opinion, and he didn't have one. He glanced up at Judith who was continuing to do an excellent impersonation of Alexander, grasping Scarlett's hand, coughing dramatically in the direction of some cigarette smoke, staring intensely at each person and speaking very slowly with gaps between each word.

"The ... answer ... is ... very ... simple ... Oh, Christ, this is too much like hard work; why would anyone talk like that? I'd forget what the hell I was talking about by the time I reached the end of the sentence, and anyone listening would have lost the will to live. OK, it's simple: we ignore the cuts, like we did with blocking, only this time we have everyone on our side."

"We don't do the cuts?" said Scarlett in amazement. "None of them?"

"It's either all or nothing. Unless of course you want to lose all your lines and we keep ours? We could make Edith into a mute."

Scarlett shook her head quickly.

"Fine. So that's my plan. Do we want a secret ballot or will a show of hands do?" Not waiting for an answer Judith went on, "All those for ignoring Alexander's cuts raise their knives." Five knives went up. Adam was still using his to eat. Judith looked at him questioningly. "Are you not with us or merely desperate to finish your lunch? I'm sure we can get you a doggy bag."

"It's not that," said Adam nervously.

"Oh My God it speaks!"

"I mean, I'm with you and all, but there's one problem, unless I missed something, which of course I might have done."

"What's that then, Einstein?" Judith asked somewhat crossly. She couldn't foresee any problems.

"Echo. She doesn't know anything about this, does she? If we all start ignoring the cuts and she doesn't, then it's not going to work … is it?"

"Well, what do you know, not only does it speak but it's smart." That was the nearest Judith got to an apology. "I had totally forgotten about that. Bugger."

Miranda looked at her watch; they needed to be back in five minutes. A much hurried debate ensued as they returned to the rehearsal room and plan B was put into operation.

CHAPTER FIFTEEN

Echo, contentedly full of fish and chips, was sitting on a chair in the rehearsal room looking at the cuts in her script. It was so confusing, honest it was; everyday they changed things and then wanted you to remember it all. Still, she'd had such a great time with her new friends, Lucy, Rebecca and Matthew, that it didn't matter as much any more. It had been cool having a laugh as they ate, even if she wasn't sure what was funny. She supposed it was this English sense of humour everyone kept going on about. It was the same as this *Blithe Spirit* play; it was meant to be funny but she couldn't see it herself. After all, it was about ghosts and everyone knows ghosts are real scary. And there was lots of shouting and Echo didn't like shouting; it upset her.

The door to the rehearsal room opened and the other six actors walked in. After being asked out by Lucy, Echo no longer minded about being excluded from their lunch outing. She watched as Miranda and Isabelle crossed to Alexander and wondered what they were talking about; she didn't think they liked each other very much, but maybe she was wrong. Much to her surprise, Scarlett came and sat down beside her.

"Hi, Echo, I'm sorry I haven't had much of a chance to talk to you. But you know what it's like at the start of rehearsals."

Actually Echo didn't have the faintest idea, but she nodded anyway and smiled her perfect-white-teeth smile.

"Look, we're about the same age, aren't we?" Scarlett went on. "So maybe we could kind of buddy up." Echo nodded again. This was turning out to be a good day. "You don't know much about theatre, do you?" Echo shook her head. "Well, I'm relatively new too." Scarlett hated this part of her speech; having to compare her experience to Echo's was mortifying, but it was part of the plan. "And some of these more experienced actors have been telling me that it's a tradition to play a joke on the director on the second week of rehearsals." Echo's eyes opened wide: a joke? She'd always wanted to play a joke on someone. She'd seen it done so often on TV shows but never got the chance, or had the know-how. "So, do you want to go along with the gag?"

"Sure, that'd be great. Do you think I ought to ask Mommy first?"

"Come on, Echo, friends don't have to check with their mothers first, do they?"

"No, I guess not. So what's the joke?"

"You know all those cuts Alexander has been putting in this morning?"

"Yeah."

"When he comes to run through the play

this afternoon we're not going to put in any of them."

"None of 'em?"

"Not a single line. And Alexander will profess to be cross and tell us to do them, but he'll know it's a joke and that's the way he's supposed to react. What do you think?"

"I have to do the play the same as before this morning?" Echo was disappointed; it didn't seem much of a joke. She'd hoped for exploding water bombs or a whoopee cushion. But if this was a theatrical joke then she'd go right along with it.

"What are Miranda and Isabelle saying to him now?" Echo asked.

"They're dropping hints about there being a joke," Scarlett improvised. "So he'll be looking out for it, without knowing exactly where it is."

"OK," said Echo. This was sounding more fun.

Alexander clapped his hands together to call everyone back to rehearsal, much to Miranda and Isabelle's relief. They were drained trying to distract Alexander from Scarlett's coercion of Echo, by debating the relationship between Ruth and Mrs Bradman.

"You do realize he will now, in all probability, come up with some lesbian sex scene for us?" Miranda said to Isabelle as they took their places for Act One.

"Now, that would be a fresh slant," Isabelle said. "At least we might acquire some sexy negligees to wear."

"Don't bet on it. Almost certainly be full frontal nudity."

"I think that would only interest Alexander if it were men."

"True."

Alexander placed his plastic chair in front of his actors. "Now, I want a run through of the whole play – no stopping under any circumstances. Do you understand?" There was no reply. "And action!" he called.

"Oh for fuck's sake, it's 'lights up' or 'curtain up', you moron," Judith snapped. "'Action' is for films, which in case you haven't noticed we aren't doing. I understand you need a camera to make one of those."

Alexander gave her a grand look as if to say don't mess with me and once again called: "action."

Judith gave another mock Nazi salute but stayed silent. Scarlett walked on carrying what was supposed to be a tray of drinks, represented by a dirty wooden tray and a few coffee cups. Miranda followed her a few seconds later and spoke her first line, then it was Scarlett's and Miranda's and wait – wasn't there supposed to be a cut there? Alexander looked at his script. Yes, they must have forgotten about it; he told Rebecca to make a note. Now Rupert was on stage and he and Miranda were having a conversation, far too long a conversation as far as Alexander was concerned; neither was using his cuts. What the hell was going on? Were his entire cast suffering from amnesia? Isabelle and Adam had lost a lot of their lines this morning, but apparently no more. He didn't even consider, correctly, that Judith would use hers. Even his loyal Scarlett was disobeying him, and every time Echo said a line which was supposed to be cut she giggled like it was a joke. Was he going mad?

"Stop!" he called at the end of Act One.

"Sorry, Alexander, but I thought you said no stopping under any circumstances," Lucy said innocently. She'd figured out exactly what had gone on over lunch and was having a field day.

"I'm the director. I don't count."

"I'm so glad you feel that way," said Judith. "We don't think you count for much either."

"No! I don't count about stopping the play. I'm the director; I can do what I like. Why aren't you putting in my cuts?"

"We don't know what you mean, Alexander. And Lucy was correct, you did say we mustn't stop. Act Two, anyone?" Judith swept away leaving Alexander speechless: a hitherto unheard of event.

"He reminds me of George Bush on September 11th," Lucy muttered to Matthew, "when, on being informed the World Trade Centre had been hit, he stayed sitting in the school class he'd been visiting, because no one told him what he else he should do."

Even to the end Alexander vainly clung to the hope that someone would put in at least one of his cuts. Surely Scarlett, his ally, would do so in her big scene at the end. But no, not even one.

"That all went very well, I felt," Judith said at the end.

"You ignored me, you all ignored me," Alexander shouted. "How dare you."

"We didn't ignore you," Judith said. "We ignored the cuts David Lean decided to make to the movie. And much as I'm sure you'd prefer to be doing the film we are, as I pointed out earlier, doing the stage version."

"Well, there's one thing I am going to use from the film; I'm going to have a car crash on the stage and Charles is going to die. And whatever you do you're not going to stop me; Jasper is already designing the car. And if you don't like that idea be grateful I stopped him from making it into a train."

"A train?" Miranda asked. "How was Charles going to die under a train?"

"Perhaps I was going to drink too much and fall off the platform," said Rupert. "After all, didn't you say Charles was an alcoholic?"

"It's not going to be a train; it's going to be a car."

"I don't think it's going to be either," said Judith with quiet venom. "I think you'll find Charles flees the house as it falls about his ears, the way the play was written."

"You can't treat me like this. I'm going straight to Wesley." And for the second time in two weeks Alexander walked out of rehearsals.

"You're quite right, Rupert," said Judith, "it does sound horribly like snitching to the headmaster when Alexander says it. From henceforward I shall stop running to Wesley myself when I've a problem. Well, within reason anyway."

Rupert smiled. "I don't see why you'd need to, Judith; you seem more than capable of dealing with stuff yourself."

Declan grabbed his mobile and went out into the corridor. He'd better call Wesley and warn him of Alexander's impending visit.

Wesley listened to the day's news with sinking heart and then glanced at his watch. He had promised to take Henrietta out to supper tonight; she'd told him if he waited much longer she'd be too big to fit behind a restaurant table, and once the baby came there'd be no eating out for a while. If Alexander came round now he'd never get away. The phone started to ring: that might or might not be him and Wesley wasn't risking it. He switched on the answerphone, grabbed his bag and jacket and fled from his office, onto the tube and to the safety of home, mobile carefully turned off. There was one piece of good news Declan had imparted: Judith had apparently declared she would no longer be coming to him with her problems. Now, that would be a bonus, but he wouldn't count on it just yet.

Declan, the last to leave the rehearsal room, found Echo standing outside. It transpired that, since they had finished early tonight, she was waiting for Storm to pick her up at the expected finishing time.

"Wasn't that a neat joke we played today?" Echo asked Declan happily.

"Joke?" Declan asked. "What joke?"

"The one we all played on Alexander, not putting his cuts in. He was real good at pretending to be mad, wasn't he? It was the best thing ever."

"Who told you about the joke?" Declan asked.

"Scarlett. She wants to be my friend; isn't that cool? I've never had a friend of my age before. I've never played a joke before either. And I had fish'n'chips at lunch. It's been the best day ever."

Declan waited with Echo until Storm arrived, and during that time gently drew the story out of her. He was going to have to talk to Scarlett at some point, though he doubted it was her idea. There was a company conspiracy afoot and whatever he thought of Alexander, and that wasn't a lot, Declan didn't like conspiracies. Plus it wasn't fair on Echo if she was used when needed; by tomorrow they'd probably revert to cutting her dead.

Returning home after an excellent three course French meal, Wesley found several messages from Alexander on his mobile. He texted back a very simple message of his own and switched the phone back off. The message read: under no circumstances change one word of script, also no car crash – the producer's decision is final.

CHAPTER SIXTEEN

Much to everyone's surprise Alexander turned up to rehearsals next morning, held his morning séance and then announced they would rehearse Act One. There was no mention of any cuts.

One hour later he declared he had a headache and was going home immediately.

"It appears the arsenic I put in his tea was effective then," Judith said after he'd left.

"You put arsenic ..." Scarlett began, before she noticed Judith give her a withering look.

"Does nobody in this company have a sense of humour?" she said.

"Sorry."

"Or do I come across as a poisoner?"

"Oh yes," said Rupert. "I'd say, under the circumstances, it would be highly plausible."

"Rupert!" Miranda said in horror.

But Judith merely laughed. "He has a point. Now, in my opinion, since it makes very little difference whether our Führer is here or not, we may as well continue rehearsing on our own at present. If we do scenes which don't involve Madame Arcati I can watch and give notes and ideas. How do people feel about that?"

There was a general murmuring of assent.

"Like anyone is going to say no," Lucy said quietly to Matthew.

"You're probably correct, Lucy, but I thought it polite to give them the option." Lucy's eyes opened wide. Judith gave her the briefest twitch of a smile. "I may be old but I'm not applying for my hearing aid yet."

"You're not kidding," replied Lucy. "Sorry."

"Everyone is entitled to their opinions – as long as they know I'm always right." Judith's twitch of a smile had become broader. "OK, we've got work to do."

Starting from the top of the play, the scene between Miranda, Scarlett and Rupert went better than ever before. Judith understood the text and her suggestions were vastly helpful. Rupert and Miranda, already used to working together, found their repartee sparkled and were rewarded several times by laughs from the rest of the cast and stage management. As for Scarlett, she was flying high – Miranda and Rupert were a joy to work with. She genuinely believed she was their gauche maid, who performed each undertaking at a run. When Rupert, as Charles, sent her to fetch his cigarette case, she would happily have fetched it from Timbuktu if he'd desired.

"Nice sprinting," Judith said as she dashed back on carrying Judith's cigarette pack which was deputising for the case. "Ever thought of entering the Olympics?"

Adam, on the other hand, was dreading

being under scrutiny, convinced Judith was going to tear him to shreds. So nervous was he that, during his entrance with Isabelle, he tripped over his own feet and careered into Rupert. "Bugger me!"

"Why, Dr Bradman, what an offer!" Rupert said with a grin, steadying Adam. "I didn't know you cared."

"I'm so sorry, everyone."

"Stop!" Judith said. "Adam, there is a renowned piece of advice to actors from Noel himself which seems singularly appropriate at present: 'Learn your lines and don't fall over the furniture,' or in your case your own feet. Go back to your entrance and remember – if you're going to clasp anyone it should probably be the actress playing your wife, not your male host."

Adam bit his lip and he and Isabelle started again. This time he managed to stay upright, but was so nervous he spoke his lines at double speed.

"Adam," Judith's voice came calmly, "this is not a race, unless there is some event you wish to attend shortly to which the rest of us are not invited."

"Sorry, sorry."

Behind Adam's back Rupert made a 'give him a chance' face at Judith.

"Adam, come here a minute," Judith called. Terrified, Adam went over to her. "I'll make a deal with you," she said, quietly enough that no one else could hear. "I promise not to bite your head off, at least not for the present, if you promise to try and stay upright and not go through this script as if participating in a Formula One race. I know Noel's lines should go at a smart pace, but not so smart as to be incomprehensible."

"Sorry."

"Dr Bradman is a country GP, not one who's strayed from some television hospital drama, where a single doctor brings at least ten people back from the brink of death in every episode while simultaneously bringing up three orphaned children and discovering the cure for AIDS."

"I think I played one of those once," Adam said.

"Along with half of the actors in the world, I should imagine. And no doubt your lines went like an express train as you ran alongside a hospital trolley with a bleeding patient prone on it. But Dr Bradman's life will be full of old ladies with sprained ankles or colds and children with tonsillitis and earache. No doubt he spends half his days on the golf course, or doing the Times crossword. So don't you feel he'd be fairly laid-back and relaxed?"

"Yes, I suppose so. But he does work at the hospital too, so he's not stupid."

"Did I say he was stupid?"

"No. Sorry."

"Adam, if you keep apologizing like this we shall have to start an apology box: one pound for each apology. All proceeds to the Judith Gold Benevolent Fund."

"Yes, of course, sorry. Oh God, I mean … Oh fuck!"

Judith chuckled. "Now that's a sentiment I can identify with. Of course Dr Bradman isn't stupid. He's a doctor for God's sake; not a profession known for its ignorance. In my opinion Mrs Bradman is the silly, annoying, gossipy one; in fact we have typecasting, don't you think?" Adam looked at her in astonishment; was she inferring what he thought? Judith briefly looked over at Isabelle and then winked at him. Apparently she did.

"Now go back and try again," Judith ordered. "No wait. I've an idea. Do you think you should have a doctor's bag?"

"Should I? I mean, I've come to dinner, would I take a bag?"

"You might; if there's going to be a séance, you could be worried about people collapsing. But it's your decision."

Adam thought about it. He liked it. He liked it a lot. "Yes, I think that's a great idea."

Judith looked around. "Anyone got anything we could use as a doctor's bag? We don't want any of our Führer's improvisation crap."

Declan produced his briefcase and Lucy added a few items from the first aid kit they kept for emergencies: bandages, Band-Aids, eye wash, ice packs and aspirin.

"Sorry, no stethoscope," she said.

"Here," said Scarlett, detaching the headphones from her Walkman. "Will these do?"

Adam picked up the medically filled briefcase: it felt great, he felt great. Making his entrance for a third time, he stayed upright while the lines came out perfectly and at the correct speed. Judith gave him a few more suggestions, but he'd found something in himself and for the first time felt confident. Thinking of Judith's comment on his stage wife, he started to treat her as a slight embarrassment to him, which worked remarkably well. Adam was starting to enjoy himself; this was how acting should feel.

Isabelle was furious. Not only had Judith held a private tête-á-tête with Adam when she'd led Isabelle to believe she was to be her bosom pal, but now Adam was treating Mrs Bradman, her character, as slightly stupid and embarrassing.

"Judith, could I have a word?" she asked, after Adam had got a huge laugh when he made Mrs Bradman sound like a petulant child with his line about her promising to behave.

"All right."

Isabelle marched over to Judith. "I don't understand," she muttered. "Adam is treating me as an idiot."

"Really."

Isabelle studied Judith. There were several ways to say 'really,' all insinuating something different, and she had no idea which one had been tossed to her. She ploughed on regardless. "You see, it doesn't fit in with my interpretation."

"Really."

Damn, Isabelle thought, it wasn't like her not to be able to pick up on things, even when she picked them up wrong, yet this time she didn't have a clue.

"So, what should I do?"

"Go with your interpretation and see what happens I should imagine. After all, I'm only helping out; I'm not the director."

Isabelle walked back furious and embarrassed. Everything was going wrong. She had been convinced Adam was going to be easy to walk over, thereby giving her character the chance to shine. She didn't see Mrs Bradman being a bit stupid, just rather sweet and charming, possibly even a bit flirtatious.

Yes, flirtatious, she'd try that out with her next line, but that failed, as Adam neatly crushed her. So that was how it was. Isabelle addressed her next line to Rupert with a slightly coy smile; if her own husband wasn't going to flirt with her she'd try someone else's. Rupert looked slightly taken aback. As far as he knew there was no subtext about Charles and Mrs Bradman; he already had two women fighting over him in the play and that was ample. So he pointedly ignored Isabelle. Isabelle looked over to Judith, who shrugged and gave her an apologetic look, while secretly enjoying every moment. It would do Isabelle no harm to be brought down a bit.

Rehearsals came to an abrupt halt when Judith was supposed to make her entrance.

"I can't see what I look like on stage," she said. "Besides, actors should never try to direct themselves, even the very best ones."

So they skipped that scene and the séance that ensued, and continued with Elvira's ghost making her entrance.

Judith tried her best with Echo's acting, but eventually could stand no more and moved rapidly on to the start of Act Two, featuring Miranda and Rupert. Again this was successful until Echo reappeared; it said a lot for Rupert and Miranda's acting that they managed to carry Echo along and produce something watchable and even funny.

Act Two, Scene 2 consisted of a duologue between Miranda and Judith. "Do you want to skip this too?" Declan, who was keeping track of the day's events, asked.

"No," said Judith. "I'd like to do some acting today; I believe it is what I'm being paid for. Rupert, would you watch and give us any suggestions you have?"

"Of course," Rupert said, highly flattered, and while he very wisely avoided giving Judith or his wife any acting notes, he did make a couple of suggestions as to moves they could make to enhance the scene.

"Nice work," Judith said as they finished.

Miranda beamed at him proudly. "Now, let's re-do the next scene so when Miranda is talking to the ghost of Elvira, Echo is not within her sight. Do you think you could manage that, Echo?"

"Sure. Only, do I have to remember them moves too?"

"'Those moves', it's 'those moves', not 'them moves'. Don't they teach English in America?"

"But we talk English in America." Echo looked confused. "Don't we?"

"That is questionable. Right, you need to start by sitting in this chair here." Judith pointed at a rather stained plastic chair. "Then, when Miranda starts getting angry and pointing at you, you need to cross to the window while she keeps addressing the chair."

"Why would she talk to the chair when I'm at the window?"

"God give me strength! Because, Echo dear, you're a ghost and she can't see you, which is the entire point of this scene."

By 5pm they had worked through the majority of the first two acts. Judith was on stage throughout Act three, as was Rupert, so there seemed little point rehearsing it. Judith asked Declan if they could finish for the day and he saw no reason to refuse. Besides, he was pretty certain Judith only asked him because it was professional etiquette; if he'd said no, he doubted she'd take much notice.

Judith came over to Rupert.

"I can't do another day of rehearsals with that awful girl as she is now. You need to get to work. You've got an hour before her even worse mother turns up to collect her."

"Now?" Rupert asked, somewhat thrown by the immediacy of it all.

"Surely you don't need to get into character?"

"So I'm supposed to throw her on the rehearsal room floor and ravish her in front of everyone?"

"No. I'm going to clear the room, telling them I want to work with you and Echo alone, and then I'll disappear too. So there'll just be you and her. Don't tell me you need help in that department?"

Rupert scowled at Judith; she really was totally outrageous, and irresistible. She was talking to Miranda now, and Miranda was nodding in his direction. It appeared he was about to start a new role as Casanova. Slowly he wandered over to where Echo was sitting munching carrot sticks.

"A little light eating?" he said.

"Mommy was so cross when I told her I'd had fish'n'chips for lunch yesterday she made me promise to eat these for lunch instead."

"Do you always have to do what Mommy tells you?"

Echo looked round as if Storm could appear behind her chair at any moment and then whispered, "I went and had fish'n'chips again at lunch, but then I thought I'd better eat these so Mommy wouldn't find out."

"You could just throw them away," Rupert pointed out. "She'd never know, unless she makes a habit of trawling through rubbish bins. And maybe next time you'd better not tell your mother when you've done something she wouldn't like."

Echo looked at him in astonishment; such a thought had never occurred to her. "Don't you tell your mother everything?"

"Good God, no!" Rupert couldn't remember the last time he'd told his mother anything. She was married to her umpteenth husband – Rupert had stopped counting after four – and lived down in Cornwall running an exclusive hotel for ultra-rich clientele. He hardly ever saw her, and that suited him fine. Echo's mother, however, was a problem; it had to be sorted before his seduction act could begin.

"So do you think you could keep something important from your mother? For example, if you had a big secret it would be better she didn't know?"

"Like what?"

"Like if there was a guy who fancied you, but your mother would stop him seeing you if she found out."

"I don't know," Echo admitted "That's never happened."

"OK. Let's try another scenario: how about a friend? If there was someone who wanted to be your friend but your mother didn't like them, would you be able to keep that secret?"

"Like Scarlett?"

"Yes, like Scarlett."

"But why wouldn't Mommy like Scarlett?"

Christ, this was hard work. "Just pretend she didn't, maybe because she encouraged you to eat more fish and chips and chocolate biscuits."

"Oh yeah, I see."

"So you wouldn't have to tell her, would you?"

"I guess."

"You can't believe how glad I am to hear you say that."

"You are?"

Rupert glanced round. Judith had certainly kept to her part of the bargain; there wasn't a soul in sight.

"Sure. I've been watching you every day."

"You have?"

"Yes. And last night, I dreamt about you."

"You did? What was I doing?"

"What weren't you doing? It was utterly erotic."

"Erotic? Is that like something foreign?"

"No, you're thinking of exotic." Judith would love that one. "Erotic means sexy, sensual, arousing."

Echo was staring at him in total amazement; was Rupert saying he fancied her? It was so hard to know when it hadn't ever happened before.

She'd heard people on the beauty circuit and on *Acacia Lane* talking about sex though; it all sounded real weird to her. She'd seen pictures of naked men and that thing that hung between their legs was real ugly. Though Rupert was so cute, perhaps his thing was cute too. But then he was married, so maybe she was totally wrong and he was trying to be friendly like Scarlett and Lucy. She decided to say nothing and see what happened.

"You're very beautiful, Echo."

Echo smiled. She at least knew this to be true. "Thank you, Rupert. I was a beauty queen, you know."

"And understandably so. Surely you had men constantly running after you?"

"No."

"They must all have been mad." Rupert rubbed his hand gently up her arm. He felt her quiver; good, he wasn't losing his touch. "You are gorgeous." His hand moved up her arm to her back.

"Echo, honey!"

"Shit!" Rupert leapt away from Echo as Storm came through the door into the rehearsal room.

"I met one of those stage management girls in the street; she said you'd finished rehearsing early," said Storm, looking suspiciously at Rupert.

"We had a few lines we wanted to go through together," Rupert improvised. "But if you want to take her home we can do them tomorrow. Let me mark a couple of things in your script, Echo." As he bent over Echo's script pretending to write something, he whispered, "Our secret, right?" Echo nodded and smiled up at him. She had a feeling Rupert was right and this was not something to tell her mother.

Storm and Echo left, crossing with Judith and Miranda coming back in. "What the hell's going on?" Rupert demanded. "I thought you were supposed to be sorting out Storm, not letting her walk in on my seduction scene."

"I'm so sorry," Judith said. "We were busy trying to keep Declan occupied. He wouldn't go home because he had to be the one to lock up; we didn't see Storm come in until too late. Did she catch you at anything?"

"No, though she did look a bit suspicious. I'm not going any further until I have a guarantee the woman isn't going to turn up again in the middle."

"I've got a plan for that."

"Why does that not surprise me?"

"You're a cheeky bastard, Rupert, do you know that?"

Rupert grinned. "So what's the plan?"

"Tomorrow evening after rehearsals Miranda is going to take Storm out for a girls' beauty session: manicure, pedicure, you know the sort of thing."

"And where does she think Echo is going to be all that time?"

"Having extra rehearsals with me, of

course. I don't think even the stage mother from hell is brave enough to refuse to allow that. I foresee that should give you a couple of hours, depending on how long Miranda can cope with Storm."

"About 10 minutes," said Miranda gloomily. "I have definitely got the short straw on this one. What the hell am I going to talk to her about?"

"You won't have to say much. That's what beauty therapists are trained in: the art of banal conversation. Or, if really desperate, just ask her about American beauty pageants and she'll be away."

"So will I."

"Close your eyes and think of your first-night reviews."

"For this alone I should get an Olivier award."

The door opened again and Declan stuck his head in. "Have you finished?"

"Sadly not," said Miranda. "Not by a long way. But if you mean can you lock up, then go ahead. I think I've got one of Alexander's headaches, and I can only think of one solution: come along, Rupert."

"Goodnight, Declan," Judith said amiably, as she followed Miranda and Rupert out. "Sweet dreams."

Declan looked after them apprehensively. "Oh, fuck," he said loudly.

CHAPTER SEVENTEEN

"It was very odd," Scarlett said to Holly later, as they sat in their flat with a glass of wine and a bowl of peanuts. "I forgot my scarf in the rehearsal room, so I started to go back in to collect it and there was Rupert stroking Echo's arm. So I crept out again before they saw me. Do you think he fancies her?"

"Is she pretty?"

"Yes. But she's vacuous. I didn't think Rupert would go for someone like that. He's so smart; doesn't he want someone with brains?"

"Like you, for example?"

"I didn't mean it like that."

Holly raised her eyebrows. Scarlett had hardly stopped talking about Rupert since day one of rehearsals, except when she was talking about Alexander or Judith, and that was not in the same way.

"Shut up, Holl."

"Did I say a word?"

"You don't have to; it's written all over your face. Besides, Rupert's married; it seems wrong. You should see him and Miranda work together on stage; it's wonderful."

"So you'd turn him down if he asked you to sleep with him?"

"Yes! No! I don't know. Maybe. But he obviously doesn't fancy me."

"Have you tried flirting?"

"Oh, I couldn't, at least not in front of Miranda and she keeps a really good eye on him, which was another reason it was odd about Rupert and Echo; I can't believe she wasn't watching him."

"Maybe she's not as observant as you think. Why don't you at least try flirting one day when she's not around?" It was sad, Holly decided, when you had to live an exciting life through your flatmate, but there was no one in her office that anyone could either flirt or gossip with.

"Oh, I don't know if I'd have the nerve and besides, I'm no good at that sort of thing."

"Oh, pleeease." Scarlett had flirted her way through their entire drama course. The majority of men who weren't gay had, at one time or another, fallen over themselves for a date with her. Scarlett only ever selected those who she considered the most talented; talent was the most wonderful aphrodisiac in her book and it was another reason she fancied Rupert so badly. Holly, on the other hand, had settled for dating one of Scarlett's rejects for the second two years of the course and had only broken up with him after he had moved back to his native Wales to try and get acting work there. She watched Scarlett's face as it flickered through various emotions; it was almost guaranteed she was sizing up the idea of flirting with Rupert. "So?"

"So?"

"Are you going to try and have an affair with Rupert?"

"Honestly, Holly, what kind of a girl do you think I am?"

Holly helped herself to a huge handful of peanuts and said nothing.

Isabelle was on the phone to Sally, one of her theatrical acquaintances; the two of them had been in rep together many years ago and Sally was always keen to hear the latest gossip.

"Darling, would you believe our director walked out on us again today? Judith took over rehearsals which was quite wonderful, so helpful, I felt utterly fulfilled as an actress. And of course I've become her right hand woman; she rang me at home and said I was the only person she could trust. It's amazing; she's only known me for a week, but we bonded straight away. But I couldn't possibly repeat our conversation; I have to be discreet." Isabelle held the phone away from her ear as there was a screech of laughter down the ear-piece. Bloody cheek, she could be discreet, after all she hadn't told anyone else about Judith's phone call. And she'd waited two whole days to even tell Sally and look what reaction she'd got. "I'm sorry, I have to go now; I must prepare some ideas in case Alexander doesn't turn up tomorrow and Judith needs my input." She hung up crossly, turned on her lap-top and entered that day's rehearsal details into it more or less accurately; she could change anything she needed to later.

She wondered if she could phone Judith and ask her why she had been so offhand at rehearsals and so buddy buddy with that stupid Adam: honestly, falling over his own feet. Maybe she could suggest the two of them go out for dinner tonight to talk strategy. She reached for the phone and then realized she didn't have Judith's number. It had carefully been left off the contact sheet; only her agent's address and number were on that. Obviously she didn't want everyone calling her, but she, Isabelle, wasn't everyone, she was Judith's confidante. If only she'd rung 1471 when Judith had called her two nights ago. But of course a mass of other people had phoned since then ... hadn't they? Now she thought about it, she couldn't recall talking to anyone until Sally tonight and she'd initiated that call. She punched in 1471; the computer voice confirmed that her last call had indeed been on Sunday evening, however the caller had withheld their number. Isabelle hung up, trying to convince herself Judith hadn't withheld it on purpose.

She got up and made herself another gin and tonic. Running her eye down the contact sheet, she considered phoning someone else to get Judith's number, perhaps Rupert and

Miranda had it or Declan, but she couldn't face the humiliation of asking them. No, tomorrow she'd ask Judith herself and organize to go out another night. Tonight she'd make herself something to eat, watch a video and work on some ideas for tomorrow. Mrs Bradman was not going to be some pathetic joke. Her supper on the other hand was going to be pretty pathetic; the fridge was empty. She looked in the cupboard; there was a tin of caviar, and another of foie gras pâté, both bought to impress anyone who might pop round on the spur of the moment. They'd been there so long she might as well eat them before they went past their sell-by date. There was a stale loaf in the bread bin she could toast and another very large gin and tonic, with the emphasis on the gin, would round off the meal.

Wesley had invited Declan round for supper. Henrietta had offered to cook, but at the last minute had felt too exhausted and so the three of them were sitting round the kitchen table eating Indian takeaway out of foil cartons.

"Isn't spicy food supposed to bring on labour?" Declan asked. "I thought I read that somewhere."

"Oh, God, is it? Wesley asked. "Quick, take the chicken madras away from her, Declan. I can't have the baby coming early; I need to get this damn show sorted first."

"Typical man," Henrietta complained.

"You're not the one who has to carry round a bowling ball in your stomach, have absolutely no bladder control and be unable to see your feet. I put on two totally different colour shoes this morning and didn't know until one of the other women at my ante-natal class told me. If this baby wants out a couple of weeks early that's fine with me."

Wesley laughed and leaned over to kiss her. "Sorry, darling. I suppose I had this romantic idea of it arriving on the first-night of the show."

"Lord, I hope not, I wouldn't get a look in; I could be in labour in the aisles and you'd be too busy to notice!" She struggled to her feet. "I'm whacked; my bowling ball and I are going to watch TV in bed. I'll leave you to talk show stuff. Goodnight, Declan. See you later, darling, if I'm still awake."

"So," said Wesley, "Alexander has walked out again, Judith is redirecting the play and you suspect a major conspiracy. Anything else I should know before I swallow an entire bottle of Valium?"

"The good news is Judith is making an excellent job of it. The bad news is she can't really direct herself. Actually, I think she probably can, only she won't because she doesn't believe it's right."

Wesley scanned the cartons for any remnants of food. "So if we get Alexander back as director what will happen?"

"I imagine he will try and tell her what to

do, she will ignore him and do precisely as she pleases. Incidentally, she puts a lot of store by what Rupert thinks."

"So she does get on with some of the cast?"

"Very much so, she's taken a real shine to Rupert and Miranda. In fact, today she was even helping out Adam."

"Really? I was worried she'd eat him alive."

"I think he was too, his face was a picture of terror. But she called him to one side, said something to him that none of us could hear and he came back on looking as happy as a sandboy and carrying my briefcase full of bandages and Scarlett's headphones."

Wesley looked at him quizzically.

"Improvised doctor's bag."

"Ah." Wesley relaxed slightly; that was one weight off his mind. He'd been dreading Adam's imminent breakdown. However, the fact Judith was being pleasant to him was a worry in itself. Rather nervously, he inquired if she was also being nice to Echo; if that was the case maybe he should worry it was Judith heading for the nervous breakdown. Luckily, Declan could relieve his mind on that one. She was tolerating Echo, but hardly extending the hand of friendship.

"But it's the situation with Echo that's worrying me," said Declan. "First Rupert asks Lucy to take her out to lunch while the rest of the cast go off together, then Scarlett gets all chummy with her, and finally yesterday Rupert stays behind to do scenes with her, only I'm not sure it was scenes he was doing."

"Don't tell me he's trying to sleep with her."

"If he is it's pretty brazen since Miranda was outside the door with me. I don't think he'd do it so close to home."

"So, have you any ideas?"

Declan shook his head. "I've tried to talk to a few people but it's all innocence and denial. I'm afraid I've hit a brick wall. How do you want me to handle it?"

"Hold the rehearsal as normal tomorrow, or as normal as you can. I'm going over to see Alexander and Jasper first thing in the morning, and I'm not leaving there until I have some designs for the set and costumes, not to mention a long talk with Alexander. Let Judith take the rehearsal again, that way she can go over the headway she made today. If they've made a lot of progress then Alexander won't have time to undo it; perhaps he can smooth bits over and pretend he's done everything himself."

Declan nodded. "What about props? Alexander won't even let us get rehearsal ones; we're making do with anything lying around."

"Buy or borrow anything you need to for the moment, and I'll try and pin Jasper down on that tomorrow too."

"And we need a table for the séance and an illusionist for the special effects. The actors need to practice with stuff like that, as do my stage management team."

"Can you sort that out?" Declan nodded. "Order it and invoice me."

"Wesley, can I ask you something which isn't really any of my business?"

"You can ask!"

"Since Alexander is such a dreadful director, why don't you sack him and get someone else?"

"Don't think I haven't considered it. But I don't need that kind of negative publicity. If it gets round I've fired this hugely successful director I'll have reporters and gossip columnists up my arse. There'll be stories that he couldn't work with Judith, which won't do the show or her any good, and strangely I do care what people think of her. Furthermore, Alexander's not going to admit he's out of his depth and leave quietly, or Jasper either. Between them they'd probably slap a lawsuit on me for unlawful contract termination." Wesley grimaced. "No, it's easier if he's seen to be working on the show while Judith directs it; it's hardly a concept that's alien to her, let's face it. Which is another point; where would I find a good director who will take over directing a show, and Judith, with only two and a half weeks of rehearsals left? Quite frankly, I can't wait for the whole production to be over in seven months time and I can have my breakdown in peace and quiet."

"It'll be fine once we do the first performance,

then you'll forget all about the problems."

"Who are you kidding?"

"Wesley," Henrietta's voice came from upstairs. "I've dropped the TV remote control; I tried to bend down to pick it up and now I'm stuck!"

Wesley jumped up and went towards the stairs. Declan gave him a brief wave and let himself out. Outside he called Lucy on his mobile. "We have permission to get some rehearsal props, so can you liaise with Matthew and go shopping tomorrow morning for them? Don't get anything expensive, no doubt we'll end up with something totally different, so for the present get things to practice with. I'm going to try and organize a séance table."

"A proper one?"

"Yes."

"Thank God, I was beginning to think I'd end up sitting underneath a piece of self -assembly IKEA furniture all the way through Act One making it go up and down, and I have to tell you I don't look my best with a tablecloth over my head."

Echo was lying in bed by the time Declan left Wesley's; Storm always insisted she get 10 hours beauty sleep, and, being a dutiful daughter, normally she would be fast asleep, but tonight she wasn't tired. She kept thinking of Rupert's hand on her arm and her back;

she still felt all tingly. But it was odd, she felt tingly in other places as well, not only where he'd touched her. For the first time since she started rehearsals, Echo found she was excited about the following day and more than excited about the prospect of working far closer with Rupert.

CHAPTER EIGHTEEN

Wesley was leaning on Alexander and Jasper's door bell at 9.30am the following morning. No one was answering, the trendy blinds were closed and there wasn't a sound, but Wesley had no intention of leaving. Twenty five minutes later he called Declan who was setting up the rehearsal room with Rebecca, and asked if by any chance Alexander had turned up there.

"No, sorry, Wesley. Isn't he at the house?"

"I don't know, I can't get a response, but I'm not going anywhere until I do. Although by the looks some of the neighbours are giving me I'm a little worried I may get arrested for loitering with intent."

"Let me know if you need bail or a character reference."

"Thanks." Wesley could hear a clunk on the other end and then Judith's voice.

"Wesley. Is our Führer coming in or not?"

"I honestly don't know, Judith. I'm standing outside his house now, but there's no answer."

"Do you think he's done a runner, fled the country?"

"No need to sound so hopeful, and I don't imagine it's anything as exciting as that; I think he's still asleep."

"Lazy bugger. So what are we supposed to do meanwhile?"

"I did hear you were doing quite a good job at directing yourself."

"That's all very well, but I do have to act as well, you know, and I can't when I'm watching. Rupert is a great help, but he's on stage with me most of the time and so is Miranda; you don't expect me to take notes from Echo, do you?"

"Ask Declan to help you with the staging; he's taken enough understudy rehearsals in the past to tell you if something looks wrong. I take it you don't need acting guidance?" The phone went silent for a while, though Wesley could hear vague voices, then Declan came back on the line.

"Thanks, Wesley!"

"Declan, you'll be fine. Judith knows what she's doing, you said so yourself; all you need to do is sit there, make a few comments about how they could fill the stage better and she'll be happy."

"I've just changed my mind about helping you with bail."

"Fair enough. By the way, you don't know anywhere that delivers coffee to doorsteps in Blackheath, do you? I am in serious need of some and I'm not moving one inch."

"Do you want me to send Lucy or Matthew round with a thermos and some sandwiches?" Declan offered jokingly.

"It's tempting, but I think your need of

them is more desperate than mine. Now go and play director."

Declan was surprised how easy it was to be the unofficial director. He did have a good eye for staging, after years of watching other people do it, and some of his ideas were useful. What's more, Judith actually listened and incorporated them. Plus, as he and Wesley had already agreed, Judith only wanted support, not direction, and Declan was excellent at support. All in all, he considered the day's rehearsals rather a success. During the lunch break he even managed to get hold of an illusionist he and Lucy had worked with a few years ago, on a production of Ken Hill's *The Invisible Man,* who agreed to come in the following day, watch rehearsals and discuss some ideas for the ghostly effects needed.

Wesley's day, on the other hand, was not proceeding successfully at all. After two hours of alternately ringing the doorbell and phoning both Alexander's and Jasper's mobiles, there was still no reply. Finally, he saw a movement in the garden which he was fairly certain led directly on to the heath. He was darned if they were going to get away with that. Wesley took a run at the large, locked gate leading to the back and managed to half vault and half scramble over the top, landing in a heap on the other side. He was getting far too old to do this sort of Indiana Jones stunt thing, plus there was a quite serious chance of getting arrested if anyone saw him.

"Jasper!" Jasper stopped, much to Wesley's relief; he didn't want to have to rugby tackle him to the ground.

"Wesley! What a pleasant surprise."

"Hardly a surprise since I've been ringing your doorbell and phone for the past two hours."

"I'm so sorry; when we're asleep we're out to the world."

"And do you always leave your house by the back gate?"

"It's the quickest way to the shops."

Wesley, who had seen several shops on the street leading to the front door and doubted there were many on the heath, decided not to make this an issue. There were other more important issues to deal with. "I want to talk to both of you."

"Alexander's still asleep; he isn't well at all. I'm just going to get him some pain killers so if it could wait …"

"Now."

Jasper, aware this was not a request, shrugged and walked back towards the house, Wesley at his heels ensuring he didn't bolt. In the sitting room, he found Alexander lying on the sofa watching a DVD and eating a huge pile of waffles covered in maple syrup; at least he had the grace to look a little embarrassed at being caught skiving by his producer.

"Sit down, Jasper," Wesley ordered. "This is my final ultimatum and I want no arguments and no excuses, is that clear?"

Neither Alexander nor Jasper spoke so Wesley took that as acquiescence and continued. "Alexander, I want you back at rehearsals tomorrow at 10am sharp, and I mean 10am, not 10.30 or even 10.01. You are not to walk out again unless you are dying, and even then I either want that in writing, from a doctor of my choosing, or an open viewing of your coffin. I don't want you changing the script, the ending or producing a line of chorus dancing drag queens. I want to see a play the audience will recognize with the wonderful cast I have assembled, plus of course the actress, to use the term lightly, you provided. Work with the actors, help them if they need it, leave them alone if they don't. Ensure the staging looks right, give them props they can use instead of improvising and make certain they don't bump into the furniture. And talking of props and furniture, Jasper, I want your set and costume designs in my hands and I'm not leaving until I have them. Now is that understood?"

"But I've not been well," Alexander started. "I'm not up to rehearsals."

"Bollocks. Jasper, designs, now."

Jasper looked doubtfully at Alexander, who shrugged. "You'll have to give me a little time to finish them, a few last minute touches."

Wesley produced a copy of *The Complete Sherlock Holmes* which he'd already made major inroads into while sitting on the doorstep. "No problem, I've got all day." He put his hand in his pocket and produced a toothbrush. "And all night too, if necessary." He sat down in one of Jasper's designer plastic chairs. "Christ, these are uncomfortable." He moved into one which looked less like an instrument of torture. "Is there any chance of a cup of coffee while I wait?"

Jasper got up and went towards the kitchen sulkily. "Would you like anything to eat with that?" he asked sarcastically.

"Yes please, some of those would be lovely." Wesley pointed at Alexander's waffles and maple syrup. He saw no reason not to inconvenience Jasper a little, after all he was paying him a designer's fee and so far for absolutely no reason.

By 5pm Wesley had read his way through *A Study in Scarlet, The Sign of Four, The Hound of the Baskervilles* and the twelve short stories which comprised *The Adventures of Sherlock Holmes*. Jasper hadn't emerged from his studio and Alexander was reclining on the sofa playing the role of the invalid, occasionally clasping his hand to his head or producing a pathetic sounding cough.

Wesley wondered whether he should discuss the subject of understudies with him. Technically, Alexander should have a say in their casting and even attend auditions, but then they might end up with a whole lot of understudies like Echo. No, Wesley thought, getting out a notepad and starting to make a list, he'd do it himself. Normally by now they would already have been cast and contracted, but Alexander had refused to have them attend rehearsals, something about disturbing his aura, and he knew Judith preferred to rehearse without them.

"I know it's not fair on them," she'd told him once, "of course it's much easier if they can see the process from the beginning. But it's very hard to concentrate on your character when you've got someone watching your every move and expression while knowing they're dying to push you down the stairs and play your role."

Actually, no one wanted to understudy Judith. For a start she'd never been off sick in her entire career, and if she ever was the audience would probably rise as one and demand their money back. Luckily, Wesley already had someone in mind for the job; an actress called Ursula, a professional understudy in her fifties, who had covered Judith several times before and spent her many hours backstage working on the largest patchwork quilt anyone had ever seen. So he needed one male actor to cover Rupert and Adam, and two other females: a young one to cover Echo and Scarlett and an older one for Miranda and Isabelle. He'd make some calls to agents tomorrow and set up auditions. He was leaving it far too late as it was.

Wesley's list was interrupted by Jasper shimmying back into the room and throwing some papers at him. Wesley studied them. It was definitely a set: walls, a door, a French window, thankfully all quite traditional, but there was something missing. "There's no furniture."

"I'm having that made myself, someone I've worked with before. Don't worry, he's doing it at cost price as a favour to me so I'm well within your budget and it'll be there in plenty of time. The same with the costumes, all my makers have got designs and material samples."

Wesley looked dubious. Jasper produced a fairly efficient looking list of names and phone numbers. "Here are the people making my furniture and costumes; check with them if you don't believe me. Get them to fax you the designs; I don't have them any more."

"I will. Where's your phone?"

Jasper pointed to a pair of bright red plastic lips sitting on the Perspex coffee table. Wesley picked up the top lip and dialled the first number. Jasper's furniture maker confirmed he was busy making the furniture and it would be there on time, no problem. Wesley was about to ask him to fax him over the designs when in his bag his mobile started to ring. He got it out and looked at the number. "Sorry, I've got to go, my wife's on the other line. I'll be in touch soon."

He punched the answer key. "Yes, darling?"

Henrietta's voice was coming in gasps. "My waters just broke."

"What?" said Wesley, his head full of sets and costumes.

"I'm in labour, you idiot!"

"Christ. I'm on my way." Wesley grabbed his bag and was halfway out the door when he remembered the designs. He ran back, collected them and the contact list and was out the door and into his car. He'd fax them to Declan later and get him to pass them along. He'd tell him he was right about spicy food too; Indian takeaways should carry a bloody health warning.

Declan, trying to phone Wesley several times later to tell him how well the rehearsals had gone, was met repeatedly with voice mail. That was unlike Wesley; he was always reachable. He wasn't to know Henrietta had taken the mobile out of Wesley's pocket as he drove her to the hospital and firmly switched it off, threatening to leave him if he as much as tried to turn it on until the baby had arrived.

It was a shame he couldn't talk to Wesley, Declan reflected; it might have cheered him up to know how well rehearsals had gone. The cast had lapped up Judith's ideas and even Echo had made a very slight improvement. In fact, Judith had told everyone she was going to rehearse alone with Echo after rehearsals had finished for the day.

"But don't worry, Declan, you don't have to wait around for us; we're going to go back to my house to do it," she'd said.

"What about Storm?"

"Don't worry about her; Miranda's sorting that out."

Miranda was at that moment on the phone to Storm. "Hello, it's Miranda Flynn here."

"Oh right, Miranda, hi."

"I don't know whether you've heard but Judith wants to put in an extra rehearsal with your daughter this evening. Judith and I had this beauty session booked and now she can't go. I wondered if you'd be interested: manicure, pedicure, facial, that sort of thing."

"That sounds real fun, but what about Echo? How long will she be? Where will I meet her?"

"Judith's going to drop her by the beauty place when they're finished. There's a coffee bar there we can wait in."

"I don't drink coffee; all that caffeine, it's real bad for you. I don't do alcohol either."

"I'm sure they do a nice seaweed and aloe juice," Miranda said, dreading this evening more by the second. She intended to have alcohol and in abundance or she wouldn't survive. She had better get the best manicure in the world, followed by the very best sex in the world from her husband.

She glanced over to where Rupert was talking to Judith, discussing where he was going to take Echo.

"I can't exactly seduce her in your house," Rupert said. "I don't think either of us would feel very comfortable, and public places are out of the question."

"We need an empty building."

"Ah, I think I've got it," he said.

"Is it catching?"

Rupert laughed. He loved Judith's humour; it was quick and wicked. "Shall I go on?"

"Please do, Einstein."

"Our theatre is dark at the moment, isn't it?"

Judith nodded. *Blithe Spirit* was going into the Theatre Royal, Haymarket. The last production had been a flop and closed earlier than expected, so at present the theatre was unoccupied.

"I wonder what time the stage door closes when there's nothing playing."

Judith got out her mobile and Rupert found the phone number in his Equity diary; it was good to know their union produced something of use. He listened to her side of the conversation. "Hello, Judith Gold here, how are you? Yes, I'm looking forward to coming back to the Haymarket too. Oh, you're very kind. I was wondering – a couple of my colleagues are keen to come and look round backstage; is there any chance of their doing that tonight? Oh wonderful, I'll tell them. See you in a couple of weeks. Bye." She ended the call and turned to Rupert. "They'll be open until about 9pm; some of the theatre management are working until then, but only front of house, so you should have the backstage area to yourself."

"Perfect. There's nothing more romantic than the backstage of a theatre."

"Make sure it's only romance; Miranda doesn't look any too happy at the moment."

Rupert made a face. "Wait until she hears where I'm taking Echo, then she's going to be really pissed off."

"Why?"

"Where do you think I first seduced her? Backstage at the National Theatre, dressing room 203. It's open 24 hours there which made it much easier, though we nearly scared the life out of the security guy."

CHAPTER NINETEEN

Judith dropped Echo off at the end of Suffolk Street, a quiet side road which leads to the stage door of the Theatre Royal, Haymarket. Echo was so relieved that she wasn't going to rehearse alone with Judith she didn't even wonder why she was being left in the middle of a street with strict instructions to wait there and not move an inch. Ever obedient, Echo stood on exactly the same paving stone for 5 minutes until another taxi drew up and deposited Rupert on the pavement beside her.

"Shall we go?" he asked.

"I can't. Judith told me not to move an inch, and I haven't. Honest, not one."

"It's OK, you only had to wait until I arrived."

"Oh." Echo moved her feet gratefully. "So are we going to rehearse together instead?"

"In a way. I thought you might like to see the theatre we're going to be performing in before we arrive in two weeks and start hectic technical rehearsals." He glanced round; the street was deserted so he took Echo's arm in his and led her down to the stage door, carefully letting go before they walked through.

"We're with the *Blithe Spirit* company," he told the stage door man. "Judith Gold told you we were coming."

"Of course, I recognize you, Mr Blake. Welcome to the Theatre Royal. Go straight through the doors ahead of you and the stage is on your left; they've been doing some work there today so there should be some lights on. The dressing rooms are on various levels up the stairs. Do you want a master key so you can see inside them?"

"That would be great," said Rupert.

"Have a look in number ten, that's a real beauty. Judith Gold always has that one."

"I'm sure she does!"

"We've still got the gold plaque from her dressing room door with her name engraved from the last time she was here."

"Gold plaques – do we all get those?"

"I'm afraid not, Mr Blake, only number ten and number one, which is the other star one downstairs."

"Who's gonna get that, Rupert?" Echo asked, a slight note of hope in her voice. It wasn't that she hadn't had gold stars with her name on before, her mother had carried one round to put on her dressing room wherever they were, but it would be nice to have one given by someone who wasn't related to her.

"It should be the second billed actor, only Miranda and I have identical billing, so unless I want to sleep on the sofa for the rest of my life, I suspect I will be noble and let Miranda have it."

222

Dressing room one was worth craving. A big wooden door opened to reveal a spacious, elegant dressing room, with a bed, an old fashioned writing desk and a large dressing table, which, in Rupert's opinion, would just about hold all Miranda's make-up. The other rooms, as they worked their way up the floors, were perfectly pleasant, clean and well kept, but not especially luxurious.

"Which one will you have, Rupert?"

"The next one up, I suppose, here," Rupert said, pointing at a door marked seven.

"Gee, I must be real bad at math," Echo said. "I thought two came after one, not seven."

Rupert laughed before realizing Echo was serious. Quickly, he assured her two did normally follow one. "But, like a lot of things in theatre, not everything is logical."

"Where will I be?"

"I don't know, that's up to Declan to decide, but I would think it'll be me, Adam and Isabelle on this floor in seven, eight and nine and then you and Scarlett above in eleven and twelve."

"Oh." Echo looked round number eleven with its dressing table, chair and reclining chair under the window. "I guess it's OK. Can we go see where Judith is going to be?"

"Sure, we passed it on the way up; it's on the stairwell between my floor and yours."

"Geez," said Echo, as they walked in. "It's like the swellest hotel room me and Mommy ever stayed in."

The door in from the stairwell (the fact it was several flights up was its only drawback) led into a small hallway. Directly ahead was a private bathroom, a luxury in many theatres, and to the left a reception area with a fireplace, fridge and elegant antique chairs. "No doubt this is where the actor's guests wait until they are summoned," said Rupert.

"Where will our guests wait?"

"Lining up in the corridors, I expect," said Rupert, wondering how many guests Echo would have apart from that dreadful mother. Perhaps hundreds of twenty something year old ex-beauty queens would descend on the theatre. That would be something he didn't want to miss.

The dressing room itself was huge, and full of beautiful furniture, a lot of which Rupert reckoned were antiques: chairs, desk, chest of drawers, dressing table and ornate cupboard. On the far side were big sash windows with tasteful curtains, and to the right another fireplace, with decorated mantelpiece, beside which stood a very comfortable looking single bed with matching cover to the curtains. Perfect.

Rupert sat down on the bed and patted a space beside him. "Come and sit down, Echo."

Echo almost leapt across the room and threw herself down beside him, almost causing Rupert to bounce off again. He looked at her; she reminded him of an over-eager puppy.

Was he doing a terrible thing? Echo looked up at him longingly; this was definitely not a good time for his scruples to kick in, besides, it was hardly as if she was fighting him off. "Now, where were we yesterday when we were so rudely interrupted?" He started to run his hands over her. She was wearing tight jeans with a gingham top tied round her midriff. He'd work on the jeans later but the top was perfect. His hands slid up inside it and round the back to the clasp of her bra.

"Christ," he swore, after several attempts at undoing it; he was generally considered somewhat of an expert. "What the hell is this bra?"

"It's a maximum support one; Mommy has them made special for me so my breasts don't go saggy."

Rupert swiftly removed the gingham blouse and studied the bra. Talk about a turn off; it looked more like a surgical corset. "I think I've just discovered my first chastity bra. How the hell do you manage to get this thing on and off?"

"Oh, I don't, Mommy does it."

"Ah, well, Mommy isn't here, is she? Turn around." One minute later Rupert gleefully pitched the offending item into the corner of the dressing room. "Now, that's much better." He began to fondle her breasts; he had to admit they were pretty gorgeous. Maybe Storm was right about the bra, although it probably had more to do with her youth. He buried his head between them and started to lick them gently. Echo let out a moan of pleasure. He worked his way downwards, undoing the top of her jeans and running his hand down to her bottom. He was about to start moving between her legs when he stopped. Echo was lying on the bed with the most ecstatic expression on her face. He didn't need to go any further; in fact it might be as well if he didn't. If he was being honest, he wasn't entirely sure he trusted himself: a pretty young girl, an empty theatre, the star dressing room – Judith's at that, which gave it an extra thrill – it really was a little tempting. He started working his way up her body again, touching the most sensitive and erotic places he'd discovered with years of practice, and being rewarded by Echo's cries of pleasure. Thank God this dressing room was so far from the stage door, he thought. He moved so he was sitting with Echo's head on his lap and gently ran his hand through her hair.

Echo sighed with pleasure. "That feels real great."

Rupert sat her up and put his own head on her lap. "Now do the same to me," he ordered. "Remember how it felt." Echo did as she was told – not bad. Rupert glanced up at her through half closed eyes; her face was blissful. Now, if she can only do that on stage, he thought, this evening would not have been in vain.

He glanced at his watch. They'd been there for nearly an hour; they'd better get a move on or the stage door man would be getting very suspicious, not to mention Storm. He got up. "Come on, sweetheart, we'd better get that contraption back on you, because if you go home without it I don't think I'm going to be very popular with your mother."

"Is that it? I thought ..." She was gesturing vaguely in the direction of Rupert's crotch.

Rupert sat down again beside her. "No, there are other things I could have done, but I don't think I should."

"But I don't mind. I thought I would when people talked about it and I saw pictures and things, and Mommy always told me it was horrid, but I don't mind with you 'cos you're special. You can do anything you like with me."

Rupert sighed; this was what he'd been worried about. "Look, Echo, you're a very beautiful girl and any man would be tempted to have sex with you, but it should be special the first time, not some dirty old man like me."

"So that wasn't sex?"

"It was foreplay, a part of sex, which can be almost as nice, especially for women, so I'm frequently informed."

"Does that mean you didn't enjoy yourself tonight?"

"Far from it, and it wasn't easy to stop where I did, believe me. But I think I made the right choice, and when you meet that someone special you'll know too."

"So am I only another pretty girl?"

"Why, Echo, what a grown up question."

"I am grown up, I can drink and everything, except Mommy doesn't let me. So am I?"

"Sweetheart, I can honestly say, hand on heart, that I have never before had foreplay with anyone like you; I will never forget it." He ran his hand through her hair again, then got up and picked up the bra from the corner of the room. It was a more complicated effort to get it on than off and it wasn't until nearly 10 minutes later that they emerged from the dressing room fully clothed.

"Let's go and look at the stage," Rupert said as they walked down the stairs. He pulled open the door and they were in the stage right wing. Rupert took Echo's arm and led her onto the stage. There were some working lights on in the flies high above them, which were bright enough to illuminate the acting area and show the outline of the auditorium. "It's so big," Echo said. "All them people are gonna be watching us?"

Rupert smiled. "What do you think?"

"Oh gee, it's real swell."

Without thinking, Rupert bent down to kiss her; something about being together on this stage made it irresistible to him. Seeing what he was about to do, unsurprisingly since her eyes hadn't left Rupert since they arrived, Echo brought her head up expectantly and clunked Rupert's.

"I'm so sorry, Rupert, are you OK?"

Rupert nodded, smiling. "Have you never even kissed a man before?"

"Only Daddy."

"I don't think kissing your dad is exactly what we're looking for here, at least I hope not." He tilted her head and gently kissed her. It was pleasant enough, though a bit like kissing your sister. "Open your mouth a little more." He tried again. "No, not like a suction pump, I don't need to be hoovered up. Yes, good, very ... mmm."

Five minutes later as they left the theatre Rupert wondered if he hadn't gone too far. What was that old adage about casual relationships: sex was fine but kissing was emotional? He certainly seemed to have aroused something in Echo – he just wasn't sure exactly what.

CHAPTER TWENTY

Alexander turned up for rehearsals the next day, one hour late and much to everyone's disappointment. They were in the midst of the final act with Judith giving direction while simultaneously, in her role as Madame Arcati, rushing round waving bits of foliage trying to exorcise the spirits of Elvira and the recently departed Ruth.

Echo, as Elvira, was sitting on a chair affecting to be cross with Rupert, as Charles, and failing. In contrast, when she had to sound upset because he no longer loved her it was utterly believable and much to everyone's amazement, rather sexy.

"What the hell's going on?" Lucy muttered to Matthew. "Has Echo been de-flowered?"

Matthew looked at her in horror. "It wasn't me; I never touched her."

"No kidding," said Lucy, looking thoughtfully at Rupert. Whatever the reason, it seemed to be working. Even Judith was fairly pleased. There were still problems with certain lines involving Elvira's flippancy, irony not being a word featured in Echo's lexicon. But Rupert gently showed her how to say them and she copied him flawlessly, English accent and all. Initially she also copied his tone of voice, which meant for a brief time Elvira unexpectedly became a baritone.

"Hold it," Alexander commanded. "I'm the director; I'm the one to tell you how to say things."

"Of course," said Judith, continuing to direct.

"Stop! I am in charge. I'll have you know Wesley begged me on his knees to come back and save the show." This would have been news to Wesley and undoubtedly was to the cast, who stared at him sceptically. "Dickon, get Wesley on the phone."

"It's Declan," said Declan, "and I'm afraid I can't get him on the phone."

"Are you disobeying me?"

"No, I'm merely saying I can't reach him."

"What do you mean?"

Declan sighed. He'd been endeavouring to avoid informing the company he had temporarily mislaid Wesley; losing their director was one thing, losing their producer and thus their financier quite another. Actors, on the whole being a neurotic breed, would assume that a disaster had occurred, the show was going to collapse imminently and they would all be out of work. That was something no one needed at present. Now it appeared he had no choice. "I mean I've been trying his office and home phones all morning and last night with no answer and his mobile is switched off."

"Have you called the police?" Judith demanded.

Declan shook his head. "I don't think that's necessary yet; I'm sure there's a rational explanation. The last time I spoke to him he was at your house, Alexander."

"Yes, he came round yesterday and stayed for ages, even though I was dreadfully ill."

"So you were the last person to see him," Judith said. "What have you done with him?"

"What?"

"Have you murdered him and hidden the body under the floorboards?"

"Or in your garden, under the patio, isn't that the traditional place?" Rupert said, joining in.

"You could simply have quit; you didn't have to kill him," Miranda added.

"Stop it, stop it, stop it!" Alexander cried out petulantly, conscious that he was being ridiculed. "When Wesley left last evening he was perfectly well, though he rushed off, which I considered exceedingly rude of him; didn't even thank us for our hospitality when Jasper had gone to the trouble of cooking for him."

"Did he say where he was going?" Declan asked.

"No."

"Curiouser and curiouser," said Judith.

"That's from *Alice in Wonderland*!" Echo exclaimed.

"Good God, don't tell me you can read?"

"Yeah, sure I can; I even did a Spelling Bee once."

"Really? How did you do?" Scarlett asked curiously.

"I came second."

"Where exactly was this spelling bee?" Miranda enquired.

"Gee, I think it was in Florida. I know it was right after the swimwear section."

"Hardly the nationals then."

"Any chance we could get back to the mysterious disappearance of our renowned producer?" Judith asked. She turned to Alexander. "Didn't he say anything to you?"

"No, and I didn't ask."

"Full of useless knowledge as usual."

"Um, perhaps he's gone to the hospital," Adam broke in nervously.

"Why?" Judith snapped. "If he's going to be ill he can wait until after opening night."

"No, not him, but isn't his wife due to give birth soon?"

"Yes," said Declan. "But it's not due for another three weeks. I saw Henrietta the night before last and she was fine."

"But babies can come early with no warning," said Adam, who remembered a terrifying rush to the hospital for Justine's birth when ten minutes earlier his wife had been tucking into fish and chips on Brighton Pier.

"I'll make some calls," said Declan. He returned a little later when Judith was attempting to show Echo how to appear thoroughly pissed off with Rupert rather than gazing at him adoringly.

"So?" Judith demanded. "Have you found him?"

Declan nodded. "Adam was right; Henrietta is in labour."

"What do you know, it seems you're pretty smart, Dr Bradman." Adam looked down at the floor, embarrassed.

"So when is the little sprog going to make its appearance?"

"I don't know. I didn't speak to Wesley; he wasn't available. I only managed to get the information that Henrietta was a patient. I'm sure he'll be in touch when everything is well."

Unfortunately, nothing at the hospital was going at all well. In mid-labour the baby had unexpectedly gone into foetal distress. Being too late to perform a caesarean, and with only an epidural, the doctor had to use a vacuum, which to Wesley's eyes resembled a jam jar lid, to remove the baby. After what seemed an eternity, the baby emerged. A deathly silence followed.

"It's not crying. Babies are supposed to cry. Why isn't it crying?" Henrietta demanded tearfully. It was also so floppy; surely babies weren't supposed to be floppy?

Wesley watched helplessly as the paediatrician bent over their baby.

"He's clearing the airways," the midwife explained. "Your daughter was deprived of oxygen in the womb."

"Oh God," Henrietta said as their daughter was placed in an incubator and rushed off. "Where are you taking her?"

"She's being taken to NICU, the baby intensive care unit, where she will be assisted to breath."

"Is she going to be all right?" Wesley asked.

"We'll let you know as soon as there's any news. She'll be in the best possible hands."

Exhausted and tearful, Henrietta kept asking the midwife what she'd done wrong. Had it been her fault? Was the baby going to be OK? Eventually she fell asleep. Wesley sat beside her, holding her hand and feeling more useless than he'd ever felt in his life. Anyone who said producing a new show was like giving birth can never have been through what he and Henrietta had.

In the rehearsal room, after the lunch break, Judith was working with Scarlett on Edith's trance scene. Echo, who had gone out on her own at the lunch break, much to everyone's surprise, and returned a few minutes late, sidled over to Rupert. "Can I show you something outside?" she asked.

Rupert glanced over to Judith. He was in this scene, but he probably had a few minutes before Judith needed him. Asking Lucy to call him if necessary, he went out with Echo into the corridor and looked at her questioningly.

"Not here," she said, walking down to the small kitchen area a few yards away. Rupert followed her rather dubiously. "Now shut your eyes."

"Echo, what is this?"

"Please just shut them for a second."

"OK."

"Now open them."

"Christ, Echo!" Echo had taken off her T-shirt and underneath was wearing a black lacy bra with red ribbons.

"Do you like it? I went and got it in the lunch period. The lady in the store said it was the kinda thing men liked. Do you like it, Rupert?"

Rupert didn't say anything for a minute; he didn't know what to. It was very sexy, but should he say that? He knew this whole thing was a terrible idea.

Echo looked like she was about to cry. "Didn't I do good? Do you hate it? I can change it."

"No, Echo, it's lovely, truly, very sexy." Echo's face lit up. "It's only ..."

"What?"

"Nothing, it's a big improvement, honestly. As a matter of curiosity, how did you get out of your other bra? I take it your Mother didn't go with you."

"Geez no! The shop assistant helped me."

"So what's your mother going to think when she sees what you're wearing?"

"I don't care. I'm an adult and I can wear

236

what I want. So can we go back to the theatre again tonight? I wanna look round it some more."

"Echo, look ..." There was the sound of the rehearsal room door opening. Rupert picked up Echo's T-shirt and deftly put it over her head before Lucy came into the room.

"Judith's calling for you," Lucy announced, looking suspiciously at Rupert and Echo.

"We were just running over some lines," Rupert explained.

"OK." Lucy said. She watched Rupert and Echo walking back into the rehearsal room. "Funny," she said to the empty kitchen, "she doesn't look as if she has any lines on her to run over."

Alexander, having decided that Judith was making a good job directing his show, had given up trying to interrupt. He'd come into his own when they got into the theatre and he had a real stage to play with. In fact, although he continued to turn up to rehearsals, and on time, he often sat there playing on his laptop or disappearing off to make calls on his mobile. Some days he went out for lunch and didn't come back until tea. It didn't make a lot of difference to anyone except Declan, who was supposed to be ensuring he was there. But since he couldn't locate Wesley to inform him it seemed immaterial.

In this way rehearsals continued for the next week. Finally the play was taking shape. Declan had received a short message from

Wesley saying he'd be in touch when he could; his mobile was still off.

Declan organized a member of the Magic Circle to come in and show the actors some of the tricks they needed to use, and ordered the props with which to rehearse. The séance table was operated magnetically. Rupert and Adam were to wear extra strong magnets under their jacket sleeves. These corresponded with those on the lightly built table, so when they raised their arms the table moved with them. With their first attempts Rupert and Adam were like two little boys with a new toy as they made it jump up and down and whizzed it round the room.

"Very nice, children," said Judith, as the table missed her legs by inches, "but do try and remember this table is supposed to be very heavy. Whenever you have to move it, apart from in the séance, make it seem like an effort. Oh, ha bloody ha," she added, as Rupert and Adam pretended to drag it back across to its original position, wiping their brows of pretend sweat.

Matthew, who had just returned from buying more props and thus not seen the table, rushed across to help Rupert and Adam in their efforts to move what appeared to be a very heavy piece of furniture.

"Thanks, Matthew, we actors are very weak," said Rupert, winking at Adam, and they both let go, leaving Matthew easily holding it up with one hand and blushing furiously. Damn it, he always seemed to be the butt of jokes, even at school. All his training made him a good stage manager he knew, but he was hopeless with people, especially actors with sharp senses of humour. Lucy was laughing her head off; why wasn't he more like her?

"Isn't it great?" Scarlett said to Isabelle. "Everything is going so well and we're actually having fun with it."

"I suppose so," Isabelle replied, disappointed. She had virtually nothing to gossip about; everyone was getting on so well with each other. It was downright dull. And on top of that, she was the one feeling left out.

Judith had insisted they would be rehearsing on Saturday, since they were so behind. She glared at Alexander, daring him to argue with her, but he merely nodded his head – and then didn't turn up. He and Jasper had better things to do with their weekends.

At the end of Saturday's very productive rehearsal, Judith announced that from Monday everybody was to be off the book. She knew most people were anyway, but Monday was the deadline.

"What's 'off the book'?" Echo asked.

"Without the script," Scarlett explained. "You need to learn all your lines by Monday."

"I have to learn all them words?"

"Is that a problem?" Everyone jumped. They hadn't heard Judith's tone of voice like that for some time.

"But I can't." Tears were welling up in

Echo's eyes. "There's so many of them."

"Didn't you have to learn lines for TV?" Rupert asked, kindly.

"No. I got them in my ear."

"What?"

"I wore an ear-piece and somebody said my lines and they came out in my ear."

"And then you said them?" Rupert said, amazed. "Didn't that take a long time?"

"Oh, no, I was real good at it."

"Do you mean to tell me you have never learnt lines in your life?" Judith's voice was terrifyingly quiet. "A life, I might add, which may very soon be coming to an end."

By this time even Echo had caught on that something was not going well here. She shook her head nervously and looked towards Rupert for support. But even Rupert had no intention of taking on Judith at present. Isabelle licked her lips; things were looking up. Judith was about to blow, surely. Surreptitiously she got out a pencil to make notes; this was something she didn't want to forget a word of. But much to her disappointment Judith beckoned Echo over to her and whispered in her ear for a good minute. Then she turned to the rest of the company.

"See the rest of you on Monday morning," she said and, collecting her things, marched out the door.

Echo had sunk onto the floor, sobbing. Scarlett and Isabelle rushed over to her. Scarlett put her arm round the shaking shoulders.

"What did she say to you?" Isabelle demanded, pen poised. "Hey!" she added, as she found her pen and paper being firmly removed from her hands.

"Since Judith decided it was something between her and Echo, I don't think she's going to want it broadcast round every member of Equity, do you?" Rupert asked coldly, throwing the notepad and pencil into the bin of used tea bags.

"How dare you? I don't know what you're insinuating."

"Oh, I think you do," said Miranda. "I was at the Theatrical Ladies' Guild meeting the other evening and kept hearing various bits of gossip relating to our rehearsals. And it all seemed to emanate from one source: you, Isabelle. And we don't like that." In truth, Miranda probably wouldn't have minded at all if it had been favourable to her, gossip was fine when you looked good in it, but it hadn't. And she'd lost no time in telling Rupert who had merely said 'stupid bitch.' But today he had obviously decided enough was enough.

Isabelle looked around the sea of hostile faces and decided to make a dignified exit. "I'm only telling the truth, you know, and some people are interested in that."

"No you're not," said Adam. "You're a trouble stirrer and you make people's lives a misery with all your nosing around and bitching behind people's backs. And I think you'll find that all those people who listen to your gossip so avidly will then go and bitch about you to other people, because no one with any decency would want to hang around with you."

Isabelle gave him a filthy look. "You're a great one to talk; at least I can remember my lines," and she stalked out.

Adam reddened, looking round nervously at the rest of the cast, and then reddened even more when he realized they were all clapping him.

"Nice one," Rupert said. "I'm sorry Judith couldn't see that; she'd have been proud of you."

Echo was still sitting on the floor, with Scarlett's arm around her, sniffing gently.

Declan cleared his throat gently. "I'm sorry to interrupt, but I think we need to empty this rehearsal room. They'll want to lock up for the day."

"Let's go and get a drink," said Rupert. He helped Scarlett pick Echo up off the floor. "I think we could all do with one." As they left, Lucy, Rebecca and Matthew started to pack up their props. Everything had to be put away tonight as on Sundays the hall was used for Sunday school.

"It's not fair," said Lucy as she and Matthew wrapped up the antique wind-up gramophone in bubble wrap and placed it in a box. "I want to know what they're all talking about in the pub. We always miss the best bits."

CHAPTER TWENTY ONE

"What the hell do we do now?" Miranda demanded over her double gin and tonic. Scarlett had taken Echo to the Ladies to wash her face. "I cannot believe, when we've worked this hard on the girl, that we're going to be foiled by this. How can she never have learnt a line in her life? Doesn't it look awful on TV if she has to wait for every line to be spoken to her before she says it?"

"Have you seen any daytime soaps in America?" Adam asked. He'd once spent a holiday there with his wife shortly before they'd split up. It had been a miserable experience; she had spent most of the time shopping on his over-stretched credit card and he'd watched a lot of TV. "I doubt anyone would spot it."

"Echo did say she was very good at it," Rupert pointed out.

"She also said she came second in a spelling bee," Miranda said, "but it turns out to be one in a beauty pageant when probably all they have to spell is 'lipstick'."

Scarlett came out of the Ladies and joined them. "Echo's re-doing her make-up; she'll be out in a minute. Actually, judging by how much make-up she has, that might be quite a few minutes. Why does anyone that beautiful need so much make-up?"

"Beauty pageant training, I imagine," said Rupert. "Her mother probably started putting it on her as soon as she came out of the womb."

Scarlett, who had taken to wearing a fair amount of make-up herself since she'd been working with Rupert, still didn't have a make-up bag like Echo's. Even at a brief glance she'd counted three bases, five different lipsticks and glosses, six mascaras, several eye pencils and countless powders, with and without sparkle.

"What did you learn about the showdown?" Miranda asked.

"As far as I could gather, Judith told her she was a total moron, that she shouldn't be allowed near a stage and if she didn't learn all her lines by Monday she would be on a plane so fast she wouldn't have time to pack a suitcase. Also, according to Echo, Judith warned her she might be sued for impressing an actress. I think she meant impersonating an actress."

"Do you think she'll have her fired?" Adam asked.

"I'm not sure we'll have much choice," Miranda said. "We can hardly have her going on stage with her script."

"Can we recast her role in a week?" Scarlett asked, anxiously.

"It's possible," said Rupert. "In weekly rep

people learn roles that quickly all the time, though that's hardly the same as a West End production. In addition, all the publicity has gone out. If we change actresses now it's going to look bad and there are enough damaging stories going about already."

"And of course you feel sorry for her, don't you, darling?" said Miranda tartly. "Or is it that you want to screw her?"

Scarlett and Adam looked at each other in embarrassment. Rupert sighed. "No, I do not want to screw her, as you so delightfully put it, but yes, I suppose I do feel sorry for her. We all know she should never have got this role in the first place, but now she has, she's trying very hard and we ought to give her a chance."

"How, darling, by giving her an ear-piece? Or are we to imitate *Singin' in the Rain* and have someone say her lines off stage while she mimes to them? Then at least we wouldn't have to hear that appalling accent."

"I don't think dubbing would work very well on stage, besides she'd still have to learn her lines in order to mime them, but the ear-piece thing isn't a bad idea."

"You're not serious?" Miranda stared at her husband as if hoping he was going to declare a joke. "But Coward's lines are supposed to come fast and light, not with great dramatic pauses while someone gives the ghost her lines."

"If we could get someone who knew the

play exceedingly well and could start the line before she needed to say it, it might be possible. It would be worth a try."

"I think you're crazy."

Rupert turned to Adam and Scarlett. "What do you two think?"

"I think we should try," Adam said, surprising himself for the second time that day with his confidence to express his opinions so openly. "What have we got to lose? If it doesn't work, we're in the same position we are now. She isn't a great Elvira, but she looks pretty and she's so much better than she used to be. That first scene with you, Rupert, when she's flirting and running her fingers through your hair, is quite electrifying now. And she's going to look fantastic. I think she could be passable if we could work an ear-piece."

Scarlett was listening to what Adam was saying with two thoughts running through her head. The first was what Adam was saying about Echo being much sexier with Rupert and thinking how she'd seen them together in the rehearsal room. Had that got anything to do with it? The second thought was about a feed for Echo.

"I know someone who might do it," she blurted out when Adam had finished. "Someone who could feed Echo her lines: my flatmate Holly. She's an actress, a very good one, but she's working in an office at the moment and she hates it. So anything would be better than that, plus she knows the play so well because she's run all my lines with me and heard me talk about you all, so she'd feel right at home."

"How nice," said Miranda. "And are all these things you tell her about us like the things Isabelle tells people?"

"Oh, no!" Scarlett stopped, trying to think exactly what she had told Holly. "Well, I suppose some of them are the same, because they are what happened, but I don't make anything up. And I never say anything bad about you, because I think you're all wonderful."

"How charming," Miranda said.

"Stop it, Miranda." Rupert ignored the glare she gave him. "So, can this Holly be located and produced tonight? We need to take action now if we're going to make it work."

"She always has her mobile on in case anyone phones her for an audition," Scarlett said. "Shall I get her to come here?"

"I'm not entirely sure the pub atmosphere is conducive to an experimental theatrical experience. What do you think, Miranda, how about we all go back to our place?"

"Why not? We can continue with our efforts to emulate *Singin' in the Rain* and stand around in the kitchen singing *Good Mornin'* and then go tap dancing over the sofa."

"Your sarcasm is duly noted, darling."

"Can I play Donald O'Connor?" Adam asked. "Only, I have a great affinity with him, apart from the fact that I can't sing, dance or run up walls."

"So what's your affinity with him?" Rupert asked.

"Neither of us ever gets the girl."

Echo emerged from the Ladies, so Scarlett took her mobile outside the pub to track down Holly, something she did with little difficulty since Holly was sitting in the flat watching re-runs of *Friends*. Five minutes later she was up and running out the door, before she had to stop and call Scarlett back after realizing she'd hung up without getting Rupert and Miranda's address.

Echo meanwhile was calling Storm to tell her she was going home with Rupert and Miranda, stressing the Miranda bit as instructed, to practice her lines. Storm immediately demanded to be included but Echo, taking a deep breath and looking over at Rupert for confidence, had told her that she would rather go on her own thank you and that someone would bring her home afterwards.

"Bravo!" Rupert said as she hung up. Echo beamed with pleasure.

"Careful, darling," Miranda muttered as they walked out the pub. "We only wanted her to get a little crush on you, not fall madly in love."

"Oh, don't be so ridiculous," Rupert snapped.

Holly, having blown most of her last week's wages on a cab to get halfway across London, arrived only ten minutes after Rupert,

Miranda, Adam, Echo and Scarlett. All the way in the cab she had been practicing her opening sentence.

"Hello, I'm Holly. I'm so pleased to meet you and how kind of you to invite me to your lovely home." No, too gushing.

Or "I'm Holly. I believe Scarlett spoke to you about me. I hope I can be of some assistance." No, sounded like she was a plumber come about a leaky tap.

Or "Hello, I'm such an admirer of both your work, what an honour to have the opportunity to work with you." No, too corny.

Unfortunately, when Rupert opened the door all that came out was: "Hello, I'm here to be an ear-piece, I mean talk to an ear-piece. Oh shit."

"That must make you Holly," said Rupert, smiling. Holly nodded, silently cursing herself. It was just that, in spite of seeing him on TV and hearing Scarlett go on about him, in the flesh Rupert was genuinely gorgeous. "Would you like to come in, or do you feel more comfortable on the doorstep?"

"Oh, sorry." Holly walked in, mortified, and trod on Rupert's toe. "Oh, I'm so sorry." Could she possibly make more of a fool of herself?

"No problem. I shouldn't stand with my feet so far apart; Miranda is always berating me for it. It's the tennis playing stance; I can't seem to get out of the habit of it. Come on in." Rupert led the way into a large sitting room which seemed to be full of people, though

249

when Holly calmed down she realized there were actually only four. Rupert introduced her to Miranda, Adam and Echo. Scarlett got up and hugged her. "Can you believe it?" she whispered. "This is going to be so much fun."

Holly looked round nervously for the infamous Judith; Scarlett hadn't mentioned on the phone which of the cast was going to be there. Thank God, the room seemed a Judith-free zone; this was stressful enough without the actress, known for eating lesser actors for breakfast, breathing down her neck.

"So how is your ear-feeding technique?" Miranda asked, running her eye up and down Holly; she wasn't as pretty as Scarlett or Echo thankfully, though she was still young and female and Rupert was Rupert.

"To be honest, I've never done anything like this before," Holly admitted, causing Scarlett to raise her eyebrows in frustration. She really had to give Holly lessons in selling herself.

"Scarlett says you know the play well," Rupert encouraged her.

"Oh, yes. And I love the part of Elvira; it's wonderful."

"That's a good start. Now, we don't actually have a microphone and ear-piece, so we'll have to pretend. How about we run the first scene between Elvira and Charles and see how it goes? Echo, give Holly your script so she's got all your lines marked. Holly, you'll need to say Echo's lines a few seconds before she has to say them. OK?" Holly nodded nervously. "Don't worry if you don't get it right first time; it'll take a bit of practice."

Rupert was correct; it took a lot of practice. At the first few attempts Echo came in far too early or too late, either trampling on Rupert's lines or leaving large gaps.

"Jesus," Miranda said after one particularly protracted pause. "The audience will think it's the interval and go to the bar if we have gaps that long."

"Sorry," said Holly and then got in such a state she read the wrong line and jumped the scene by about half a page.

Adam sympathetically gave her a glass of water, quietly pointed out where they were and gave her a smile. "You're doing fine," he said. "You should have seen me on the first day of rehearsals."

Holly smiled back gratefully, took a large mouthful of water and started again. After about an hour she began to get the hang of it, and Echo had been right; she was excellent at picking up the lines. She was also excellent at mimicking them, which meant she copied Holly's interpretation and accent to perfection.

"Christ," Rupert said to Miranda as they took a break. "Why the hell didn't we think of this before? We could have been rehearsing Holly all this time and not have bothered about Echo."

"Ah, but you're forgetting darling, she also needs to have the ability to express the correct emotions on her face, something which she appears to be doing much better since your little theatre trip the other night. However, since she's not so good at showing anger towards you, perhaps you should tell her your little seduction scene was a joke and see how effective that is."

"Don't be a jerk, Miranda. That would destroy her."

"Don't flatter yourself, darling."

Rupert ignored her and produced a takeaway menu from the local Indian restaurant. "Is anyone apart from me hungry?"

At midnight, after five hours of rehearsal and a large amount of Indian food, Rupert insisted on paying for a taxi for Holly, Scarlett and Echo to get home. He didn't offer one to Adam; he knew it would only embarrass him. He was far happier making the fifteen-minute walk to catch a night bus.

"How do you think we should tell Judith about this?" Miranda asked as she and Rupert cleared up. "Shall I call her in the morning?"

"How about we get an ear-piece first thing on Monday morning and show her? We could have a quick practice before she arrives."

"You mean I have to get up even earlier?"

"Not if you don't want to. I can do it with just Echo and Holly. You can come in at your normal time."

"Are you insane?" snapped Miranda, who

had absolutely no intention of missing out on this event. "Wake me when you get up. Only don't expect me to be pleasant at that unearthly hour."

"I never do, darling," said Rupert eating a left-over vegetable samosa with his fingers. "I never do."

CHAPTER TWENTY TWO

Judith, arriving on Monday morning ready to do battle over Echo, was surprised to find her and Rupert running through their first scene with no script in sight. Obviously her threats had worked. She continued watching while Miranda joined them for the following scene; it wasn't bad. Rupert had done wonders with the girl, whatever method he'd used. She was hardly good, but she was one step above bad and had the advantage of looking beautiful and slightly ethereal. In addition she was excellent at throwing herself at Rupert.

"So it can learn lines, can it?" she asked as they finished the scene.

"Not exactly," said Rupert, looking over to the corner of the room where a young girl, who Judith hadn't noticed before, was huddled over a script.

"You see, Judith, we had this marvellous idea," Miranda said, determined not to miss out on the glory in spite of the fact she'd been negative over the whole notion. "We decided to try what Echo was used to: the ear-piece. Holly there is saying her lines to her; Echo hears them through an ear-piece and says them."

"Really?"

"Yes. It took a lot of practice, we were at it all Saturday night until the early hours, but eventually Holly got it right."

Poor Holly was mortified. 'This is Holly who eventually got it right' was not the way she'd wanted to be introduced to the great Judith Gold.

Scarlett, torn between not wanting to upset Miranda and yet wanting to stick up for Holly, tried desperately to think of something to say to appease both sides. However, to everyone's amazement, including his, it was Adam who came in first. "Holly did brilliantly. I mean, you weren't aware of her feeding the lines, were you?"

Judith shook her head. "No, I'm impressed. Congratulations, Holly is it?"

Holly nodded.

"And Dr Bradman," Judith went on. "You're getting positively opinionated. We should give you doctors' bags more often."

Adam smiled. He couldn't believe how much he was beginning to like Judith, even her sarcasm. And he loved the way she always referred to him as his character. She didn't do that to anyone else; it was almost as if she understood he needed that.

"What do you think?" Scarlett asked.

Judith stood and deliberated for a while. It wasn't ideal, and it certainly wasn't professional. Everything inside her was screaming 'no'. But then she looked round at her fellow actors, and how hard they'd worked for this and felt touched. Touched? Hell, she was getting soft. In truth, it wasn't all her fellow actors, it was Rupert. He'd gone to so much trouble with Echo, even risking his marriage at her suggestion; how could she throw that away?

"Has anyone asked Wesley if he's willing to pay for a voice-over actress, or is Holly donating her services for the good of the show?"

Holly, who would have donated her services for this chance but wasn't sure, since she'd quit her office job, how she would pay the rent, was relieved when Rupert pointed out she could also be Echo's understudy.

"We've checked with Declan and they haven't employed one yet."

"Well," Judith said after a long pause, "it seems I'd better start working with Holly in her interpretation of Elvira; God knows it can only be an improvement. Declan, you'd better tell Wesley we have an understudy before he employs another one. If, of course, you can find him."

Suddenly, much to everyone's amazement, Judith shrieked with laughter. "Tell me, Echo, I don't suppose your mother is actually very intelligent with a wry sense of humour and a knowledge of Greek mythology?"

"Huh?" said Echo looking, as usual, at Rupert.

"I don't think Rupert is going to be able to answer that question," said Judith. "Unless, of course, he has some relationship with your mother that we are unaware of." Rupert made a face at her. Judith grinned slyly and continued. "So does anyone else realize the irony of Echo's name?"

There was a silence and then Matthew nervously raised his hand. Judith looked over at him. "Finally, someone in this room with an education. Please enlighten these ignoramuses."

Matthew went red and wished he'd kept his hand down, but it was too late now; everyone was looking at him. "OK. Let's see. Echo was a mountain nymph, and she kept Hera, the Queen of the Gods, talking for ages and thereby stopped her from catching Zeus, her husband, being unfaithful. As a punishment Hera deprived her of speech apart from the ability to repeat the last words spoken by someone else."

"Excellent," said Judith. "I bet you went to Eton."

"No, it was Harrow, actually."

"Nice to know your parents got their money's worth. Now can you all see the irony?"

There was a general agreement. "I can't," said Echo. "I don't know any Hera or Zeus."

"Oh, for fuck's sake," Judith snapped. "Matthew, please explain it to her."

"You seem to be very knowledgeable, presuming you didn't go to Eton or Harrow," Rupert said to Judith, as Matthew slowly went through the story again with Echo.

"I read a lot. I love to learn things. I can't bear these actors who have no other interests besides acting; it's incredibly dull. How many ways are there to discuss the perfect way to play Hamlet, for fuck's sake? Moreover, you wouldn't believe how often Greek mythology comes up in crosswords and I don't like failing to finish any kind of puzzle – or problem."

"Oh gee, so you weren't talking about me." Matthew had finally succeeded in explaining the myth to Echo.

"If we were you'd have to be several thousand years old," Judith pointed out, cuttingly. "And I know Americans are at the forefront of plastic surgery but that would be a miracle."

"So what happened to that other Echo?"

Judith gestured towards Matthew to continue the story. "Oh, right, um, she fell in love with Narcissus, but he didn't return her affections so she faded away until only her voice remained. Or there's another story that she spurned the advances of Pan who caused her to be torn to bits by shepherds."

"Gross," said Echo.

"But they say Earth hid her remains which continue to sing and imitate other sounds."

"Which is where we get the word echo, as in a cave, then?" Rupert asked, fascinated.

"I suppose so," said Matthew.

"So after that bit of trivia, shall we get back to work?" said Judith. "Now, come along, Holly, let's see what you can do. How good are you on saying lines flippantly?"

"OK, I think," said Holly, terrified that it appeared she was going to have a one-to-one rehearsal with Judith.

"That certainly makes you one up on our beauty queen."

Isabelle looked over jealously; why did Judith never give her the time of day? Now she was paying attention to a nobody, a line-feeder.

She saw Rupert approaching. She smiled; perhaps he had come to apologize about last night. He sat down beside her.

"Isabelle, I hope this conversation is unnecessary, but the fact Echo is going to be using an ear-piece CANNOT be known. If it gets round, every single one of us is going to be a laughing stock and I don't intend that to happen. That means we tell no one, and that means no one, not just one little friend. Do you understand?"

"What are you insinuating?" Isabelle sniffed in the dramatic way she'd used in several plays. "I don't know where you've got all these ideas about me."

Rupert stood up. "Don't you? Well, I suggest you prove it. If I hear one word about this subject from an outside party I don't think you're going to find *Blithe Spirit* a very enjoyable experience."

"What makes you think other people won't talk?"

"Because I trust them, and they're not stupid."

"Are you suggesting that I am?"

"I am merely suggesting you keep your mouth shut for once."

Rupert stalked off, leaving Isabelle in almost genuine tears. Had Rupert just threatened her? What right had he to give her orders? Perhaps if they'd seen fit to include her in their ear-piece scheme she might feel less inclined to spill the beans. Then again, much as she hated to admit it, Rupert was right about them being a laughing stock and Isabelle disliked ridicule more than she liked gossip. For the first time in her life Isabelle made a conscious decision to keep a secret.

Declan made a note about understudies and Holly. He'd tell Wesley, if he ever got hold of him. The mobile was still switched off and the hospital was giving out no information.

Wesley's mobile was, in fact, still in his car in the hospital car park. As soon as Henrietta had been allowed out of bed, he and she had sat in NICU day and night, watching their tiny baby girl fighting for her life, surrounded by tubes and monitors. The nurses had asked them if they had a name for their daughter, but Henrietta refused to give her one. "If she dies it'll be even worse if she had a name," she said.

"She's going to be fine," said Wesley, wishing he truly believed it. How could anything so frail survive?

He'd made a couple of trips home, to collect clean clothes and make calls to family and close friends who needed to be kept up to date.

The answerphone had been flashing frantically but Wesley had been unable to face wading through all the messages or the pile of letters on the doormat. He'd retrieved his briefcase from the car thinking he'd just go through it quickly; he'd recalled there was something pending in it. But as he'd flipped the clasp open, the phone had rung and he'd heard Henrietta's voice come over the answerphone: "Wes, come quick, I'm sure she just smiled at me." So he'd dropped everything and left. The briefcase stayed where it was, containing the list of understudies to be employed and the details of the set and costumes to be checked out.

Luckily, Echo had her understudy and Judith was making sure she was up to scratch. After the initial terror, Holly, like Adam, found Judith's suggestions exceedingly helpful. She handled Elvira's flippancy well and Echo had no problem copying her tones perfectly. There was only one slight problem left with Echo's performance now:

"Echo, stop looking as if you want to jump on Rupert and tear all his clothes off," Judith said. "It's not that kind of play and we aren't working for the Royal Court."

Echo giggled, which did not help Judith's temper. "Oh, for fuck's sake, sort it out," she snapped to Rupert. "I'm going to have a cigarette."

"Go on, sort it out, Rupert," Miranda mimicked.

Rupert scowled at her. Miranda was being a real pain. He understood she was jealous and it wasn't easy for her, but she had agreed to the plan, and this behaviour wasn't helping anyone. Besides, under the circumstances, he considered he was behaving very honourably. He turned to Echo. "Come on, let's try the scene where you get angry and tell me that you made love to other men."

"I did?" Echo asked. "Why would I do that when I had you?"

"You didn't have me," Rupert said. "Elvira had Charles; that's a totally different thing." Echo merely beamed up at him.

"Look, this is a play and we're actors playing roles; that's it."

Echo moved closer to him and whispered, "But we weren't play-acting the other night, were we?"

Rupert brought his voice down to a low mutter. "Yes. That's exactly what we were doing. We were acting Elvira and Charles backstage in a theatre. OK?" Rupert was aware he and Echo were causing some speculation in the rehearsal room; he only hoped Isabelle didn't have a hidden microphone planted near them. "Echo, perhaps what I did the other night was wrong, but I wanted you to discover how it feels to be passionate."

"And I have."

"But it's only acting. You're sweet and

beautiful, but I have a wife whom I love."

"But she's real mean to you."

Rupert, aware of Miranda glaring at him, smiled. "Yes, well, that's the way our relationship works."

"Why?"

"That's a good question and I'm damned if I know the answer. But somehow it does."

"So you don't like me?"

"Of course I do. But can we just be friends?"

Echo's face lit up. Rupert smiled. Most girls he'd dated would slap his face at that old cliché but Echo was completely unaware of it. It was amazing how anyone could be so naive in this day and age. "You wanna be my friend, honest?"

"Honest, Echo. And I'm going to help you be a wonderful Elvira on stage too."

"Rupert?"

"Yes."

"Can I be in love with you on stage as Elvira and you as Charles? That's acting, right?"

"Now that, Echo, is an excellent observation. And yes, of course you may, in fact please do. Remember, though, that Elvira is in love with Charles only when she first materializes. By the end she gets pretty fed up with him and the whole situation, and that's what you need to work on."

"Or Judith is gonna be mad at you, huh?"

"Echo, I don't think you're nearly as stupid as you make out."

"I think I am," Echo said sadly. "I just get moments of insinuation."

Rupert laughed. "Well, you keep those moments of insinuation or intuition or whatever you like. Now, Judith's back from her cigarette break, so can you try and play Elvira as thoroughly pissed off, as if I've been horrible to you?"

"But you never are."

"For goodness sake, Echo, that's because I'm trying to help you. But if you can't be bothered to learn then I give up. I've had enough with everyone blaming me for your mistakes. If you can't do it, then go back to America, see if I care. Oh, and that bra you bought is ridiculous. Now get on with it."

The scene, with Echo half in tears copying Holly's angry vocal interpretation of the lines, was a surprising success. Even Judith declared, "That wasn't bad, was it, Alexander?" thereby rousing the director from a daydream where he was making his Oscar winner's speech while this cast grovelled at his feet and Judith begged for any role, however small, on his next movie.

"Yes, great. Nice work, Echo. You see, I knew she'd be wonderful when I cast her."

This remark was greeted by the deathly silence it deserved. Judith made a mental note that it would be the last time she tried to bring Alexander into the equation.

Declan opted to call a lunch break before war broke out again. Judith announced her intentions of getting scampi and chips from the pub if anyone wanted to join her. Miranda leapt up, while Scarlett and a doubtful Holly and Adam started collecting their things. Isabelle decided she'd tag along; surely no one would snub her. Echo remained sitting on the chair from the last scene looking bereft. Rupert crouched beside her. "You OK?"

"I thought you were my friend."

"I am."

"But you told me I couldn't learn things and should go back to the States and you wouldn't care. And that you hated my bra."

"You didn't know how to act being angry because I'd never been horrible to you, so I was horrible to you."

"You were acting?" Echo stared at him in amazement. Rupert nodded. "Gee, you were real good."

Rupert raised his eyebrows. "Thank you, it's good to know I haven't been wasting my time all these years."

"Huh?"

"Never mind. The point is, you were good. Try to absorb how it felt being angry and use it. I can't keep snapping at you each time we do that scene."

"So I have to remember how it feels to be passionate and pissed. Shucks, it's so hard."

"You're doing fine, Echo. Oh, and in this country you should probably say 'pissed off'; 'pissed' means you're drunk, and as far as I'm aware Elvira is not an inebriated ghost."

"So you're still my friend."

"Yes. Now come to the pub and I'll buy you a Coca Cola."

"Mommy doesn't let me drink Coca Cola."

"Ah, but Mommy isn't here. Go on, live dangerously."

Echo giggled. "OK." They started to walk towards the door. "So you don't really hate my bra then?"

"Quite the opposite, I think it's very sexy and, believe me, if I wasn't married I'd be tearing it off you right this moment and seducing you on the tea table."

"Gee," said Echo, looking at the tea stains, spilt milk and biscuit crumbs thoughtfully. "Wouldn't that be awful messy?"

"Americans: you're obsessed with cleanliness! Live dangerously, Echo."

"OK. You know what else I wanna try that Mommy never let me?"

"No," Rupert said, wondering if he should be apprehensive.

"Death by Chocolate cake. It was always on menus in diners Mommy and I went to for salads and it looked real good. Do you think they'd have it in the pub?"

"If they don't, we'll find you some before we finish this show; that's a promise," said Rupert in relief. He started to put his arm round her but changed his mind. He didn't want to suffer Death by Miranda Flynn.

CHAPTER TWENTY THREE

On the last day of rehearsals before they moved
into the theatre, Alexander resolved to make a
speech and show his authority. Judith may be
under the impression she was directing this
play, but as far as Alexander was concerned
that was only because he had let her. It was
for the good of the production that Judith be
kept happy; those had been Wesley's instructions. But enough was enough. So, after their
morning séance bonding (something even
Judith hadn't been able to dispose of except in
Alexander's absence), he cleared his throat and
started to speak in his slow trademark manner.
Then, deciding he didn't want Judith making
comments during the pauses, he settled for a
steady but pause-free manner of speech.

"I would like to say this last month has
been a voyage of discovery for all of us."

"He's not kidding," Miranda muttered to
Judith.

"Now we are to start on the final leg of
our little journey, taking up residence at
the Theatre Royal, Haymarket where, after a
period of technical and dress rehearsals, we
will be inviting our audiences to join us in
our expedition and see where it will lead us
and them."

"At this rate it will be leading them straight to the exits," Judith drawled.

Alexander ignored her. "So I want a complete run through of the play today, with a break for lunch, after which I'll be giving notes."

This was their third run through and unquestionably the best. Everyone was perfect on their lines and moves, and Holly's feeding of Echo was flawless. There was a growing confidence within the cast, as if at last they knew what they were doing.

At the end, Alexander gave them an hour's lecture on motivation and depth of feeling, before calling a tea break where Judith gave constructive notes as well as congratulations. "I never thought we'd achieve this much," she said. "But everyone has worked very hard and, praying nothing calamitous befalls us at the theatre, we might have an accomplished show on our hands. However, we must all be aware, especially those of you less experienced, that a theatre is a very different space to a rehearsal room. Everything needs to be bigger and projected to three layers of audience, both vocally and physically. That is apart from you Holly; if you start projecting the audience is going to be very confused. Now, Echo, do you know what I'm talking about with 'projection'?"

"Kinda. I guess. Not really."

"Holly dear, you have another job when we get to the theatre next week. Show Echo how to act to an audience. I take it they teach that sort of thing at drama school."

"Yes, we learnt all that," Scarlett broke in, in case Holly failed to sell herself.

"How clever, Holly: ventriloquism," Judith said, pointedly, and Scarlett silently cursed herself.

"One last thing, again for those people who are newer, and that includes those who consider they have learnt everything at drama school." Holly gave Scarlett a sympathetic smile; Judith was taking great pleasure in twisting the knife. "There is so much stopping in technical rehearsals it can feel you've lost your performance, that the comedy isn't working any more and you wonder why the hell you ever became an actor to begin with. But that's normal. Use those rehearsals for their intended purpose. If you aren't in your light, you miss a quick costume change, can't find a prop or the sound effect doesn't work, that is what these things are designed to sort out. So mark your performance, get a feel for the space and save the real acting for the dress rehearsal."

Alexander, feeling he should be doing the pep talk, called everyone back into rehearsals and launched into another speech.

"Now, next week will be very tiring for us all, especially of course for me since I have to be there constantly, arriving before you actors are called and staying long after you've left."

"That'll be a first then," said Judith. There

was a ripple of laughter round the rehearsal room. Even Echo got that joke.

"So," Alexander continued, peeved, "I suggest we break early today, and have a good long rest over this weekend."

Declan glanced at his watch. It was only 4 pm; they were supposed to be rehearsing for another two hours. He looked at Judith, waiting for her to comment, but to his amazement she didn't. Perhaps she was planning something behind Alexander's back. Almost as if she could read his mind she smiled at him, shook her head, and mouthed: "I'm tired."

Whether she was tired of fighting with Alexander or from the demands of rehearsals Declan wasn't certain, but he suspected the latter. It was a concept no one had considered: Judith was not young and she'd been acting, directing, fighting and scheming non-stop for the last month. No wonder she was in need of a long weekend before the pressure of next week.

Declan was about 75% right. Judith was shattered. She was desperate to go home, curl up with Max X and sleep for at least 12 hours. But she also had plans to meet Rupert and Miranda for brunch on Sunday to discuss the week ahead. The first preview was on Friday, which meant they had four days to do the technical rehearsal, a horrible time-consuming affair, and at least one dress rehearsal, preferably two. It wasn't that

Rupert and Miranda were essential to her, but she took pleasure in their company, even if Miranda could be a tad cloying. Besides, she wasn't going to get the play out of her head, so she might as well spend time with people who understood that.

With the exception of Alexander, who intended to sleep, eat and have sex with Jasper, and Lucy, who never let work get in the way of her social life and planned to make the most of her last free Friday and Saturday nights, everyone was intending to spend the weekend working on their roles. Adam's daughters had offered to help him with his lines, Scarlett and Holly were going to work with each other, while Isabelle ... well, Isabelle was at a bit of a loss. Normally, she'd be on the phone, imparting the latest gossip, but now she had her vow of secrecy to keep. Instead she'd try and find a way of making Mrs Bradman less of an idiot; that should keep her busy. Declan too had a lot of work to do. He had finally heard from Wesley. His daughter was still in intensive care, but out of danger, yet neither he nor Henrietta were leaving the hospital without their baby.

Echo was the only one leaving London and the play behind, though even she was smuggling her script into her case. Storm, feeling alienated from this slightly unknown, rebellious daughter, and horrified when she'd seen the new black bra, was taking her to Bath for the weekend. She'd been told it was a very old-fashioned place and had visions of staying in a country estate where she and Echo would re-bond, surrounded by characters from a Jane Austen novel. Not that Storm had ever read a Jane Austen novel, but she'd seen lots of versions on TV. She had dreams of Echo marrying someone like Mr Darcy, in the guise of Colin Firth, and living in a stately mansion surrounded by green fields and sheep.

Alexander, realizing no one was protesting his suggestion for an early break, was collecting his bag when Miranda interrupted. "Wait a minute, before we go, what about our costumes? I haven't had a single fitting."

"No problem, it's all under control. Jasper has sent everyone's measurements to the makers. It'll be a surprise when you arrive at the theatre on Monday."

"And the set?" Rupert asked. "We haven't seen any designs or a model. It would be helpful to have a couple of days with a vague idea what we're going to be working on before we start. It's supposed to be Miranda's and my home in the play, and it should appear we've lived there for years. It's going to look ridiculous if we don't have a clue where the doors and windows are or where we keep the drinks."

"That too will be a revelation. All I can tell you is that they are both going to be in total keeping with the period of the play."

"Thank God," said Judith, realizing she'd been so caught up with acting and directing she hadn't given a thought to sets and costumes. "If I got there and found I was wearing a Roman toga and the set was comprised of a whore house I would make good my earlier threats and kill you very slowly and very painfully."

"I promise it is period through and through. And Jasper has done a wonderful job; he's so talented."

"Is that in bed or out?" Judith enquired.

Alexander glared at her, endeavouring to produce a suitably sarcastic reply. Judith crossed her arms and gazed back at him. Alexander hadn't learnt a lot in the last month, but he had learnt he couldn't win with Judith, so after a few seconds he gave up and went back to his address.

"As I was saying, it's going to be a wonderful surprise for you."

It can safely be said that on arrival at the theatre on Monday morning the company unquestionably received a surprise. On the other hand, it was hardly the wonderful one Alexander had prophesied.

"What," said Judith, as she walked onto the stage, "the fuck is that?"

CHAPTER TWENTY FOUR

"Welcome," Jasper said, as he fiddled with the furniture on the set, if it could be considered a set. Instead of the elegant home of Charles and Ruth Condomine, this place was a shambles. Everything was threadbare. The carpet had the appearance of being marched over by several hundred army regiments, and a Persian rug, which covered part of it, was full of holes. The sofa was patched, the sideboard scratched and pictures hanging on the walls had pieces of broken glass hanging from the frames. In the upstage left corner some of the wall had crumbled off, leaving a gaping hole. The French window was covered in sticky tape in a criss cross pattern and long black curtains hung either side.

"So?" Jasper asked. "What do you think?"

"I think I'm going to be sick," said Judith. "And I repeat my earlier question. What the fuck is that?"

"It's the set."

"Alexander assured us it was going to be authentic," Miranda said.

"And it is; I've done all my research, haven't I, Alexander?"

"Absolutely," said the director, emerging from the stalls. "A typical house of 1941,

274

the date the play was written. We've got the wartime blackout curtains and some damage from a nearby bomb." He pointed at the part of the missing wall. "And they wouldn't have been able to get new carpet and rugs, so we broke them down to look threadbare – that was an expensive authentic Persian rug, but we sacrificed it for art. You see, totally authentic."

There was an awful silence. Finally Judith spoke. "*Blithe Spirit* was written in 1941. Noel wrote it as an escape from the war, so people could come to the theatre as a distraction from threadbare carpets and bomb damage. It was never meant to be set in 1941, you total and utter moron."

Alexander was temporarily flummoxed; how the hell was he supposed to know that? It hadn't been stipulated in his script and he'd read it – twice. The only date mentioned was the one when it was written: 1941. If Noel Coward hadn't intended to set it then, why hadn't he mentioned it? What was he, a mind reader? He opted to bluff his way through. "I'm well aware of the author's intentions, but I'm the director and I have decreed this exciting new production is going to be set in 1941."

"But then Charles would be at war, not wandering around writing novels and holding séances," Rupert pointed out.

"I thought of that," said Alexander. "He was in the army but he's been invalided out:

shrapnel in the leg. Look, Jasper's even found you an original walking stick." He brandished it, beaming.

"But I haven't been rehearsing it that way. I can't suddenly change my whole performance from being a debonair English writer to a wounded war soldier with a limp."

"Of course you can," Alexander said smoothly. "You're an actor. And don't you see how pertinent this whole play is to the war? People are being constantly killed in battle or raids, so a medium like Madame Arcati would be in constant demand by those struggling to contact their late loved ones. In fact, I had this brainwave that Elvira could have been killed by a bomb. Wouldn't that be poignant?"

"Yes, apart from the fact she's supposed to have died a number of years previously so, unless there was a mini-war prior to 1939 which none of us were aware of, I don't think that's very credible. There is also the small matter of the script relating how she died of a heart attack laughing at a BBC programme while recovering from pneumonia."

"We can always change that line."

"Declan?" Judith, surprisingly, hadn't spoken throughout Rupert's argument with Alexander.

Declan emerged from the wings where he and Rebecca were trying to work out the sound cues. "Yes, Judith."

"Where is Wesley?"

"He's still at the hospital."

"Which hospital?"

"I'm not sure we should bother him. Maybe I could help."

"Which hospital?"

Declan handed over the details. She turned on her heel, grabbed her mobile and disappeared. The rest of the cast continued to stare at their set. "I can't believe it," Miranda said in shock.

"I know, isn't it wonderful?" Jasper said, sticking up a *Careless Talk Costs Lives* wartime poster. "Why don't you go and check out your costumes? You are so going to love them!"

"Why does that statement fill me with doom?" Isabelle asked.

"We may as well investigate," said Rupert. "How much worse can it get?"

"Shall I answer that question?" said Adam.

Miranda flew off to her graceful number one dressing room next to the stage which Rupert had so correctly prophesied she'd expect, while the rest of them trudged up the stairs to their respective quarters.

In his dressing room Rupert found a Captain's army uniform adorned with a multitude of medals. Charles appeared to have won not only the Victoria Cross, the Military Cross, Distinguished Service Order and Military Medal (Rupert had spent countless hours as a child, when not playing tennis, in the Imperial War Museum), but also the Distinguished Service Cross, which

Rupert was fairly certain was a naval award, the Purple Heart, which was for Americans, and his favourite of all – the German Iron Cross. He knocked on Adam's dressing room door next to his, and produced the Victoria Cross, the Purple Heart and the Iron Cross. "Hey, look. Charles has been fighting for the British, the Americans and the Germans! He's a triple agent."

"Or a triple threat: he acts, he sings, he dances, he fights for three countries!" Rupert laughed. "At least you look smart," Adam continued. "Get a load of my costume." He reached into the rail behind him and produced a white dress shirt and black dinner jacket with blood smeared down the front. "Apparently Dr Bradman was operating in the hospital in the clothes he was coming to dinner with the Condomines in. I'm like something out of *The Texas Chainsaw Massacre*."

"Oh, Christ, I'm sorry, Adam."

"It should make for pleasant dinner party conversation."

"It could explain why Madame Arcati won't eat red meat."

"I like your thinking."

There was a shriek and Miranda came running into his dressing room, panting from the stairs she'd run up and carrying a darned floral dress. "Look!" she exclaimed. "It's hideous, I won't wear it, I won't!" Flinging it down on Adam's floor she demanded Rupert did something.

"Miranda, I may be able to do a lot of things, but producing a dress out of thin air is not one of them."

"It's all very well for you, at least you get to wear a uniform."

"Yes, and he's been fighting for the British, Germans and Americans," said Adam.

"Who cares? He can fight for the Foreign Legion for all it matters to me. I need to look glamorous. Would you believe Jasper has even left a pencil in my room to draw lines on my legs to pretend they're stockings like they did in the war? How can anyone look glamorous with pencil lines on their legs?"

"Darling, you'd look glamorous in anything, and can I draw on the lines please? The idea seriously turns me on."

"Really?" Miranda was slightly mollified. "But I still want a proper costume. If this is all that idiot designer is going to provide, I shall find one myself, at least for the dinner party. Even if it is 1941 the war has only been going two years; I'm sure Ruth would have some decent clothes left from before it started."

"I'm sure she would," said Rupert. "The same as I doubt the carpets and sofa would be threadbare unless Charles and Ruth have a multitude of heavy wearing guests. But that's Alexander for you; never does anything by halves."

"So what are we going to do?"

"For the present, wait and see what Judith

says once she's phoned Wesley."

At the hospital Wesley and Henrietta, sitting by the side of their daughter's incubator, were astounded to hear Judith's voice saying, "It looks perfectly healthy to me; I mean, it's drooling and crying so it's obviously not dead. Crisis averted. Now Wesley, perhaps we could have your attention to another pressing crisis."

"Judith, what are you doing here? Aren't you supposed to be at the theatre?"

"Where do you think the crisis is? I tried to phone, but none of the staff at this place seem to be interested in finding you, even when I informed them who I was."

"I wasn't aware any of you knew which hospital we were at; how did you?"

"I tortured Declan. Now are you coming?"

"Judith, I'm sorry, I know this is lousy timing, but if you've got a problem can you get Declan to deal with it? Or even you. I gather you've been doing a terrific directing job."

"Wesley, our moronic director and designer have set the play in 1941, complete with bomb damage, blackout curtains and the notion that Elvira was killed by a bomb. It is Monday and we have our first preview on Friday night. Miracle worker though I may be, I cannot rebuild a set, remake costumes and order a hit man to dispatch the director and designer in that time. Neither can Declan. You

280

are the producer, we need you, now, or you may as well kiss goodbye to your investment in the play and any thoughts of sending little whatsitsname," she pointed to the baby, "to private school, university, or even giving it pocket money."

"They've set it in 1941?" Wesley said. "Why?"

"It was the year it was written."

"But it wasn't set then."

"You know that, I know that, the whole cast knows that, but evidently our director doesn't. Didn't you check the designs? Declan said that was the reason you went over to Alexander and Jasper's house."

"Oh, shit." Wesley put his head in his hands, thinking of the designs and contacts Jasper had given him, sitting in his unopened briefcase at home. "I'm so sorry, Judith. I did have some blueprints to chase up, but then Henrietta went into a horrendously complicated labour and the baby was delivered barely alive and I haven't been able to think of anything else."

"Marvellous. So is there any chance I can now drag you away to deal with our minor catastrophe? Or shall we cancel the whole show, after most of us have worked our bollocks off to attempt to save it? Yes, of course, let's do that."

"Judith, I am sorry, truly I am, nevertheless I can't ..."

Henrietta touched his hand. "Go."

281

"But ..."

"We'll be fine. Rescue your mobile from the car where I seem to recall I threw it. I'll phone if there's any news."

Wesley looked at her doubtfully.

"Go."

"Come on," Judith said, "you have your wife's permission." Wesley sighed and got to his feet. As Judith reached the door she turned back to Henrietta. "I'm sure little Blythe will be fine; as babies go I've seen worse." Before Henrietta could say anything in return Judith had left. Wesley kissed Henrietta, gave another look at his daughter and followed Judith.

"Blythe?" he said.

"You can hardly call her anything else under the circumstances. Moreover, it's a lovely name."

"Over my dead body."

"That may be fairly soon, Wesley dear. There is a bunch of irate actors awaiting you and the words 'lynch mob' and 'tar and feather' come to mind."

"Oh joy!"

Back at the theatre, Wesley was inundated with complaints, questions and demands he create miracles. Adam was the only one who remembered to ask about the baby.

He had to admit the set was a disaster and at this late stage there was virtually nothing he could do. In addition, since the set was so firmly fixed in 1941, the costumes had to mirror that.

Leaving Alexander and Jasper hanging gas masks on the set, he suggested the cast and he have a meeting in Judith's sumptuous dressing room. As they piled in, Echo couldn't resist bestowing a beaming smile on Rupert as she headed for a seat on the bed. Miranda, catching the smile, was about to glare at Rupert, but decided to keep her venom for the problems in hand.

"First of all I owe you all a huge apology," Wesley said. "I should never have permitted this set to be built or the costumes designed without checking on it first. I did battle to get answers from the outset, which proved more difficult than anticipated, and when I eventually got a vague outline I didn't follow it through. And for that I am sorrier that I can say."

"It's all very well being sorry, but what are we supposed to do?" Miranda demanded. "Can we get another designer in now?"

"Even if we found one willing and able to work that fast, we couldn't build it by Friday," Wesley said. "I'm afraid we're stuck with it."

"What about the costumes? I can't wear darned cotton frocks; I want elegance. Surely we can all go to Angel's and hire some stunning 1930's outfits?"

"Miranda, the set is so firmly established in 1941 we have to use costumes which complement that."

"But that's not fair."

"No, but I'm afraid we have little choice."

"Only because someone fucked up," Miranda said, tearfully.

"Yes, and I can go on grovelling forever but that's not going to help."

"So what is going to help?" Isabelle chimed in. "I've got a lousy part, the least I want is decent costumes."

"I like my costume," said Echo, happily. Rupert grabbed Miranda as she moved menacingly towards her.

"Look, I know we are working under adverse circumstances here," said Wesley, "but perhaps you can make this work. Regard it as a new interpretation, and technically it is the director's call where, when and how a play is to be performed."

"Even when he's a total moron?" Judith demanded.

"Think of him as innovative."

"Bollocks. It's spoiling the whole point of the play. Is that all you can come up with?"

"Alexander wants me to play the whole thing with a limp and a stick," Rupert complained.

"And he's trying to rewrite the lines," Scarlett added.

"He is?"

"Yes," Judith retorted. "Or perhaps you don't care about that either. Some fucking producer you are."

"Stop it!" There was a temporary silence as everyone looked at Adam. "You seem to forget Wesley nearly lost his baby, and that is far more important than this play. What if he

284

didn't get a chance to check the designs? He was in hospital checking whether his daughter was going to live or not. Whether this play is a success or a disaster is important to all of us and God knows that includes me, but it isn't a matter of life and death. We ought to be a bit more considerate and give Wesley some slack."

"So what do you suggest, Dr Bradman?" Judith asked.

"Um, well, I suppose a compromise, like Wesley said. As long as Alexander doesn't change any of the lines, we can still make it a great production. Ignore the supposed war happening around us and behave like people in the country probably did in 1941, going about their lives as normally as possible. Perhaps Rupert could have a scar to represent a war wound rather than a limp. And Miranda could get a decent frock for the party from a costume place, and that sort of thing."

"I don't believe I'm hearing any of this. I've never been involved in anything so unprofessional in my life," Judith snapped. "Is this what we've been brought to? Maybe I'll retire now and sod the show. Sue me, for all I care, Wesley."

"Sue you? I'll be too busy fighting off my own law-suits from furious backers and audience members who have been promised your presence on stage." Wesley rubbed his eyes. "We need you Judith. With you we can survive, without you – I don't know."

"Thanks," said Rupert.

"Sorry, Rupert. I haven't had much sleep recently; I'm not at my most succinct or tactful. I need each and every one of you. Please hang in there. I'll talk to Alexander and Jasper and see what I can save. Also, I swear if I ever do another production I will offer everyone jobs and the choice of director, if of course you'll ever work for me again."

Judith snorted. "If you don't spend all your money on little Blythe."

"Blythe," Scarlett said. "Is that your baby's name, Wesley? It's so cute."

"No, it's not!"

"Oh, sorry."

"Yes, it is," said Judith. "What else can he call her?"

"Virtually anything but that," Wesley replied. "So, how about it, will you stick with me?"

Scarlett, Echo, Adam and Isabelle were nodding before he'd even finished the question. Rupert looked at Judith who shrugged. "Seems like we're in," she said.

"Miranda?"

"Can I really have a decent frock?"

Despondently, the company prepared for the technical rehearsal. The two dressers employed for the show had been in the theatre for a couple of hours familiarising themselves with the costumes and setting them in the dressing rooms. Fred, or Freda as he was affectionately known, was Judith's dresser and, having previously worked with her countless times, coped with her moods and moans with ease.

"What am I supposed to do with these?" Judith demanded, holding up a pair of enormously baggy culottes.

"You could knot the legs together, blow into them and use them as a floatation device like we did with our pyjamas in swimming class. Or wait, here's an idea ... you could wear them."

"I'll look like a frump."

"And Madame Arcati was known for her fashion sense?"

"Oh, piss off, you're fired."

"Again?"

Cassie, the dresser responsible for the rest of the cast, was being given instructions by Miranda. "Between you and me these costumes are not going to stay, however they'll have to do for the moment. Now, I have two impossibly quick changes, both in Act Two, so I trust you can cope."

Cassie, who had coped with 'impossibly quick changes' for the last fifteen years, never yet failing to do them within the timescale demanded, nodded and took the relevant costumes to the small cubicles covered with heavy black curtains and specially designated for quick changes in the wings. She set them on the short clothes rail and checked around: a small table and chair to set things on, good, but no lights. They always forgot about the lights. She'd need to speak to the electrician and get a bulb put in; she was sure Miranda would be the sort to want to check her make-up.

On talking to Rupert she discovered he had changes at exactly the same points as his wife.

"But I'm on after Miranda both times," he said, "so help her change first and I'll start on my own."

"Are you sure that's OK?"

"It'll be the most peaceful solution, believe me. Besides, it's easier for us men; we don't tend to have complicated fastenings up the back."

"I had to lace a man into a full Victorian corset once," Cassie said.

"Remind me to have that conversation with you sometime."

Cassie laughed. She liked Rupert instantly.

You couldn't help it; he had the ability to make people feel at ease. In the ten minutes she was in his dressing room he had extracted a potted history of her life, something half the actors she had worked for had never bothered with in ten months. Adam seemed sweet too, if rather quiet. That was hardly surprising she thought after Fred had filled her in on his history. The poor guy was probably in a state of sheer panic; she'd make certain to give him plenty of space. No, she didn't foresee the men being a problem on this show.

The women on the other hand were a different story. "Is Miranda getting new costumes?" was Isabelle's greeting to Cassie. "Because if she is I should be too."

Cassie replied, truthfully, it wasn't her job to sort that out, but did Isabelle need help with any changes?

"I only have two scenes and they're ages apart so I have plenty of time to change from one set of rags to another," said Isabelle, bitterly. "I don't know what possessed me to take such a tiny role. I thought at least I'd have attractive costumes."

"But I love this one," said Cassie, picking up the less ugly of the two dresses. "Look at the way the colours blend."

"Really?" Isabelle studied it more closely. "I suppose it could be worse. That must be for my second scene; shall I try it on?"

"Why not," said Cassie, taking it off the hanger. Granted it was fairly ugly, but it was important to make actors feel good in their costumes, however many white lies had to be told. Leaving Isabelle a little happier, Cassie went to check on Scarlett, hoping a simple maid's costume wouldn't cause so many problems. She found two girls in the dressing room, putting out their personal effects.

"Hi, I'm Cassie, your dresser," she said. "I'm looking for Scarlett."

"That's me," said Scarlett, sticking a *Blithe Spirit* poster on the provided cork board. "This is Holly, Echo's understudy."

"Oh, yes." Cassie, Fred and the other backstage staff had been required to sign confidentiality clauses forbidding them to reveal Echo's use of an ear-piece.

"This is a new one on me," Cassie had said as she and Fred signed. "Usually these things are to stop you selling a story where the big male movie star you're dressing is sleeping with the entire female ensemble."

"Or the male ensemble," Fred had retorted. "Don't be sexist, Cassie darling."

"I'm pleased to meet you, Holly," said Cassie. "If you need anything let me know."

"Thank you," said Holly, gratefully. She was finding it disconcerting being part of the company, and yet not. As her fellow actors went onto the brightly lit stage, she would be huddled in the dark wings with a torch, muttering someone else's lines. Still, Scarlett had sweetly insisted she share her dressing room, even though Declan had allocated

290

her one upstairs with the other understudies, when they had some. A West End show opening with no understudies was unheard of and the first thing to do on Declan's list, when he had time.

As Cassie emerged from Scarlett's room she met Tasha, the wig girl, coming along the corridor looking almost tearful and clasping a mug of coffee. "Hey Tasha, how's it going?"

"Judith, Miranda and Isabelle all hate their wigs. And Echo's ghastly mother keeps saying that Echo has such lovely hair she doesn't need a wig. I tried pointing out her hair may be lovely but it hardly looks 1930s which is when Elvira would have died, but she doesn't listen. It's a total nightmare. I'm hoping that coffee will get me through, though at this rate I may have to resort to alcohol."

"Are the wigs awful?"

"Miranda's and Isabelle's are essentially beautiful wigs, and expensive since they're real hair. But the styles Jasper has created aren't flattering, plus he's insisting they wear snoods for the dinner party, and knotted headscarves for the day scenes."

"What about Judith's?"

"It's a fucking disaster," said Fred, who was carrying a bag adorned with a large sticker proclaiming: 'I'm not really a lesbian'.

"Hello, darlings, I thought I heard the smell of bitching and the sound of coffee. I'm going out to get Judith a triple espresso and possibly a large bottle of scotch. Do either of you require anything?"

"A can of coke, please," said Cassie.

"Chocolate," said Tasha. "Any sort as long as it's large. I need cheering up."

"So what's wrong with Judith's wig?" Cassie asked again.

"She looks like a rooster," Fred said. "Doesn't she, Tasha?"

"Fred!"

"Well, she does. The wig is bright red and I mean bright, like a bad henna job and it's short, in tufts. And on top of that, her first costume consists of a red and orange floral blouse which clashes beautifully."

"I don't understand," said Tasha. "What is the designer playing at? Is there something I'm missing here?"

"What he's playing at, Tasha darling, is sleeping with the director. And believe me, if you sleep with that you deserve to get a job, even with no talent. On the other hand, I wouldn't mind sleeping with Jasper, he's gorge."

"Perhaps you should, Freda," said Cassie. "You might be able to influence his designs."

"I'd love to influence more than his designs, but I suppose I could start there. Meanwhile I'd better go and procure Judith's caffeine fix before she completes her transformation into a Gorgon. So, one coke and one extra large chocolate bar, right?"

The girls nodded and Fred disappeared downwards, moaning gently that at his age he shouldn't have to endure this amount of stairs. Cassie's calling after him that they could install a stair-lift especially for him was greeted with a reply of which Judith would've been proud.

"I'd better go and see Scarlett about her hair," said Tasha.

"Is she having a wig?"

"Thankfully no, she's using her own hair. It's to be up in a bun to start and loose for the final scene: nice and easy – I hope."

Cassie left Tasha at Scarlett's door and made her way along the corridor to Echo's room where she came upon Storm being removed by Declan. "Sorry, nobody not involved in the show is allowed backstage during the performances or rehearsals," he said politely but firmly.

"Where am I supposed to go?"

"Wherever you like as long as it's not in this theatre."

"You mean I can't even watch?"

"No," said Declan, not wanting Storm giving notes from out front.

"Echo honey, are you gonna be OK without me?"

"Sure."

"But I've always been there with you; you need your Mommy. What if you get real scared?"

"I won't."

"You can call my cell phone if you need me."

"Thanks Mommy, but I'm good."

"I'll see you out," said Declan, escorting Storm to the stage door and on her departure instructing the stage door keeper to ban her until they'd finished each day.

Cassie helped Echo to put her dress on. Thanks to her character dying several years before the war had started and thus not being bound to rationing restrictions, Echo's dress was exquisite: a silvery silk and chiffon dress cut on the cross with tiny diamante jewels on the straps and the hem.

"Do you think Mommy was mad?" Echo asked, admiring herself in the mirror.

"I don't know your mother so it's hard to say, but I'm sure she'd want what's best for you."

"I guess."

"You only have the one costume, so you don't need me for any changes, what about a drink in either of the intervals? Tea, coffee?"

"I'm not supposed to drink them."

"OK. What about water?"

"What's Rupert having?"

"Black coffee."

"I'll have one of them too."

Cassie turned away to hide her smile: another Rupert devotee.

"Cassie!" Cassie could hear Miranda's voice even up three flights of stairs. "I need help with my jewellery."

"See you later, Echo," she said.

"OK. Hey, Cassie, are you gonna be here with me everyday?"

"Yes."

"Cool, so we're gonna be like friends?"

"I suppose so, yes."

"Cassie!" Cassie ran down to sort out Miranda's necklace clasps.

"Ladies and gentlemen of the *Blithe Spirit* company, please make your way to the stage for the technical rehearsal. Thank you," Rebecca announced over the tannoy at the scheduled rehearsal time. The cast, in make-up, wigs and costumes, returned to the stage. Rupert was sporting a large scar down his cheek, which Tasha had put on him. "I rather like that," Miranda said. "It makes you look terribly heroic."

"It's better than a limp, anyway," Rupert said, proving his point by limping across the stage.

"It would certainly upstage the rest of us," said Judith.

"Judith, if I crawled across the stage minus both legs, arms and half my head, I still couldn't upstage you."

"I'm glad you know your place! Talking of places, where is our Führer?"

"Um, I don't think he's here," said a voice from under the séance table.

Miranda peered underneath. "Matthew, what are you doing under there?"

"I'm checking that the table is going to work properly. Again."

"Obviously more dedicated than our Führer," said Judith. "Where did you say he was, Matthew?"

"I didn't, I mean, I'm not certain or anything, but I think I heard him and Jasper mutter about going out for coffee."

"WESLEY!"

"Good God, Judith," said Rupert, ruefully rubbing his ear. "I wish you'd warn us when you're going to project so stridently."

"I don't intend to be ignored. WESLEY."

"I'm here, Judith; what's the problem?"

"We appear, once again, to have lost our professed leader."

"Oh, hell."

Wesley was waiting at the stage door when Alexander and Jasper returned. The look on his face made even Alexander a little wary. "I have a mutinous cast on stage waiting for you. I do not expect you ever to leave the theatre again in the midst of rehearsal. I trust that's clear."

"But we needed coffee," Jasper whined.

"Bring a thermos."

The technical rehearsal finally started four hours later than scheduled and after lunch. Rather than ask the actors to change out of their costumes and wigs, when they hadn't even used them on stage, Wesley ordered in twenty large pizzas for everyone to share. Cassie and Fred brought round towels for the actors to protect their outfits.

"Do you think it's going to make any difference to this tat?" Miranda demanded, eyeing a piece of pizza thoughtfully.

"If you smear pizza into your frock and

stink of oregano and tomato sauce for the rest of the day Charles is going to divorce Ruth in the first scene and elope with Edith," said Rupert.

Scarlett looked up hopefully.

"I don't think it'll show up on mine," said Adam, looking at his blood stained suit.

"Here," said Declan, bringing over a pizza to Cassie, Fred and Tasha. "Make sure you have some before the cast eat the lot; you know what actors are like about free food. Where's Libby?"

"She's up in the wardrobe," said Cassie. "I'll take some up to her."

Cassie found Libby on the phone to Angel's costume hire. "I'm trying to sort out some new costumes for the first scene," she sighed, as she put down the receiver. "Wesley came up earlier and asked what I could do. Unfortunately, it seems the National Theatre, the Young Vic, and several reps are doing World War II plays at the moment, while the Imperial War Museum is holding a D-Day theatrical special, so we don't have much scope. But I'm going over there this afternoon to see what I can find."

"Are you going to get anything new for Isabelle as well as Miranda?"

"Yes."

"Thank God!"

"Ah, do I detect a hint of rivalry?"

"You could say so."

"I'll bear that in mind."

Tasha came up as Libby was about to leave. "Wesley took one look at everyone's wigs and asked me to redesign Miranda's and Isabelle's into decent 1940's styles."

"Is that possible?" Libby asked.

"They're good wigs so it shouldn't be a problem, though I need to get some period designs to copy. But Judith's I can't do anything with. If she doesn't want to look like a cockerel, as Fred so delightfully put it, she'll need a new wig."

"How long will that take?"

"If we have one made it'll take weeks. So we might be forced to buy an acrylic one off the peg."

"She'll love that."

Tasha threw herself down on a chair and shut her eyes. "I'm beyond caring."

The tannoy system spluttered into life. "Standby on stage please to begin the technical rehearsal. This is your Act One beginners call: Miss Flynn, Miss Montgomery and Mr Blake. Act One beginners to the stage. Thank you."

"Come on, Cassie," said Fred, sticking his head round the door, "they're starting and we don't want to miss any of the carnage."

"I'm not very good at bloodshed," said Cassie.

"Then, my darling girl, I have a hunch you're working on the wrong show."

CHAPTER TWENTY SIX

"OK, people, let's go, let's go." Alexander was walking round the stalls carrying a megaphone.

"He really does think he's directing a film, doesn't he?" said Rupert. "Where the hell did he get the megaphone from?"

"I tried to get him to use a microphone," said Declan, "but he insisted on the megaphone."

"If he calls action again, I shall personally stick his head in a clapperboard," snapped Judith, who was sitting in the wings even though she didn't appear for a while.

"A sort of cinematic guillotine," Rupert said. "How very fitting."

Fortunately for Alexander, though to Lucy's disappointment, who'd been prepared to dash out for a clapperboard, he seemed to have learnt that lesson from earlier rehearsals. "Curtain up," he called. Rebecca cued the curtain, it rose and Scarlett made her entrance carrying a drinks tray.

"Can we staaaap," Alexander called. Along with his film director's megaphone he appeared to have developed a Hollywood director's American accent.

"What's he stopping for?" Miranda asked. "Nothing's happened yet."

"Scarlett, make your entrance a bit slower. We want to appreciate the comedy of you struggling with your tray."

"OK," said Scarlett, returning to the wings and coming on again more slowly.

"Staaaap. Scarlett, a little less slowly this time."

Ten minutes later, Scarlett had made her entrance at eight different speeds and was thoroughly confused. "Perhaps I should go on backwards," she muttered as she came off to try once more.

"Oh for fuck's sake!" Judith snapped. "I'm going into the stalls. Perhaps I can gag the idiot so we can advance past the first five seconds of the play, otherwise somebody get me a clapperboard." Lucy looked up hopefully as Judith disappeared through the pass door leading to the auditorium.

"Don't even think about it, Lucy," said Declan.

Judith found Wesley had beaten her to Alexander and was demanding the director continue with the play. "If you're unhappy with Scarlett's speed you can return to it if we have time later in the week, or during previews. If we don't make any progress soon there won't be time to have any previews."

Sulkily, Alexander moved on to Miranda's entrance and continued to brood, so Rupert managed to make his entrance and play the scene with Miranda and Scarlett without interruption.

"Can we staaaap." Isabelle and Adam had made their entrance and not even spoken before Alexander's new American drawl brought them to a halt. "Don't tell me we need to go faster," Isabelle muttered. "I can't do speed in these heels."

"OK, Dr and Mrs Bradman, you look too confident at your entrance. Look nervous, like you haven't been here before and you're wary of the whole evening."

"But we have been here before; Charles and Ruth are acquaintances of ours," Adam said.

"Oh. Yes ... nevertheless you're troubled about doing this séance thing."

"But one of my first lines is to say how excited we are about it," Isabelle said.

"You can be excited and troubled. I'm the director and I want wariness; please do as I say."

Adam and Isabelle gave up arguing, left the stage and re-entered resembling lowly servants crossing the threshold of the house of their cruel master, which sent Rupert into gales of laughter. "Dr Bradman, get down on your knees and treat me with the respect I deserve," he called out, "while I ravish your wife and then throw her out to a life of destitution and possibly with child."

"Can you please take this seriously?" Alexander commanded.

"Why? You aren't," said Judith from right behind him. Alexander jumped.

"Shouldn't you be preparing to make your entrance? Madam Arcati is on in a page or so."

"Which, at the rate you're going, will be next Christmas. And while we're on the subject of entrances, please inform me at what speed you require me to make mine and I'll ensure I have my pedometer to guarantee I'm spot on."

"Good point. Yes, considering you've come on your bicycle, I think you should come in very fast as if you're still on it."

Judith raised her eyebrows and returned to the wings. When she eventually made her entrance she rushed on making pedalling movements with her legs and ringing an imaginary bell. The cast on stage gave up any semblance of focusing and began to laugh hysterically, while Judith continued her circuit round the set careering wildly into anyone in her way.

"Is that always going to happen?" Echo asked Holly as they sat watching in the stalls, being the only two cast members not on stage at that point. "She didn't do that before."

Holly shook her head. "I don't think so; Judith's making a point."

"Gee, what a pity, it's real funny. Hey, if she's not gonna do it, do you think I could go on like that?"

"No," said Holly firmly. "You're supposed to be a ghost."

"Don't ghosts ride bicycles?"

"No."

"How do they get around?"

"I have no idea; they sort of apparate."

"Oh, I see. So I make my entrance by apparating?"

"Yes."

"OK. I can do that, I guess. Holly?"

"Yes."

"What's apparating?"

Holly was saved from continuing this absurd conversation by Declan speaking quietly to Alexander. Alexander nodded and picked up the megaphone. "Seems like we have to break for supper, people. So I want to start where we left off when you get back."

"I hope Judith will make an identical entrance after the break," Lucy said to Rebecca. "It's the most fun I've had for days."

"OK, everybody," said Declan, "you have fifteen minutes to get out of costume and wigs, an hour for supper and fifteen minutes to get back into costume. So please be back on stage in an hour and a half. Thank you."

"Fuck that, I'm not getting out of all this crap for an hour," said Judith to Rupert and Miranda as they left the stage. "I'll get Freda to buy me a salad; I'm not particularly hungry anyway. What about you two, anything you fancy while he's out?"

"A salad would be lovely," said Miranda. "Whatever you're having. So it's easier for Freda," she added hastily.

Rupert smiled; Miranda never quit. "Do

you think Fred would mind if I was a little different? I'd love a burger and fries. I need something substantial."

In spite of the hysteria at rehearsal, it was not a cheerful meal. They had only reached page nine, and pages one to eight hadn't been very successful. Even Rupert's cheerful disposition was suffering under such conditions.

The evening didn't go much better. Alexander seemed to be using the technical rehearsal to redirect the play, rather than for lighting, sound and props. This was a total nightmare for stage management who would be responsible for these things when the show was running. At one point, Scarlett made her entrance to announce dinner in total darkness and Alexander said nothing until Rupert pointed it out.

"I'll sort that out later," said Alexander. "Don't worry."

"All the more reason to worry," Rupert muttered to Adam. "If the audience can't see Scarlett they'll think Charles and Ruth have a ghostly dinner herald."

As they finally reached the séance scene Alexander called out, "OK, people, staaaap."

"What now?" Judith enquired. "Would you like us to play the whole scene in slow motion?"

"No, I want to break for the night."

"But we still have an hour left," Declan said.

"I know, but I think we should get an early

night and start with the séance scene fresh in the morning, because I feel that scene will require all our emotive output."

"OK, everyone break," Declan said. "Please be back on stage in costume and wigs ready to start at 10.30am. Thank you all very much for today. Have a good rest."

The cast cleared the stage in seconds. "It's a funny thing about actors," Lucy said to Matthew. "They all say acting is their life and moan when they don't have a job, but if anyone lets them go early or there's a chance of a performance being cancelled you don't see them for dust. Stage management, on the other hand, claim no such thing, yet we are the ones who never get to leave early. See, here's Declan with a list of things I'm sure we'll be doing tonight."

"I don't mind; I think it's exciting getting a new production ready."

"You'll learn, young Matthew, believe me. Yes, Declan, what can we do for you?"

"I'd like to run through the séance scene for technical things like lighting and sound so we're perfect for tomorrow."

"Won't Alexander mind if we do that without him, I mean, isn't he supposed to involved?" Matthew asked.

"He's not going to know, is he?" Lucy said. "I imagine he's left the building, hasn't he, Declan?"

"Within about 30 seconds of my calling the official break."

"Besides, he has no idea what he's talking about with technical stuff. What am I saying? He has no idea what he's talking about full stop. Come on, let's get on with it; I'd like to get to the pub before last orders. What do you want us to do?"

"Could you and Matthew stand in for the actors?"

"All of them? I know we're exceptionally talented but ..."

Declan made a pretend swipe at Lucy's head. "If it isn't too much trouble, perhaps you two could wear Rupert and Adam's magnets and operate the table. I'm going to sit in the stalls and try to foresee any problems while Rebecca cues the lights and sound."

By the time they left the theatre that night, the stage management considered they had ironed out any possible glitches.

The following morning a large amount of their hard work went for nothing when Alexander changed his mind about what he wanted and began to re-block the action. At one point he sat Rupert and Adam beside each other, resulting in the table, its magnets uneven, toppling over on one side, squashing Isabelle into her chair.

"Can't Miranda wear the magnets instead of Adam?" Alexander called out.

"Where can I hide them under this dress?" Miranda snapped. "I think the audience might work out the trick if they see a large magnet stuck on my wrist."

"OK, Adam, move back to where you were originally."

"If anyone can remember where that was," Judith said acidly. "It's like playing musical séances."

By the time they had worked through the scene to Alexander's liking and Holly had ensured Echo had made her entrance in the correct place, it was 8pm on Tuesday night. By dint of Wesley insisting Alexander continue every time he wanted to "staaaap" they actually managed to get to the end of Act One by the time they broke that night.

"We'll be lucky to get one dress rehearsal at this rate," Judith said. She'd invited the cast into her dressing room for a quick drink before they went home.

"But we will get one, won't we?" Scarlett asked.

Judith shrugged. "Who knows?"

Scarlett paled. "But if we don't, what if it all goes wrong at the first performance? Will the audience ask for their money back?"

"Serves them right for coming to a preview," said Miranda. "That's the point of them; it's a work in progress."

"Do they pay any less?"

"Who are you kidding?" said Judith. "It used to be the norm, but now it's very rare; occasionally special deals are offered for previews on shows which aren't selling at all. But on a potentially successful play like this one forget it; producers wouldn't make so much money, would they?"

"But Wesley doesn't seem like that."

"Every producer is like that; it's in their job description. Come on, I'm going home to dream of séance tables."

By Thursday night, in spite of Wesley's goading, Alexander had not reached the end of the play. Wesley looked at his exhausted and utterly fed up cast and made a decision. He called the whole company, actors and backstage team, down to sit in the stalls and sat on the front of the stage, facing them.

"OK. I'm going to call you all in tomorrow morning, which I'm aware I shouldn't with a performance tomorrow night, but we must finish the technical. This I intend to do by lunchtime," he glared at Alexander, "so in the afternoon we can do a sort of stagger-through dress rehearsal. Needless to say, this means undertaking our first performance in front of an audience without a proper dress rehearsal. I realize how unfair this is on all of you, so I am willing to offer the audience their money back and inform them tomorrow night is an open dress rehearsal. Normally I would propose they come another night, but since we're completely sold out for the whole six month run this is the only option."

"Absolutely not," said Judith. Wesley looked at her in surprise. He'd been certain she'd jump at the idea. In fact, he'd mainly suggested it to keep her happy. "You are quite correct, we aren't ready to perform in front of an audience tomorrow, but I'm damned if anyone is going to be aware of that. Giving them their money back is admitting to failure and I won't tolerate that. I'm sorry if the rest of you feel differently, but I'm afraid my answer is no."

There was a general consensus of agreement; Isabelle was the only one slightly disappointed. Listening to Wesley speak, she'd half prepared how she'd impart this gossip.

"OK, that's great," said Wesley. "I appreciate your confidence, and I'll do everything I can to help it go smoothly. Now, go home, get a good sleep and I'll see you in the morning."

Scarlett and Holly followed Rupert up the stairs. "Rupert, if Judith had agreed to refunding the audience wouldn't Wesley have lost a lot of money?" Scarlett asked.

"Yes. This theatre holds about 900 people; if you times that by the seat prices we're talking at least £30,000."

"But Judith said producers would never agree to lose money."

"I'll tell you two girls a secret if you promise never to repeat it."

Scarlett and Holly leant forward eagerly.

"Judith is very occasionally wrong." He grinned and disappeared into his dressing room.

CHAPTER TWENTY SEVEN

No one was certain how Wesley did it, the odds on favourite being a loaded pistol in Alexander's back, though Scarlett was on the side of blackmail and Lucy a gay mafia hit man, but the technical run-through was finished by lunchtime. Wesley then organized sandwiches to be sent in so they could start the afternoon's stagger-through as soon as possible.

"Why is it called a stagger-through?" Echo asked Lucy.

"Because everyone staggers through it, hoping for the best, and if nothing goes wrong it's a miracle."

Miranda and Isabelle were in a much improved mood since Libby had managed to get them some elegant evening frocks for the first scene.

"Your dress is gorgeous," said Miranda as they stood side by side in front of the mirror outside the door to the stage, secretly thinking how much lovelier her maroon gown was than Isabelle's black and gold.

"No, Miranda, yours is simply stunning," Isabelle replied, reflecting that maroon dresses shouldn't be worn by people with auburn hair and how her black and gold would show up better on the drab set.

Jasper had gone into a sulk as soon as he'd noticed his designs had been supplanted and was refusing to come out of the gents. This upset no one but Alexander who spent precious rehearsal time whispering endearments through the locked door in an effort to placate him.

Libby had not been so successful with Judith, who refused all the outfits she'd brought from the costumiers and was wearing a pair of land army dungarees she'd acquired from a role in a movie thirty years ago. "I can see Madame Arcati as a land girl, can't you?" she said to Rupert. "Toiling the land between contacting the dead. It's no less incongruous than anything else in this production."

"Very attractive; I'm sure Charles would take you in the hay barn anytime."

"Promises, promises! Incidentally, is your scar getting bigger?"

"Yes, I'm afraid so. I persuaded Tasha to make it a little longer and more dramatic; I'm going for the sympathy vote. You don't mind, do you?"

"Christ no, this production has gone beyond subtlety. Besides, I agree with Miranda that it's heroic and quite sexy."

"Madam Arcati, please control yourself; Charles is a twice married man."

"Ah, but by the end both your wives are dead, and Madam Arcati is a single girl, you know!"

Rupert laughed. "Would you like a scar the

other side as well and maybe one across my chin?"

"Now that is going too far; you'd look like Herman Munster."

Judith had additionally brought in a land girl hat which she wore over her own bobbed hair, scooping it up in the 1940s snood Miranda was no longer using. "It's better than looking like a cockerel," was her only comment.

Tasha had successfully restyled Miranda's and Isabelle's wigs to their delight, but there was nothing she could do with Judith's.

Adam was relieved to discover he had been given a new white dress shirt; the blood was now only on the dinner jacket where it hardly showed. Now he could start feeling more like a doctor and less like a mass murderer.

A stagger-through was an apt description of the afternoon's rehearsal. In spite of requests not to stop the show unless absolutely necessary, Alexander did so several times; this prevented the actors from getting an un-interrupted run and caused them to lose their concentration. Adam even fluffed one of his lines. On the technical side, mostly thanks to Declan and Rebecca, the show ran fairly smoothly, though instead of dim lighting for the séance the cast were plunged into total darkness with the result that Judith fell over Rupert, and later the gramophone didn't work, thereby losing a visual gag. In addition, Miranda panicked over her first quick change with the result that she missed her entrance in spite of Cassie's best efforts. There is little a dresser can do if the actor insists on whirling their arms round like windmills crying out, "shit, shit, shit, I'm not going to make it." If she did that again this evening Cassie was going to hold her arms down by force and snap at her to keep calm; that usually worked.

Wesley ordered in more food before the evening show, but none of the actors were very hungry. The nerves were kicking in horribly and no one felt prepared for an audience.

Rupert, needing some air, and to escape from Miranda and Judith's complaints, was walking past the front of the theatre when he stopped in amazement. Outside there was something which strongly resembled an unexploded World War II bomb and beside it stood Alexander grinning proudly.

"What the hell is that?" Rupert asked.

"It's a World War II bomb."

"Yes, I'm aware of that. But what's it doing outside our theatre?"

"On the first night of *Blithe Spirit* in 1941 the audience had to step round a bomb crater to get into the theatre – I read that. So I'm recreating it for our audiences."

"Terrific. But a) this isn't 1941 and the audience aren't going to understand why the hell there is a bomb outside the theatre, and b) it was a bomb crater and not an actual bomb. If it had been a bomb the performance would presumably have been cancelled."

"Yes, but I wanted something more obvious."

Rupert sighed, somehow that didn't surprise him.

"If I dug a hole in the street it would look like the rest of London."

"You do have a point there. Alexander?"

"Yes?"

"It is a dummy, isn't it? We're not going to have an unexpected explosion in the middle of the show and end up with half the audience being rushed to hospital, are we?"

"NO! I mean no, of course we're not. Obviously it's a dummy. Do you think I'm stupid?"

Rupert didn't bother to answer that question, and walked back to the theatre frowning. There was something in the way Alexander answered that last question he didn't trust. He wondered whether he should mention this to Judith or Miranda but decided they had enough to worry about. He'd content himself with reporting the theatre's new bomb décor.

Judith, in spite of all her experience, still suffered from appalling first-night nerves, but not to appear weak she kept it to herself. Only Fred was aware of her terror as she strode up and down the dressing room muttering her lines and occasionally banging her head against the wall. "Why the fuck do I do this to myself, Freda?" she demanded. "Why don't I retire like any normal person of my age?"

"Because, Judith darling, you adore every moment once you're out there."

"Why can't I be more like Judi Dench? She's always so relaxed before she goes on stage."

Fred, who often wished Judith was more like Judi Dench, a delightful actress to dress, said nothing.

"This is going to be my last show, do you hear me? I'm going to do movies from now on, nice little cameo roles with few lines and no live audience."

"Yes, Judith. Whatever you say."

"Oh, fuck off and give me a cigarette."

"You're not allowed to smoke in the theatre, you know that."

Judith opened the window of the dressing room wide and stuck her head out. "Now I'm not inside the theatre, give me a fucking cigarette!"

Fred fetched a packet from the stash he kept for her, lit it and passed it out the window. "Just don't fall out while you're giving yourself lung cancer. Remember we don't have any understudies yet."

"Get out!"

Miranda was re-doing her make-up for the third time; it helped her to relax. Besides, with the lack of glamour on this show she had to augment it with make-up. She had forced Tasha to put the wig on four times before she was happy with the way it looked and then all she said was, "I suppose that will have to do."

This meant Tasha was late getting to Isabelle who pursed her lips and said, "I suppose Miranda kept you re-doing her wig. That's fine; I understand I'm not nearly as important. Tell me, is she very nervous?"

Scarlett was already sitting on the set, fully dressed, when Rebecca announced the half hour call. She wanted the 35 minutes to get her head together and feel she was Edith. Holly was sitting in the wings muttering her lines into the microphone which was to go in Echo's ear, so Rebecca could do a final sound check.

"Hi." Holly looked up to see Echo standing beside her.

"Wow, you look beautiful, Echo." Tasha had helped Echo with her make-up, so she now resembled a pale ghost rather than an over-made-up beauty pageant queen; combined with the flattering dress and wig, Echo was a truly stunning Elvira.

"Gee thanks, Holly. Do you think Rupert will think so?"

"I'm sure he will."

"Really? Should I go show him?"

"No, I wouldn't. Leave him some time to concentrate before the show."

"Oh. OK."

Holly looked at Echo's disappointed face; she certainly had got a bad case of the Ruperts. Not that she could blame her; Holly certainly wouldn't throw him out of bed – as if she'd get the chance!

"Everyone's like so weird tonight, Holly. Why is that?"

"They're nervous."

"Why?"

"It's the first show in front of an audience."

"Oh. Should I be nervous?"

"Not if you aren't naturally, no."

"But I don't wanna be different."

"We're all different."

"Even Rupert?"

"Especially Rupert!"

Rupert was putting on his Captain's jacket, now minus the German Iron Cross and American Purple Heart, when there was a knock on the door.

"Come in, darling," he called out, expecting Miranda ready to moan about something.

"Thanks, gorgeous," said Adam, sticking his head in.

Rupert laughed. "Sorry, I was expecting Miranda."

"The story of my life," said Adam, trying to smile. "Look, I'm sorry to bother you, but I wondered if you could help me. I can't seem to do up my bow tie for some reason; I don't normally have a problem and I didn't want to bother Cassie." He held the offending article in hands shaking so badly Rupert was amazed he'd managed to open the door.

"Sure, come over into the light." Rupert deftly did up the tie and then looked at Adam's face. "Christ, are you all right? You look as

317

white as a sheet. You haven't been putting on Echo's white ghost make-up, have you?"

Adam shook his head. Suddenly his legs turned to jelly and he caught hold of the dressing table to steady himself. Rupert grabbed his arm. "Here, sit down." He helped him into a chair and crouched beside him. "What's wrong?"

"I fluffed my line this afternoon."

"I'm hardly surprised with Alexander demanding that we 'staaaap' every few minutes. Any of us could have done the same thing."

"But you didn't, it was me. What if I do it again tonight? You may have heard I have a slight reputation for such behaviour."

Rupert's heart sank. That was all they needed, an actor with cold feet. "Adam, you're going to be fine. Honestly. I've been rehearsing with you for the last month and I have total confidence in you, OK?"

"I'm sorry, Rupert, but what if I was wrong and I'm not ready to go back on stage yet?"

"You've waited twenty five years. If you wait another twenty five you'll be performing on a Zimmer frame!" Adam smiled weakly. "That's better. Now, once you get that Doctor's bag in your hand and all that blood on your jacket, you'll be well away."

"I hope you're right."

"I'm virtually always right – only don't tell Miranda!"

There was another knock on the door and

Cassie stuck her head in. "Do either of you need any help getting dressed? I'm sorry I'm rather late checking on you. I got a bit held up."

"I imagine my wife has been keeping you busy. But I think we're doing all right, aren't we, Adam?"

Adam nodded.

"Great, I'll see you in the interval," said Cassie, leaving. "Have a fabulous show."

"Thanks."

"I'd better go and finish getting ready," said Adam.

"Good idea, and don't worry, OK? Apart from anything else if you do get into any difficulty I'm on stage with you most of the time so I can easily feed you your line."

"Thanks."

"Ladies and gentlemen, this is your five minute call, you have five minutes. Thank you." Rebecca's calm tones came over the tannoy system.

Rupert took a quick look at himself in the mirror, left the dressing room and headed down to the wings to look for Holly. Echo was standing beside her trying to look out at the audience through the curtain.

"Echo, be careful. The audience are going to be very surprised if they catch sight of a white face peering through at them," he said.

"Geez, could they see me?"

"First rule of theatre, Echo: if you can see the audience, the audience can see you."

319

"Oh, right. I'll learn that; I learn real fast, don't I, Rupert?"

"Yes, you learn real fast."

"Do I look good?"

"You look beautiful." He gave her a quick kiss on the top of her head. Echo looked as if she'd won the lottery. "Have a terrific show tonight." Echo smiled. "Holly, could I have a quick word with you?"

Holly nodded, annoyed at how excited she was at the request. Rupert took her arm and led her into a small room off the stage right wing, out of sight of anyone else. "I need to tell you something in total confidence; I know I can trust you, can't I?"

"Absolutely."

"You may have heard something about Adam's history; it doesn't matter whether you have or not, what does matter is he's having a slight panic attack and convincing himself he's going to forget his lines."

"Oh God!"

"Exactly. Now, I'm certain he'll be fine once he gets going, and since I'm on stage with him most of the time, except for his short scene with Miranda, I can feed him his line by reversing it, if necessary." Holly looked at him questioningly. "For example, if his line was, 'I wonder what Madame Arcati will be doing tonight,' I can say, 'Don't you wonder what Madame Arcati will be doing tonight?' and that should get him back on track – hopefully."

"I see. Do you know all his lines?"

"I think so; I pick up things fairly easily. However, it might not be possible for some reason: if it would make no sense for Charles to say the line for example or if I'm not on stage. In those circumstances, could you prompt him? You're following the script, aren't you, even when Echo isn't on?" Holly nodded. "Do you think you could manage that?"

"OK," said Holly, warily. Although she was pretty good at feeding Echo, she was still terrified something might go wrong and this was one more problem.

"Good girl. I'll tell Rebecca you're going to do that. Normally that would be her job, but she has enough to worry about with all the cues on this show." He smiled at her. "What would we do without you, Holly?"

Returning to the wings, Rupert found the whole cast had assembled, regardless of when their entrances were. Alexander pushed his way through them. "I'm just going to make a speech," he said, dashing on stage before anyone could stop him.

"Fuck!" said Judith.

"Ladies and gentlemen," Alexander began. "I would like to welcome each and every one of you to this evening's performance of *Blithe Spirit*. As you are aware, this is our first preview and thus extremely special for us. But I believe this will be an unforgettable evening for you all."

"He's not wrong there," said Judith.

"For the last month the actors and I have been sharing a journey of exploration. Tonight you, our wonderful audience, are going to be sharing this journey with us to an unknown destination."

"I think I'm going to be sick," said Miranda.

"Who's going on a journey?" asked Echo.

"There is every chance we may have to stop, so please bear with us and remember, this is a work in progress."

"Why doesn't he just tell them it's total crap and destroy us altogether?" Miranda said despairingly.

"I can disclose to you, our audience and fellow travellers, that standing in the wings beside me I have a cast of terrified actors, so please give them your support. Now I can officially welcome you to this exciting production of *Blithe Spirit*." Alexander walked into the wings, beaming at the success of his speech. Judith walked over to him and slapped him round the face as hard as she could.

Alexander looked at her speechlessly.

"How dare you? How dare you tell the audience we're terrified? We may all be shitting ourselves, which thanks to you we probably are, but you never tell the audience that. NEVER! To them we should be Madame Arcati, and the Condomines and the Bradmans, not quaking actors. You've completely destroyed our credibility as characters, not to mention actors, you total fucking imbecile."

Rupert gently drew her away before she wrestled Alexander to the ground and did him permanent damage. She was almost in tears with rage.

Declan came over. "Judith, are you OK? We really need to take the curtain up; the audience is getting restless."

"Where's Wesley? How could he let Alexander do that?"

"I don't think he knew; I certainly didn't. He suddenly rushed on there and started speaking," said Declan, aware Wesley wasn't in the building. Henrietta had phoned to say she was being allowed to take their daughter home and Wesley had shot out of the theatre to collect them with strict instructions that Declan was to tell no one of his absence. "Anyway, I'm not sure how many people would have heard. Alexander's not used to projecting and he didn't have his megaphone."

"Rubbish, he has a voice like a foghorn; in all probability they heard him at Her Majesty's Theatre across the road."

"Judith, we have to start."

"Fine, go ahead, how much worse can this evening get?"

"Great. Scarlett, are you ready?" Scarlett gripped her drinks tray and nodded. "OK, Rebecca, we can go."

"Standby ladies and gentlemen," Rebecca called out. "The curtain is about to go up."

CHAPTER TWENTY EIGHT

"Listen, laughs," Rupert said, during Scarlett's business with the tray and dialogue with Miranda. "Halleluiah! Perhaps it's not going to be such a disaster."

"It will be if you don't make your entrance," said Judith.

"I'm going, I'm going." Rupert's entrance was greeted by a round of applause, not popular with Miranda, who had received no entrance round. Judith was also rewarded with one. This audience seemed determined to enjoy themselves in spite of Alexander's speech; the laughs were plentiful and loud. Rupert and Miranda were playing off each other perfectly; Adam was relieved his lines were coming out acceptably and his repartee with Isabelle was working well, while Judith could do nothing wrong.

The actors started to relax slightly. Perhaps the old adage, that a bad dress rehearsal means a good performance, was working for them tonight. They had almost reached the end of Scene One where Scarlett, as Edith, announces dinner, when Alexander, standing at the back of the stalls, pushed the button on a sound system he had prevailed upon the sound engineer to set up earlier. Over the speakers came the unmistakeable sound of an air raid siren. The cast froze. The audience looked round apprehensively.

It was impossible to carry on with the siren blaring out. Rupert turned to the other actors, shouting over the din, "Ruth, Madame Arcati, Dr and Mrs Bradman, Edith, I think we'd better make our way down to the cellar until this air raid is over." He opened the door and waved the rest of the cast through. The audience laughed, relieved it seemed to be part of the entertainment. They'd already had to scramble over a bomb to get into the theatre, so why not this?

"What the fuck is going on?" Judith shouted at Rebecca in the wings. "Get that racket off."

"It's not me; it's coming from front of house. Declan's on his way there."

The siren suddenly cut off in mid-wail as Declan pulled the socket from the wall. The audience laughed; this was evidently another part of Alexander Columbus's innovative direction. Declan dragged a complaining Alexander out into the foyer with dire warnings about messing with the sound system again.

"Quick, get back on," Judith said.

"Where shall we go from?" Miranda asked.

"Start at the top of Scene Two; it'll make more sense than going back."

"But we're supposed to go in the blackout, with coffee cups."

"Improvise," Judith snapped, taking her

coffee cup and strolling back onto the stage. Miranda and Isabelle followed suit. Rupert and Adam, who weren't on for another couple of pages, pulled up their sleeves so Lucy and Matthew could put the table magnets on their wrists. On stage Judith was ad-libbing: "Don't you just hate those air raids, Mrs Condomine? It disturbs my aura so."

"I'm so sorry, Madame Arcati. I hope it didn't spoil your dinner," Miranda returned.

"Not at all, it was quite delicious. Now, shall I tell you about my control?"

"Please do."

"Nice one," Rupert whispered to Adam. "They've got back to the script and only lost a couple of lines."

"Yes."

"Come on, we're nearly on."

Adam followed Rupert through the door into the Condomine's living room, but his concentration had gone. He looked round the stage, yet it was as if he wasn't on it, but floating quietly above. He could see himself standing on the set below with the rest of the cast, but he couldn't move or utter. Everyone was staring at him; he knew he should be speaking but what was he supposed to say? Did it actually matter? Everything up here was so peaceful.

"Oh no," Holly thought, and quietly gave him his line. Nothing happened. Adam continued to watch it all from what seemed like another world. He heard Holly say his line, but was powerless to repeat it. Rupert, hearing Holly's prompt and realizing there'd been no effect, reversed and modified Adam's line: "Madam Arcati, Dr Bradman was saying, as we came in, how he hoped you were in the mood."

Judith jumped in with her line, then Miranda, and the scene continued, while Rupert wandered nonchalantly over to Adam and pinched him hard, without the audience being able to see. Adam's eyes came into focus and he felt himself return to his body. Rupert was looking at him anxiously. Where the hell were they? Oh, yes, Judith was going on about the cuckoo sounding angry. After that, he had to move some furniture round to prepare for the séance, and a line, a line about the furniture, yes that was it, he was back in it now.

He waited for the sound of the cuckoo which followed Judith's line. Unfortunately, when Rebecca cued it, the sound system, possibly because Alexander had been fiddling round with it earlier, jumped several cues and instead of a pissed-off sounding cuckoo there was the loud doorbell peel from Act Three.

"Were you expecting anyone, Ruth darling?" Rupert ad-libbed quickly to Miranda.

"I don't believe so. It's probably someone from the village collecting for the war effort. I'm sure Edith will answer it; I told her we weren't to be disturbed."

"Nice save," Lucy whispered to Matthew. Poor Rebecca was bent over the sound system, desperately trying to get it back in order.

Amazingly, the séance scene went well. Rupert and Adam negotiated the table perfectly and Rebecca had succeeded in resetting the sound system so the child's voice reciting Little Tommy Tucker and the gramophone playing Irvine Berlin's *Always* played at the correct time.

The audience response to the scene was wonderful. Echo, watching in the wings, was so busy laughing with them she would've forgotten to make her entrance if Rupert and Judith hadn't exited at that point and pushed her on. Judith stormed up to her dressing room, signing to Declan she wanted to see him in the interval, while Rupert went back on stage to finish the act and do his first scene with Echo. At least with her he knew she wouldn't forget her lines, unless Holly drifted off, and he really did enjoy the way she ran her fingers through his hair as the curtain came down on Act I.

"Good luck," said Fred. "Her majesty is not happy." He was sitting outside the dressing room as Declan and Rupert came upstairs to see Judith in the interval. Rupert had taken pity on Declan and volunteered to come with him. They found Judith throwing anything she could find around the room. Rupert ducked a large pillow.

"Where the fuck is Wesley?"

"I'm sure he's around somewhere, Judith, but I don't know exactly where."

"You're lying, Declan. He's not here, is he?"

Declan couldn't think what to say. "I don't fucking believe it." A coat hanger flew across the room.

Fred put his head round the door. "I heard a coat hanger, was that my cue?"

"Get out."

Fred picked up the coat hanger and got out.

"Where is he?"

"He's picking Henrietta and the baby up from the hospital."

"Thank goodness there's some good news around here," said Rupert. Judith glared at him. "Honestly, Judith, what could he do anyway? I'm perfectly sure he didn't know about Alexander's speech or the air raid siren. If he'd been here he'd probably be having a heart attack by now with the stress."

"Good!"

"Judith."

"The rest of us will probably end up with one at this rate so why should he escape?"

"Because he pays us our wages?"

Fred stuck his head round the door again. "Rebecca's here; is it safe for her to come in?"

"What do you think I'm going to do, eat her?"

"Who knows? Come in, Rebecca darling."

"Judith, Rupert, I'm so sorry about the muddle with the sound. I don't know what happened. I've triple checked the system so it should be fine from now on. And Matthew and Lucy are re-checking all the props and effects so we shouldn't have any more technical errors."

"Fantastic. How about human errors?"

"I'm going to see Adam, now," said Rupert.

"And is Echo going to be having such a 'cool time' with the audience," Judith did an excellent impression of Echo, "that she'll keep forgetting to go on?"

"I'll tell Holly to make sure she cues her entrances too," said Rupert.

"I'll do that if you like," said Rebecca. "I need to go and apologize to the rest of the cast about the sound, but I can do it after that. You need a break."

Rupert thought about it; he'd love to sit down and have the coffee Cassie had promised to bring him. But he wanted to thank Holly for trying to give Adam his line. "No, I'll do it, that's fine. How long do I have until the end of the interval?"

"Five minutes. But I can give you a bit longer if you like and cut the second interval shorter, if that's OK with Declan."

"Absolutely, I'll tell the front of house manager so the bar staff go faster next time!"

Rupert ran downstairs to talk to Holly who was still sitting on her seat in the wings, going through the script. Certainly she'd cue Echo on, no problem. She blushed when Rupert thanked her for trying to help Adam. "I didn't know whether I should say it again; I thought maybe I wasn't loud enough."

"It was fine, I heard it, but I don't think Adam was on our planet at that point. You did great." He leant over and gave Holly a quick kiss; she blushed with pleasure.

On the way back up to talk to Adam, Rupert heard Miranda shouting in her dressing room. A few seconds later, Cassie came out carrying Miranda's costumes for her quick changes.

"I'm sorry, is Miranda being a total pain?" he asked.

"She's just panicking a bit because she didn't make it on this afternoon for her quick change."

"Yes, I caught the end of that when I came off for my change. She never learns that panicking doesn't help. Try slapping her if she does that again tonight, that should work."

"I had considered that."

"You have my permission."

"Did you have time to drink your coffee?"

"I didn't, sorry."

"I'll make you a fresh one for the next interval."

"Cassie, I love you."

"Yeah, they all say that; ten minutes later they've forgotten my name!"

"Never!"

Adam was sitting on the floor in his dressing room when Rupert went in. "Something wrong with the chairs?" Rupert enquired.

"Not as wrong as there is with me. Rupert I'm so, so sorry."

"Forget it. I'm a typical actor, any excuse to have more lines, even if they are someone else's."

"Thank you for pinching me the way you did."

"Normally if I pinch a girl like that I get slapped in the face; to be thanked is a new experience." He sat down on the floor beside Adam. "What happened? I'd say you looked like you'd seen a ghost, but maybe that would be a bit obvious under the circumstances. How about like a rabbit caught in headlights?"

"I suppose it was a bit like that. I felt as if I wasn't in my body; that I was watching myself and you lot from above."

"The way the show is going tonight it's probably the best place to see it from. Unless you're Echo, who was seeing it so well from the audience's point of view she nearly forgot to go on."

"She didn't!"

"Luckily Judith and I exit at that point and noticed. Judith pushed her on so hard I thought she'd shoot straight across the stage and off the other side."

"Is Judith furious with me?"

"I think her venom at present is aimed at Wesley who had the audacity to leave the theatre in order to collect his wife and daughter from the hospital."

"The baby's being allowed home; that's wonderful news." Adam looked happy for the first time that evening.

The tannoy crackled into life with Rebecca's voice: "Ladies and gentlemen, this is your Act Two beginners call: Miss Flynn, Miss Montgomery, and Mr Blake your calls please. This is your Act Two beginners call. Thank you."

Rupert got up. "I've got to go. I'll see you out there. No sirens this time."

"You hope!"

Act Two was a comparative success; even Miranda's change went fairly smoothly, once Cassie had grabbed her arm and shouted at her to keep bloody still. Miranda was so unused to people talking to her in such a manner, she stood motionless while Cassie put the costume on her.

"Did you slap her?" Rupert asked when she came to change him.

"No, I just yelled. It worked."

"Please don't yell at me. The way I feel tonight I might cry!" Rupert raised his eyebrows at her.

Cassie helped him on with his jacket. "I'll bear that in mind."

There was only one final, minor, problem. Echo threw the vase into the fireplace, as rehearsed, where it was supposed to smash; instead it bounced back out of the fireplace and rolled towards the audience, much to their glee. "Bugger," said Lucy. "We're going to be in trouble with Judith later."

Rupert had completed his second quick change when Adam came into the wings for his next entrance. Rupert grinned at him and produced a large safety pin from his pocket. "Just in case!"

Rupert's distraction tactic succeeded and Adam entered too busy trying not to grin to worry about his lines, and even got a sizeable laugh from the audience at his impersonation of Charles's inability to concentrate. He and Isabelle made their exit leaving Rupert and Miranda on stage; that was his part finished now, thank God. He returned to his dressing room and lay down on the floor. He'd made it, though only just; what on earth had possessed him to have some form of out of body experience? That was a new one even for him. God knows what Judith was going to say.

After a few minutes he sat up and dialled Wesley's home number; at least tonight had yielded one bit of good news. After four rings the answerphone picked up. "Hello, Wesley it's, um, Adam. I, er, wanted to say how thrilled I was to hear you've been able to bring your daughter home. That's wonderful news, I ..."

"Adam, hi, sorry, I was screening my calls; I thought it might be Judith. Incidentally, how did you know about the baby? I told Declan not to tell anybody."

"Rupert told me. I'm sorry, I didn't realize it was a secret."

"So much for discretion. How's the show going?"

Adam paused. "We'll fill you in tomorrow; enjoy being a proper dad tonight. There's nothing like it, not even theatre."

"Oh, God, is it going that badly?"

"No," Adam lied. "We're just coming up to the second interval; listen, you can hear the audience response." He held the phone up to the relay system through which the audience could be heard enthusiastically clapping the end of Act Two. "I'm going to leave you in peace now, or what peace you can have with a baby! See you whenever you're back."

"I'll be there tomorrow; if I'm not I'm sure I'll find Judith on my doorstep."

Surviving Act Three with ease, the cast were relieved to find the reaction at the curtain call was friendly and heartfelt.

"I think they felt sorry for us," Miranda groaned. "Surely they couldn't think the performance was any good?"

"I suppose it was fairly entertaining for them, watching us make complete fools of ourselves. Rushing to air raid shelters, reacting to eerie door bells ringing, throwing bouncing vases and, thanks to Alexander, knowing we were all terrified," said Judith. Adam was relieved, though surprised, that she made no mention of his blunder; it was hardly as if she could've missed it.

"I thought it was swell," said Echo. "It's so much more fun than doing TV; the audience thought I was funny."

"Glad to know somebody does," said Judith.

"I wanna do theatre for ever and ever now."

"With that prospect I am definitely retiring after this play."

Alexander came rushing through the pass door from the auditorium, with an equally elated Jasper. "Did you hear that reaction? They loved it. We're a hit. Didn't you adore my air raid siren? The genuine surprise on your faces was perfect; the audience felt they were there with you, living the play. That's what I call spontaneity."

Rupert, Miranda, Adam, Isabelle, Scarlett and Holly stared at him in stunned silence, while Judith wandered over to the props table, picked up the vase which had failed to smash earlier, and brought it down hard on the back of Alexander's head. It broke spectacularly. "Now that," she said as Alexander looked at her in dazed surprise, "is what I call spontaneity."

CHAPTER TWENTY NINE

Wesley, after a stressful evening with Henrietta either because their daughter was crying or because she wasn't and might've stopped breathing, was not impressed to be woken at 2am by Alexander claiming Judith had tried to kill him.

"But she didn't."

"That's hardly the point."

"It's exactly the point. If she'd killed you I would have a dead director, a leading lady in jail and, ergo, no show. However, since you are obviously alive and well enough to call me I can't say I care very much."

"But I might be concussed or brain damaged."

"I doubt anyone would notice the difference. Goodnight." He hung up on the spluttering director.

"Who's that?" Henrietta asked sleepily from beside him.

"Alexander. Apparently Judith tried to kill him."

"Good for her. I'm going to check on the baby." She got out of bed and went over to the cot in the corner of their room where their daughter slept on, oblivious to the theatrical predicaments which surrounded her. "How did Judith try to kill him?"

"Smashed a vase over his head, I think. I've no doubt I'll hear the details tomorrow."

"It's Saturday tomorrow; is there a matinee?"

"No, not after a first preview; we need the afternoon to work on any problems arising from that."

"Do you think there were a lot?"

"Judith tried to murder Alexander, so I'd say that was a strong possibility."

"I wish I'd seen that," said Henrietta.

"I'm rather glad I didn't, I might've felt duty bound to stop her."

The actors had been called for 1pm, to give them the morning to rest, but Adam, turning up an hour early at the theatre, was alarmed to find a note waiting for him at the stage door. It seemed Judith had arrived even earlier.

Dr Bradman,

> *Please come and see me in my dressing room on arrival.*

Judith

Adam clambered up to his dressing room to leave his bag and gather his nerves. The flight of stairs from his room up to Judith's seemed endless. He tried to picture little Millie's face (the happy place Dr Bennett had suggested he adopt in times of stress), but Judith's face kept fusing with Millie's, which was horrifying and he stopped the visualization abruptly.

"Come in," Judith's voice replied to his trembling knock. He walked in through the receiving room and towards the inner sanctum feeling he was on the way to his execution. 'Dead man walking', wasn't that the expression? He found Judith hanging out the window, smoking. "Dr Bradman, come in. Please sit down." Adam sat down nervously on the bed. Judith stared at him for a while. Adam could feel himself sweating. "Rupert sets great store by you," she said eventually. "And I set great store by Rupert."

Adam gulped. "So do I."

"That's why I've stuck by you and not made a formal complaint to Wesley." Adam said nothing; he didn't know what he could say. "But you make me nervous, and I don't like that. I don't want to look at a cast member and discover they have wandered off to their own planet. You can understand that, I presume."

"Yes."

"Do you want to tell me exactly what happened?"

"I'm not sure I can ..."

"It's not an optional request."

Adam tried to explain the best he could; it sounded even more stupid than when he'd tried to enlighten Rupert. It didn't help that he was so nervous he kept stuttering and falling over his words. When he had finished, Judith looked at him for a few seconds. "I don't suppose, while you were floating around in this other world, you discovered the meaning to this production, did you?"

"I'm afraid not."

"Is this going to happen again?"

"I don't know." Judith was silent. "Look, if you want me to resign, I will. I understand that me messing up is the last thing any of you need at the moment. You need an actor you can rely on and be an asset to the show and to the company. It's not a big role; I'm sure Wesley can find someone to replace me fairly quickly, if you can bear to work with me until then."

"But Dr Bradman, you are an asset to the company. You're considerate and unselfish, qualities actors aren't best known for possessing. If I wanted to get rid of someone on the grounds of bad company interaction, Isabelle would already have her P45. But I don't give a toss about relationships off stage; we can downright loathe each other for all I care as long as everyone pulls their weight on stage. Rupert is convinced you won't fuck up again and I am inclined to trust his judgement. I also trust his ability to cover for you if necessary, like he did last night." Judith climbed off the window sill and came to sit beside Adam on the bed. "BUT, and this is a big but, I am going to speak to Wesley about getting a decent understudy for you ASAP, with the proviso that if you freak out again he will play Dr Bradman while you understudy. I'm sorry, but it's a tough business."

"It's perfectly fair," said Adam. "I'm sorry I'm letting the rest of you down; maybe I should never have come back into the business."

"That would be a waste; I happen to consider you a good actor. If you weren't, believe me, you'd be out. But replacing you would be a loss for the show."

Adam tried to stammer out his thanks for this huge compliment, but Judith cut him off. "Now fuck off and leave me to concentrate."

Adam was halfway through the receiving room when Judith called after him. "What happened to you was twenty five years ago; it doesn't mean it's going to happen again."

"Right."

"Make sure it doesn't." Judith settled back on the window sill and lit another cigarette.

Adam scrambled down to his dressing room, half elated by Judith's compliments and half wary of his possible demotion to understudy. He almost collided with Scarlett and Holly who were climbing up to their room.

"Hey, Adam," said Scarlett. "Have you seen Alexander?"

"No."

"He's got his head completely covered in bandages; he looks like the invisible man."

"Only, sadly, he's not invisible," said Rupert coming up behind them.

"Do you think he's really hurt?" Holly asked.

"No," Rupert replied. "If he was he'd be lying in hospital playing for sympathy with all the male nurses. That vase was made for breaking; it's not dangerous."

"What a shame," said Scarlett.

"Why, Scarlett," said Rupert. "I thought you were an Alexander Columbus fan. I seem to recall you extolling his virtues."

Scarlett looked embarrassed. "I guess I didn't know as much as I thought I did."

"It's a wise actress who knows that; you must be growing up," said Rupert.

"I am grown up – well past the age of consent!"

Rupert laughed. "You're going to leave a string of rampant actors in your wake, little Miss Scarlett. See you girls later. Are you coming, Adam?" He and Adam walked off down their corridor leaving a disappointed Scarlett.

"Damn, I was enjoying that; I think Rupert was flirting with me, don't you, Holl?"

"I don't know, yes, maybe."

"I'm going to have to make a pass at him soon if he doesn't make one first or I'll go crazy. He's so gorgeous."

"You wouldn't, would you?"

"What, have a fling with him? Of course I would."

"No, I mean make the first move; what if he turned you down?"

Scarlett, who hadn't even considered that concept, laughed. "Dear Holly, you're such a romantic. You'd only be happy with a knight in shining armour sending you bouquets of flowers, taking you to expensive restaurants and not touching you until after your wedding night. Someone like Rupert isn't going to turn down sex with no complications, trust me."

Holly followed Scarlett upstairs, thinking about what she'd said. Was Rupert like that? She hoped he wasn't; it made him less chivalrous. Or did she feel that way because she would be so envious of Scarlett if she did get her fling?

At his dressing room Adam stopped with his hand on the door knob. "Thanks for sticking up for me with Judith, Rupert."

"Ah, you've seen Judith."

"Yes, I was summoned to the inner sanctum when I first arrived. I must have lost about half a stone in nerves. I offered to resign, but she wouldn't let me."

"I'm bloody glad to hear it."

"But I may get demoted to understudy if I mess up again."

"You won't," said Rupert. "Judith likes you."

"I'm not sure she does. I make her nervous."

"She'd hardly give you the time of day if she didn't."

"She says she doesn't care who likes who; it's only what happens on stage that concerns her."

"And you believe that? Come on, I'll run your lines with you before we're called on stage for rehearsals."

"I couldn't ask you to do that."

"You didn't, I offered. Besides, it won't do me any harm either."

Adam smiled; he very much doubted Rupert had ever worried about lines in his life – he was so damned confident.

Wesley was greeted by the bandage-clad Alexander, and had to turn away to stop himself openly laughing. "I didn't realize there was a mummy in *Blithe Spirit*."

"It's not funny," Jasper protested, holding an ice pack in a spot where Alexander's ear might be. "He's been seriously injured; it could've been fatal."

"Yes, of course." Wesley tried to be serious but it was hopeless. He was tired and stressed; if he didn't laugh he would probably cry.

"I hope you don't expect him to rehearse this afternoon," Jasper continued. "He can't even speak properly."

"He managed all right at 2am when he woke me to relate his near death experience," said Wesley.

"It's got worse since then."

Wesley peered through the bandages. "How can you tell?"

Declan emerged from the stage. "Wesley, it's good to see you. How are Henrietta and the baby?"

"They're both doing well, thanks. How are you? You look like you slept even less than I did last night."

"No, I didn't get much," Declan admitted.

"There were a few problems that needed to be sorted."

"Let's go to your office and you can fill me in. Incidentally, why is there a large bomb outside the theatre?"

"Ladies and gentlemen of the *Blithe Spirit* company, this is your call to the stage for this afternoon's rehearsal. Full company to the stage, please. Thank you." Rebecca turned off the tannoy after her announcement and reached for her coffee. It was going to be a long day.

Scarlett, as usual, was the first to arrive on stage. Even last night's fiasco hadn't dampened her enthusiasm. Echo was surprisingly last down, no doubt thanks to having got fully dressed in her Elvira costume and make-up. She'd also put on her wig, but without Tasha to help her it sat askew on top of her own tresses. She looked at the other actors in surprise. "Gee, you guys aren't dressed."

"That's because it's a rehearsal," said Miranda. "Holly, I thought you were supposed to be filling Echo in on theatrical behaviour."

"Sorry," said Holly. "I didn't think about that."

"Why should you?" Rupert said. "You're not telepathic."

Miranda glared at him; she'd give him hell later for showing her up in front of everyone.

"So I don't have to get dressed for rehearsals, even when I'm on stage?" Echo asked. "But I did before."

"Those were technical rehearsals, for God's sake," Miranda replied. "They're completely different."

"Geez, I'm never gonna get it all right."

"No, dear," Judith said, "I think that's highly likely. And please take that wig off – it looks as if you have something nesting on your head."

"Come along, everybody, we need to start rehearsing." Jasper's voice came over the dreaded megaphone. "I've got a list of notes for you."

"Why is our designer, no, I'll rephrase that, the director's boyfriend masquerading as a designer, taking our rehearsals?" Judith asked curtly.

"Alexander is in too much pain to talk, so he's going to whisper to me and I shall relay it."

"I don't think so."

There was a brief muttering from the stalls before Jasper came back on the megaphone. "Alexander is the director and that's what he wants to do."

Judith, with an amazing agility, jumped off the stage, grabbed the megaphone off Jasper, put it to his ear and shouted "I said I DON'T THINK SO!" Jasper clutched his ear in pain. "Is there anyone from stage management around?" Judith called out. Matthew emerged from the wings nervously. "Ah, Matthew, can you disassemble this contraption?"

"Oh, yes, absolutely."

Judith handed it up to him. "Please do so immediately."

"How dare you?" Jasper shouted. "I'm going to hospital to have my hearing checked out; I may be deaf for life."

"Sadly for the theatrical world, such a disability won't stop you from designing."

"Come on, Alexander darling, I think you should get a second opinion on your head wounds." Director and designer stormed from the theatre in unison.

Judith smiled. "Wonderful, two obstacles temporarily removed. Now, can someone give me a hand back onto the stage? I'm far too old for this athletic stuff; I think I might have done my organs some permanent damage. Thank you," she continued, after Rupert and Adam had gone to her rescue. "Right, shall we get on with rehearsals? Unless anyone has any objections, I have a list of scenes we should work on." No one had any objections. "First, I've got a few notes, starting with Act One: Scarlett, make your first entrance at the speed you feel happy with, otherwise you're worrying about velocity and not acting; Miranda and Rupert, you can afford to go faster with your first scene, it's fine already but that will enhance it; Isabelle, can you be more gushing on your arrival thereby making it easier for Dr Bradman to be more embarrassed by you." Isabelle scowled. "I'm aware you hate it, but it is the way the part's written as far as I'm concerned. Dr Bradman, try and actually feel my pulse when I pass out instead of looking as if you're admiring it, however flattering that may be; Miranda, you can get even crosser with Rupert at the end of the Act One …"

"No problem," Miranda said, dryly.

"Rupert, get up faster when you initially hear Elvira's voice; Holly, can you cue Elvira's lines about Ruth a little sooner and say them with more bitterness, so Echo can imitate them, and Echo, could you try and bear more resemblance to a ghost and less to an elephant. Whenever you approach Rupert you literally stomp across the stage. I'm sure half the audience would also like to stampede across the stage to reach him, but this is a drawing room comedy and not an orgy."

"What about you?" Echo asked. "You haven't gotten yourself any notes."

Isabelle looked happy for the first time; this could be fun. But she was disappointed. Judith threw her head back and laughed.

"That, Echo dear, is because I am like Mary Poppins: practically perfect in every way. Now, shall we get on with rehearsing? We have a show tonight and with Alexander stuck in A&E there will be no one to make apologizing speeches to the audience for any fuck ups – thank God."

CHAPTER THIRTY

The applause which greeted that evening's performance was extremely responsive, with many of the audience even standing up to cheer.

"Why were they standing?" Echo asked as they came off stage.

"It's called a standing ovation," said Scarlett, who, having dreamt her entire life of receiving one, was on cloud nine.

"Either that or they were leaving to get their last trains," Judith said. "This play is far too slow; we need to speed it up. Everyone must pick up their cues faster, and Declan, can we cut down the intervals?"

"The theatre won't like that; they make a lot of money from drinks and it takes a while to serve a full house."

"Get them to hire more bar staff. Two twenty-minute intervals is absurdly long; the audience will have forgotten the plot. We must reduce them to fifteen, tops. Has anyone else got anything they need to discuss tonight or shall we wait until Monday?"

The consensus was to wait until Monday. Everyone was exhausted; Sunday, their one day off, had never seemed so precious.

"Can I remind you all there are interviews

for everyone at 1pm on Monday?" said Declan.

"I don't do interviews," said Judith. "And it's hardly like we need the publicity."

"I'll do it," Miranda said quickly.

"OK. I believe the idea was to do individual ones," said Declan. "And then a group photo."

"Forget it," Judith said. "Echo isn't doing an interview on her own. Scarlett and she can do it together. You know, the 'two youngsters starting out' angle."

Scarlett looked a little disappointed; her first interview and she had to share it with Echo. However, disobeying Judith was not an option.

"Why can't I do it on my own?" Echo asked. "I can talk properly."

"It's not that you can't talk, dear, sadly, but what you say. Good night all, make sure you rest over the weekend. See you on Monday."

The cast was out of the theatre within half an hour; Judith, Rupert and Miranda were held up at the stage door by members of the audience asking for their autographs. Judith scribbled her name as fast as possible and leapt into her taxi. Rupert and Miranda spent longer, dedicating each autograph to the person asking.

"It must be wonderful working with such a director as Alexander Columbus," a pretty young girl said, waving her programme under Rupert's nose.

"It's unquestionably an experience I'll never forget," said Rupert.

"Well, you were wonderful."

"Thank you very much."

"You were flirting with that girl," Miranda accused him as they got into their taxi.

"I was being polite Miranda; there is a difference."

No one had plans for the following day except to sleep, eat something that wasn't sandwiches, and sleep again. Even Echo refused to go jogging with Storm in the afternoon. "But we always go," Storm protested. "You'll get fat if you don't take any exercise."

"Not on carrot sticks I won't," Echo muttered from under the duvet. Rupert had kept his promise and produced a piece of Death by Chocolate cake for her during rehearsals. Having once discovered the pleasures of chocolate, Storm's healthy eating plan was no longer of any interest to Echo.

The interviews on Monday went reasonably well. Judith, as promised, failed to turn up, much to the assembled reporters' disappointment. An interview with Judith Gold was a rare event; ones with Miranda Flynn were two a penny. But there were consolations: Rupert was always charming, and Scarlett and Echo were of interest as fresh faces. Scarlett, as per Judith's instructions, did most of the talking while Echo smiled prettily.

"So, Echo, how do you find acting on stage

as opposed to TV?" asked a female reporter.

"She loves it," said Scarlett quickly. "She was saying the other day how much fun she's having."

"Is it very different, Echo?" the reporter persisted, stressing Echo's name and daring Scarlett to answer the question.

Echo looked at Scarlett. Scarlett nodded at her. "Yes, it's very different."

"How is it different, Echo?"

"I am having fun."

"And you didn't have fun on TV?"

"I am having fun here. And I have friends, don't I, Scarlett?"

"Yes, it's an extremely friendly company; we all get on perfectly."

"Even with Judith Gold? She has the reputation of being difficult."

"Well...." Echo began.

"Judith is wonderful," Scarlett broke in. "She's so professional, and funny and clever; an inspiration to all of us, isn't she, Echo?"

"I am having fun."

Adam kept his distance from the reporters, much relieved that no one seemed interested in him. In theatre circles stories such as his unfortunately stuck around; in the rapidly changing world of newspapers it was instantly forgotten.

Isabelle would also have been largely ignored if it wasn't for the fact she had no intention of allowing that to happen. Overhearing the female reporter flagging in her attempt to dig up gossip on Judith from Scarlett and Echo, Isabelle later cornered her, introducing herself as Judith's great confidante. The woman grew instantly interested and Isabelle acquired a personal fifteen minute interview.

Miranda, having completed her own interviews, noticed Isabelle shaking hands with the reporter as they finished talking. She didn't like the look of that one bit, especially since she recognized the woman as a gossip columnist. God knows what Isabelle had been saying.

Once the reporters had gone and the photographers taken endless shots of the company on stage, smiling, arms round each other, Judith arrived to take the afternoon's rehearsal. "Echo, throw that vase as if you meant it, we all know it can break dramatically even if the set is less wooden than our director's head; Rupert, can you be a bit nastier to Echo over her infidelities and Echo, stop smiling at him, you're supposed to be angry with him at that point; Miranda, when you rush on after your quick change try not to look so flustered, the audience aren't supposed to realize what you've been doing; Dr Bradman, be careful not to carry your doctor's bag as if it was a handbag or there'll be rumours about you and Charles, and Scarlett, the key you sung *Always* in last night was so high-pitched I think the glasses in the bar were in prospect of shattering."

"I'm sorry. I realized I'd started too high, but I didn't think I could stop and start again when I'm supposed to be in a trance."

There was a crash at the back of the auditorium and two figures entered.

"Oh, look," said Judith. "It's Tweedledum and Tweedle-even-dummer."

"I've come to hold the rehearsal," Alexander said, walking towards the stage, his head still swathed in bandages.

"Really? And pray, what did you think about the show on Saturday night? Please feel free to give us your un-humble opinion on the performance – oh wait, you weren't here. How exactly do you intend to give us notes without seeing the show?"

"I intend to work from the beginning and see how we go from there. Scarlett, please make your entrance."

"Your entrance is fine, Scarlett," Judith said. "Let's go from where you announce the Bradmans."

"Scarlett, from the start please."

"Scarlett, please announce the Bradmans."

Scarlett looked back and forth at Judith and Alexander. Her instinct was to obey the director but ... She took a deep breath and went to the door to announce the Bradmans, silently praying this wouldn't be the end to her career.

"How dare you?" Jasper squealed from the stalls. "You wait, you'll be sorry. Come along, Alexander, your genius is obviously not appreciated."

"When you find it we'll try and appreciate

it," Judith called after them. She bowed as the cast and Lucy gave her a round of applause. Isabelle made a mental note of the exact expression Judith had used; it was far too good to get wrong.

"Oh, Lord," Rupert said. "I don't think I can take much more of this hilarity; I'm all laughed out. You made a good choice there, Scarlett."

"She would hardly still be here if she hadn't," said Judith. Scarlett smiled weakly; she wasn't wholly sure that was a joke. "Now, I'd actually like to go from the top of the show, so, Scarlett, could you get your tray? Yes, does anyone have a problem with that?"

"You wanted to go from the top all along?" Miranda asked. Judith inclined her head slightly.

Rupert shook his in admiration. "You're a total and utter minx, Judith Gold."

"Thank you. Yes, Echo dear, you're wearing your confused expression?"

"You didn't want to go from the top of the show and now you do. I don't understand."

"No, dear, it's called irony; I don't believe you have it in America."

"We don't? Oh, I see. Kinda."

Monday night's preview only had two minor hitches. Firstly Adam tripped over one of his lines and although he got straight back on track, the look Judith gave him in the interval would have put terror in the most fearless of men.

The second involved props. When Judith, and later Rupert, came to eat the cucumber sandwiches in Act Two, they discovered their fare had grown to gigantic proportions more suitable to an American deli than an elegant English afternoon tea.

"What the fuck are these?" Judith demanded in the interval, brandishing one of the offending sandwiches.

"Cucumber sandwiches," said Matthew, who had made them. "Is there a problem?"

"They're enormous."

"Oh, yes, see, I thought they were too small before to register from the back of the auditorium."

"Right, and now they're so big I can't get them in my mouth. Contrary to the rumours, I am not an ogress."

"I'm so sorry."

"I'm surrounded by idiots. And you're not helping," she added to Rupert, who was laughing.

"It was such a wonderful sight watching you trying to cram this doorstep into your mouth and endeavouring to talk afterwards, pure joy. I do love live theatre."

"And I suppose you managed it easily?"

"I have a big mouth; ask Miranda."

At the end of the show, Declan, sitting in the company office, received a call from a reporter. After listening for a couple of minutes he told him there was no comment.

"What's the matter?" Wesley was in the

office reading the show report Rebecca wrote every night stating each performance's comments and problems. The way this show was going, the combined show reports were going to be longer that the complete works of Shakespeare.

"We're in big trouble."

"What else is new? Tell me." Declan told him.

There was a knock on the door. It was Fred, panting. "Do you have to have an office in the basement? I'm too old for all these sodding stairs. I've been sent to get the whole company, in whatever state they're in. Judith has heard something on the radio and she's not happy."

"Have you any idea what she heard?" Wesley asked.

"Oh yes, and by the looks on your faces I suspect you have too. I tell you, the shit's really going to hit the fan now and how very messy that's going to be."

As Wesley and Declan reached Judith's room they met the other members of the company, in various states of attire, arriving. "Have you any idea what this is about?" Scarlett asked Declan.

"Possibly," said Declan. "But I'm sure Judith will fill us in."

Rupert, who'd been in the shower, was clad only in a towel, much to Scarlett, Holly and Echo's delight; Miranda was still in her costume having been looking at herself in the mirror since the show came down; Isabelle was in her dressing gown; everyone else was dressed to go home. Lucy, who had been about to leave the theatre and not amused to be stopped, was wearing her coat.

Judith stood at the end of her dressing room facing everyone. "I was listening to an arts programme on the radio; our play was the main topic of conversation."

"Isn't that good? Miranda asked. "Surely that was the point of all the interviews we did. Incidentally, was I mentioned?"

"Not as far as I recall, but since I'm not your agent I don't really care." Miranda pulled viciously at a loose thread on her costume. "No, it was all about Echo."

"Oh gee, that's real nice."

"No, Echo, it is not 'real nice' at all. Not unless you want it broadcast on national radio that you are using an ear-piece."

There was a deathly silence in the room. "Did they actually say she was?" Wesley asked. "Because Declan got a call from a reporter wanting to know if it was true."

"Did he now, and what did you say, Declan?"

"No comment."

"How original, no doubt that'll instantly stop the stories."

"Sorry, it threw me; I wasn't expecting it."

"Who was? Well, perhaps somebody was. According to the radio the information hasn't been substantiated, but had come from an inside source. Would anyone care to own up?"

No one spoke, but there was a general look toward Isabelle. "It wasn't me," she said.

"Indeed," said Judith. "So Louella, our gossip expert, is apparently not responsible for this. So who else could it be? Scarlett, did you let Echo alone with the reporters at any point?"

"No! And the only thing she kept saying was she was having fun."

"Are you, Echo dear? We must put a stop to that. I take it you didn't talk to anyone?"

Echo shook her head vehemently. "Honest! You said I shouldn't and I don't wanna make you mad; you're scary when you're mad."

"Keep thinking that way, dear. OK, Scarlett, since you were with Echo that gives you an alibi too. Dr Bradman?"

"The reporters had no interest in talking to me and the feeling was mutual. I went nowhere near them."

"Rupert and Miranda, since this whole thing was your idea I presume you wouldn't leak it. Wesley and Declan, I can't see you doing it. Fred I trust emphatically."

"And we've all signed confidentiality clauses," Lucy said. "If any of us leaked it we could be sacked and sued, which, quite frankly, would not be worthwhile. Besides, the press rarely bothers to talk with anyone backstage. We're of no interest to them."

"Dear me, it seems no one did it," Judith

said. "Where's Hercule Poirot when you need him? But if he were here, I suspect he'd eliminate each suspect until there was only one left." She glared at Isabelle.

"You're wrong, all of you. How about Holly? Perhaps she doesn't like being a secret voice and decided to spill the beans."

"I'd never do that!" Holly was horrified. "I love this show and wouldn't do anything to harm it."

"Another denial. Isabelle, it seems you're running out of other suspects."

"How come when they deny it you believe them, but when I deny it you don't?"

"I can't imagine."

"There's another thing," said Miranda. "I saw you with one of the reporters from the gossip papers. What were you talking about?"

"The show generally, how it was going and things like that. I wanted to have my own interview – everyone else did." She looked round the sea of angry faces.

"How could you?" Rupert said. "The one time we asked you to keep quiet."

"But I didn't."

"At least the real Louella Parsons had the courage to acknowledge her gossip," said Judith. She got out a bottle of scotch and poured everyone except Isabelle a glass and passed them round. "Are you still here?" she said pointedly as she walked round Isabelle. Isabelle turned round and ran from the room.

Everyone drank their whisky in silence. Holly made a face; she wasn't keen on whisky. Quietly she poured it on a pot plant behind her, hoping she wasn't committing flora murder. Looking up she realized Rupert had noticed; he raised his eyebrows at her and she blushed.

Echo sipped at her drink, choked, and then gave a huge smile. "Wow, this is cool." She took a big swig before Rupert leant over, took her glass and poured it into his. "I think that's enough. The last thing we need is to have Elvira with an ear-piece and a hangover."

Judith was smoking without even bothering to hang out the window; Declan automatically started to say something and thought better of it.

"Look," Wesley said. "We don't know this story is going to go any further."

"Oh, come on, Wesley," Judith blew a large smoke ring. "An actress in a prestigious West End production using an ear-piece? No one is going to let that drop. Damn Alexander. If he hadn't employed an imbecile who can't learn lines in the first place we wouldn't be in this mess."

"Do you mean me?" Echo asked, in rather a small voice.

"No, I mean the fucking Archbishop of Canterbury."

"Oh, right. Can't he learn lines either?"

Judith banged her head against the wall. "Give me strength. Oh, let's get the hell out of here. Perhaps if we all live in Wesley's cloud cuckoo land, this will all have blown over by the morning."

At her flat Isabelle sat bleakly on her sofa. What the hell was she going to do? It was clear she was universally hated by the company; how could she go back to the play knowing that? Yet if she walked out now, citing mental cruelty or harassment, her career would, in all likelihood, never recover. And theatre was her life; she couldn't imagine living without it. On the walls hung framed posters from previous shows, every one signed by her fellow cast. Staring at them, she wondered whether each of them had also hated her.

She opened her own bottle of scotch; sod Judith, who needed her? Damn it – she did. All she'd wanted was to be one of her cronies. What had she done that was so awful? She might be a gossip but she wasn't vicious, was she? Besides, even if she might occasionally have gone too far, she'd always done her job professionally and wasn't that all Judith was interested in? Even in this shitty part with a moronic director and lousy costumes, she'd done her best. Meanwhile Adam, who'd botched his lines on stage, seemed to be Judith's golden boy. No, that wasn't right, the golden boy was Rupert; he could do no wrong. At the thought of Rupert, Isabelle felt a stab of pain as she recalled his angry face.

Rupert virtually never got angry, so why did it have to be with her? Why not that shrew of a wife, or that idiot American girl? It was so unfair. Everything was unfair. She poured herself a second drink, knocked it back and followed it with another. Then she took her empty glass and threw it at one of her theatre posters. Life was bloody unfair.

CHAPTER THIRTY ONE

The following day the ear-piece story had been picked up by several papers and Declan arranged for the actors to be smuggled in through the front of house entrance to avoid the waiting press at stage door.

"I don't suppose you could actually learn your lines, could you, Echo?" Miranda asked. "Then we could truthfully deny it. You've heard them often enough; how hard can it be?"

Echo looked terrified. "No I can't! I don't have to, do I, Rupert?"

"Not if it's impossible; it was only an idea to get us out of a sticky situation."

"Oh, that's very helpful, Rupert."

"Miranda, we can't force her." Privately Rupert considered the notion of Echo struggling with lines, in addition to Adam, one problem too many, even for him.

"Perhaps we could say she was hit over the head and has brain damage," said Miranda. "Then she'd have an excuse."

"I don't wanna be hit over the head."

"You're not going to be, Echo," said Rupert.

"Don't be so certain," Miranda growled. Echo moved away from her warily.

Wesley finally put out a press release stating that there had been a misunderstanding over the way the ear-piece was used. It had been designed to cue Echo to her entrances, something she'd got used to whilst working in television.

"Not bad, Wesley," said Judith. "Though you may go to hell, lying like that."

"Hell could be worse than this?"

Eventually the afternoon's rehearsals started. Alexander was still missing, presumed suffering, so Judith got out her own notes.

"Has anyone seen Isabelle?" Adam asked.

"I thought there was a lack of bitchery in the air," said Judith. "Obviously can't face us. Never mind, we can manage without her at present."

"What if she doesn't come back tonight?"

"She will; she's not stupid enough to risk her career. She's evidently making her point by sulking through rehearsals. Declan, phone her, will you? Tell her to get her arse in here."

"Actually, I have tried, but there's no reply."

"Silly cow! I suppose she'll come in later; I hope you'll give her a proper reprimand." She stopped and looked out into the auditorium. "Declan, who are those people out there?"

"Our understudies: we finally got them contracted today."

"I hope they're quick learners." She looked pointedly at Adam. "Perhaps we should go through your scenes, Dr Bradman, so your understudy can see what happens."

Adam bit his lip.

"Jesus, Judith," Rupert muttered to her. "Why don't you totally destroy him while you're at it?"

"It's not my problem; if he keeps stumbling he has to go, good actor or not." She raised her voice. "OK, let's go from the Bradmans' entrance."

"I don't have a wife," Adam pointed out, again.

"Bugger, I forgot. OK, we'll leave that for a moment and go back to it when she deigns to arrive. Let's work on the final scene. Rebecca, can we have the set ready to be destroyed for the finale? It seemed slow last night. Charles was stuck for ages waiting for his ghost wives to wreak havoc."

"Give me a couple of minutes," Rebecca called out, as Lucy and Matthew prepared the special effects.

Three hours later and there was still no sign of Isabelle. Declan had phoned her constantly to no avail; he'd never had a show where contacting people had been so problematic. He was on his umpteenth attempt at 5pm when Wesley came into his office. "Still no luck?" Declan shook his head. "Damn, what if she doesn't come in tonight? She was pretty upset yesterday."

"I thought I might go to her flat; she can hardly refuse to talk to me if I'm on the doorstep. If necessary, I'll drag her in."

"Good idea, thank you. Get a cab and put it on petty cash. I'll hold the fort here. You never know, she might be on her way."

It took Declan about 45 minutes to reach Isabelle's flat. There was no answer when he rang her bell. He continued to try for five minutes before ringing the bell of the flat upstairs where a woman answered. No, she hadn't seen Isabelle, but she had a key to her flat; she normally watered the plants when Isabelle was on tour. Declan ran up to the woman's flat, collected the key with thanks, and gingerly let himself into Isabelle's, calling out her name. The sitting room was empty, as was the kitchen. "Isabelle." He pushed open the door to her bedroom. "Jesus Christ." Isabelle was lying on the bed, an empty bottle of scotch and an empty bottle of sleeping pills beside her. "Isabelle!" He tried to shake her awake, but there was no reaction; her pulse was faint. Recalling some basic first aid, he placed her in the recovery position, before picking up the phone and calling an ambulance. Waiting for its arrival he kept talking to her: "Come on, Isabelle, don't give up, please don't give up."

Rebecca was calling the half hour when Declan phoned Wesley from the hospital. The cast, aware that Isabelle still hadn't arrived, were on the stage wondering what the hell was going on.

"How can she do this to us?" Judith said.

"Of all the fucking unprofessional behaviour. Well?" she asked, as Wesley got off the phone.

"Isabelle won't be performing tonight."

"I'm going to kill her."

"She might have saved you the trouble, Judith. Isabelle took an overdose; she's in hospital."

There was a horrified silence. "Is she going to be all right?" Scarlett asked, in a whisper.

"I don't know. Declan is going to stay with her and keep us up to date."

"We did this to her," Adam said. "We may have killed her."

"All we did was to tell the truth," Judith said.

"Are we sure we jumped to the right conclusion?" Rupert asked, fully aware of his own curt conduct to Isabelle. "She kept denying it."

"Of course we did," said Miranda. "Who else would have leaked the story?"

"Gee," Echo said. "I don't think that was Isabelle."

"You mean it was you, you little idiot? Who the fuck let Echo talk to the press?" Judith demanded.

"No, it wasn't me," Echo sniffed, backing away from Judith. "Honest, I wouldn't do that, I'm not that stupid."

"You could have fooled me."

"Judith, you're not helping," said Rupert. "Echo, who told the press about your earpiece?"

"You're gonna be mad if I tell you."

"You haven't seen mad yet."

"Judith!" Rupert glared at her. "Echo, we're not going to be mad." Judith snorted. "At least, I'm not going to be mad, but it's vital we know."

Echo took a step closer to Rupert so she was out of Judith's arm range; this took her perilously close to Miranda, so she moved to Rupert's other side to be between him and Adam. "OK. It was Mommy. She got talking to one of them reporters outside the stage door; I think she was feeling a bit left out 'cos she's not allowed in the theatre, and she didn't realize it was a secret 'cos I always used one at home. I expect she thinks we all wear 'em."

"I fucking hope not; if she told the press that, I'm going to shoot myself," said Judith. "That is, after I've shot your mother."

"She didn't mean to get anyone in trouble, honest. Please don't be mad."

"Why the hell didn't you tell us before?" Miranda snapped. "You were there when we were blaming Isabelle."

"I didn't know then. Mommy only said about it last night. I was gonna tell Isabelle when she came in, but she didn't come and I didn't know what to do. I'm real sorry." She was sobbing now. "What if she dies and it's all 'cos of me?"

"It's OK," said Rupert, putting his arm round her. "It's not your fault."

"Of course not." Miranda shot a venomous

look at Rupert. "We can't blame little Miss Innocent."

"Miranda, for once in your life, can you keep your mouth shut?"

"How dare you." Miranda ran at him, her arm raised as if to strike him. Scarlett's mouth fell open and Echo gave a little scream. Rupert quickly removed his arm from Echo and caught Miranda's before it could do any damage, bringing it down by her side; it was hardly as if he hadn't had any experience with this behaviour.

"This domestic scene is all very lovely," Judith broke in, with an unusual display of tact, "but what are we going to do about the show?"

"How can we think about doing one?" Scarlett asked in horror.

"Haven't you heard, dear, the show must go on? Though fuck knows why this one should. Does anyone have a problem with that?"

"It does seem heartless somehow," said Adam.

"Fine, sod the lot of you, see if I care." Judith stalked off.

Wesley went to follow her, but Rupert stopped him. "I'll go." He caught up with her on the stairs.

"What do you want?" she demanded, keeping her back resolutely to him.

"Judith, I understand about your professionalism and I admire it enormously, but you must realize how upset everyone is about Isabelle."

"How the fuck do you think I feel?" she said, turning round to reveal tears in her eyes. "I was the one who turned on her most last night and wouldn't even acknowledge her presence. How guilty does that make me feel? If she dies I'll be responsible."

"No more than any of us; we all presumed she'd done it."

"But I'm the head of this company; I should be setting an example."

Rupert raised one eyebrow. "We should all behave like you?"

Judith smiled faintly. "If you did we'd have a thoroughly professional show, no offence, Rupert. So do you believe we should cancel too?"

"I'm not sure anyone wants to cancel. We're all in shock; no one knows what to do. But no, I don't think we should in principle, though with no understudies I'm not sure we have an alternative."

"We do have understudies," said Judith, thoughtfully, "but since they only started today I don't see Isabelle's being ready in twenty minutes. I suppose she could go on with the script, though that looks unbelievably tacky."

"Besides, she wouldn't know any of the moves; she'd be all over the place, especially in the séance scene. We'd be tripping over each other as if Alexander was still directing!"

"Heaven forbid. Come on, let's go back down." She wiped her eyes briefly. "Do I look normal?"

"Absolutely: no one would ever know you had any emotions."

"Bastard!"

On stage, Scarlett, Holly and Miranda were talking in low voices; Adam sat alone, shell-shocked, while Echo, still in tears, was being plied with tissues by Lucy. All stared at Judith as she sat on the Condomine's worn sofa.

"Look," she said. "I am aware most of you feel I'm being a hard bitch expecting to push on with the show under the circumstances, but I want to share something I was taught when I started in theatre. Out there are people who have chosen to come and see this play for a variety of reasons: a birthday; first date; anniversary; engagement; maybe they have a loved one in hospital like Isabelle and need a temporary release. There might even be someone terminally ill who has come to have a laugh and forget their troubles. Noel wrote this play for people to escape from a God-awful war; don't we owe it to our audience to try and put some escapism in their lives?"

"Wow," said Scarlett, neatly summing up the effect of Judith's speech on the company.

"However, having said that, we have no prepared understudies, so unless we send one on with a script we will have to cancel, won't we, Wesley?"

"It looks like it. I'd better go and make an announcement. Some of the audience are already in their seats; they aren't going to be happy."

"I might be able to do it."

Every pair of eyes turned on Holly. "I watch it every night, so I think I know the moves and I certainly know the lines."

"Go Holly," said Scarlett, impressed her friend was finally selling herself.

"But what about Echo's lines?" Wesley asked.

"Elvira and Mrs Bradman aren't on at the same time, except after the séance scene when Elvira first appears, and then all she does is drift about silently. If I run round straight after I exit I should be back at the microphone in time to feed Echo. It's the same with Mrs Bradman's second scene; as soon as she leaves Elvira enters." She looked at everyone's amazed faces. "I mean, if you think it's a good idea."

"Holly to the rescue again," said Judith. "Wesley, it seems you have been saved from an audience lynching. Dr Bradman, what do you think of your new wife?"

"I think I stole a child bride," said Adam, with a smile. "But otherwise I'm certain she'll be fantastic."

"Holly, go up to wardrobe," said Wesley. "See what Libby can do to make Isabelle's costumes fit in ten minutes. Get Tasha to try and age you a bit with make-up. I'd better ask front of house to hold the curtain as long as possible. God, I wish Declan was here; I'm not made of company manager material."

"I'll deal with it," said Rebecca calmly,

going through the pass door to talk to the front of house manager. The cast dispersed to get ready. Wesley picked up the phone and dialled Declan's mobile, which went to voice mail; no doubt hospital policy demanded it was switched off. He left a message asking for any news and relaying how distraught the company was.

Declan was using the hospital payphone to try and locate some relative or friend of Isabelle's; he'd had the foresight to bring Isabelle's bag to the hospital and was working through her mobile contact list. So far he was drawing a blank. He could locate no relatives, and no one he spoke to seemed interested in Isabelle's plight, or at least not enough to come to the hospital, though several were curious as to her malady. Declan had merely cited stomach problems. The only person who turned up was the upstairs neighbour and Declan got the impression she and Isabelle weren't particularly close. "Can you stay here in case there's any news?" Declan asked her, so he could go outside and use his mobile. He glanced at his watch; the show should be about to go up, if they could have one without Isabelle.

Wesley answered the phone instantly. "Declan, is there any news?"

"Not really. What about you, have you cancelled the show?"

"No."

"But how …"

"Holly's playing Mrs Bradman."

"Good for her. I suppose the show really does have to go on."

"If you'd heard Judith's speech you would have gone on yourself in a wig and frock to produce a magical experience for the audience."

"You can explain that to me later. I can't find any relatives or friends of Isabelle's; the only person to show any interest is a neighbour who I feel is here only because it's the most exciting thing that's happened to her for years. But maybe I could leave her with Isabelle and come back for the rest of the show, if you need me."

"We do need you, but no, if you don't mind, I'd rather you stayed with Isabelle; Rebecca and I can cope. I feel it's the least we can do."

"I agree. I'll phone if there's any news."

"Oh, Declan, there's something else you should be aware of; Echo's mother leaked the story to the press."

"Christ, what a mess. Does everyone know?"

"Oh yes, the air here is rife with guilt."

Ten minutes after the advertised starting time, Wesley walked nervously onto the stage – in spite of his early acting experiences he hated having to make speeches. That would normally be Declan's job. "Ladies and gentlemen, I'm sorry to have kept you waiting so long. Unfortunately, Isabelle Whiteside was rushed to hospital this evening with stomach problems, so, at very short notice, the role of Mrs Bradman will be played by Holly Brooks. Thank you."

There was a smattering of applause as Wesley came into the wings, shaking. Thank God it wasn't Judith or Rupert he'd had to announce were off; he hated it when the audience groaned or booed. "Not bad, but don't give up the day job," said Judith.

"Thanks for the vote of confidence. Be grateful I didn't make a speech like Alexander's."

Judith pointed to the vase which was on stage ready to be broken by Echo later. "Remember I'm a mean hand with a prop; consider yourself warned."

"Standby ladies and gentlemen, the curtain is going up," Rebecca called. Scarlett picked up her tray, gave a wink to Holly and made her entrance.

"Oh God, I think I'm going to be sick," said Holly and rushed to the nearest loo.

CHAPTER THIRTY TWO

Luckily Holly wasn't sick, but she had enough butterflies dancing in her stomach to have their own ball. Adam squeezed her hand as they stood in the wings.

"Here we go," he said, as Scarlett raced across the stage to announce the Bradman's entrance to Charles and Ruth.

"I can't remember the lines. What do I say? I can't do it."

Adam gripped her arm and moved them towards the door onto the stage. "Yes, you can," he muttered, and gave her the first of Mrs Bradman's lines. In her desperation to speak before she forgot it, Holly jumped in too early and spoke over Rupert's line. Rupert, so used to the unexpected on this play, didn't bat an eyelid. But it flustered Holly, who had to stop herself from apologizing. She sat on the sofa as directed and listened to Adam testify how she'd promised to behave. She gave a girlish giggle and declared how excited she was and that her husband had no need to caution her. Being much younger than Isabelle, she came across as naively innocent and the audience responded to it; even in her panicked state Holly felt a rush of pleasure as she received her first laugh.

But that feeling was short-lived when Judith, as Madam Arcati, made her entrance and was introduced to Mrs Bradman. Holly smiled at Judith while supposedly informing the other characters that she and Madame Arcati had met before, in shops. Unfortunately, rather than 'shops', it came out as 'ships'.

"Indeed," said Judith. "You must remind me sometime which ship we last met on."

Rupert, who was supposed to be offering cocktails, had to turn upstage with the drinks shaker so the audience couldn't see him laughing. Poor Holly was gutted. She got through the rest of the scene, but she'd lost her angle on playing the role, so busy was she concentrating on the lines.

At the end of the scene all the actors exited the stage. The women were to go straight back on, once Lucy and Matthew had done the scene change. Adam quickly grabbed Holly. "Don't let it throw you; we all make mistakes and I should know. What you're doing with the role is wonderful, you're a joy to work with, so go and give it your all, OK?"

"OK. Only, what's my next line?" Adam gave it to her.

"Holly," Miranda hissed. "We're on." Holly shot onto the stage, leaving Rupert and Adam to have the magnets attached to their wrists.

"Nice speech," said Rupert.

"Well, you didn't help; you were openly laughing over the ship line!"

"I know, it was an awful thing to do to

the poor girl, and I shall apologize later, but honestly, I couldn't help it. Judith's line was a classic; the idea of Mrs Bradman and Madam Arcati having all these meetings on ships, like a sea-faring WI."

"Perhaps they're undercover agents for the navy," Adam said, setting Rupert off laughing again.

After Adam's brief pep talk, Holly found herself easing back into the role and earning some appreciative laughs. She was an excellent actress, better than Isabelle, even if she was about 20 years too young, and Adam had been truthful when he'd said she was a joy to work with.

As soon as she made her final exit for Act One she dashed over to her stool in the wings and started to give Echo her lines. It had been the oddest sensation to be on stage with Echo even though she wasn't speaking. There was one moment when her eyes involuntarily started to travel towards the supposedly invisible Elvira, checking she was in the correct place, but Adam had given her arm a squeeze and she'd promptly focused on him.

Adam had given her a quick thumbs up sign as they'd finished, Scarlett had been jumping up and down with excitement in the wings and even Judith made the effort to track her down in the interval and tell her she was doing a good job.

"Now, that is the equivalent of winning the Pulitzer prize," said Scarlett as Judith left their dressing room. "I'm not sure I've ever had a compliment from Judith; I think the nearest thing was 'Not bad, Scarlett.' You're honoured."

Holly smiled. What Judith had said was a huge compliment and something she'd never forget. But it was Rupert coming to give her a hug and a kiss as she finished giving Echo her lines at the end of Act One which completely made her day. That and the end of the show where the cast insisted she took a solo bow while the audience gave her a huge cheer. Thankfully her scene in Act Two had gone with no hitches.

As the curtain finally came down and the audience were leaving, Wesley came on stage with a bunch of flowers he'd dashed out to buy in the interval.

"Wow, thank you," Holly said, half in tears. "Thank you all so much, you've been wonderful; it's been an amazing evening." She stopped suddenly, horrified that she'd forgotten. "Apart from Isabelle, that is."

"Go ahead and enjoy your triumph, Holly," said Wesley. "Declan phoned; Isabelle is going to be fine."

"Christ, what a case of *Much Ado About Nothing*," said Judith, stalking off to her dressing room, where Fred was the only one to see her sink down and put her head in her hands with relief.

Isabelle had finally regained consciousness at 9pm that evening, and found Declan sitting beside her in the ward she'd been moved to from A&E.

"Hi, welcome back. How are you feeling?"

"Like shit," she croaked. "So I didn't even manage to kill myself, or is this some kind of hell?"

"Similar, it's an NHS hospital, but you're very much alive, thank God."

"I didn't do it, Declan, I didn't leak the story, I swear it."

"We know; it was Storm."

"Oh."

"There're going to be a lot of grovelling people when you come back, starting with me. We should have listened to you."

Isabelle gave a brief smile. "I guess once you get a reputation in this business it sticks. But why did Storm do it? Surely she didn't want Echo to appear stupid?"

"I don't think she realized it was anything out of the ordinary. I gather Judith nearly had a stroke when Echo announced her mother was probably under the impression you all used them."

"I can imagine her face. What time is it?"

"Nine o'clock."

"At night?" Declan nodded. "My God, the show!" Isabelle struggled to sit up, her head pounding. A feeling of nausea swept over her and she gagged.

Declan passed her a sick bowl and helped her to lie down again. "I don't think you're going anywhere for a while."

"But what about the show? There aren't any understudies."

"Holly is playing Mrs Bradman."

"Oh. I see. So I am totally dispensable."

"We didn't have much choice."

"No. I really screwed up. But I wasn't thinking very clearly; I'm not used to total animosity." Declan looked at the floor uncomfortably. "I'm sure they're thrilled to have Holly instead of me." She looked at the tube going into her. "What's this for?"

"They've been monitoring you and pumping you with liquid to clear out your system."

"It'll take more than a bit of liquid to do that," Isabelle said, wryly, "after twenty years of rep and touring, living on midnight takeaways and spending hours in pub lock-ins. My system is probably 50% alcohol and 50% chicken korma."

Declan smiled at her. "I'm more of a prawn curry man myself. Are you OK if I go outside and use my mobile to call Wesley and tell him you're all right? Everyone will be incredibly relieved."

Isabelle nodded and Declan left. She doubted anyone cared if she lived or not. Of course, she could hardly blame them. She'd made the worst blunder you could in theatre, regardless of the circumstances, and failed to turn up for a show when there was no cover – only evidently there had been. Still, Judith was hardly going to bother with her now. Any small fantasy of her and Judith sharing a table and chat at the Ivy was shattered. She felt a lump in her already sore threat. Panic seized her. Dear God, her throat, what about her throat? Frenziedly she pushed the call button beside her. After a few seconds a cheerful Irish nurse appeared. "Good evening, Isabelle, good to see you back with us."

"Nurse, this isn't going to affect my voice, is it? I'm an actress; my voice is my life."

"That's a line you don't hear often." Isabelle reddened; it did sound rather melodramatic. "But no, you'll be fine; it's only a tube they put down your throat to clear your airways. The doctor will be round in the morning to see you, as will one of our therapists to have a chat."

"You mean a therapist as in a psychiatrist? I'm not crazy."

"It's standard policy in attempted suicide cases."

"It wasn't suicide, it was ..." Isabelle tried to remember the expression she'd used while playing the solicitor of an attempted suicide victim in some awful play in Torquay. "I know: a cry for help."

"There you go then; you cried, we help."

Declan was on the phone to Wesley when he saw Isabelle staggering out of the hospital towards him. "Hang on, Wesley. Isabelle, what the hell are you doing?"

"Leaving. They want me to see a shrink."

"Wesley, I've got to go, Isabelle is trying to go AWOL." Eventually, with much persuasion, Declan got an exhausted Isabelle back into her hospital bed where she fell asleep almost immediately.

"I'm sorry, I didn't see her leave; we're so busy tonight," the nurse said.

"How long will she need to stay in for?"

"The doctor can tell you that tomorrow morning. But it'll be at least 24 hours so we can monitor her. Does she have anyone at home to look after her?"

Declan thought of his attempts to track down friends and relatives and shook his head.

"You should go and get some rest yourself and come back tomorrow; she'll probably sleep until then."

Having discovered an approximate time for the doctor's visit in the morning so he could be there, Declan left Isabelle to sleep. He considered heading back to the theatre, but when he'd phoned Wesley everyone was having a drink in Judith's room to celebrate Holly's performance and he wasn't in the mood for that. Much as he was delighted for Holly, he couldn't help but think of Isabelle lying forlornly in her hospital bed.

"When's Isabelle going to be back?" Wesley asked.

"I'm not sure; I'll talk to the doctor in the morning. I wouldn't think for at least two or three days." He could hear Wesley relaying the message. "I think I'm going to go home now, if that's OK. I want to be back in the morning to see the doctor."

"Of course, thanks for dealing with everything. I'll talk to you tomorrow."

"Do you think she'll want to come back?" Adam asked, as Wesley hung up.

"Of course she will, what else does she have to live for?" Judith retorted.

"Isn't that rather the point, under the circumstances?"

"Dr Bradman, stop being so practical. She's made her point; now she'll come back here as a total martyr and dine out on the story of how badly we treated her for years to come. Oh joy."

"Judith, you are such a cynic," Wesley sighed. "I'm going to head off; I'm shattered."

"You're shattered? You haven't had to give your life blood on stage tonight like we actors have," Judith said. "As a result you can all piss off out of my dressing room so I can go home – except you, Dr Bradman." The room emptied in seconds.

"They could use Judith to call time in pubs," Rupert said to Miranda as they walked downstairs. "One look from her and people would be throwing back their drinks and running for the exits in record time."

"You'd know more about that sort of thing than I would, darling." Miranda preferred the elegance of wine bars to pubs. "But I don't think there'll be any last orders at our place tonight! I could drink an entire bottle of anything strong."

"I'm with you there, darling. I hope Judith

isn't going to gripe at Adam too much; he did really well tonight."

"Oh, for God's sake, Rupert, he's a grown man. I don't know what's got into you over him – people are going to start talking."

"He's a friend; remember them, darling? I expect you had some once upon a time, before you considered them all competition."

"Drop dead."

"I love you too."

In Judith's dressing room Adam was fingering the pot plant, which seemed to be thriving on the scotch Holly had poured into it last night.

"Dr Bradman, you did a good job with young Holly tonight; feeding her lines, calming her down, giving rousing speeches." Adam looked at her surprised. "Yes, amazing though it seems, I am aware of people other than myself. If you can do it for Holly, you can certainly do it for yourself. So I want no more fluffing or nerves from you. This is not a request or a suggestion; it's an order. Do you understand?" Adam nodded mutely. "It's all in your head, so clear it out of there or I'll do it myself with something a lot heavier than that stage vase."

"Yes, Ma'am," Adam said, with a salute.

Judith laughed. "Look at you taking the piss, when a month ago you couldn't even meet my gaze. I'll tell you something else; you were a different person on stage tonight."

"Yes, I felt different, the way I did 30 years ago."

"It's about bloody time. Now, go home and have a rest, we need to do some rehearsing with Holly tomorrow."

"But she was good, wasn't she?"

"Under the circumstances she was brilliant, but she had no rehearsal; there are things we need to work on."

Adam was halfway back to his dressing room when Judith's voice came down the stairs. "Welcome back to the acting profession ... Adam."

CHAPTER THIRTY THREE

"Honey, I didn't know it was wrong," Storm said that night, taken aback by Echo's coldness. "I dunno what's so bad; it's hard to learn all them lines, why should anyone bother if they can have an ear-piece?"

"Because they do, Mommy, it's what normal actors do. I'm not normal; I'm a freak. If I wasn't then none of this would've happened and Isabelle wouldn't have taken them pills. I may not be smart but I do know that. I know you didn't think what you said was wrong, but why did you talk to them reporters? I told you I wasn't allowed to 'cos I'm too dumb, so what makes you think you're any better?"

"Honey, I don't like the way you're verbalizing. Nor your behaviour. It's like you're not my little girl no more. It's them people, the actors and stage managers, they're making you go rotten. I don't wanna do this no more; we should go home."

"Like, quit the show?"

"Yeah."

"Mommy, what are you talking about? I can't quit. I'd be letting everyone down. Besides I wanna do it. I may not be too good, but I'm working real hard and I love it."

"Echo, I'm your mother and I wanna go

back to the States. Maybe we could get you onto TV again or a big Hollywood movie."

"Mommy, no."

"Echo honey, how can you argue with me? I'm your mother; I only do what's best for you. Please go to bed now. You've upset me. I'm gonna call the airlines for a flight real soon, so start packing."

Echo silently walked to her room, waited for her mother to go to sleep, then crept out to the phone and rang a number from the *Blithe Spirit* contact sheet.

"Yes," came Miranda's sleepy voice.

"Gee, did I wake you?"

"Why would you wake me, it's only 3am."

"I'm real sorry, but I had to wait for Mommy to go to sleep and she took ages."

"How fascinating. And did you phone me entirely to illuminate me as to your mother's sleeping patterns?"

"Huh?"

"What do you want?"

"Please can I talk to Rupert?"

"Can't it wait until tomorrow?"

"No, it's real important."

Miranda prodded Rupert hard in the side; she didn't see why he shouldn't suffer. "It's your girlfriend, darling."

"Who?"

"Your great sexual conquest: little Miss America."

Rupert rolled over and took the phone from Miranda.

"Hello? What? Echo, calm down a minute, I can't understand you." He listened for a few more minutes. "Echo, you are a grown up woman; your mother cannot force you to do anything you don't want. She certainly can't drag you onto a plane back to the States; that's kidnapping. No, I know you're not a kid, but it's still called kidnapping even if you're 103. No, I know you're not 103 either. Just say no; you can do it. Look, if you're not there for rehearsals tomorrow I'll call the police, I promise. Now go to sleep and don't worry."

"What was that about?" Miranda asked. "Wanting to arrange another love tryst?"

"Miranda, I wish you'd let that drop. You did agree to the idea if you recall."

"Not one of my better decisions. So what was it then?"

"Storm wants Echo to leave the show and go back to America. She thinks we're a bad influence on her precious daughter. Echo was in a state because she doesn't want to do that; I was endeavouring to tell her she was old enough not to have to follow Mommy's rules."

"You'd better not tell Judith; if she thought there was a chance we could get rid of Echo that easily she'd be down at Heathrow buying her and Storm plane tickets."

Echo hardly slept at all. Going against her mother was a whole new experience. Choosing her own underwear had been one thing; refusing to pack and get on a plane was another. Finally, she got up at 6am, sneaked out of the flat and wandered round London for hours, getting utterly lost; Storm, as a rule, wouldn't allow her out alone. In her wanderings, she found a wonderful underwear shop and spent all the cash Storm allowed her on several pairs of sexy knickers. She eventually arrived at the theatre five minutes late for rehearsals, which produced a vile look from Judith and raised eyebrows from Rupert.

"I was wondering if I should be alerting the airports," he muttered to her.

"Oh, no, you don't have to, I'm here."

"Yes, I noticed. So you managed to stand up for yourself?"

"Kinda. I got up real early and left while Mommy was still asleep."

"That would explain the ten or so messages the stage door keeper, Wesley and Declan have all been receiving from her, demanding to know where you were."

Echo looked horrified. "Oh gee, what am I gonna do?"

"We'll sort something out."

Echo's day did not improve. That evening, as she wafted through the French windows to make her first entrance, her dress got caught on a nail Jasper had stuck there, intending, but forgetting, to hang something on it, and no amount of gentle plucking would release it. Having learnt at least enough to realize she would be unable to play the entire scene from the French windows (apart from anything else she didn't want to miss her favourite bit of stroking Rupert's hair), she grabbed the dress in both hands and gave it an almighty yank. The dress tore with a loud ripping sound, leaving half the lower part still on the nail in the door. The audience gave her a huge round of applause and gasps of appreciation as a pair of silk white lacy knickers were revealed.

"Somebody from wardrobe to the stage immediately please, a member of wardrobe to the stage. Thank you," Rebecca said into the tannoy.

Libby, Cassie and Fred, who, having nothing much to do in Act One, had been sitting in the wardrobe chatting, arrived breathlessly together. Rebecca pointed out Echo who was continuing the scene, knickers on view.

"I can't mend that," Libby whispered, "it's shredded. She'll have to have a new one. But bring it upstairs in the interval, Cassie, and I'll try and cobble it together for the rest of the show."

"But can ghosts have their clothes fixed?" Fred asked. "I mean, they're dead, aren't they; do they have some ghostly tailors in the other world waiting to repair things?"

"And ghosts are likely to walk around showing their underpants?"

"Thank God she was wearing some," Cassie whispered. "I've dressed people who don't."

"That's more information than I needed, Cassie darling."

"Don't get all prudish with me, Freda."

"It's amazing that they had La Perla knickers in the 1930s."

"How do you know they're La Perla?" Cassie asked. "On second thoughts, don't tell me, I don't want to know! At least they're sexy; can you imagine if she was wearing up to the waist granny knickers which had gone grey in the wash?"

Holly, having made her exit, shot past them on her way to feed Echo her lines. Adam, who came off with her, was spluttering with laughter. "Oh, that was so hard; I mean, I'm not supposed to be able to see Elvira, but it's not easy to keep your eyes off someone who's wandering around half naked. I don't know how Rupert and Miranda are keeping it together."

"I'm not sure they are," said Cassie, looking at Rupert who was openly grinning every time he caught sight of Echo. Miranda, to whom Elvira was supposed to be invisible, was faring slightly better, but not a lot. And the audience, fully aware this was not part of the direction, were helpless with laughter.

Miranda exited and joined Adam at the side of the stage to watch Rupert and Echo's scene together.

"Bloody Rupert, he's so obviously laughing," Miranda complained. "It's lucky Judith isn't watching; she'd do her nut."

"Actually, I think she is." Adam pointed to the other side of the stage where Judith stood, arms folded, watching with her face twitching in amusement. "I don't think Rupert can do much wrong in her eyes."

"Hmph."

Libby managed to temporarily stitch the dress together, with the aid of a quantity of Wonderweb. However, as Fred had predicted, ghosts having their frocks mended was a novelty, with the result the audience screamed with laughter as Echo reappeared and gave her a round of applause. Echo was so thrown by this she gave a little curtsy and got torn off a strip by Miranda in the second interval.

"I'm sorry, but all them people clapping when they don't normally, I did it without thinking."

"What else is new? God, why didn't Rupert tell you to get on that sodding plane with your mother?"

Echo's face fell. "But I didn't wanna go. I like it here."

"How flattering, but if you ever do that again I'll set Judith on you."

"I won't, I promise." Echo scuttled upstairs.

Storm had spent the entire day attempting to contact her daughter. But Echo wasn't answering her mobile, the stage door had orders not to let her in, and once Declan had confirmed Echo was safely in the theatre, he too refused to take her calls. He did, however, inform her that if she tried to take Echo out of the show Wesley would sue her for breach of contract. Miserably, Storm stood outside the theatre until the end of the show. When Echo eventually came out she was accompanied by Scarlett and Holly and announced her intention of staying the night at their flat. This had, in fact, been Rupert's idea after seeing how stressed Echo was, and fully aware that Scarlett would do anything for him.

"But, Echo honey, you've never spent a night away from me before."

"Well, it's 'bout time I did," said Echo, having been coached by Rupert. "I am a grown up person and I can do what I like. I am staying with this play and if you don't wish to join me, then you can return to America." Echo finished her prepared speech proudly; who said she couldn't learn lines? Then she added as an afterthought, "If you go back to the States I can move in with Scarlett and Holly."

Scarlett and Holly exchanged horrified glances; an odd night was one thing – having Echo as a permanent flatmate was quite another. Luckily for them, Storm had no intention of releasing her hold on Echo. "OK honey, maybe I did act kinda hasty. I guess you should stay do the show, only please come home with me now."

Echo gulped; she wasn't used to winning against her mother, but she was getting used to knowing what she wanted. "Maybe tomorrow, Mommy. Tonight I'm gonna stay with my friends and watch TV and do each other's hair and make-up and eat chocolate and popcorn, and ..." Echo thought back to all those TV shows she'd dreamt of being in where girls had sleepovers, and tried to remember what they did. "And things."

"Oh, I see. OK, honey, if that's really what you want. Only, will you two girls make sure Echo goes to bed early? She needs her beauty sleep."

"Mommy, I shall go to bed when I'm ready." Echo nervously waited for Storm's chastisement and was amazed when it didn't come. Still, there was no point in pushing her luck, so she linked arms with a rather surprised Holly and Scarlett, like the publicity stills she'd envied from *Friends,* and set off down the street.

"Echo honey, remember chocolate is bad for your skin," Storm's voice reverberated behind them.

"Can we find a store which has the biggest chocolate bar ever?" Echo asked. "And I'm gonna eat the whole thing and not floss after."

CHAPTER THIRTY FOUR

Isabelle rejoined the company three days later, only two days before the official first-night when the critics were invited. She looked fairly awful: pale and gaunt. But, contrary to Judith's predictions, she didn't behave like a martyr, merely politely accepted the company's apologies and got on with her role. Much to her surprise she'd thoroughly enjoyed her session with the hospital psychiatrist; the woman had invited her to talk about herself for as long as she wanted, something Isabelle had never found a problem with. Whether the psychiatrist learnt that much about Isabelle was questionable, but she certainly experienced a crash course in theatre gossip.

Holly, who after the initial terror had thoroughly enjoyed her five shows as Mrs Bradman, found it horribly flat to return to relaying someone else's performance. This feeling was accentuated when, on the night Isabelle returned, a party was held for the cast by a banking firm who had invested in the show. The event was to start with drinks in the front of house bar, and then continue with a meal in the private room at the Ivy. It was a cast-only invite, which pissed off the wardrobe, wigs and stage management departments, especially Lucy who hated to miss out on free social events. "They'd get a pretty lousy show if we weren't there keeping it together," she complained. "But no one ever thinks about backstage people; we aren't important."

"I don't mind," said Matthew. "I wouldn't know what to say."

"You don't have to speak to them, just enjoy the free food and drink. Honestly, Matthew, you have a lot to learn about theatre."

The cast-only invite also did not include Holly.

"I expect it's only an oversight," said Scarlett when she received her own personal invitation. "You should turn up anyway; I'm sure no one would mind."

"No," said Holly. "They want to hobnob with the cast; they wouldn't know who I was. Anyway, I'm not very good at these social gatherings like you are; I'll go home and get an early night."

"Are you sure?"

"Totally."

Once she knew the cast had gone to the bar, and everyone else had left the theatre, Holly crept down to the stage and sat on it, arms round her knees, staring out into the auditorium. She could almost imagine the ghosts of former actors around her; this theatre had so much history and in her own tiny way she had been a part of that. If she closed her eyes she could hear applause from hundreds of audiences throughout the years; theatre was the most amazing thing in the whole world and she was incredibly lucky to be in it. She must never forget that.

"Reliving your former glory?" said a voice from the darkness at the back of the stalls.

"Rupert! You made me jump; I thought you were at the bankers' party."

"I was, but I'm making a bid for freedom. It's awful in there: loads of men in suits talking about PEPS and off-shore banking, without a single decent girl to flirt with. I can't take it any longer; I have to break out." He started dashing through rows of seats in mock desperation. Reaching an emergency exit he grappled with the chains and padlock before throwing himself to the ground and pretending to have convulsions. Holly giggled. Rupert looked up at her from his prone position. "I don't suppose you happen to have an escape tunnel on your person, do you?"

Holly shook her head. "Sorry, I'm right out. But I heard a rumour Alexander was starting one – to get into the theatre."

Rupert grinned at her and got to his feet. "What's your excuse for party skipping?"

"I wasn't invited. I'm not a member of the cast any more."

"That's ridiculous, of course you are; I'll go and sort that out right away." He turned back towards the bar.

"No, please don't, I'm not actually bothered,

especially if they're as boring as you say. I'm much happier sitting here daydreaming."

Rupert walked down the aisle until he reached the front of the stage, climbed onto it and sat beside her. "It's a pretty special theatre, isn't it?"

"It's beautiful. I feel so privileged to have acted here, even if it is only for five shows."

"You're a good actress, Holly; you'll be back here again, perhaps as the star."

"No, that'll be Scarlett; she's the beautiful, successful one. At drama school she was always the student who got the leading roles and won the awards."

"You have more talent."

"You're just saying that to make me feel better."

"No, I'm not, and for your information Judith thinks exactly the same. As for Adam, since you've been acting opposite him he's a changed man."

"Really? Gosh, thanks."

"Look, do you want a lift home? I brought the car in today; it's in the car park round the corner."

"But you live miles from me."

"I enjoy driving at night; it's peaceful and empty. Come on."

"But how will Miranda get home?"

"She'll get a cab, or the way some of those bankers are fawning over her she'll probably get a lift in someone's limo."

"Are you sure you don't want to go back? I

mean, there's the meal at the Ivy too."

"I'm perfectly sure; I hate that kind of thing. Miranda, on the other hand, loves it as, by the look of it, do Scarlett and Echo. I saw several men literally drooling over our American ghost; they'll be shocked when they realize she comes complete with Mommy. And Isabelle isn't doing badly for someone who was at death's door a few days ago; when I left she was filling in some grey haired old guy on theatre etiquette. Adam, on the other hand, keeps looking around as if hoping for an emergency escape chute!"

"What about Judith?"

"Good God, she wouldn't be seen dead at a thing like this. By now she's probably in bed sticking pins in an Alexander voodoo doll."

"Wasn't it compulsory though, as part of the investment deal? Put money in the show and you can socialize with the cast."

"And who do you think is brave enough to force Judith? Unlike the rest of us, Judith doesn't believe publicity and promotion are part of her job; she considers she's an actress, and she acts, end of story." He took Holly's arm. "Let's get out of here before they discover we've done a runner; I've shown my face, that's enough. My wife, your flatmate and our ex-beauty queen will be happy for hours, believe me."

Holly wandered down the street while Rupert signed autographs for people who'd been devotedly waiting for him since the curtain came down. He caught up with her as she reached the car park. "Wow," said Holly, as Rupert pushed the button to release the alarm on a two-seater green sports Jaguar. "What a beautiful car."

"Thank you."

"Is it old? Sorry, that sounds slightly insulting."

"I think the word is classic, but yes, she's a 1958 model." He ran a hand over her lovingly before opening the door for Holly. She slid in feeling like Grace Kelly in *High Society* or *To Catch a Thief.* She longed for someone she knew to see her as Rupert pulled out of the car park and headed to North London.

"Shall I put the roof down, Holly, or will you be too cold?"

"Oh no, not at all, I'd love it."

The wind whipped through her hair as they drove out of the West End; now she knew why Grace Kelly wore headscarves in the movies.

Rupert, glancing sideways, reflected how adorable she looked with her hair flying everywhere and her eyes shining; he'd felt the same way as he'd stood at the back of the auditorium earlier watching her sitting on stage. She had an appealing quality that enchanted him.

Holly directed him to an area he'd never been to before, and wasn't keen on revisiting.

"I'm sorry, it's not terribly nice round here," Holly apologized, "but it's cheap. That's our place over there. Above the kebab shop."

Rupert drew up outside. "There you are, madam, door to door service."

"Thank you so much. Um, I don't suppose you'd want to, I mean, I'm sure you'd rather get back to Miranda, or go to bed." Rupert raised his eyebrows questioningly. "That is, your bed." Oh God, this was not going well. Still, she'd started so she'd better finish. "But since you've come all this way, could I give you a, um, coffee?"

"A um coffee would be lovely." Rupert closed up the roof and put the car alarm back on.

"We'll be able to hear if anyone touches it," Holly said. "You can hear everything from our front room, including orders for shish kebabs and chips."

Holly led the way along the peeling corridor and up the worn stair carpet to the flat. The place was a mess; why hadn't she tidied up before they'd left that morning? Rupert watched her, smiling, as she gathered together piles of clothes, shoes, make-up and magazines and threw them into a cupboard. "I'll go and make your coffee." She disappeared into the kitchen and came back a few seconds later holding a piece of paper. "I'm so sorry; I got you up here on false pretences." She held out the piece of paper on which was scrawled: To buy: coffee, milk, sugar, bread, cereal, fruit, biscuits. "We haven't been very organized with rehearsals and everything. I can't even give you normal tea since we haven't any milk. I think we have herbal though; would you like one of those?"

"No thanks, I've never been one for drinking nettles and dandelions – it makes me feel like a slug or a rabbit."

Rupert picked up one of Scarlett's publicity photos from the coffee table and sat down on the armchair. "Nice pictures, where are yours?"

"In my cupboard, I don't get much use for them."

"Can I see?"

Holly disappeared off to her bedroom, glad to get a chance to check herself in the mirror: good grief, what a sight. She ran a brush through her hair, put on a bit of make-up and then wiped it off again in case it looked too obvious. Rupert was asking to look at her photos, not for her to model for him. She dug into her cupboard and brought out a half empty box of 10 X 8 publicity photos and the contact sheet of all the pictures the photographer had taken. She'd sent out over a hundred already to varying casting directors and agents with no results. A few bothered to answer in the negative; most she never heard from, even though she always included a stamped addressed envelope. Acting was a depressing business, and an expensive one. She took the contact sheet and a 10 X 8 out to where Rupert was flipping through a copy of *Nicholas Nickleby* which was lying on the table.

"Is this yours?" he asked. "I can't quite picture Scarlett reading anything more than *Vogue*."

Holly felt she ought to defend her friend, even if Rupert was correct. "Scarlett's very smart you know."

"Being smart has nothing to do with it; it's a matter of personality. Miranda once tried to read *Anna Karenina* because she thought it would improve her persona and after one chapter gave up because the names were too complicated! She is also a great fan of *Vogue*. So I take it this is yours?"

"Yes," she sat down on the sofa. "I love Charles Dickens; I know that sounds rather pretentious, but ..."

"It's not in the least pretentious, he writes brilliantly. I used to read them between tennis matches; there's so much hanging around you wouldn't believe it. A match you consider is going to be a three setter suddenly turns into a five setter and you have another hour or two to kill. I think I've read every one of his novels but *Bleak House*. I always got stuck over the wards in chancery stuff."

"But once you get through the first few chapters it gets much easier and there are such wonderful characters in it, almost as good as *Nicholas Nickleby*, though that's my favourite. Apart from anything else Nicholas is so heroic; the way he protects poor Smike and his own sister, Kate, is wonderful."

"You're rather a romantic, aren't you, young Holly?"

Holly blushed and handed over the photos. Rupert looked at them. "Not bad, but, to be honest, they're not really you. You're trying to look sexy like Scarlett."

"And I'm not?"

"You're very sexy, but in a completely different way. Scarlett is going for the vamp look, which is the kind of roles she's ideal for; personally, I think she's too glamorous to be playing Edith. You're sexy in a sweet, innocent way; the way that would make men long to hold you and cherish you – and then rip all your clothes off. You should have photos which reflect that. And take your eyes; they're huge and wistful but you hardly notice them in these photos. Look, I'll show you."

He got up, moved over to the sofa and sat down next to Holly who immediately jumped up again. "How clever, a seesaw sofa, one down one up," Rupert said laughing.

"I, er, just realized I never got you anything to drink; I'm sure we have wine, oh, no, you're driving, um, fruit juice or water, though we don't have any bottled stuff or ..."

Rupert took her hand and gently drew her down beside him. "To be honest, sweetheart, I'm not actually thirsty." He ran his hand down her face, stopping at her eyes. "You see these are amazing, especially at the moment when they appear to be open twice as wide as usual." He continued down her face until he reached her lips which he started to kiss softly. Holly couldn't believe this was happening to her. Her heart was beating so fast she wondered if she was about to have a heart attack; it would certainly be a hell of a way to go. But things like this happened to Scarlett, not to her. Perhaps it was a dream; she used her old childhood trick of pinching herself.

"It's definitely not a dream," Rupert said, smiling.

"Are you sure you're really a man?" Holly said, embarrassed. "You notice everything."

"A slur on my manhood; I shall just have to prove myself." Rupert lifted her up, took her into her bedroom and laid her on the bed. Carefully, he removed the old teddy and fluffy rabbit which lived on her pillow and placed them on the dressing table, facing the wall. "I prefer not to have an audience," he said. Deftly he began to remove her clothes. Holly struggled up.

"Wait," she said.

"What's wrong; do you want me to stop?"

"No! I mean, not really, only, you're so experienced and I'm not ..."

"You aren't ...?"

"Oh God, no. But I've only ever had one boyfriend, so I might be a disappointment to you."

"On the contrary, it merely means I have less to live up to. Now come here you gorgeous, sexy, talented creature."

When Scarlett arrived home two hours later, she found Holly sitting on the sofa wrapped up in her duvet with the biggest smile on her face.

"Hi Holl, I thought you'd be asleep by now."

"I wasn't tired," said Holly, happily. Rupert had been the most amazing lover, at least in her limited experience. Both considerate and funny, he'd relaxed her completely and yet touched her in places and ways she hadn't known existed. As a result, when he'd entered her she'd cried out with pure pleasure.

"That should wake them up in the kebab shop: one orgasm, to take away," Rupert had muttered, buried in Holly's breasts. "Oh, God, you have such a beautiful body."

"I do?" Holly had tried to look but all she could see was Rupert's back and bottom, which was of far more interest.

After a while Rupert had regretfully rolled out of bed, had a quick shower and replaced his clothes. Holly had lain on the bed watching him. Rupert had leant over and kissed her.

"Goodbye, little Holly, thank you for a wonderful evening. I'm sorry I have to love you and leave you, but you understand, don't you?"

Holly had nodded; she understood all too well. Rupert was married, she was a one night stand, but she didn't regret it for a minute. This was a night she'd treasure forever.

"So, what do you think?" Scarlett's voice cut in.

"What?"

"The banker I've been telling you about, who wants to take me out. Have you been listening?"

"I'm sorry, I was miles away."

"Honestly, concentrate, this is important. I was trying to tell you he's got a single friend so we could double date."

"No thanks, Scarlett, I'm not interested."

"Oh come on, Holl, you could do with having some sex."

"I'm fine on that front, believe me." Holly snuggled closer into the duvet, which smelt wonderfully of Rupert, and smiled.

Rupert opened his front door to be greeted by a pair of stilettos being thrown at him.

"Miranda, what the hell are you doing?" Damn, he hadn't counted on her being back yet.

"Where have you been?"

"I've been to the pub if you must know. I didn't think you'd be back for hours."

"Obviously. While the mouse is out the cat will play."

"Isn't that the other way round?"

"Don't be pedantic. You've been screwing someone, haven't you?"

"Don't be ridiculous. I told you; I've been to the pub."

"No you haven't; you smell clean as if you've just got out of the shower, which of course you would have if trying to cover up a sexual encounter."

"I always have a shower after the show, as you're fully aware."

"That was hours ago; if you'd been in a pub

you'd smell of smoke and beer. Don't try and fool me, Rupert, I know you too well. So who was it? Couldn't you resist little Miss Beauty Queen, or that tart, Scarlett?"

"In case you didn't notice they were both with you when I left the party; the whole cast was apart from Judith – are you accusing me of sleeping with her?"

"Nothing would surprise me; I've ascertained over the years of our marriage that you'd sleep with anything in a skirt. Judith might be a challenge."

Rupert walked past Miranda. "I've had enough of this fantasy; I'm going to bed."

"Don't you dare ignore me," Miranda shrieked, throwing herself at him. Rupert grabbed her and carried her kicking and screaming to the sofa.

"Stop it, Miranda, you're working yourself up into a total state over nothing."

"Come off it, Rupert, you can't fool me."

"Maybe, for once, you're wrong."

Miranda stopped fighting for a minute. She would never win in a physical fight; Rupert was far too strong, one of the things she normally found so attractive about him. "Yes, perhaps you're right."

Rupert released her arms. "Thank you."

Miranda quietly reached behind her, picked up a candlestick and smashed it down on the side of his head. "But I don't think so."

CHAPTER THIRTY FIVE

Rupert woke up in the spare room the following morning with a killer headache. He groaned, got out of bed and looked at himself in the mirror. Luckily, the candlestick hadn't drawn blood. He'd half anticipated Miranda's move last night and started to bring his hand up to protect his face. Still, he had acquired a reddish purple bruise on his cheek and above his left eye, giving the impression he was wearing dark red eye shadow.

Bloody Miranda! Not that he was blame free. What the hell had possessed him to play around so close to home? It wasn't fair to Miranda, or to Holly. He'd have to apologize to the girl later, though it wouldn't be easy; Miranda would be watching him like a hawk for the next few days trying to figure out the truth. He couldn't even blame it on being drunk; he'd been stone cold sober. It was pure temptation, which, as Oscar Wilde so adeptly put it, was something he'd never been able to resist. And Holly was so tempting. He could hear Miranda stamping around in the kitchen. That was alarming in itself; normally she never surfaced until he'd brought her tea. Sighing, he set off to try to make amends – atonement apart he wanted to borrow her make-up to cover his bruise.

"Forget it," was Miranda's reply as she slammed a cup of coffee down on the table so hard the liquid jumped out.

"Do you want everyone to know you hit me?" Rupert demanded.

"Why shouldn't I? And I can tell them why; I might even see a guilty face among them. If it wasn't Echo or Scarlett maybe it was Lucy. I've seen her looking at you; I'm sure she wouldn't say no, plus she wasn't at the party last night."

"You can look all you like, Miranda, but you won't find anyone because there wasn't anyone. And do you really want our sex life brought up in front of the entire company?"

"I don't care." Miranda shoved some bread in the toaster and turned up the dial.

"You'll burn it if you put it on that high."

"Piss off. I know how to cook toast in my own home, thank you."

Rupert shrugged, went to have a shower and take several Neurofen. A few minutes later he heard Miranda swearing and the smell of burnt toast wafted in to him.

"Christ, what happened to you?" Judith demanded, as Rupert came onto the stage that afternoon for rehearsals.

"Miranda hit me," Rupert said flippantly so everyone laughed: a perfect double bluff.

"Fine, don't tell us," Judith snapped. "At least it won't be out of place with this ridiculous war time theme; no doubt Charles got hit with a piece of flying shrapnel. It'll add authenticity to your scar."

Holly looked at him from the side of the stage, her heart beating. Rupert steadfastly ignored her and she felt a surge of disappointment. Honestly, what had she expected, that he rush straight over to declare undying love? He probably wasn't even aware of her being there.

Holly was wrong; Rupert was extremely aware of her and feeling utterly heartless in his lack of acknowledgement, but with Miranda glaring at him it was the safest option.

"Rupert, are you with us?" Judith asked.

"Yes, sorry." The cast and stage management, with the exception of Miranda, looked at him in amazement; Rupert not concentrating was a first.

"The blow to your head hasn't affected your brain too, has it?" Judith asked. "The last thing we need on this play is yet another brain-dead individual."

Rupert grinned. "No, I think I'm still compos mentis."

"What's compost mentis?" Echo asked.

"Something you'll never be," Judith said. "And it's 'compos' not 'compost', you imbecile, it's Latin – though actually in your case compost is more appropriate."

Echo sighed; however hard she tried she was never going to learn enough. She must remember not to ask Judith questions; she should wait and ask Rupert or Holly later.

"OK," Judith continued, "let's get on. The performance last night was good; we're finally getting in shape and I'm no longer having nightmares about the impending critics. Talking of which, since we open the day after tomorrow, I think we should freeze the show, after a couple of improvements I want to put in tonight."

This was too much for Echo's new resolve. "We're gonna do it in a freezer?" she asked in horror.

There was a silence as everyone waited for Judith to explode, but instead she leant forward and said very seriously, "Yes, Echo, we're going to get a big walk-in freezer and take the audience in there with us, but we can't do it until tomorrow as we have to warn them to bring warm clothes. It's a theatrical tradition that we have to do one performance like that; if we don't we'll all come to a horrible and painful end."

"Honest?" Echo looked appalled.

"Yes, honest. So you might want to bring a thick coat in tomorrow to put over your frock, maybe even a scarf and a woolly hat – I'm sure you'd look very cute. Moving on: the changes I want to put in involve the scene with Charles and Ruth and Edith over breakfast at the top of Act Two. After that I want to work on the end of Act Three. So Rupert, Miranda, Scarlett can you take your places? Rebecca, are you set up ready to go?"

"One minute," Rebecca called out, cuing

in the correct sound and lighting state for the start of Act Two. Lucy and Matthew were setting up the breakfast table.

Adam looked at Holly. "Do you think we should enlighten Echo before she's in John Lewis tomorrow morning checking out fridge-freezers?"

"Do you think Judith will mind?"

"I doubt it. Where did Echo go?"

"She left the stage; she's probably gone up to her dressing room, trying to work out which coat she should wear for the big freeze."

"More stairs," said Adam as they climbed up. "I'm getting too old for this job; if I worked in an office they'd have lifts."

"And office hours and office politics and the office Christmas party," said Holly, thinking of her temping experiences. "Be very glad you're not."

"All right, Miss Pollyanna, I'm very glad that I'm here climbing stairs for a living and not working in an office," Adam smiled. "But I'm still relieved I'm on the floor below you girls." He knocked on Echo's door and they went in. Echo was sitting at her dressing table looking worried.

"Do you think my coat should be white tomorrow so it looks ghostly?" she asked. "'Cos I don't have one, only pale pink."

"Echo," Holly said. "Judith was teasing you; we aren't really going to do a show in a freezer."

"But she said about freezing the play."

"That means you don't put in any more changes," Adam explained. "Normally, a show is frozen at least one night before the official opening so no one has to worry about any new bits."

"So we won't die horrible deaths if we don't do it in a freezer?"

"No." Adam smiled.

"Aw shucks, I'm never gonna learn all the stuff you guys know."

"Oh, Echo, you're having to pick up things incredibly quickly, that's all," Holly said kindly. "I spent three years at drama school learning what you're trying to pick up in a month."

"And I've been acting for thirty years," Adam added. "Well, on and off, and I'm still learning."

"But Judith knows everything."

Adam smiled. "Judith certainly thinks she knows everything, but for God's sake don't tell her I said that. And you're right, she does know a lot, but then she's been in this business for longer than any of the rest of us. You could learn a lot merely by watching her."

"But she's playing Madam Arcati and I'm playing Elvira; ain't it gonna look weird if I copy her?"

"No, don't copy her for God's sake; just watch the way she captures the audience or the presence she has by only walking on the stage."

"OK," Echo said doubtfully and then beamed. "I'm real glad about the freezer thing though."

Cheering Echo up helped Holly to take her mind off Rupert slightly, who seemingly continued to ignore her. He was, in fact, attempting to work out a time when he could talk to her privately. He'd intended to steal out between the afternoon's rehearsals and the evening show under the guise of getting food, but Miranda had insisted on coming with him and proceeded to complain the entire time that she was tired.

There was only one point Rupert could think of to see Holly secretly: while Miranda was on stage playing a scene with Judith. Echo wasn't on stage either so Holly wouldn't be busy. It wasn't a long scene and during it he had a costume change, but if he did the change swiftly he would have a few minutes.

Cassie, having done Miranda's quick change in the wings, was somewhat taken aback, on her way to help with Rupert's, to discover him already changed and dashing over to prompt corner. Honestly, actors, she thought, picking his discarded costume off the floor. Rupert must've been in a hurry to do something; he was normally careful with his clothes.

"Holly?" Rupert crouched down beside her stool in her dark corner of the wings.

"Rupert!" Her face lit up.

"Look, I wanted to apologize for last night."

"Oh, please don't! It was wonderful, one of the best nights of my life, honestly."

"Thank you, I'm very flattered, but all the same I shouldn't have done it. It was reckless and thoughtless, though completely and utterly delightful. I'm sorry I've been outwardly ignoring you today and now doing this clock and dagger stuff, but I daren't have Miranda see us together. She's already highly suspicious, and if she realizes it was you I was with last night, she'd make your life hell. I don't want you to go through that, it's no fun, believe me."

"She knows you, um ...?"

"Had sex with someone?" Rupert smiled. "She suspects, although I totally denied it. Unfortunately, she was there when I got home last night."

"But Scarlett didn't get home for hours. Didn't Miranda stay at the party?"

"From what I could gather, through the verbal tirade I received, the men were paying more attention to Scarlett and Echo; Miranda doesn't like to play second fiddle, so she left in a sulk."

"How awful, that must have given you such a shock." A horrible thought occurred to her. "Oh my God, so she did give you that black eye?"

"I'm afraid so."

"How dreadful, it's all my fault."

"Stop that at once, Holly," Rupert said, almost crossly. "You did nothing. The fault was entirely mine."

"But if I hadn't accepted a lift home ..."

"Holly, I don't give up that easily, believe me. I've wanted you since you first arrived on my doorstep announcing you were there to be an ear-piece!"

Holly blushed, at a loss of what to say. "Is your eye sore?"

"Surprisingly no. It's more a case of looking worse than it is. Typical actor: anything for effect. I had far worse bruises being hit by tennis balls or rackets from angry players. But the cause of this one is between you and me, OK?"

"Of course, I'd never say a word about any of this to anyone, I promise."

"You're one in a million, Holly, do you know that?"

"I don't think I am; it's only that I wouldn't want to hurt you."

He ran his hand gently down her cheek. "What about you?"

"I'll get over it."

Rupert bent over and gave her a kiss. "God, you're lovely, Holly; you deserve a lot better than me. Damn, I've got to go, that line sounds familiarly like my cue." Rupert dashed off to make his entrance.

"But I don't want a lot better than you," Holly muttered to his departing back. At that moment she didn't feel she'd ever get over it. She took a deep breath, switched on the microphone and prepared to feed Echo for the next scene.

By now the lines were starting to sound vaguely familiar to Echo, so she was slightly surprised to hear something she didn't recognize, but who was she to argue?

"Standby for Act Two, Scene Three; Miss Whiteside and Mr Lane this is your call please; dressers standby for Miss Flynn and Mr Blake's quick changes. LX cue 52 standby. Thank you." she announced clearly.

Rupert and Miranda, on stage with her in mid-discussion as to Madam Arcati's visit to Ruth, stopped dead in their tracks.

"Fuck," Holly muttered. She gave Echo Elvira's line again, but to no avail.

"LX cue 52 go," Echo said, puzzled. This definitely didn't sound right.

Holly, realizing the calls were coming from Rebecca, who was too busy with cues to be aware of the problem, dropped her microphone and dashed over.

"Rebecca stop!"

"What?" Rebecca asked.

"What?" Echo repeated dutifully.

Holly pulled Rebecca's hand off the call switch. "Echo is picking up your calls not my lines."

Rebecca looked at her briefly and then onto the stage where Rupert and Miranda were frantically ad-libbing a row between Charles and Ruth, while Echo stood fiddling with her ear, hoping the correct lines would return.

"OK," she said calmly. "Matthew, fetch someone from the electrics department; I can't use the tannoy to call them if Echo is picking it up." Matthew sped off, colliding with Declan who had come running up from his office.

"What the fuck is going on?" Judith demanded. She had reached her dressing room for a break before her next entrance, heard total gibberish from Echo and immediately returned to the stage.

"We seem to have a technical problem," Declan said.

"Fuck!"

Rebecca and the electrician were bent over the sound system.

"We'll have to bring the curtain down; Miranda and Rupert can't go on like this indefinitely," Declan said.

"Wait," said Holly. "Listen to Rupert."

"It seems, Ruth dearest," Rupert was continuing to ad-lib, "that Elvira has decided to sulk today and is refusing to speak. I am aware, since you can neither see nor hear her, that such behaviour makes little difference to you. However, she informed me earlier that …" and he proceeded to paraphrase the entire scene.

This explanation gave Miranda, as Ruth, the motive for her angry tirade and stormy exit. Rupert remained on stage with a silent Echo.

"Elvira, there's nothing else to say in your present mood," Rupert improvised, thereby cutting a page of duologue. "I'm going after

Ruth and there's not a thing you can do about it. Why don't you play the gramophone while I'm gone?" He stressed the word 'gramophone' in the hope Echo would remember that piece of business without Holly to tell her. Luckily, it involved no dialogue. Echo beamed; this she could remember. She put the record on the gramophone and placed the needle on it; the music started. Scarlett, as Edith, entered, removed the needle and then screamed and fled as the invisible Elvira switched it back on.

"Bring the curtain down," Declan said to Rebecca. "We'll have to have an interval at the end of this scene; it won't look odd." Rebecca nodded.

"Echo has been broadcasting LX cues to the audience," Miranda pointed out. "Nothing will seem odd to them after that."

"Lucy," Declan continued. "Go round front of house and warn them they're about to have an extra interval." Lucy ran through the pass door to inform the astonished bar staff there was going to be an unexpected mass exodus.

The entire company, all by now in the wings, stood in stunned silence as the curtain came down. Then Rupert staggered back onto the stage and collapsed in a heap on the sofa, while everyone congratulated him.

"If I'd wanted to perform a one man show I'd have gone to the Edinburgh Festival," he complained with a grin.

"Excuse me," Miranda said acidly, "I suppose I did nothing."

"It was only a joke."

"It's not funny."

"I'm sorry, you were fantastic, darling," Rupert said. "It's amazing how realistic our improvised argument scene was."

Miranda scowled at him.

"It was brilliant," Holly said without thinking.

"Thank you," said Rupert with a brief nod in her direction. Holly silently cursed herself and hoped Miranda hadn't noticed her comment. But it seemed Miranda was too busy chastising Rupert.

"Now, is Echo going to be able to speak for the next scene or are we going to perform the rest of the play in mime?" Judith enquired.

"Hopefully, we should be able to sort it out," Declan said, with a lot more confidence than he felt. Neither the electrician nor Rebecca were sound experts and they could hardly hold the play up while they brought one in.

"Shall I have a look?" Matthew asked quietly.

"Why? Do you know what's wrong?" Judith asked.

Matthew gulped. "I ... I might. My uncle is a sound engineer. I used to help him set up sound systems for pop gigs when I was a teenager."

"Rebecca, move," Judith said. "Let the boy wonder have a shot."

Matthew huddled over the system; everyone else moved away a little to give him some space.

"Every day I assume things can't get any worse and yet, staggeringly, they do," Judith said. "Apparently, rumours that this play is cursed are spot on."

"There's a curse?" asked Isabelle.

"Oh look, Louella has woken up. Yes, supposedly there's one because the play deals with conjuring up the dead. The threat refers especially to the role of Madam Arcati since she's the Medium. I believe Margaret Rutherford, who created the part, was so close to a nervous breakdown she had a doctor in the wings; more recently another actress developed a tumour, then her replacement walked out with exhaustion. So if you hear about a body floating in the Thames tomorrow morning, it may well be mine."

"Don't even think about it," Rupert said. "Or we'll be holding a séance to return you for the first-night. You're not escaping that easily; if we've got to suffer so have you. But, if you knew about this curse, why choose to play the role?"

Judith gave Rupert a wicked look. "I like to live dangerously."

Rupert laughed. "Any curse that tried to cross you would probably come to a very nasty end."

Matthew came over, nervously. "Oh, God," said Judith. "Don't tell me you couldn't fix it?"

"Oh yes, I've fixed it, I was just worried about interrupting your conversation."

"For fuck's sake, I'm not that frightening, am I?" She glared at Rupert. "Don't answer that! So what was the problem?"

"Somehow the frequencies got switched over."

"Was it something I did?" Holly asked, anxiously.

"No, it's something that happens occasionally. You're lucky it was only theatre calls you were getting; I've known microphones pick up police radios, taxi bookings or even flight control towers."

"Oh, marvellous," Judith said. "So at any time we could have Elvira requesting a pick up from Hampstead, taking a 999 call or trying to land a jumbo jet."

"It's pretty rare," said Matthew.

"Pretty rare? Oh, that's all right then," said Judith with a beaming smile, then at the top of her lungs yelled, "NOT!"

"Judith," Declan said. "The audience is only the other side of the curtain, you know, and it's not soundproofed."

"And I should care because?"

"Because you do," Declan said.

"Sadly, you're right, Declan. But consider this: Echo could be responsible for landing aeroplanes. Don't you think our audience should be made aware of this? Some of them may be flying off on holiday tomorrow. They've already sat through a disastrous show tonight; surely they don't deserve to suffer any more?"

"I don't understand," Echo sensibly whispered to Holly. "I don't know nothing 'bout aeroplanes."

"I'll explain later," Holly whispered back.

"Are we going to have the normal interval as well as this one?" Rebecca asked.

"We can't," Judith said. "This next scene is so short, the audience will literally have sat down and they'll be up again. It'll be like having yo-yos out there."

"Can we do without the interval though?" Declan tried to work it out. "If we only have a curtain drop and leave the lights off in the auditorium, we can do the changes to the set quickly. What about you, Rupert? You have a costume change."

Rupert shrugged. "I can do it fairly fast if Cassie's in the wings with the costume."

"No problem," said Cassie.

"What about you, Rebecca, are all your cues set up to run straight through?"

"It shouldn't be a problem; I'll talk to LX now to ensure they don't bring up the house lights."

Declan nodded. "Fine, I'll tell front of house."

"Excuse me," Miranda said, "but I have a complete costume change into a ghost, and I have to do my make-up to look ethereal."

"But you don't come on until the end of the scene," Rupert said.

"That's hardly the point, it's still a time consuming change and I'm used to having an interval to do it in."

"Perhaps tonight you could get unused to it."

Miranda glared at him, wishing she had another candlestick to hand.

"It would be helpful," Declan said.

"Fine, but don't blame me if I look like crap," she snapped and then turned to Echo. "It's entirely your fault anyway; you're nothing but trouble." Echo backed away fearfully. "I'm going to perform my earlier change now when I'm not going to be pressured. Cassie, can you help me please, if of course Rupert can spare you?"

"I'd watch out tonight, Rupert," Judith muttered to him as Miranda marched off. "I'd say you stood a strong chance of receiving another black eye."

She and Rupert looked at each other for a second before Rupert gave her a brief nod of assent. "I should've known better than try to fool you, Gold. And I'm touched by your concern for my welfare."

"Fuck your welfare! I just don't want to act with someone who bears a strong resemblance to a panda."

CHAPTER THIRTY SIX

At the end of the show Rupert, exhausted after rewriting a large chunk of Act Two as he went, was surprised to find Echo outside his dressing room.

"Can I come in?"

Rupert sighed, thinking of Miranda. "It might be better if we stayed out here."

"Oh, OK."

"What can I do for you?"

"I wanna learn my lines."

"What?"

"I've been nothing but trouble 'cos I can't learn my lines. If I learnt them I'd stop being the dumb one and be like you guys. Would you help me?" Rupert tried to hide his smile; it would take a lot more than learning lines to make Echo like the rest of them.

"Echo, we open in two days, don't you think you've left it a little late? Maybe after we open you could have a try."

"But I wanna do it now; I think I kinda know them. See, when I got them funny lines tonight I knew they were bad."

"But you still said them. If you'd been really confident you'd have said the correct ones and ignored your ear-piece."

"Oh, gee, I guess so." Echo's eyes filled with

tears. "I'm always gonna be dumb, aren't I?"

To hell with Miranda, Rupert thought, and put one arm round Echo's waist, tilting her face up to his with his free hand. "You're not dumb, you've just got a lot to learn. But the most important thing is how hard you're trying and that you care about the play. You do, don't you?"

Echo nodded. "I've never done nothing better, even when I was Miss Teen America and my photo was in all the papers, and I had a crown. I wanna act in theatre forever, only maybe without Judith and Mir ..." She stopped. "Gee, I mean without Judith."

Rupert laughed. "Don't worry, Echo, I'm not in the least offended if you aren't fond of my wife; between you and me there are occasions when I'm not either. But as far as your lines go: stick with the ear-piece until after we've opened tomorrow and then go ahead and memorise them if you can. I'll happily help you, though I think the best person to ask would be Holly."

"You're so swell, Rupert." Echo threw both arms round him and was ecstatic as she felt Rupert return the hug. Adam came out of his dressing room and turned away embarrassed.

"Go and get out of your costume, Echo," Rupert said, releasing her. "Poor Cassie is probably waiting to collect your laundry before she can go home. And don't worry about the lines thing, OK?"

Echo sniffed and regretfully headed upstairs to her dressing room. It'd felt so good to be held like that.

"Rupert, I know it's none of my business," Adam said, gesturing towards Rupert's black eye. "But you didn't ... you know ... with Echo, did you?"

"You're suggesting Echo socked me?"

"No, that Miranda did because you slept with Echo."

"Why, Adam, what kind of an actor do you think I am?"

"One I'd happily swap with."

"Why?"

"You have complete confidence, you're a wonderful actor, Judith adores you, you have girls falling over themselves and you can play tennis!"

"Oh yes, the tennis thing is so useful in this business; how many plays do you know which involve a match on stage? But if we're playing admiration games: you are also an excellent actor, your confidence is growing daily, I imagine girls would throw themselves at you if you'd give them the chance instead of sticking your head in the sand and I'd say Judith was growing fond of you too. So that leaves one thing I have that you don't and that's Miranda, who, at present, I would gladly loan you."

"Christ, no, she scares the life out of me!"

Rupert laughed. "Her bark, as they say, is worse than her bite."

Adam looked dubiously at Rupert's eye. "Indeed. So don't tell me, she barked and you walked into a door and got that shiner."

"Absolutely, you wouldn't believe how vicious the doors in our house are." Adam looked at him cynically. Rupert sighed, so much for his earlier double bluff: Holly, Judith and now Adam. All he needed was for Isabelle to guess.

"Look, Miranda and I have always had a pretty volatile relationship, sometimes I win and sometimes she does. This time I was too slow off the mark. But no, I swear I did not sleep with Echo. As far as I'm aware she's untouched by human hand – well almost. Are you interested?"

"Rupert, she's younger than my daughters!"

"There's nothing wrong with that, as long as she's not your daughter of course; that would be perverted. I, on the other hand, am not related to your stunning-looking daughters in any way."

"Don't even think about it, or I'll blacken your other eye."

Rupert went into his dressing room laughing.

Miranda stared at herself in her dressing room mirror; she could swear there were at least two more lines under her eyes than yesterday. It was Rupert's fault for getting her in a state, resulting in a lousy night's sleep. She'd kept him under surveillance all day and got nowhere. It was conceivable he hadn't been unfaithful, but improbable. Theoretically it might not be a member of the company; what if he had gone to the pub, as he'd stated, and picked up some tart there? Very unlikely, it wasn't his style. If she'd any sense she'd have left him years ago; she didn't know exactly how many times he'd cheated on her, but doubted it was in single figures. But there was a major obstacle to following the divorce path: she loved him. Or, to be precise, she lusted for him; she wasn't convinced she did love him that deeply any more. But she'd never met a man, and she'd had a fair few before her marriage, who had the same effect on her as Rupert. In one deft movement he could have her squirming in ecstasy, and the advantage of their constant rows was the most amazing make-up sex – apart from last night. No amount of lust could make Miranda have any immediate contact with her husband if she suspected he'd slept with another woman.

Maybe she should get herself a lover; that would teach Rupert. Be escorted by some successful and gorgeous playboy, though watching the bankers drooling over the youthful Echo and Scarlett last night made her realize it might not be as easy as it once was. It was so unfair; men were often considered sexier as they got older, while the reverse applied to women. In addition, actors could go on getting great roles until they died, whereas actresses found the opposite; once you'd stopped being the pretty young ingénue or the sexy vamp, roles dried up.

Occasionally, when she looked at Scarlett she hated her because she was reminded of the young Miranda: pretty, sexy and ambitious, with a whole career of wonderful roles ahead of her, whereas this Miranda could look forward to playing batty old ladies on TV murder shows. Miranda gave her auburn hair a tweak: well, maybe she wasn't ready for geriatric grey-haired roles yet, but she was unlikely to be cast as a twenty something year old again, at least not without a lot of soft focus camerawork.

Of course Kathleen Turner had been older than Miranda when she starred in *The Graduate* in London, where queues formed round the block to watch her naked. Perhaps she should ask Mike to find her a play with nudity and have men ogling at her through opera glasses; that might make Rupert jealous. No, the trouble was it wouldn't; he wasn't like that. He'd simply laugh and say, "Make sure you have a thick dressing gown in the wings, those old theatres are draughty." It was a no win situation with Rupert; he was too easy going, nothing got to him, or if it did, he'd laugh it off within an hour.

Bastard!

Scarlett, unaware of Miranda's resentment of

her, was getting ready to go out on a date with the rich banker she'd picked up last night. "I wish you'd come too, Holl," Scarlett said, breathing in to do up the skin tight cerise dress she'd bought before rehearsals that morning. "His friend is dying to meet you."

"No thanks. I appreciate it, honestly, but I'm not interested." Holly was looking forward to having the flat to herself to reflect on the previous evening's events. Besides, what man could possibly be of interest to her after Rupert?

"Suit yourself. Do I look OK?"

"You look stunning. Where are you going?"

"The Ivy. That's why I want to look so good: my first meal at the Ivy as a West End actress with a date who can afford to pay."

"You managed to get a table? I thought there was a three month waiting list unless you were famous."

"I used Judith's name."

"Won't they be surprised when you turn up and Judith doesn't?"

"I shall inform them that I'm her co-star to whom she gave her table since she was too exhausted to use it. I'm sure they won't mind."

No, they probably wouldn't, Holly thought. Scarlett would flash them a smile and doubtless get a table next to Jerry Hall and Mick Jagger. If she tried that trick she'd almost certainly be escorted out by the doorman and barred forever from the premises.

Scarlett teetered down the stairs in her high heels to meet her date. Holly stayed in the dressing room listening to people leaving. After about 15 minutes she figured the coast was clear and returned to the stage. She picked up the sling Rupert wore in the second act, and his prop cigarette lighter, and, holding them closely, sat on the set, reliving the moment when he'd joined her last night.

"Oh dear, so it's you, is it?" Judith was standing in the wings, arms crossed.

Holly jumped to her feet. "I'm sorry, I thought everyone had gone."

"I stayed behind; I do occasionally. I enjoy being on stage when it's deserted."

"Me too," said Holly. "I sort of imagine the ghosts of people who've acted here in the past."

"Some of us aren't dead."

"Oh, God, I'm sorry. You've acted here before?"

"Several times, it's one of my favourite theatres."

"I can see why, it's beautiful. I love looking out there, daydreaming." Holly gestured into the auditorium. "That sounds corny, doesn't it?"

"Yes, but you're young; you'll soon become cynical like the rest of us." Judith smiled and then gestured at the cigarette lighter and sling in Holly's hand. "Are you now being an ASM and checking the props as well as being voice-over person, unofficial understudy and

435

general all round good egg?"

"No, I was only …"

"He's a lovely man, Holly, but a heart breaker. Be careful he doesn't break yours."

Holly went bright red. "I don't know what you mean."

"Holly, I have a huge respect for you, you're a smart girl, so please don't treat me as if I'm an idiot."

"I'm sorry, but really …"

"Your loyalty is laudable, and believe me I have no interest in details, but Rupert didn't get that black eye for no reason. I presume Miranda isn't aware you are the guilty party, though God knows why not; she's been behaving like Sherlock Holmes all day. I'm surprised she didn't make you girls take a lie detector test."

"I think Miranda only suspects Echo and Scarlett and maybe Lucy. I'm not sure she's aware I exist, or if I do that I could possibly be of interest to Rupert."

"More fool her; I can see precisely why you would appeal to Rupert. And to be honest, if he's going to screw around with anyone I'm glad it's you and not your tarty little friend or that moronic beauty queen."

"Thank you." Holly found a tear was rolling down her cheek.

"For fuck's sake don't get weepy on me – I don't do counselling, it's not part of my contract."

Holly took a big breath, and managed to stop

the tears. "Of course I'm not weepy; I mean, nothing happened to be weepy about, did it?"

"Good girl. Discretion is the greater part of valour and all that crap. All we'd need to finish us off completely would be if Miranda and Rupert broke up, or Miranda walked out of the play. Now, I'm going to head home, I'll see you tomorrow."

"Judith, could I ask you something?"

"Go ahead."

"Why do Rupert and Miranda stay together? They seem so incompatible."

"Fuck knows. Goodnight."

A mile away, in his 1958 Jaguar, Rupert drove Miranda home in silence.

Unknown to Judith and Holly, they were not the last to leave the theatre. Isabelle was sitting in her dressing room also intending to be the last there, or hopefully the second to last. To pass the time, she was entering the day's events in her laptop diary. Speculating over Rupert's black eye, she stopped to reflect on her therapist's suggestion that she should consider an alternative method of expression to gossip. Perhaps she should take that advice. No one had been anything but kind since her return, but she was fully aware it was through guilt not friendship. No point in risking further hostility. She highlighted all mention of eyes and hit delete.

Isabelle had continued to see the hospital

therapist privately, and thoroughly enjoyed her sessions, sometimes not drawing breath for the entire hour. She'd even invited the woman to the first-night as her guest, but the therapist had declined on professional grounds. So Isabelle was dateless for the biggest theatre occasion of the year. She certainly wasn't asking any of her so called acquaintances since not one had bothered to visit her in hospital. You could tell who your true friends were in a crisis and apparently she had none.

Declan was sitting in his office, going over Rebecca's show report. Christ, he hoped that sound problem wouldn't recur; he was going to call the system's experts in tomorrow to double check, though Matthew had been brilliant. There was a knock on the door. "Come in," he called, surprised. He'd been under the impression everyone else had gone ages ago. Isabelle stuck her head round the door. "Hello Isabelle, is something wrong?"

"Poor Declan, do people only ever come to see you when there's a problem?"

"As a rule, yes."

"Well, I've come to offer to buy you a drink; I feel it's the least I can do after what you've done for me."

Declan's heart sank. All he wanted was to go home, have a good sleep and try to anticipate any problems which might crop up tomorrow. But Isabelle looked so vulnerable and lonely that he opted for a compromise. "I tell you what, I've got a bottle of scotch in my desk; let's have a glass of it here."

"OK."

Declan poured them each a small amount into a tumbler. "So how are you doing? Settling back in?"

"Yes, it's a bit odd; I don't feel quite the same as I did before."

"That's understandable. But the company are being OK with you?"

"Absolutely, I think they feel like they're walking on egg shells and that any moment I might take a suicide leap from the flies onto the stage. Adam especially seems to be permanently monitoring me and offering me cups of tea."

"He's a nice guy."

"Yes, he is." She cleared her throat nervously. "So are you."

"Thank you." Declan gave a mock bow. "It's all part of the company manager service."

Isabelle swilled the whisky round in her glass nervously; this was proving harder than she'd anticipated. She changed tack. "Are you bringing someone to the first-night party?"

"God, I haven't even had time to think about that. I suppose I'd better do so. I hate first-nights: the pressure for the show to be perfect, and then the parties are always full of D list celebrities who have nothing to do with the play and have eaten any food there was before us lot get there."

"Yes," Isabelle said, thinking of her dilemma.

"There's pressure in a lot of ways, on and off stage. So you haven't anyone special in your life?"

"No," Declan said carefully, not sure where this was leading. "Not exactly, there's an old friend I have a sort of on/off relationship with."

"Oh, I see. Only, I was wondering if you'd like to be my sort of date."

Shit, shit, shit, Declan mentally groaned, desperately trying to think of a way of getting out of this. "Isabelle, I'm highly flattered, I really am, but ..."

Isabelle got up quickly, almost throwing her glass down. "Forget it, Declan. I shouldn't have said anything; it was stupid of me."

"Isabelle, wait!" Declan followed her onto the stairs outside his office. "Look, I am going to ask Robin, this sort of girlfriend, because we go back a long way, and she'll never let me hear the last of it if I don't, but I would be delighted to escort you as well."

"Thank you, but I don't want to be a gooseberry."

"Once you see me in my tux you won't be able to resist!"

Isabelle laughed for the first time in days. "Won't your friend, Robin, mind?"

"Hey, you asked first – she'll just have to share."

"Thank you, Declan; you are one special man." She gave him a brief peck on the cheek and then virtually ran out of the theatre in embarrassment. Declan shook his head disbelievingly; soon he was going to wake up and discover this entire show had been some terrible nightmare. He reached for the phone to call Robin to ask her to double date with Isabelle.

After that he called Wesley; he could hear the baby crying in the background.

"Oh, Christ, it never lets up, does it?" Wesley muttered after Declan had filled him in on the evening's events. "Thank you once again for dealing with everything. You'll never want to work for me again after this, will you?"

"Only on the condition it's on a four hander play with actors who get along, a director who knows what he's doing, and no technical problems."

"Sounds good to me. Anyway, I'll be in tomorrow for back up in case you encounter any new catastrophes."

"Thanks."

"Wesley, it's your turn to change Blythe," Henrietta called out, carrying the screaming baby into the room where he was on the phone.

"Blythe?" Declan asked.

"Yes, it sort of stuck. We've been through every name we could find and nothing else seemed to suit her."

"I can't wait for Judith to hear that!"

"Mm, she'll be unbearable. Not only has she taken over my production but also taken over naming my baby. But if I'm being honest, pain though Judith may be, she's probably saved this production from what could have been a total disaster. I hope in 20 years or so Blythe might be very proud of being named by Judith." Blythe's screams got louder. "However, at present I think she's only interested in a clean nappy. I'll see you tomorrow." Wesley hung up and went to get the bag of Pampers.

Scarlett, even though she had managed to talk her way into keeping the table at the Ivy, and had turned a few heads as she walked in escorted by her banker date, wasn't having much fun. In comparison to Rupert the man was dull, knew little about theatre and lacked the wicked charm her fellow actor possessed. If she had been with Rupert she'd have turned every head in the place, and maybe made the cover of *Hello* magazine. She spent most of the meal planning a very special first-night present for him.

CHAPTER THIRTY SEVEN

Judith woke up far too early on the morning of the press night; nerves had that effect on her. The final preview had gone amazingly well, though every time Echo received a line from Holly she left a space before repeating it while ensuring it made sense. At the end of the play Judith gave her short shrift about that: "If you elongate this play any further it will run longer than an uncut *Hamlet*."

"And that's bad, right?" Echo made a mental note to ask Holly who this Hamlet was and why anyone should want to cut him.

Judith got up and made herself a cup of tea. Max X curled round her legs and she bent down to stroke him. "Oh Max," she sighed, realizing her hands were shaking slightly as she poured milk into the mug, "why do I put myself through this every time? Maybe it is time to retire, but then what would I do with myself?"

"Meow." Max looked hopefully at the pint of milk. Judith poured some into his saucer and then sat down to write first-night cards for the company. She'd already bought everyone a bottle of champagne. It wasn't a gift especially appropriate to the show but that was too bad; she had better things to do than tramp the streets searching for items symbolic of a play about séances, acrimonious marriages and ghostly wives. Besides, it was very good champagne and she'd included bottles for every person involved in the production, not merely the actors. After she'd finished the cards she'd take a walk to clear her head and then go into the theatre early, at about 3pm. The company were meeting at 4.30 for a morale boosting session. This would normally be taken by the director but, since Alexander seemed, mercifully, to have completely disappeared, Judith presumed it would be up to her.

Miranda prided herself on her first-night gifts and had bought each member of the cast (she rarely bothered with anyone else) a silver cigarette lighter engraved with the name of the show, the date and her name.

"Good grief," Rupert had exclaimed, on finding the receipt in the Asprey's bag a few days before and discovering she'd put it on their joint credit card. "I'd better take out a second mortgage."

"Don't be so bloody tight," Miranda had sworn. "My gifts are known to be the best."

"Of course they are; no one else can afford anything like this. What if no one smokes?"

"They can light candles with them – don't be so contrary, Rupert."

Rupert had tracked down a poster for the original production of *Blithe Spirit,* which he'd had copied and framed for each person in the company. The excitement of first-nights proved an aphrodisiac for both Rupert and Miranda and they spent the whole morning in bed until Rupert said they'd better stop before they had no energy left for the show. Miranda immediately leapt up to try on her first-night outfit for the umpteenth time, while Rupert began to make the bed.

"Are you sure it's all right; I don't look too tarty?" Miranda, privately competing with Scarlett and Echo, had chosen an outfit rather young for her.

"Darling, you look wonderful, as always. You could wear sackcloth and ashes and still look stunning."

"Thank you, Rupert."

"Of course, you would never wear such things since, as us mere mortals are aware, you're never wrong about anything."

"You bastard." Miranda threw one of her Jimmy Choo shoes at him. Rupert ducked, laughing. "Sorry, I couldn't resist it." He moved towards her. "And there's one more thing I can't resist." He pulled the dress carefully off her and threw her back on the bed.

Adam woke up expecting to be terrified, but instead he felt strangely elated, as if he'd finally discovered how to live again. On the table in his bedsit was a pile of wrapped ghostly sound effects CDs which he hoped were a suitable and amusing first-night gift.

Isabelle had spent ages trying to work out her presents; she didn't want to get it wrong, yet couldn't think of anything clever. Finally, she opted for Fortnum and Mason's hampers, which she could ill afford, but she didn't care; no one could sneer at her for a basket from the Queen's grocer.

Scarlett and Holly had spent hours discussing what they should do. In the end they went halves on a bottle of wine for everyone on which they stuck a special ghostly *Blithe Spirit* label created, at Scarlett's request, by her banker beau on his computer.

Scarlett was so overexcited Holly had difficulty stopping her from rushing into the theatre at lunchtime. "What are you going to do if you go in now?" she asked.

"I don't know, absorb the atmosphere, go over my lines, check the tickets are at the box office for my parents."

"You can do all that later; why don't you have something to eat first?"

"How can I think of food at a time like this?"

"Because you're going to look very stupid if you fall over in a dead faint halfway through."

"Fine!" Scarlett grabbed a mouldy looking orange.

"Oh, that'll make all the difference."

Echo spent three hours of her day at the hairdresser and beautician's with Storm. "But, Mommy, I wear a wig in the play," Echo pointed out. "What's the point of making my hair look good when no one's gonna see it?"

"They'll see it at the first-night party after. You gotta look your best for that 'cos there'll most likely be hundreds of photographers there. This is your big chance to show you're a ... a legimitate, letimigate, a real theatre actress, so you can't have your roots showing. No, we want a brighter red," Storm addressed the manicurist who was doing Echo's nails. "How about the Natasha? That's a real vibrant colour."

"I don't think I should wear nail polish for the play."

"Are you crazy, Echo? You gotta look good on stage; there's gonna be important people watching. What do you think, should I go for a darker red polish with my gold dress, like the Kylie, or even the Monica?"

"Sure, Mommy, whatever."

Storm frowned and quickly stopped. Frowning and smiling created lines and were not to be encouraged; something she was forever telling Echo. A blank face led to a perfect face. Still, it was hard not to frown at Echo who was showing utter indifference in preparing for tonight, unless it was in regard to events on stage. They'd been to all the best designer shops in London and Echo hadn't cared for anything Storm had suggested.

"I want something plain, but a little sexy," Echo had explained. "Not real fussy like that." She'd pointed to Storm's suggestion of a long orange ball gown with layers of netting and bows all round the top. "I'd look like an angel on top of a Christmas tree."

Echo had finally found the perfect dress: maroon velvet cut on the cross with a slight slit up the side. Much to Storm's chagrin she'd found it in Marks and Spencer's.

"Promise you'll tell them it's Armani," Storm had begged.

"OK, Mommy."

Rebecca, Matthew and Lucy were carrying out a check of the props and scene changes when the cast arrived, having fought their way through a forest of flowers which had arrived for them all at the stage door.

"Wow," said Scarlett, finding several bouquets with her name on the cards. "Here's one from Wesley, and from Mum and Dad, and my banker. Isn't it thrilling – a real first-night like we always dreamt of at drama school? I bet the rest of our class are green with envy. Oh my God, there's even one from the head of our school; I can't believe he's sent me flowers!" She gave Holly a hug. Holly was pleased to discover she too had flowers from Wesley. She wondered whether the rest of her class would be that envious of her role in this play. Yes, of course they would; to be involved in such a high profile production in whatever capacity was amazing.

"I wish people would stagger sending flowers," Judith complained as Fred carried bouquet after bouquet upstairs to her dressing room. "You can't move for days in the dressing room for the damn things, never have enough vases, then within a week they're all dead and the dressing room is as bare as a baby's arse. People should send cards telling you flowers will be arriving in say two or three weeks' time."

"You're such a romantic," Rupert said.

"Romance is very overrated – I am merely practical, my dear Rupert."

Echo was wandering around carrying Miranda's cigarette lighter and Judith's champagne. "I don't understand," she said.

"Nothing new there," Judith replied. "And what are you wearing on your nails?"

"Nail polish. Mommy made me put it on."

"And I'm making you taking it off – NOW."

"I've got some nail polish remover in my dressing room," Scarlett said. "Come on, I can get it off in a minute."

Echo followed Scarlett upstairs. "But why is everyone giving presents? It's not like Christmas, is it?"

"It's a theatrical tradition, to give first-night cards and presents."

"But I didn't know," Echo wailed. "Nobody told me."

"Don't worry, no one will mind."

"But I mind."

Judith's pep talk was brief and to the point: ignore everything Alexander had ever said; concentrate on what they were saying; listen to their fellow actors; keep it light; keep it fast; give it everything they had, and best of all, enjoy themselves. After she'd finished, Echo rushed out to find gifts. It was too late to find anything appropriate for the play, and her choice of shop was limited, as was her budget, dictated by Storm's allowance. Finally she settled on the biggest chocolate bars she could find from the Spar on the Haymarket. Walking back she noticed a commotion outside the front of the theatre and went to investigate. There were people clasping cameras, no doubt waiting for any celebrities who might be attending the first-night. Some were obviously professional photographers, one subject on which Echo was an expert. Talking to several of them was Alexander, with Jasper right beside him. Echo moved a little closer to listen.

"Of course I had no idea of the kind of behaviour I would have to endure on this production: the egos; the tantrums; the cruelty. If I'd been a lesser man I would have given up. But," Alexander gave his trademark pause for effect, "I ... had ... a ... dream, and I continued to pray I would be allowed to realize it. But no, it was dashed to the ground and I was stripped of my dignity. I am still hoping tonight, perhaps, there will be a little of that dream left on stage for you, my beloved audience, to share, but I fear the worst. Those so-called actors will have ruined it."

Echo crept away quietly before Alexander or Jasper saw her and then ran back to stage door. Of course, not being smart she might be wrong, but what Alexander was saying didn't sound good.

"Rupert!" She started up the stairs to his dressing room. From below her Miranda's dressing room door opened.

"I'm in here, Echo," Rupert called out. Echo hurried back down into the dressing room to find Rupert, Miranda and Judith.

"What do you want?" Miranda demanded. "Can't you leave my husband alone for a moment? We're trying to have a private conversation."

"But it's real important – I think."

"What's wrong, torn another dress?"

"Miranda, stop it," Rupert said. "What is it, Echo?"

"Alexander and Jasper are talking to the photographers outside the theatre and I don't think they're being real nice about us."

"Fuck," Judith said. She opened the dressing room door and shouted down to Declan in his office to come up to Miranda's room. Heart sinking, Declan arrived in seconds.

"Alexander is front of house giving unwanted interviews. Get round there and stop him."

Declan disappeared, wondering what the hell he was going to do, freedom of speech and all that.

"Did I do good?" Echo asked, rather nervously.

"Yes," Rupert smiled at her. "You did very good. Thank you."

"Oh, pleeease," said Miranda, miming

sticking her fingers down her throat.

Declan found Alexander holding court on the steps of the theatre. "Ah, Mr Columbus," he said. "Could I have a word?"

"I have nothing to say to you. You've treated me abysmally, and I'm going to tell everyone about it. Look." He brandished a leaflet in front of Declan's eyes.

I HAVE BEEN OUTCAST FROM THIS PLAY
SUPPORT THE DIRECTOR: BOYCOTT THIS PRODUCTION
THE ACTORS IN THE PLAY ARE ANIMALS

"You can't hand these out; they're libellous – and illiterate. You can't be 'outcast' – it's a noun not a verb."

Alexander looked nonplussed for a second and then continued to distribute his handout. "Try and stop me," he hissed to Declan.

Declan attempted another approach in a low voice. "Look, Alexander, you haven't been cast out; it was your choice not to return to rehearsals."

"Only after that witch attacked me." Alexander addressed the group around him once more. "Do you know, ladies and gentlemen, I was brutally assaulted by Judith Gold, your renowned so-called theatrical treasure?" There was a muttering from the crowd which was growing ever larger as passers-by stopped to see what was happening.

Declan tried to make light of it. "Now, Alexander, you know Judith was only fooling around, it was a stage vase designed to smash, and totally harmless."

"Harmless? I don't think so! I still bear the scars."

"Really? Where?"

"You're not going to silence me, Dylan, I will be heard."

Declan gritted his teeth. "I don't doubt it."

Wesley, alerted by Judith on his arrival at the theatre, appeared at Declan's side, much to the company manager's relief.

"Good evening, everyone," Wesley said. "I'm Wesley Barrett, the producer of the play tonight. In case you haven't gathered this is our director, Alexander Columbus, who I gather is having a bit of a joke with you."

"I'm what?"

"Alexander keeps us in stitches in rehearsals, never knowing what he's going to come up with next, never serious: the perfect director for a comedy."

"He sounds pretty serious now," said one of the photographers.

"That's his speciality. He once revealed he models himself on Jack Dee and think how dour that comic appears. In addition it's great publicity for us; look what an interested crowd he's drawn. But I'm afraid I'm going to have to drag him away now as we need him backstage; some of the actors require last minute advice." Wesley gripped Alexander's arm and turned him away from the spectators.

"What are you going to do, kidnap me?" Alexander hissed. "Believe me, I won't take this sitting down."

"No, you won't; there's hardly a seat left for the entire run, so frankly, whatever you say is going to make no difference to the box office. However, as director you are paid a retainer for the play's run: if you renounce your involvement we would no longer have to pay you. The same would apply for Jasper's design credit if he persists on handing out those leaflets. If you are willing to relinquish your rights, please feel free to continue your protest."

Alexander took Jasper to one side and after a few seconds of muttering they collected what leaflets remained and, with false smiles to the crowd to suggest it had been a joke, they disappeared in the direction of the nearest pub. It had been a hard choice for them: artistic integrity over money, and it had taken them all of 30 seconds to opt for the latter.

Wesley turned to what was left of the crowd. "Ladies and gentlemen, I'm sorry for the mis-understanding; sometimes Alexander's idea of a joke leaves something to be desired. But I hope those who see *Blithe Spirit* tonight or in the future find this to be a very superior production. Thank you."

"Nice save, Wesley," Declan said. He glanced at the producer as they walked back to the stage door – he looked shattered.

"Thanks, though I can't guarantee Alexander won't go back to complaining when I'm not watching."

"But as you said, it won't affect the box office."

"I know, and I also know people say any publicity is good publicity. But I can't bear to see a cast that has worked as hard as this one has being slagged-off by an idiot who doesn't know his arse from his elbow. Especially when it's my fault he was employed in the first place."

"You weren't to know."

"First rule of theatre, Declan: if you're going to employ someone, in whatever capacity, ensure you check out their work first. Going by reputation or vogue doesn't mean they're any good. I wonder how many other producers who have employed Alexander have encountered similar problems, but would never admit to it, the way I'm not. A sort of *Emperor's New Clothes* scenario: no one wants to be the individual who admits to not understanding his work when actually there's nothing to understand."

Declan laughed. "That's a very good point. Perhaps we should start an Alexander Columbus survivors' support group."

At the stage door they had to walk over more flowers which had arrived. Piles of cards practically covered the stage door keeper's doorway. Fred and Cassie were carrying things up to the dressing rooms when they had time.

"Who the hell has sent me a cactus?" Judith demanded.

"A prickly plant for a prickly person maybe,"

Fred suggested, putting it on the table.

"Fuck off," Judith said. "And put it some place out of the way."

"OK." Fred moved it into the shower and then withdrew to the window seat on the stairs so Judith could work through her nerves on her own and he could act as a doorman to stop her being disturbed.

Five minutes later Judith put her head out the door. "Freda, could you ask Rupert to come up if he has a moment?"

Fred looked at her in surprise. "Are you feeling all right?"

"Go!"

Fred knocked at Rupert's door: silence. There were voices from Adam's room next door so he tried there. Rupert was perched on Adam's windowsill and both were laughing at a chilli plant sent by a local restaurant, obviously after their custom, to every cast member. "Rupert, Judith said if you could spare a moment, could you pop in."

"OK." Rupert got up. "See you later, Adam."

"You're privileged," Fred muttered as they walked upstairs. "In all the years I've dressed Judith she has never let anyone in her dressing room in the hour before curtain up on a press night."

Miranda, climbing the stairs to get Rupert to massage her shoulders for relaxation, found an empty room. Adam, hearing her calling out, relayed Judith's request; within seconds Miranda was also on her way to Judith's room.

"Sorry," Fred stopped her, "Judith is not receiving visitors."

"But my husband is in there."

"By Royal Command: don't blame me, I only work here."

Miranda tried to push past him, but Fred blocked the way. "Sorry, dear, it's more than my job's worth."

Fred might be camp, but Miranda wasn't sure she could outmanoeuvre him and she certainly didn't want some sort of embarrassing scuffle on the stairs. So, giving him a glare of which Judith would be proud, she turned and stormed back to Rupert's dressing room to await his return. How dare Rupert be so bloody popular when she'd been the one putting herself out to keep in with Judith? All Rupert did was laugh at her efforts.

Rupert found Judith curled up in a tiny ball on the bed. He decided not to go for the obvious 'are you all right?' since an eminent actress in the foetal position was most likely not. Instead, he sat down on one of the dressing room's antique chairs and began talking about the Australian Open Tennis Tournament which was starting soon. Who he thought would win, which players he knew still competing, why he'd enjoyed it as an event and the nerves he'd had before a match.

"Were you really nervous? I can't imagine you ever being ruffled by anything." The ball uncurled itself.

"OK, you got me! Truthfully, no I wasn't, which is probably why I never made the grade. Normally I was too busy chatting up the ball girls to worry about the game, but I thought I'd try an allegory."

"That was an allegory?"

"I haven't the foggiest. Tennis players don't get much of an education; we're a pretty thick breed. Allegory, alligator, it's all the same to me."

Judith smiled. "Bollocks, you're one smart cookie, Rupert Blake." She was silent for a few seconds, studying Rupert thoughtfully. "I don't usually admit this, and I'm having second thoughts about doing so now, but if I don't I may spontaneously combust."

"That could be messy. Please feel free to confide your innermost secrets; I am the soul of discretion. Unless it's that you murder your leading men on press night and bury them in the dressing room, in which case, I'd rather not know."

"Damn, you've caught me out."

"I wondered what the funny smell in here was."

"Bloody cheek, this dressing room smells fine, although the aroma of lilies from all those bouquets reminds me of funerals, and God knows I go to enough of those nowadays. I only ever buy black clothes; it saves time."

Judith broke off for a minute. Rupert waited patiently.

"God, I wish I was at home curled up with Max."

"Max? Is there a male skeleton in your cupboard?"

"Max, or to be precise Max X, is my cat and my sanity. I've acquired a Max at the most important milestones in my life. Cats are much easier than people."

"Yes, but not to have sex with; all those claws are lethal and the fur balls get stuck in your throat."

In spite of her tension Judith threw back her head and roared with laughter. "You are totally depraved, Rupert, and I like that in a person." She paused again and then took a deep breath. "OK, here goes, admission time: I'm terrified, Rupert. I know every actor gets nervous before a press night and I'm up there with the best of them, but this is different. I have so much riding on this."

"Judith, you're fantastic. We all do our best, but, to be honest, when you're on stage the rest of us might as well be reading the proverbial phone book."

"I thought Echo was – oh no, wait, that was the stage management cues."

Rupert laughed. "You've done a great job there too; can you remember what she was like when she started?"

"You did your fair share on that front," Judith pointed out. "As did Holly."

"And you helped Holly. She thinks you're wonderful."

"A subject on which I believe you are an expert." Rupert had the grace to look surprised and then embarrassed. Judith really didn't miss a trick. "Now, returning to the matter in hand: I deeply appreciate all your compliments on my achievements, but essentially that's my point. At the end of the day, I've taken over this production for good or bad, thanks to being lumbered with a director who's had numerous lobotomies. That imbecile is now out there bemoaning his appalling treatment and, I assume, my ruthless behaviour. So people will be judging me as an actress and director and waiting for me to fuck up on either or both. I know I can act, but I've never directed before; maybe I'm crap. What if I ruined everything?"

"Judith, from what I've heard you've been directing everything you've been in for years. The difference is other directors don't walk out when you take over, so you're less aware of it."

Judith stared at him, stunned. "I can't believe you said that. Are you suggesting I'm a megalomaniac?"

"No, I'm suggesting you're a bloody good director. Every one of us realizes that, even Echo. This play has been a hell of a tempestuous ride, but I, for one, wouldn't have missed it for the world. It's been scary, funny, stressful, exhilarating and a fantastic learning curve. Tonight you need to forget about directing and concentrate on your performance. Every time we perform this play I look forward to your entrance and each scene I do with you is a joy."

"You sentimental bugger!" Judith was startled to hear an emotional crack in her voice. "Now piss off and leave me to prepare."

"Yes, Ma'am." Rupert pulled his forelock. "Does this mean I'm not going to be buried under the floor boards?"

"No, I'm saving that for Echo if she starts declaiming LX cues."

"Think of it this way, Judith: in four hours you can be tucked up in bed."

Rupert walked back to his dressing room to find Miranda sitting at his dressing table. "What did Judith want?"

"Just to chat, say good luck, that kind of thing."

"I wasn't even allowed in; I was physically barred by that camp old queen. Perhaps it is her you're screwing."

"Yes, darling, we had a quickie in her dressing room, with Fred waiting outside to clear up afterwards. Honestly, Miranda, can't you think of anything else?"

"I got a bunch of beautiful red roses from Ben Miller."

"How nice."

"Ben Miller, who played my husband on that telly thing I did last year."

"Yes, I know who he is: good actor."

"Aren't you jealous?"

"No, why?"

"Because he sent me roses."

"So?"

"Oh, you are impossible." Miranda stormed downstairs.

Rupert glanced at his watch and then went down to Declan's office. "Can I use your computer to go on the internet?" he asked.

"Sure, strange time to check your emails though."

"That's not exactly what I'm after," Rupert replied, Googling pet shops. Fifteen minutes later, he'd been assured a kitten would be delivered to Judith's house the next day. "Please write: 'another milestone and another Max'," he said. "Don't sign it; she'll know who it's from."

Holly had done fairly well with first-night gifts; some people had remembered her and others hadn't. Echo had given her the biggest chocolate bar and thrown her arms round her. "You're so cool, Holly. Thanks for everything you done for me and for being my friend." Isabelle, who realized too late she'd forgotten Holly, gave her a bag of groceries from Tesco's rather than the Fortnum's hamper. Rupert, Adam and Judith had all included her, but she did not receive one of Miranda's lighters.

"Hey, here's another one for you," Scarlett said, holding up a blue Tiffany's bag. She hunted through the piles. "I haven't got anything like that."

Holly opened the bag. Inside was a Tiffany's box with a card attached. Amazed who could be sending her anything from Tiffany's, Holly pulled the card from the envelope:

For Holly,

Thanks for being a girl in a million, I shall never forget you.

With all my love, a secret admirer

Hands trembling, Holly opened the box. Inside was an exquisite necklace with a blue jewel in the centre.

"Is that a sapphire?" Scarlett asked in amazement. "I guess if it's from Tiffany's it must be – I don't think they go in for fake gems." She studied the card. "An admirer, who is it, Holl?"

"How should I know? It says secret admirer; I presume they want to remain secret."

"But you must have some idea."

Holly shook her head untruthfully. "Can you help me put it on? I don't think I can do it myself, my hands are trembling too much."

Scarlett did the clasp up. "It's a clever fastening; it won't come off easily".

Holly, who had no intention of ever taking it off, except maybe to have a shower, fingered it happily and smiled. She must thank Rupert, but secretly, especially as Scarlett was already horribly curious. At that moment there was a knock on the door and Rupert himself put his head in. "I seem to have acquired some of your cards, Scarlett," he said, handing over a pile, "and some for Echo. You couldn't be an angel and pop them in to her? If I catch her in her underwear I'll have her mother chasing me with a rolling pin!"

"Sure," said Scarlett, disappearing with alacrity. This gave her the perfect opportunity to prepare Rupert's first-night gift.

Left alone with Rupert, Holly suddenly became tongue tied and looked at the floor. Rupert smiled. "Do you realize how much trouble I went to, stealing Scarlett's and Echo's cards from stage door so I'd have an excuse to see you? And you're not talking to me."

Holly looked up in horror. "Oh no, it's not that, I'm so sorry, how rude of me. It's just this is so beautiful." She held up the necklace. "I couldn't think of anything to say which would even half express how I feel. It's, oh I don't know: Supercalifragilisticexpialido-cious. Isn't that the word to use when nothing else will do?"

"Yes, if you're Julie Andrews, but I get the gist! I'm glad you like it."

"I can't believe you bought it for me."

Very gently Rupert bent over and kissed her. "I meant everything I said in the card too; you are very special. Now, I'd better fly; Miranda is already on the warpath because Judith wanted to see me and not her! Have a great opening night, Holly, and remember

464

you may not be on stage, but you are a very integral part of *Blithe Spirit,* OK?"

"OK."

Rupert disappeared back to his dressing room to start getting dressed. Opening the door he discovered Scarlett, lying on the floor, wrapped only in her dressing gown. "I'm glad it's you," she said, gradually pulling off her dressing gown to reveal she was stark naked. "I was worried it might be Cassie."

"Sod Cassie, what about Miranda?" Rupert demanded.

"She's safely downstairs; I checked first."

"Scarlett, what are you doing?"

"I'm giving you your first-night present; don't you like it?"

"Whether I like it or not is irrelevant." Rupert placed the dressing gown over her. "You can't seriously be suggesting we have sex in my dressing room fifteen minutes before the play starts with a theatre full of critics, can you?"

"Well, no." Scarlett was a little disappointed with Rupert's reaction. "I thought I'd give you a taster of what you could expect later – we could take a rain check for the actual sex. Maybe at the end of show party. I've booked a room at the Waldorf since the party is there; we could sneak upstairs when no one was looking."

"Scarlett, please get up and put your clothes on properly."

"But ..."

"I'm very flattered, really I am, but I'm afraid I have to turn down your kind offer. In case you haven't noticed, I am married to Miranda who is hardly going to be ecstatic if I have an affair with someone playing her maid and who is probably young enough to be her daughter, though for Christ's sake don't mention the latter to her."

"She wouldn't have to find out."

"You don't know Miranda; she's pretty quick on the uptake, believe me." Rupert absently rubbed the fading bruise on his cheek.

"I could be very discreet, honestly. It would be our secret."

"No, Scarlett, thank you but no, totally and utterly."

Scarlett got off the floor, wrapping her dressing gown round her angrily. "Don't you fancy me?"

"You're attractive, Scarlett, but you're not exactly my type."

"Why not?"

"You're too confident and ambitious; I already have a wife like that. If, and I say if, I was to have an affair I would choose someone who was more vulnerable."

"I could play vulnerable."

Rupert laughed. "Yes, I'm sure you could play anything you wanted, but the answer is still no. And since we're on the subject of acting, don't you think it would be an idea to go and get ready? I don't think Noel Coward envisaged Edith wearing a slinky dressing gown and fuck-me make-up. And I would also like five minutes alone to try and get my head around my own role."

Scarlett stormed up to her dressing room. "Bloody men."

"What's wrong?" Holly was going through Elvira's lines for the hundredth time that day, trying to remember every note Judith had given her.

"Rupert turned me down for sex. He said I wasn't his type, that I wasn't vulnerable enough. And he kept saying Miranda might find out even though I told him I could be discreet."

"Not very discreet – you just told me," Holly pointed out.

"You don't count."

"Thanks!"

"I mean you're not going to tell anyone."

No, Holly thought, I won't. I am discreet. And Rupert slept with me and turned down Scarlett! That was an awful way to think about your best friend, but it did feel good.

"Why are you smiling?" Scarlett demanded. "I've been rejected, what's so funny about that?"

"Sorry."

"Just because you've got a secret admirer. I bet you wouldn't mind if it was Rupert, would you?"

"In my dreams," said Holly truthfully.

Isabelle knocked rather nervously on Adam's door. "Come in," he called out.

"Sorry, I didn't mean to interrupt. I wanted to say have a great show."

"Thank you, Isabelle, you too."

"You know, I still think Mrs Bradman is a pretty lousy part, but if I've got to have a husband putting me down all the time, I'm glad it's you."

"Oh, thank you very much." Adam was taken aback by this new Isabelle.

"Perhaps you could mention that to Judith, what I just said, with you being so friendly. So she doesn't think the worst of me."

Adam smiled inwardly; so that was what she wanted. So much for a great change of heart! "Judith and I aren't exactly bosom buddies, you know."

"But you seem ..."

"She tolerates me. Rupert is the one to speak to if you want a mediator."

"I don't think Rupert likes me very much."

"I don't think Rupert dislikes anyone."

"Maybe you could have a word with him then."

"Isabelle, if you cut back on the gossip and bitching and behaved normally you wouldn't feel so alienated."

"But that is normal."

Adam shrugged. "Whatever you say. Now I must go through my lines before I go on."

"Of course, I'll leave you in peace, unless ... would you like me to do them with you?"

Adam studied Isabelle's face, searching for an ulterior motive; there didn't appear to be one. "Thank you, Isabelle; I'd appreciate it."

"Ladies and gentlemen of the *Blithe Spirit* company, this is your Act One beginners call: Miss Flynn, Miss Montgomery, and Mr Blake your calls please. Standby: stage management, electrics, wardrobe and wigs. Flyman to the flies. This is your Act One beginners call. Thank you." Rebecca's calm tones came over the tannoy system.

"I'm rather nervous," Matthew admitted to Lucy. "It's silly when I'm not even going on stage, isn't it?"

"Yes, very silly."

"I wonder how the actors feel."

"Probably like they want to change careers. Have you got the bucket ready?"

"Bucket?"

"In case any of them are sick."

"Sick?"

"With nerves, didn't you know that? On first-nights actors are so scared they come off and throw up in the wings and it's the job of the most junior ASM to hold their heads into the bucket and clear up afterwards."

Matthew looked at her horrified. "No, I didn't realize; I'll go and get one." He charged off, careering into Declan.

"Oh, God, is there a problem?" Declan asked, his heart sinking.

"No, at least I don't think so. I'm getting a bucket in case the actors are sick; Lucy said they might be."

"Lucy," Declan called across to her, "stop

winding Matthew up, we need all our wits about us tonight."

"So I don't need a bucket?"

"Not unless anyone has gastric flu, which as far as I'm aware they don't. Of course, the way this production is going all seven actors may be struck down with it within 10 minutes of curtain up."

Miranda, Scarlett and Rupert were standing in the wings waiting to start. The front of house manager came through the pass door to announce they finally had front of house clearance. "OK, Rebecca," Declan said to the DSM.

"Scarlett, Miranda and Rupert standby please," Rebecca called out. "Standby LX cues 1-4, standby tabs."

Scarlett gripped her tray of cocktail glasses, hoping her hands weren't trembling so much she'd drop anything, and waited for the curtain to go up.

In her dressing room Judith, who didn't appear for a few pages, stared at herself in the mirror. "Oh fuck," she muttered. "Here we go."

CHAPTER THIRTY EIGHT

Scarlett's entrance received a smaller laugh than at the previews, but she'd been warned of that possibility. Press night audiences tended to be quieter; critics had that effect even though the rest of the audience consisted of friends, relations and professional first-nighters. Even Rupert's entrance round was comparatively restrained, while Miranda's consisted only of a couple of friends fully aware there'd be no further press night tickets if they failed in their ovation duty.

The critics were not entirely to blame for the slightly muted start. The audience had been considerably unnerved by several odd experiences on entering the theatre. Their first obstacle was being forced to step over and round the bomb crater to which Jasper had added several disembodied limbs, human hair and a glass eye. On reaching the auditorium they were greeted by Alexander and Jasper handing out gas-mask boxes, ration cards and directions to the nearest air raid shelter. Jasper was further attired in a tight SS costume, thereby causing some confusion as to whether Noel Coward had written a play wherein England had been successfully invaded; a notion emphasised by Jasper proffering swastika armbands.

News of this activity had been relayed backstage, and Wesley had hurried round to check it out. But, apart from firmly forbidding Jasper to hand out any more arm bands before he caused a political backlash, there was little he could do. It was hardly illegal, was in keeping with the production and, as far as he knew, wasn't coming out of his budget. "I suppose we should be grateful Alexander isn't dressed as Hitler," he'd muttered.

"More likely to be Eva Braun," Judith had snapped.

"But why is Jasper wearing an SS uniform?" Matthew had asked. "Surely he knows it was German and this play is set in England."

"Probably thinks he looks sexy," Lucy had replied. "With those tight leather boots and all: very kinky. No doubt he wears it in bed for Alexander, complete with a whip."

By Judith's entrance the audience had warmed up and she received such a rapturous round she had to wait several seconds before she could say her first line.

"I hate the bloody things," she'd moaned on the first preview. "What's the point in clapping before you've even opened your mouth? It only interrupts the play."

"I like them," Miranda had said. "Surely it shows they respect you as a performer?"

"Bollocks. It means they recognize you off the telly."

As the play continued, the response

became more vociferous. By the time the cast finished the séance scene, and Madame Arcati was collapsed on the floor, the audience were helpless with laughter. Judith couldn't help but relax slightly; no one could crucify her with this reaction, surely. She wouldn't go as far as to admit she was enjoying herself but, climbing up to her dressing room after her exit, she was aware of looking forward to Act Two. Her feet ached though; she seemed to have been on them for hours, so she decided to relax them in the shower. A few seconds later there was a shout. "Freda, get this fucking cactus out of my shower!"

"And what do you want me to do with it?" Fred demanded.

"Try finding our so-called director and then use your imagination."

Adam and Isabelle came off shortly after Judith: Adam relieved the hardest part was over; Isabelle miffed that she had so little to do now.

Miranda stayed in the wings after her exit, watching Rupert and Echo. Rupert was on great form tonight; it thrilled her just to see him work. And every minute of acting opposite him tonight was a joy. It felt as if sparks were flying off them.

Echo was doing impressively well too, and there was a small appreciative murmur at her beauty as she wafted around the stage. As she gently ran her hand through Rupert's hair at least one critic became slightly aroused. The curtain came down on Act One to appreciative applause as the audience headed out to the bar. Rupert and Echo came off stage.

"That was so cool," Echo said, jumping up and down. "They think we're swell."

"Don't get carried away," Miranda said, dryly. "The critics can still be vile, whatever the rest of the audience think."

"That's right, darling, think positive," Rupert said.

"And thinking positive is going to get Echo good reviews? I don't think so."

Echo's face fell. Rupert smiled at her.

"Ignore my wife, Echo; I shall be charitable and put her remarks down to press night nerves. You're doing great."

"Oh yes, take your little girlfriend's side."

"Come on, Echo, let's leave Miss Negativity here, and go upstairs. There's a cup of coffee in my room with my name on it."

In the wings, Holly stretched herself on her stool. "Aren't you going up to your dressing room?" Rebecca asked.

"No, I think I'll stay here and check over Act Two." Actually, Holly couldn't face listening to Scarlett alternatively raving about her West End debut and moaning about Rupert's rejection.

"Can I bring you something to drink?" Rebecca offered.

"I'm fine, thank you."

Adam came down before the end of the

interval and spotted Holly. "Not leaving your post?"

"I'm going over the lines again. I know it's stupid when I can use the script, but I don't want to stutter or get any of the interpretation wrong because Echo will copy it exactly."

"You won't; you're doing a fantastic job. It's a shame you're not on stage with us, but you are in spirit."

"Thank you. Aren't you a little early? You're not on for two scenes."

"I couldn't concentrate on anything else. I've been attempting the easy crossword and after it took me several minutes to find another word for angry, in five letters starting with c and ending with a double s, I knew my mind wasn't on it."

"Especially when the answer is in the title," Holly said. "As in 'cross' word."

Adam slapped his forehead with his hand. "I didn't even think of that – point proven! So, in such a state, I figured I might as well watch from the wings and soak up the atmosphere. Did I just say 'soak up the atmosphere'?" Holly nodded, smiling. "Good Lord, I sound like Scarlett! No offence meant, Holly, I know she's your friend."

"None taken; she is a bit intense occasion-ally."

"So, who are your guests tonight? Any special man on the horizon?"

"No," Holly said, wistfully dreaming of Rupert dumping Miranda in order to take her.

475

"I asked my parents because I knew they'd be excited by a West End first-night, even if their daughter isn't actually on the stage. What about you?"

"My two daughters: Hattie and Justine. I wanted my granddaughter to come too, but Justine was worried she'd shout out 'Grandpa' when I came on."

"Judith would've loved that; she'd probably have had her shot at dawn!"

"Quite. So if you have no male escort at the party, other than your father, may I be permitted a dance?"

"I'm not a very good dancer; I was always the worst in movement classes at drama school. I seem to have several left feet and they all go in different directions."

"What a coincidence – I have several right feet, so we should match perfectly."

"In which case, my feet would be delighted to accept your feet."

Rupert, Miranda and Scarlett had arrived in the wings ready to start Act Two.

"There you are, Holl," said Scarlett. "You didn't come up to the dressing room."

Holly repeated the excuse about practicing lines. "And Adam's been keeping me company."

"I've booked her for a dance at the party."

Rupert was taken aback to discover he felt mildly jealous, a virtually unknown emotion for him.

"How sweet," Miranda broke in. "But we do

have a play to finish first, if anyone else is interested. Some of us still have a major part to perform. It might be helpful to prepare."

"No rush," Rupert said. "The audience always takes forever to return from the bar on press nights. Besides, you're the one who has to start on stage."

"Fine, I'll be professional then." Miranda marched on stage and took her place at the breakfast table. Scarlett collected her tray of bacon and eggs, which Matthew had been cooking on a small hotplate in Declan's office. Rupert turned round and gave Holly a large grin, then watched as her face lit up. God, he was such a swine – he just couldn't help himself.

"Standby please," Rebecca called out. Rupert turned back and stood by to make his entrance, leaving Holly fingering her necklace.

Boosted by a drink, and with no sign of the strange SS officer and his companion, the audience returned for Act Two even more responsive. Miranda and Rupert's breakfast argument went so flawlessly Echo was determined not to let them down as she performed Elvira's mischievous tricks – that vase was going to break tonight whether it liked it or not. Imagining she was a baseball pitcher, she threw it with such force it shattered completely. One piece flew into Rupert's hair and another down the front of Miranda's blouse. Echo only stopped herself from giggling at the thought of the dressing down she'd get from Judith and Miranda. Even Rupert limited himself to a slight twinkle as he carefully removed the fragment. Miranda opted to remove her piece when not in full view of the audience.

The following scene, as Rupert was waiting to enter with Adam, Cassie dashed over, waving his sling. "Thought you might need this," she whispered.

"Cassie, you're an angel," Rupert said, quickly putting it over his arm. "I totally forgot, most unlike me."

"You probably had other things on your mind," said Adam.

"I can't imagine what! I'd certainly have felt exceedingly silly talking about the sling you made me wear, waving an arm devoid of one."

"Oh, I don't know; it would merely show what a lousy, disobedient patient Charles is, something I've always suspected."

"Some friendly, family doctor you are!"

"Rupert?"

"Yes."

"Don't you normally wear it on the other arm?"

"Bollocks!" Rupert quickly switched it over.

Adam only had a few lines in this scene while Isabelle had a short scene with Miranda a couple of pages before, but they both exited together and didn't reappear. Adam was thrilled how effortless his performance and lines had been; in spite of the nerves, it had felt incredible. Twenty five years ago he would never have believed he'd feel that way again. He turned to Isabelle. "Well done, Mrs Bradman."

"Thank you, Dr Bradman. I'm going to open a bottle of champagne. Why don't you join me?"

"We've still got to do the curtain call; I don't want to be tipsy."

"How hard is it to walk on stage, bow and walk off again?"

"I want to relish every moment of it. I've waited a long time for this."

"A single glass and I promise you'll remember every second."

Adam realized he was sounding rather priggish. "You're right; thank you, that would be lovely."

"It's alright for some," Rupert complained as he came up to his dressing room in the second interval to find Adam and Isabelle drinking champagne in Adam's room. "Some of us still have to do Act Three."

"The advantage of being supporting players," Isabelle said. Already on her third glass, she found she was caring less and less about the size of her role. Adam was keeping to his resolution and slowly sipping his first and only one.

"You'd better save me a glass for the end."

Holly, having drunk a large bottle of water

to keep her nervously dry throat lubricated, decided she'd better go to the loo in the second interval. Stage management, having set up for Act Three, had also gone for a break, so there was no one to see two figures creep into the wings through the pass door from the auditorium, and quietly put the finishing touches to something they had prepared earlier.

Judith and Rupert stood in the wings ready for Act Three to start.

"Are you happy yet?" Rupert asked.

"I'm never happy."

"You must have been a cheerful child!"

"I was a wartime child; we didn't do cheerful."

"OK, I'll rephrase the question: are you satisfied with the way the play is going tonight?"

"I shall be satisfied once the curtain has come down. Talking of curtains, I think Rebecca is about to raise ours. Are you interested in standing by on stage, or shall we leave the audience to study our hideous set actor-less?"

"Yes, boss, I'm a-going, boss," Rupert said, walking onto the set backwards, bowing subserviently to Judith as he went.

"Just make sure you get it right or I'll be getting the whip out later," Judith called after him.

Rupert raised one eyebrow at her. "Oh good, I thought you were never going to offer."

"Rupert, Judith, are you both ready?" Rebecca asked calmly, wondering if she was ever going to be able to take the curtain up.

"Sorry," said Rupert, grinning at Judith before he took up his position of mock sadness, as he pretended to mourn the death of his second wife, mistakenly killed by the ghost of his first, whilst being secretly relieved. The curtain rose on Charles looking mournfully at a picture of Ruth, before he threw it aside and burst into a jitterbug, a piece of business Rupert and Judith had invented. The audience loved it.

Judith made her final entrance; Madame Arcati had turned up in a bid to dematerialise Elvira, an experiment resulting instead in Ruth's materialising. Scarlett, waiting to enter for the play's denouement, couldn't believe how well it was going; so much for bad press nights. The reviews were going to be fantastic, she knew it. She could envisage herself swept off to Hollywood on the strength of them. She was going to be more famous than even Judith. Maybe then Rupert would want her.

As Madame Arcati ultimately solved the problem, after a mass of unsuccessful incantations, waving of greenery, sprinklings of salt and pepper, and involving Edith as the catalyst of the entire scenario, Scarlett reluctantly made her exit; she could have stayed on stage forever.

Longing to share her elation, she went over to Holly who was gratefully laying down her microphone, Echo having also finished bar the curtain call, which she could just about manage without instructions. "Well done, Holl – Echo has never sounded so good." Scarlet gave her friend a hug.

"Thanks," Holly said, feeling guilty for her earlier unkind thoughts about her friend.

Judith made her final exit. "Thank fuck for that," she said, taking a large swig of water from the bottle Fred was holding for her. "Next time I do a press night like this Freda, I want neat vodka in this bottle."

"I thought you were retiring after this."

"Piss off."

Rupert remained alone on stage to bid farewell to his now invisible dead wives as they created havoc around him. Lucy and Matthew were standing at their posts ready to pull ropes, push levers and other mechanics to make books fall off shelves, gramophones play on their own and objects fly round the room, theoretically caused by Ruth and Elvira. Rebecca gave them the cue to start the effects. After each one Charles addressed a few more words to his unseen wives, which gave the two ASMs time to reach their next position. Rupert, dodging a flying cushion, spoke his second to last line; there was only one effect left to go. As Lucy prepared to pull out the peg to collapse a bookshelf, she found it was jammed. How odd, the peg looked as if it had been tampered with. As she struggled to free it, the horribly familiar wail of an air raid siren yet again filled the air.

"Not a-fucking-gain?" Judith hissed in the wings.

But this was far from the only effect. The siren was followed by the drone of a plane and the whoosh of a bomb dropping.

The rest of the cast, gathered for the curtain call, stared at each other stunned.

Matthew had rushed to help Lucy and, as the plane droning grew louder, the peg finally came free. But instead of the shelf collapsing, a picture crashed to the ground, glass spraying everywhere, and the entire set began to shake. From the flies high above the stage, chunks of plaster came crashing down. Rupert sensibly ducked under the table as pieces of the set came hurtling towards him. The stage was full of dust; the audience began to cough while Rupert put his handkerchief across his mouth. There was no doubt in anyone's mind they were experiencing a realistic mock up of a full scale World War II air raid. The surround sound system Alexander had earlier organized front of house gave the audience the sensation of being fully involved in the attack.

Wesley, who had been sitting out front watching, came dashing through the pass door. "What the hell is going on?" he shouted over the noise.

Declan shook his head. "I haven't the

foggiest, but I have a good idea who's behind it."

"I'll bloody kill him." Wesley smashed his fist against the wall. He didn't recall ever being so angry before.

"You'll have to join the queue," said Judith, in a tone which made Echo take several steps away from her through force of habit.

"Should I bring the curtain in?" Rebecca asked.

"No," Judith said. "If we finish like this no one will know what the fuck is going on. We need to resolve this one way or another."

"But how? There's only Rupert on stage," Scarlett said.

"Exactly, can you think of anyone better?"

"Ah yes, the world according to Saint Rupert," Miranda said, bitterly.

"He's real clever," said Echo. "I wouldn't know what to do."

"No dear," said Judith with her eyes firmly fixed on the stage.

Holly got off her stool and stood next to Adam, staring anxiously at Rupert. She felt Adam squeeze her hand; he was as tense as she was. She returned the squeeze. Even Isabelle found herself gripping Matthew's shoulder while Lucy, still clutching her peg, was stunned into a sort of silent prayer.

After about 30 seconds the sound effects grew silent and the set stabilized; the audience stirred uncertainly. Those in the first few rows were brushing plaster dust off their hair and clothes. Rupert emerged from under the table and stared about. Through the dust and smoke he saw the shocked faces of his fellow actors in the wings. After this he was asking for a wage rise, not to mention danger money. What the hell was he going to do? To ignore what had just happened and finish the play the way it was written wouldn't work now; it would be a total anti-climax. But wasn't totally re-writing Noel Coward some kind of theatrical crime? For a second he had a brief stab of envy for Tim Henman; he could hit a few bad balls and walk off court and try harder on the next match. He'd saved enough problems on this show; why couldn't he just quit for once? Walk off and leave the problem for someone else. Do a John McEnroe and throw his racket down shouting, "You cannot be serious!" Then his eyes locked with Judith's; he couldn't let her down. He didn't want to be a great tennis player – he wanted to be a great actor and great actors never gave up.

He walked over to the French windows which had blown open and stared out. "That was close," he said. "I had no idea we were on the German bombing run." Then he looked upwards. "Quite frankly, Ruth and Elvira, compared to Hitler your earlier pitiable efforts with gramophones and cushions are hardly going to frighten me." The audience laughed, now under the impression this was part of the action. "As I said previously, my dear wives,

I am leaving this house, and you and Adolf can have it." He paused for a minute looking at the devastation. "Or at least, what's left of it. Goodbye." Rupert stopped and gathered his breath for the correct last line. "Parting is such sweet sorrow." He walked to the door and gave one more glance at the chaos round him as the curtain slowly came down.

EPILOGUE

The Times: First Night Review
Coward goes to War
Last night's performance of *Blithe Spirit* at the Haymarket Theatre was familiar and yet unfamiliar. Surely this play, though written during the Second World War, was about an earlier time when the horrors of air raids and death were shadows yet to come? But director Alexander Columbus has instead set his production in what appears to be the midst of the Blitz. The set resembles a house with more than its fair share of bomb damage, which raises the question as to whether the Condomine's home was in fact in London, Liverpool or Coventry, not a country village where the Luftwaffe were unlikely to waste bombs. In fact Charles (Rupert Blake) makes this very point, after emerging from a simulated air raid, in lines which have nothing to do with Noel Coward. Neither does the air raid, though the effects are frighteningly authentic and should be snapped up by Imperial War Museum for a future exhibition. This poses an interesting question: where is the line between theatrical effects and fair ground rides?

So does this change of the setting work? No, not in my opinion. In spite of Charles being dressed in an officer's uniform complete with scar, having presumably been invalided out, and Madame Arcati (Judith Gold) looking fetching in a land army outfit, the lightness of touch does not feel real with strife looming overhead. Surely if we were in mid-war there would be quantities of soldiers slain in battle lining up to use Madame Arcati as a medium to speak to their mourning relatives, not merely one spoilt dead wife (Echo)?

Most of the cast struggle valiantly to make the play work, chiefly by ignoring the setting. Judith Gold was obviously born to play Madame Arcati. Both eccentric and menacing, this is one Arcati I wouldn't like to cross and it makes a refreshing change from previous actresses who have played it merely for laughs, as a total oddball or a type of gypsy fortune teller. If you go and see the play for only one reason, Miss Gold is it. With acting of such calibre as hers there is always a risk that it can unbalance the show, but this is not the case.

Rupert Blake is an admirable Charles, whether battling with a duet of dead wives or sheltering beneath a table battling with an unseen Adolph. His scenes with the excellent Miranda Flynn (as his wife Ruth) are a prime example of how Coward should be played. There is also a sexual frisson between them missing in other productions, so we can understand why, in spite of their differences, they would have married.

There is admirable support from Adam Lane as Dr Bradman, a perfect country GP, and from Scarlett Montgomery as Edith the maid.

But overall this is like a Beethoven concerto played with half the wrong notes.

The Guardian: First Night, Blithe Spirit

This Spirit is not only Blithe but exciting

Hooray for Alexander Columbus. This director who has given us previously refreshing interpretations of familiar plays here lends his talents to *Blithe Spirit*. Ignoring the surface frivolity of the script, Mr Columbus has instead caught the deeper feeling of loss and mortality brought about by World War II. The curtain rises on Jasper Fleming's excellent war-torn set. Charles (Rupert Blake) is nobly clad in uniform complete with large scar, no doubt heroically received in battle; Madame Arcati (Judith Gold) is a land girl, while Dr Bradman (Adam Lane) has clearly come straight from a hospital full of war wounded. Yet these characters continue as if the war around them was not happening, thereby making the play much more profound and frightening. And the idea of the spirit world versus the world of war and horror is brought home perfectly as a major air raid interrupts the smaller destructions produced by Charles's two dead wives. Mr Columbus's concept gives emphasis to the oft held view regarding the claims the deceased have on those still living.

The cast all give stellar performances, though at certain points they do not seem completely at one with their director. Yet, in general, this is a brave and laudable production which should surely earn its director great acclaim.

Evening Standard: First Night, Haymarket Theatre

Great Acting: shame about the Direction

I have to confess, when I entered the auditorium to find a pretty young man in full SS uniform handing me a gas mask, I was extremely intrigued. Had I the wrong theatre, and strayed into *Springtime for Hitler*? This was not *Blithe Spirit* as I knew it, though I'm sure Noel Coward would not have complained at such an attractive sight. Sadly for this male critic, the SS Officer made no further appearance in what was a rather unusual evening.

Most of us are acquainted with the story of *Blithe Spirit*: a novelist married to his second wife after the first dies, asks an eccentric medium to hold a séance as research for his next book, with the result his first wife reappears to comical and sometimes disagreeable results. As far as I recall, there was no mention of World War II which is where director Alexander Columbus has elected to set this version, complete with such an authentic air raid several members of the audience looked nervously at the map handed out with our gas masks detailing the location of the nearest shelter.

There is no reason to set the play at such a point in history, and it makes nonsense of the behaviour of the characters. Would Charles and Ruth be holding an elegant dinner party to do research for Charles's book if there were air raids overhead and Charles had obviously been injured in the war, unless Ruth had been the source of the large scar across his face? This might not be a far fetched theory, since the strongest parts of this play are the marital tiffs between Charles and Ruth which contain a stinging venom. In fact the performances from real life couple Rupert Blake and Miranda Flynn are so believable it is hoped this is not suggestive of their offstage marriage.

And in the war wouldn't Edith, the maid, (Scarlett Montgomery) be working in a factory or on the land, not serving cocktails or eggs and bacon? And precisely where did this household receive such a glut of eggs and bacon in a time of shortages? Furthermore, would Charles have left them rather disinterestedly on his plate if they were his entire weekly ration? Perhaps this director has discovered a sub-text where the Condomines keep chickens and pigs in their garden? But somehow the idea of Ruth in her elegant dress picking her way through a hen house to collect the eggs doesn't ring true.

But there are plus points, for instance the sight of Judith Gold dressed in a Land Girl's outfit rather than the usual eccentric knitted or frumpy costumes Madame Arcati is generally issued with. Though at her age, should she really be tilling the land? Along with Rupert Blake and Miranda Flynn, her performance is the other reason to see this production. She takes a role which everyone associates with Margaret Rutherford and makes it her own. She is at once eccentric, slightly wicked and enormous fun. Her incantations during Act Three had the entire audience, this reviewer included, in fits of laughter. Gold, Blake and Flynn are performing Coward how it should be, in spite of the director's bizarre ideas. And it is a pleasure to see Adam Lane back on stage as Dr Bradman, a handsome young actor, I recall, when we were both starting out on our respective careers. For such a first-rate actor, this is a surprisingly small role, but played to perfection. It is a shame this, by and large, acclaim for the cast could not be said for Echo, the actress (and I use the term loosely) who is playing Elvira. Unknown over here (for which we should be grateful), she appears to have mastered the correct accent and vocal interpretation for the role. However, she wafts around the stage looking very pretty but utterly vacant. It's almost as if she was giving a radio performance. Someone needs to tell her she has to act with her face and body, not merely her voice.

See this play for the acting, forget about the direction. And if that SS officer is interested, I can be contacted C/O this newspaper.

The Daily Telegraph: Blithe Spirit, Haymarket Theatre

Coward Gold

What a joy to have Judith Gold back in the West End, and in a role so perfectly suited to her talents. When Noel Coward was writing *Blithe Spirit* back in 1941, he could have been writing it for this actress (brief note to the director: it was written in 1941, not set then; the ridiculous notion of setting it mid World War II doesn't merit any further discussion). In Miss Gold's first appearance, instead of the 'jolly hockey sticks' manner of Margaret Rutherford and Peggy Mount or childlike quality of Dora Bryan, she swoops in with a slightly mischievous smile on her face, so the audience are always wondering if perhaps she is aware of the real reason she has been asked. Is everything she does a slight act? She certainly controls the people around her, putting the inane Mrs Bradman (Isabelle Whiteside) down with aplomb. There is also an almost flirtatious quality to her when she addresses Charles or Dr Bradman. There is a faultless piece of interplay when she winks at Charles, who does a seamless double take and then looks anxiously over to his wife. Never has the séance scene been performed to such comic effect, while the argument between Madame Arcati and Ruth was perfectly played. Noel Coward would doubtlessly have cheered this production's acting and acerbic bite since this play is often considered to express his woman hating homosexuality. Others consider the character of Charles to be Coward's direct voice and opine that Charles also hates women, but Rupert Blake's performance does not follow that route. His is a very heterosexual Charles and there was strong sexual chemistry between him and both Ruth and Elvira. Rupert Blake continues to prove what an excellent performer he is; there is a good chance by the time he reaches Judith Gold's age he may be as fine an actor.

Miranda Flynn's confused, panicked and angry Ruth is a perfect foil for him and makes the audience wonder how long their marriage would have lasted if Elvira hadn't solved the problem by accidentally killing Ruth. Here is a marriage to which Relate should offer its services.

After a lamentably long absence, Adam Lane has returned to the stage as a very believable family doctor, and there seems to be a genuine friendship between Dr Bradman and Charles which I have not been aware of in previous productions. Perhaps it is something Noel Coward would have applauded. In contrast to the returning prodigal there is a newcomer (Scarlett Montgomery) as Edith. Miss Montgomery gives a performance which gives her nothing to be ashamed of, but she is too sexy and bubbly to be this slightly dense maid. You feel she would have seduced some poor innocent villager as soon as look at him. It is a bit like asking Joan Collins to play a pit miner.

That is a minor quibble in comparison to the performance of another newcomer, not only to theatre but to these shores (though apparently a big name in her native USA, even if none of my fellow American critics could enlighten me as to exactly who she was): the strangely named Echo. Although she recites the lines in a vaguely believable manner, she appears to come from the Sylvester Stallone Two Expression School of Acting: while Sly could act tough looking up and act tough looking down, Echo can smile (very prettily) and she can get angry and stamp her foot (also very prettily). Still, she looks beautiful and one of my colleagues, seated directly in front of me, leant forward at her every entrance. Luckily for Echo she is surrounded by actors of such a high calibre that they carry her along with them so she appears better than she probably is.

This production of *Blithe Spirit* is a pleasure; as long as you ignore the direction and setting.

The Independent: First Night, Blithe Spirit, Haymarket Theatre

Cowered by Coward

Alexander Columbus has opted to stage his new production of *Blithe Spirit* during World War II for which there is no discernable reason whatsoever, unless he's under the impression that since Noel Coward wrote it in 1941, that was its intended setting. Surely Coward wrote it to lighten the dark days of wartime London, not emphasize them? Luckily, with the exception of a rather realistic air raid, which frightened my young son who had accompanied me to the extent of inducing nightmares, it makes little difference to the play. The actors seem to be working on the original text with an easy confidence and walking around Jasper Fleming's bomb ravaged set as if there was nothing unusual about it. Only Charles has to make some acknowledgement of the hostilities, as it is him who is left alone on the stage as the air raid breaks.

People say no one enjoyed Coward like Coward, so it would be interesting to discern how he would feel about this production. He constantly pointed out to amateurs that his plays appeared easy to stage, but were in fact fiendishly difficult. Certainly his plays are particularly susceptible to the whims of directors, unlike, say, Shakespeare who can withstand most abuse, and Mr Columbus is a perfect example of directing failure.

With luck, Coward would give him and his designer a dismissive look and move on to enjoying the perfectly timed comedy and acting. Judith Gold is utterly confident in her role as Madame Arcati, and the best I've seen (unlike the majority, I've never been a fan of Margaret Rutherford in the role on film). It is part innocence yet part minx and she and Rupert Blake (Charles) work skilfully together. Blake's real-life wife, Miranda Flynn, here plays stage wife Ruth and her uptight, angry performance is a perfect foil for his nonchalance and weary detachment, the result of living with two nagging women for so long. The scene over breakfast, where Ruth struggles to accept Elvira's materialization, is a perfect piece of theatre business. It is a shame Echo, as Elvira, lacks any depth in her role, uses virtually no facial expression and moves as if on a catwalk. Even raising one arm seems to take all of her concentration, as if she is expecting to be given marks out of ten. Scarlett Montgomery, as Edith, gives a fine performance in her theatre debut, though perhaps her lack of experience is shown up slightly by the stalwart acting surrounding her. Adam Lane and Isabelle Whiteside play the supporting roles of the Bradmans.

The Sun

Cor Blimey Nice One Echo

A star was born at the Haymarket Theatre last night, at the latest revival of *Blithe Spirit*. The mysteriously known Echo shimmered her way onto the stage and charmed the audience as a ghost called Elvira. In spite of being American, her British accent was perfect and her delivery, whether being comic, evil or petulant, was charming. Her almost vacant expressions were ideal for that of a ghost and in the scenes where she flirts with her ex-husband Charlie, the theatre was electrified. The lucky actor playing opposite her (Rupert Block) was helped in his role by playing with such a shining new talent. I predict great things for this young actress.

The other electrifying part was the air raid at the end, when the whole theatre seemed to shake. This is not normally in this play, so my colleagues tell me, but I think it should be added to all future productions – it makes you wake up. Also in the cast was Judi Dench.

Erratum

We have been requested to point out a few errors in our review of *Blithe Spirit*. The name of the character in the play is Charles, not Charlie, the actor playing him is Rupert Blake, not Block and Judi Dench is not in the production in any capacity. Her role is instead taken by Judith Cold.

The Stage

Blithe Spirit: Haymarket Theatre, London

Blithe Spirit was Noel Coward at his wittiest and is a play beloved of repertory and amateur companies all over the UK. This production, however, offers a first-rate cast. The story is of writer Charles Condomine, who invites a medium, Madame Arcati, to hold a séance for research purposes at the home of him and his wife Ruth. Also invited are Dr and Mrs Bradman. During this séance the ghost of his first wife, Elvira, is brought back, though she's only visible to Charles. This leaves plenty of opportunity for comedy as the invisible Elvira causes havoc to Charles's life and marriage before she kills Ruth while attempting to kill Charles. For some reason this production has been set in the Second World War. Judith Gold, one of our finest actresses, plays Madame Arcati.

Also giving good performances are Rupert Blake (Charles), Miranda Flynn (Ruth), Adam Lane (Dr Bradman), Scarlett Montgomery (Edith), Echo (Elvira) and Isabelle Whiteside (Mrs Bradman).The director is Alexander Columbus and designs are by Jasper Fleming.

The Observer
A tired old ghost rises yet again
Noel Coward has never been a favourite
playwright of mine so this production of
Blithe Spirit is no better or worse than any
other. Judith Gold plays Madame Arcati
with her usual aplomb, Rupert Blake is
suitably handsome as Charles and Echo
(is that really her name?) suitably pretty as
Elvira, but the play is so dated and clichéd
with Coward's obvious bitterness against
marriage and women in general. Why are we
constantly forced to sit through hackneyed
old plays when there are so many exciting
new playwrights around? The programme
notes inform us that Noel Coward wrote this
play in six days – I felt I'd been sitting in the
theatre for a similar length of time.

To the Arts Editor of The Observer
Dear Sir/Madam,
 Why the fuck do you send a reviewer to
see a play who admits in her opening line
she does not like the playwright? It's hardly
going to produce an unbiased review. To me it
shows total unprofessionalism on the part of
both the critic and yourself for sending her in
the first place. The theatre is a hard enough
medium to keep afloat in today's world;
critics like yours obviously have a desire to
utterly destroy it. I suggest you find someone
with less bias and an interest in the classics

to send to future revivals; do I presume she would also consider Shakespeare to be passé? Thankfully, with no seats to be had for the entire 6 month run, it makes no difference to our business, only to our irritation.

Yours,
Judith Gold.

Personal Biographies:

Judith Gold: Madame Arcati

Judith Gold trained at RADA and began her career at Oldham Rep.

Theatre credits include: *Arms and the Man; A Winter's Tale; Private Lives; Anthony and Cleopatra; Hay Fever; Hedda Gabler* (Olivier Award); *The Rivals; The Three Sisters; The Magistrate; Separate Tables; Major Barbara; The Circle; Time and the Conways; Mary Stuart; The Daughter-in-Law; Wild Oats; Who's Afraid of Virginia Woolf?* (Olivier Award); *Star Quality; The Man who Came to Dinner; An Ideal Husband* and *Peter Pan.*

She made several movies in America, most of which she considers totally forgettable, and won a British Academy Award for her role in *Don't Knock it Until You've Tried it.*

Miranda Flynn: Ruth Condomine

Miranda was spotted, playing Sally Bowles in *Cabaret,* by a renowned agent whilst still at drama school. Since then she has experienced an exciting and varied career encompassing theatre, film and TV. She was delighted to have been involved with the work of Alan Ayckbourn, performing in several of his plays, her favourite role being that of Poopay, the dominatrix, in *Communicating Doors*. Since then she has appeared in plenteous other comedies including *Present Laughter* and *Clouds*, straight dramas including *The Glass Menagerie* and *Jumpers* and musicals including *The Fantasticks* and *Gypsy*, where she was proud to play the stripper Gypsy Rose Lee. On television she starred in the drama series *Whose Love is it Anyway?*, played Oliver's mother in a BBC adaptation of *Oliver Twist*, and an evil murderess on *Midsomer Murders*. She is married to actor Rupert Blake, whom she met whilst playing Ophelia opposite his Hamlet at the National Theatre, and is happy to be getting the chance to work with him again on this production.

Rupert Blake: Charles Condomine

National Theatre work: *Man and Superman; The Front Page; The Importance of Being Earnest; The Birthday Party; Hamlet.* West End Theatre: *Journey's End; A Life in the Theatre; The Boys Next Door; Prelude to a Kiss* and *Someone to Watch over Me.* Film includes: *Gotcha; The Pennsylvania Story* and *Alien Attack.* TV includes: Lynda La Plante's *Revenge!* and *Make Mine a Double.*

Isabelle Whiteside: Mrs Bradman

Isabelle has appeared in the West End and in repertory theatres all over the country. She was also fortunate to be part of Derek Nimmo's foreign touring company, bringing theatre to the Far East. Roles include: Muriel in Alan Ayckbourn's *Woman in Mind*; Helene Hanff in *84 Charing Cross Road;* Mavis in *Stepping Out;* Maggie in *Hobson's Choice*; Linda Loman in Arthur Miller's *Death of a Salesman;* Miss Skillon in the farce *See How they Run*; Vera in Agatha Christie's *Ten Little Indians* and Grizabella in *Cats.* Her favourite role to date has been that of Miss Shepherd in Alan Bennett's *The Lady in the Van,* a role originally created by Maggie Smith, an actress whom she was honoured to follow. She is especially excited to be working with another of her heroines, Judith Gold, in this classic Noel Coward play. On TV Isabelle played a murder victim on both *The Bill* and *Morse* and would like in any future TV roles to stay alive past the first few pages.

Adam Lane: Dr Bradman

Adam Lane appeared in *Dangerous Corner, Sleuth* and *Caught in the Act* in rep; a tour of Noel Coward's *The Vortex;* and in Neil Simon's *Brighton Beach Memoirs* in the West End. For the Royal Shakespeare Company:

A Midsummer Night's Dream and *Othello*. TV: *Fifteen in the House, Emergency Room* and *The Bill*.

Echo: Elvira

For the last 10 years Echo has been the young star of the hugely successful and popular US TV soap opera, *Acacia Lane*, receiving more fan mail than the rest of the cast. Before that Echo was a regular winner of beauty pageants all over the States, picking up prizes from most beautiful baby to Miss Teen USA. Echo is excited to be acting on stage in the West End like other big American movie stars. She would like to thank her mother, Storm, for being so supportive in her career.

Scarlett Montgomery: Edith

Scarlett trained at Guildford School of Acting, where her roles included: Hedwig in *The Wild Duck;* Daisy in *Daisy Pulls it Off;* Roxane in *Cyrano De Bergerac;* Annie in *The Real Thing* and Cinderella in *Into the Woods*. Her favourite role was that of the robot Jacie Triplethree in *Comic Potential*, for which she received the school's award for best comedy performance. She is thrilled to be making her professional stage debut with *Blithe Spirit*.

Alexander Columbus: Director

Alexander Columbus first came to prominence with his innovative production of *Twelfth Night*. He followed this with *Romeo and Juliet* and *The Cherry Orchard* at the National Theatre, and *The Sound of Music* in London's West End where he was finally able to depict his long held theory of an affair between Maria and the Mother Abbess. His future plans are a production of his own work *Dracula: Blood Will Out* and *The Rocky Horror Show* with an entirely naked cast. Following that he intends moving to Los Angeles where he is confident he will be much in demand. He would like to dedicate this production to his mentor and inspiration, Jasper, with all his love.

Coming soon

to a bookshop near you

Judith Gold, Rupert Blake

and full supporting cast

return in

Climbing the Curtain